THE ULTIMATE TRIUMPH

Ruth Freeman Solomon

THE
ULTIMATE
TRIUMPH

G. P. Putnam's Sons, New York

FOR THREE SOLOMONS:

Nellie King, Joshua Ben, Jared Freeman

*I should like to thank my husband,
Doctor Joseph C. Solomon, for the information
he gave me, which I do understand. And I
thank our son, Doctor George Freeman Solomon,
for his research, which I do not understand.*

Part I

VIENNA

MEDICINE was what Dan wanted. From the beginning, he had done brilliantly at Harvard's Medical School, then excelled in his residency. And finally, even on the analytic couch, he knew it was what he had always wanted. It took time, a long time and a lot of resistance, before he relinquished his defiance and let that brilliant mind go back. Back to the time of his childhood, to his parents, to his early memories. And even then, Dan's unconscious knew how to choose to his liking.

> DAN: "My mother, whom I revered, said to me: 'Dan, my son, I'd die happy if you were a doctor.'
>
> "I could see by the look on her face she was talking about father, too. She did not have to say anything for me to understand her suffering."
>
> A.: "Do you think she always suffered? What about your father?"

But this is what really happened.

The room, with its quiet colors and solid furniture, was warm and filled with the treasured possessions of a six-year-old—a sword, a jumbo freight train with engine, cars, and tracks, a coloring set, a turreted castle complete with sword-bearing knights on mounts. And there were picture books, and racing sets, and stuffed animals scattered across the thick blue pile rug. Young Dan, in his walnut bed, was not asleep. Across in the spacious upstairs sitting room, where one's eye immediately fell on the Savonnerie carpets, silk needlepoint, antique porcelains, and velvet hangings, a very unfriendly conversation was taking place between Miriam and Andrew Gunther.

"You knew my business. I told you about it."

Protesting, Miriam answered, "But I married a soldier. That was bad enough. The 'business,' as you call it, came later—after our daughter. Consequently, I had no choice. You didn't even consult me. You said, 'I only want you to understand that the sale of munitions is like any other business —totally dependent upon supply and demand, and human nature being what it is—' That sentence, Andrew, you left unfinished; because you believed in armed persuasion; you went on to explain, with your usual smile, 'When you come right down to it, what's the difference between the man who sells the gun and the man who pulls the trigger? War is war.' "

The argument continued until they were screaming at each other.

Finally Andrew said in exasperation, "A hell of a lot you've got to complain about. I've given you everything you wanted and more. You don't spend your life going from one dreary garrison house to another. The children will go to good schools and. . . ."

Miriam, in tears, could not argue anymore. She went to the door. "Are you coming to bed?"

"Later."

Miriam looked up at him. "The children; do you realize—can you imagine—Dan's disillusionment when he learns where the money comes from and starts seeing you as a merchant of death?"

Andrew stood up. "Get out."

That, somehow, did not seem to faze her. "Andrew, don't you see—"

"Perfectly. You should have found a rabbi—or maybe a doctor."

"If only you were a doctor, I'd ask for nothing more. I'd die happy knowing my children have a father whose profession the whole world admires."

After an angry silence, Andrew said, "Go to bed, Miriam. I'll see you tomorrow."

Miriam's face lost some of its color. She gave her husband a hurt, knowing look, and, with a sob in her voice, said, "Good night, Andrew. Give my regards to your—to your current—" In horror of the word "mistress" she closed the door. She went directly to Dan.

She sat on the bed and looked down at the boy soberly. Then she whispered in his ear, "Mother loves you." It sounded like an accusation.

"Father doesn't love you." The boy pretended deep sleep, and in the morning, he remembered nothing. There was a reason—there has to be for everything.

The two young Americans were facing each other in the train as it chugged steadily through low-lying fields, past the tree-lined embankment of the Danube, toward Vienna.

"Christ, women are strange!" His brown eyes went to hers. "I thought if it was right for me, it would be all right with you."

"You have so many private places, Dan."

"Not from you, Jenny."

"You're an excellently trained physician, Dan. Do you really want to switch to psychiatry now?"

"Let's say I find the human mind fascinating. What's wrong with that? Why does psychiatry terrify you?"

Jenny put her hand into Dan's. After some thought she spoke. "As I understand it, psychiatry will enmesh you in the lives of unhappy people. You'll be on call to any woman who wants to complain about her husband, or brag about her own sexuality, or involve you in some bizarre fantasy. You'll come to me weary with listening to the damn eroticism of females. There'll be nothing left that's special for me alone."

Dan gave her an amused look. "How does a nice girl like you—?"

Just then, the conductor called out, *"Wien, Wien. Wien Westbahnhof. Alles heraussteigen!"*

Thankful that the train was pulling into the station, Dan kissed Jenny on the tip of her pretty nose. Then he stood up and reached for their suitcases wedged in the iron rack above. Thus, on a warm mid-September night in the year 1930, Dr. Daniel Gunther, having completed a two-year rotating internship and a pediatric residency, arrived in Vienna with his twenty-year-old bride. He, eager and confident, focusing on his own skills and ambition.

Dan offered his hand. The customs official was quicker than he looked. He quickly pocketed the five-dollar bill and the Gunthers cleared customs at once. The people standing around envied the Americans. Jenny gave no sign that she saw, but she felt regret that Dan contributed to corruption because the man in uniform had the power to detain them indefinitely.

Dan went around with two porters to pick up their luggage. After he took his seat beside Jenny in the taxi, he said, "You look like you need food. What about supper?"

At the mention of food, Jenny relaxed a little. She turned her face and nodded. "That wasn't much we had on the train."

It had taken over two days for them to make the journey from Paris to Vienna, with three changes. Staying with Princess Marie Bonaparte, they had enjoyed a golden warmth that only the city on the Seine can offer. Vienna seemed more somber, more of a bastion—as indeed it had been against the Turks not so many centuries before—more inaccessible to the non-European eye, with its domes, spires, and ornamented façades above the dark, twisting streets. The princess had recommended lodgings to them, a small hotel, as pleasant and clean, and she supposed it was still so. "It's not in the best part of town," she told Dan in Paris, "but it's near the Kinder Ubernahmstelle where you'll be working with Charlotte Bühler in your observation of children." Jenny was not overjoyed, but she went along with the idea. It was good for Dan to be near the hospital. "If," she acquiesced, "you're to be a student, I had better learn to be a cabbage."

"Just what I've always wanted, a cabbage," Dan replied with a grin.

To the princess' trained ear, there was a veiled protest in Jenny's remark. At least she was not happy about it. The princess decided to take another look at Dan's wife. She saw a finely molded flower, five foot two or three, weighing about one hundred pounds, with big, dark eyes and shoulder-length coppery hair worn loosely. The girl had on a sunny-colored, low-necked dress of sheer wool ending above the knees in a swing of pleats. The flowing chiffon scarf around her neck was long, and at a time when a lot of makeup was the style, she wore only a little lipstick—and that, pale pink. Suddenly not so sure about the pension, the princess damned the professions that don't care what they do to the wives. But her thoughts were soon back to Dan and his training.

The restaurant they found close to the Gasthaus was on a small cobbled alley, which was dark and oppressive; the meal they ate and washed down with sour wine was hardly Vienna's best.

The Gasthaus in the next street needed fresh paint. Upstairs, the room they were shown was grim. A frayed shade and a wilted curtain on the one narrow window. Everything except the streaked mirror was pushed against a wall—the bed, the wooden desk, the two straight chairs with stained seat covers. Jenny made a great effort to concentrate on the one decent piece of furniture in the room—a really good carved chest, solid.

Dan grimaced. "Is this all you have?"

"Please, Herr Doktor, don't judge," the landlord pleaded. "I promise, tomorrow, you move upstairs. There I have a large room, nicely furnished, and with a view."

Jenny raised the window shade and looked out at the misty, dimly lit street—dull, drab, totally neglected. Not quite a slum but certainly poor and old. A street of small shopkeepers and clerks. Her voice was hardly audible. "A view of what?"

Dan reached for her hand. "Why don't we go to a downtown hotel?"

"Send him away," Jenny said. "And give me your pajama tops. I don't want to unpack."

"Are you willing to spend the night?"

"It's a bed. It looks reasonably clean."

The room made Jenny shy. She wanted to whisper, to tiptoe. The wall that divided this room from the next must surely be thin so that whoever is in the next room will hear. It was like being spied upon. The room had the opposite effect upon Dan. He wanted to make love to her.

They talked while they were undressing. Then Dan waited, with the door open, until Jenny came out of the bathroom across the hall. "It's untidy and has no bath," Jenny said, holding out her soap and towel to him. Alone in the bedroom, she lit a cigarette.

Lying beside her, Dan gathered her close in his arms. His face against her hair, he whispered, "I love you." He sensed her unwillingness. "What's the matter?"

"I'm tired."

Dan's hand touched the small of her back. Caressing gently, he let her sleep. Presently he detached himself from her and rolled over.

Jenny awoke. *It's a nightmare, a stupid nightmare. Tiny monsters were not swooping up and down my belly. What made the torture worse was that the creatures were biting.* Jenny edged herself toward the light: *Be calm, be calm.* She seized and pulled the string. Her nightmare was infinitely real. Jenny screamed.

Dan opened his eyes and swung his gaze on Jenny, who, in utter despair, begged, "Get them off me, please!"

By the time Dan realized he was looking down at bedbugs, he had Jenny in his arms. She was crying. He carried her into the hall water closet, and, there in the iron sink, washed her clean.

Tears still in her eyes, Jenny asked, "What about you?"

Dan grinned at her. "They liked only you." But he went back to the sink and scrubbed himself thoroughly. Then, lifting Jenny off the bare tile floor, he carried her back to the room. "We're leaving now."

Jenny stared at him. "Thank you, Dan."

The proprietor pulled his pants on over his nightshirt. He reached the small downstairs lobby, wondering why the Americans were running away in the chill of the gray dawn. There was absolutely no sense to it. Dan explained briefly.

Shaking his head in sadness for what his pension had become—once a princess had taken short sojourn there—he turned his eyes, sadly apologetic, onto Dan. "I promise you, Herr Doktor. In a few hours. . . ."

"No," Dan interrupted, shaking his head.

"Just give me the chance and I'll. . . ."

Dan sighed heavily, "Sorry."

The proprietor's thoughts turned to the poor Polish students, always behind in the rent. The Indians and the Arabs brought street women into their rooms. They gave the place a bad name.

The proprietor felt he should do something generous. He cranked the phone and called for a taxi. He then lowered himself into the chair, dropped his head, and stared down at the floor.

"Thank you," Jenny said softly. Dan had no notion of the aching compassion she felt for the weary old man.

The ancient Ford moved slowly, its driver pitting himself against his vehicle, the fog that blinded him, and the dampness blowing up from the gray Danube. The Café Edison that headquartered the American Medical Association of Vienna was closed when they got there, as a gray dawn touched the sky. They pulled up in front of a workman's café.

Jenny said, "Not again. I want good coffee. I want a proper bath and a hot breakfast. Let's check into the Imperial."

Dan opened the taxi door. "Come!" He held out his hand to help her. Not until they held mugs of steaming hot coffee did he give his answer. "While we're here, Jenny, let's live like students. We're not tourists any longer."

He took her hand and as the warmth of his hand reached into hers, she softened. "The coffee is good."

"More?"

"Please."

When the waiter brought the coffee, Jenny asked for black bread and cheese.

With a grin on his face, Dan said, "After we've looked in at the Edison and seen who's there, we'll see what rentals are available near here. If nothing suits you, we'll live at a good hotel until we find something. Fair enough?"

"Eminently fair, Herr Doktor." Jenny waited, "There's no use sitting here. Let's drive around the neighborhood. There must be something to see besides factory buildings, poultry shops, and sidewalks heaped high with empty crates."

Twisting and turning, the old car struggled along bleak streets not yet alive except for a few shabby pedestrians, kerchiefed women with their deep baskets, and a beggar still stretched on a curb bench, under one of the city's gas-lit lamps, elegant reminders of a richer past.

"So this is gay Vienna—the most civilized city in Europe? Looks more like the Western Front in 1918."

"Wait, *meine Liebe*," said Dan. "Soon Vienna will look like Vienna should look. You'll see."

Jenny followed Dan into the Café Edison, and they climbed a flight of uncovered stairs bare even of paint or varnish. This brought them to an open space which—in spite of corner booths, tables and chairs, a wall clock, the usual tiled stove, and a bulletin board—had the appearance of an empty warehouse.

The man who approached them was short and round, with a smooth clean-shaven face, also round. He had deep, piercing, slightly mad El Greco eyes. He was extravagantly and flamboyantly dressed. That he was a man of vanity was obvious. Studiously ignoring Dan, he held out both hands to Jenny.

With a laugh, Jenny laid her cool hands against his damp palms. "You must be Lewis Miller."

Still Miller gave no sign of noticing Dan. "I regret that I missed your wedding. I hope the Georgian urns took some of the weight off my absence."

Jenny said, "I'm mad for them. We both loved them."

He gave Jenny a faint smile, released her hands reluctantly, and turned to Dan.

"You're a lucky man, Dan. It's good to see you." Lewis Miller gestured toward another room. "Come meet the others."

Surprised at first, Jenny thought over Lewis Miller's behavior of a few minutes ago. It was a disguise, a cover-up. She knew he was genuinely fond of Dan; he obviously did not trust himself to show it openly.

The six men around the table, which was covered with a checkered cloth, rose to their feet as they approached. Lewis Miller reached for a chair and held it for Jenny. "Coffee and schnecken first," he said, speaking to them all. "Introductions come later."

Jenny could feel their eyes. She hesitated briefly, glanced around with a smile, and lowered herself into the chair. With answering smiles, the men took their places.

Miller looked in the direction of Julius, headwaiter and undisputed ruler of the Café Edison, and ordered.

"Herr Doktor," Julius asked, with a flourish, "you want me to serve before Frau Doktor Tascha arrives?"

"Yes."

A big man with red hair and calm eyes winked at Julius. "I'll tell her you tried."

"Thank you, Herr Doktor Reilly. I should like her to know."

To the average person, the fixed silence in which the men sat could have been torture. Dan was relaxed. He even enjoyed the silence, because it gave him the time to gather his own impressions. Jenny took her cue from Dan, not questioning the silence.

Lewis Miller took a schnecken. It was the signal for everyone to begin speaking. He swung around in his chair. "Let me introduce new friends —Jenny and Dan Gunther, old friends of mine. Now it's not because I am the senior member here but. . . ."

The talk around the table drowned his words. Leaning over to Dan, Lewis Miller said seriously, "Listen to our friend Brotman. Sir Abe, as we call him. He likes nothing better than shedding light on our shortcomings and heaping shameless praise upon himself."

Abe Brotman chuckled. "You're maligning me. And Tascha isn't here yet to stand up for me."

Abe looked over to Dan. "I'm in a special position to do the honors because I, unlike your friend here, regard my comrades and fellow neurotics impartially." Abe wanted nothing so much as to impress Dan Gunther. *And damn Tascha*, he thought, *Just when I need her, she's late*. He took his glass and swallowed a little water. "Well, let's start with me."

"By all means," Lewis Miller said with alacrity. "Just start."

Resentment, barely noticeable, shone out of Abe's eyes. Making himself give a short laugh, he spoke brightly. "Glad to oblige."

Jenny struggled with her feelings. These were brilliant men. But they seemed to be playing some game. Abe seemed manly. Maybe a bit below average height but not frail. His eyes glittered with intelligence. He's attractive, Jenny decided, even good-looking in an intense sort of way. Why is he so defensive? Why is Lewis treating him badly? Why are the others silent? Was Abe afraid to fight back?

Finally—it seemed a long time, although it was only seconds—Jenny spoke up. "What is the explanation of the 'Sir'—I mean. . . ."

"Well, after I got my MD degree, Mama considered plain Abe disrespectful. But in our New York neighborhood, especially on our street, practically every family had a doctor, a judge, a lawyer—at least an accountant. Mama said, 'What am I to do—lean out of the window and yell to the whole East Side, My son, the doctor? That's commonplace. Therefore, I'll call him Sir Abe. It adds class.' "

The others were glad to have the often-told story over with.

Jenny smiled and said, "I hope to meet your mother someday."

"Sure, someday, when I'm on Park Avenue making money." Feeling good now, Abe turned back to the introductions, interrupting the bits of indifferent exchange among the men.

"The face of misery belongs to Al White. Like most of us, he's taking the cure." To Jenny, he explained, "Analysis. He thinks he's the reincarnation of Freud born before his time.

"Bill Reilly is our Irishman. He's no ordinary drinker; otherwise, he suffers no emotional unbalance. Maybe," Abe said, as if the thought just came to him, "he's wasting his time."

Bill ground out his cigarette. With a big grin on his face, he said to Jenny, "I have many good Irish qualities—wasting time is not among them."

Jenny smiled. "I could have guessed that."

"I'm Tony Fuller. I comment upon myself. I have no wife despite many chances."

"Why don't you tell them?"

Tony turned to Lewis on his right. "About what?"

"Your music."

A smile lit up his face.

Lewis Miller said, "We've interrupted again. And I want Dan and Jenny to understand that the crazy world of analysts is like no place they know, that not all of us can turn off the faucet when we leave the couch." He leaned toward Jenny. His chin on his hand, he said, "You'll catch on."

She made no answer.

Abe's eyes went to the man sitting directly opposite him. "Dr. and Mrs. Gunther meet Jerry Blake, our resident goy." As Dan was thinking, *What in hell does that mean?* Abe indicated the last man at the table. "Peter Rice—mistaken, misguided, and off the track." Abe tapped his head. "Up here. He thinks that there is such a thing as psychotherapy without analysis."

Looking more closely, Jenny saw that he was uncomfortable. He wore baggy trousers and an ill-fitting sports jacket of drab green, and the clothes did not become his olive complexion that showed scars of severe teen-age acne. Still, he was not a homely man. He impressed Jenny as a nice man, and she liked him. Peter Rice would have been pleased had he known that. But Peter knew very very little about affection and not a thing about women.

Rice turned toward Dan. "All my training is in organic medicine. I am—I was a neurologist. Until a few months ago I didn't know anything else."

"I understand," Dan answered. "I might have stayed with the purely organic side of medicine but for Lewis. He urged me to take the plunge."

Abe turned his face to Peter. "I pointed out your error. I'll help you correct it."

Only Lewis Miller had an inkling. *Poor Peter,* he thought. *He sees himself through Abe's eyes—inferior.*

Dan contemplated the three empty chairs, and Abe, who was watching him, noticed.

"I was just coming to them. That one"—he pointed—"belongs to my wife, Tascha." A note of annoyance crept into his voice. "She's never this late. Why didn't she telephone me?"

"Maybe she overslept. I often do."

Abe's gaze shifted to Jenny. "Not Tascha." Then, making the words sound halfway between a compliment and a criticism, he said, "If I had an idea where bargains have been advertised and prices listed, I'd know where she is. But she knows her way about Vienna." Quite plainly, he was proud now as he said to Jenny, "My Tascha is queen bee around here, you know."

Jenny saw this as a loaded remark and one to which she had no ready reply. Lewis Miller was already talking. His voice rose in emphasis. *"Was!* And that only by the consensus of her own opinion."

Abe was satisfied that Jenny got the message. "Well," he said, "that brings us to Joe Garafalo, our darkly handsome, slightly demented Italian. Smart as a whip—his consuming passion is to get into bed with every. . . ."

It was Bill. "Joe's broad achievements are his private affair."

"It's compensation for his ears. One protrudes slightly," Abe jested.

Jenny laughed. "Natürlich."

Bill thought: *She's all right.*

Abe wasn't sure what he was feeling. He wanted to say something rough and unpleasant to Jenny. When he did speak, however, it was pleasantness itself. "The last chair is reserved for Piotr Dubinsky. We're stuck with him as he is with us."

Dan asked with promptness, "Why?" When Lewis Miller's mouth started to open, Dan said, "For Christ's sake, doesn't anyone else here talk besides you and Sir Abe?"

"Sometimes I do. We're all free to. Today, because Lewis has a prior claim and a well-intended proprietary attitude toward you, we decided beforehand to let him and Abe do most of the talking."

Dan ruminated for an instant. So this was Jerry Blake, the reputed goy. The meaning eluded him. He put it away for another time. Refraining from comment, he asked, "Why is Dubinsky among you and still apart?"

Jerry Blake said, "Among us—period?"

Dan grinned. "Of course."

Even as Jerry Blake said of the absent stocky Russian, "He's a Red," he realized Dan was his kind of man, one he could reach in his language—because the subtleties, the submerged hostilities, the smug smartness, the fake submissiveness, the shrewd subterfuge, were not his style. Nor were they Bill Reilly's.

Lewis Miller made it his business to explain Piotr for whom he had a profound fondness.

"Today it is psychoanalysis that is attracting the brilliant and the sophisticated." He added, "And the neurotic. However, give the devil his due. Marx was aware that behind the conscious motives are other motives—buried ones—but, all the same, these unconscious drives are true causative factors. Freud, too. . . ."

Tascha Brotman walked in. Like Jenny, she wore a sweater and a pleated skirt. But, whereas Jenny's was the best money could buy, hers was not bad for the money.

"I'm here," she announced, and as Dan raised himself, she slid down into her chair, crushing her cigarette into an ashtray. She reached for a raisin on Bill's plate, eyeing Jenny with intense concentration. There was no time that Jenny could remember when anyone made an appraisal so plain. She returned the stare resignedly and waited, composed.

Then Tascha smiled. A warm smile. The effect was startling. "You're all they have been saying." Her smile widened. "Well, I suppose you know that." Jenny gave her an answering smile and said, "I like you, too."

Tascha stretched out her hand and picked another raisin, again from Bill's plate. Abruptly, she turned to Dan. "So you're our handsome Dan!"

Dan gave her an admiring glance. Flapper-breasted and rail-thin. Glossy black hair. The darkest eyes, white teeth, and deeply rouged lips. The queen bee. "I'm glad you noticed," he said.

It was quiet for the minutes it took Julius to serve fresh coffee, raisin buns, hot and buttered. And, for Tascha, he had something special—cheese strudel. He adored her, for she taught him how to make ice cream sodas and introduced him to a sandwich with mayonnaise, American-style.

Dan did not expect the introductions to take so much time. The tables around them—other doctors in other specialties—emptied while they were still talking. A few of the doctors nodded in passing.

Lewis Miller, correctly guessing that Dan's was the usual reaction of the American neophyte, tapped his watch. "You had better get going. Dr. Adler likes a degree of punctuality from his dissenting listeners—it makes him feel powerful, thereby proving his striving-for-power theory as the explanation for all human behavior."

"Adler!"

"Why not? Why miss learning a little something from everyone in Vienna. We took for granted you'd like the idea and signed you up for his lectures—ten bucks a throw. Split among eight of us, it comes to a dollar and a quarter apiece; that includes the maid's tip. We meet in Adler's flat. He lectures for one hour, adding case material. Noting interest, he will sometimes run over. We pay extra. If the maid fixes coffee, we pay her a little extra."

Dan murmured a thanks, feeling that it was thoughtful of them to include him; no one needed to persuade Dan that it was useful to hear views other than Freud's. "I think I'll beg off for today and start with Adler's next lecture. I want to call first on Professor Freud."

There was deep silence and quick glances.

"Didn't you hear about Freud's mother?"

"No—unless you mean she was suffering from gangrene of a leg. Marie Bonaparte told me about that. But she said that Professor Freud's momentary dread was over, and now that his jaw sarcoma is under control, he's taking on new patients."

"Dan," said Lewis Miller. "She died a few days ago. His hideous and painful jaw prosthesis plagues him once more. He has closed his door. And, we, like cardinals, wear the deep purple of mourning."

"Wait a time," Bill Reilly suggested. "Then consult Frau Anna. She's a very sensible girl; she can steer you to an analyst who has the Old Man's blessing."

"Postpone your analysis. Hang around for a few months, and go home."

Dan looked at Lewis Miller curiously.

"That's right. Back to the States, if you want proper training."

Dan did not quite expect that.

Lewis Miller was a complex psychological phenomenon. Regularly, he behaved with considerable brilliance and frequently with considerable hostility. Time and again he used harshness to hide his true feelings.

"Because you represent the particular kind of man we need in psychoanalysis, I asked you here. I know you are eager to work with Freud, and with him only. Well, let me tell you a little of the psychoanalytic situation here in Mecca.

"Let us forget the current political temper of Europe and concentrate on Freud. He has lost control of his own discovery and all manner of side-routing is taking place. Last week—on the twelfth to be exact—his mother, who had endured ninety-five years, committed a drastic act. She died. To the world, the son behaves like a giant. He says 'No pain, no grief . . . a feeling of liberation, of release. I was not allowed to die as long as she was alive. Now I may.'

"But, in reality, Freud is a fear-filled infant. He is preoccupied only with his own health. The seventy-four-year-old cripple doesn't want to die. He wants to live, to smoke strong cigars, to work with rich patients, to revive his literary fame, to receive more and more honors. He wants, above all, revenge on those on his hate-list—the disciples in rebellion."

The explanation over, Lewis Miller stared intently into Dan's eyes, wondering if Dan had any idea how much he loved the Old Man and of the astonishingly close relationship that existed between them. He half-expected Abe, or one of the others, to say something about his real feelings—possibly to Jenny. But Abe was thinking: *You round bastard—flaunting your importance like a phallus.* Gesturing with his head toward the wall clock, he said, "The lecture—it might be too late now."

With quick good-byes, the men left. Dan made his decision to join them. He bent over and brushed his lips lightly on Jenny's hair. "Dan," Jenny called softly after him, but there was no answer. Puzzled, she glanced at Lewis Miller. He understood and shook his head. "I've heard him—dozens of times." He finished his cigarette. "Let's make our own plans."

"Will they be long?"

"Long!" Tascha whistled. "You'd better not count on seeing Dan until late. It's around eight or nine before we eat. Seven is the prescribed time for reunion."

"Let's get out of here," Lewis Miller said to Jenny. "My car's outside. We'll drive out to Semmering where I rent a villa. My housekeeper will give us lunch." He turned to Tascha. *"Auf Wiedersehen!"*

For months Tascha had entertained a curiosity about the villa at Semmering. Excluded from the gatherings there, she often heard talk of it. To pass through its high-walled garden, where Freud himself gave wisdom to the chosen, would be a solid triumph. Apprehensive, Tascha switched all of her attention on Jenny, silently willing her to agree. And Jenny would have noticed the entreaty had she been her usual observant self. But Jenny wasn't thinking of villas on the outskirts of the city. Her main desire was to get settled, to unpack, to enjoy the calm and peace of a hot tub.

Lewis Miller sensed that something other than a ride over wooded hills was on Jenny's mind. He got up from his chair and looked down at her. "It's a pity to miss my garden with the fuchsia still in full bloom. This time of year the change is a matter of days." Impulsively, he added, "For you, because this is a special occasion, I'll read aloud some really good avant-garde poetry—my own. Come." He turned his gaze to Tascha. "You, too."

Tascha jumped up, eager to go.

Jenny still sat. "It sounds divine, but I"—her voice faltered, weary—"you two go off to Semmering, please. I'll ask someone to get me a taxi." Both Tascha and Lewis realized that Jenny was close to tears. "Would either of you be able to recommend a hotel, nearby hopefully, with clean rooms and bathrooms in the suite? I. . . ."

"Jenny, *where* is your luggage?" Tascha asked.

"My steamer trunk is still at the railway station. Our valises are downstairs. The porter said he'd keep an eye on them."

Tascha shook her head. "Damn men—they're all the same!"

Lewis exploded. "You mean, you've just been deposited here, alone in a strange city, and it's up to you to find some chilly hotel?"

Jenny's response was quick, not quite defensive. "Dan meant to make arrangements. I know he was anxious to begin the lectures. I'm sure he'll be back before too long."

"I've got it. No need to make arrangements. You will move into my rooms. They're large and the view reminds one of a Dutch interior."

Tascha could only glare at him, remembering the broiling midsummer afternoon she and Abe had turned to Lewis Miller for hospitality, and his response had been, "Julius, the headwaiter, conducts a renting service as a sideline. I'm sure he will have something for you." The old hurt in her hardened. The Jennys always won. Yet watching Jenny's face, seeing a beautiful girl with a gentle smile, Tascha thought maybe just this once good fortune had nothing to do with money.

Lewis Miller studied Jenny's face, still uncertain and vulnerable now. He envisioned Dan in his bed with Jenny. "I'll take no argument from you, Jenny. You must do as I say."

Jenny rose slowly. "All right. I will move in for the day. Whether we take over the apartment for good is for Dan to say."

"I'll manage Dan. You see, I reside in the only establishment in this vicinity that brags a proper bathroom, running hot and cold water, and all the conventional paraphernalia."

"Dan did promise me a proper bathroom."

"Then that's settled." Lewis smiled. "We'll go there now and leave the villa for tomorrow."

On their way out, they delayed long enough to tack a message on the bulletin board, and then to explain to Julius that Dan was to come directly to Lewis Miller's place.

Even with the help of the porter and the porter's helper, it took almost fifteen minutes to transfer the baggage from the vestibule to the rumble seat of Lewis' Packard roadster. It was a tight squeeze. Lewis Miller and the girls settled themselves in the front with Jenny in the middle, then rode away over cobblestone streets in the bright sunshine—bright for fall, but with the beginning of coolness in the air.

Jenny leaned back against the car seat, her eyes closed, thinking about the kind of life Dan was committed to. Was it worthwhile? What would happen to her? Suddenly, she felt an enormous loneliness for California, for the unchanging rhythms of the ocean against the rocky coastline where she had gone so often as a child, for the tall house with its imposing steps and brass-medallioned front door in which she had grown up. She thought of her mother, widowed young, yet concerned for her daughter's education, and her still beautiful grandmother, whose vitality and laughter attracted young and old to explore every new dimension of life. There she had known the luxury of security and well-being. This city was not only strange but unwelcoming.

Gradually, the feeling vanished and Jenny opened her eyes to an incredible change. They were humming along a stretch of road beside the gray waters of the Danube. On the far bank low houses and factories hid a large expanse of trees and parkland. Far off in the distance was the green darkness of hills inviting discovery. Here she noticed the narrow houses were old and weathered, all charming; the entire street seemed familiar even to the old, ornate streetlamp—the kind she remembered from prints hanging in her family's home in San Francisco.

"Lewis has just cut across town," remarked Tascha. "I hope he's taking us to lunch."

He nodded, smiling. "Any objection?"

Jenny smiled, too. "I'll tell Dan to buy you a dinner in return. You pick the restaurant." Tascha looked at her, half-smiling, expectantly. "I want you and Sir Abe, too."

Minutes later they left the car to a uniformed attendant.

"I think you're going to like this place. Everyone meets here for lunch or after the opera." Lewis Miller maneuvered both girls through the elaborate foyer. The watchful Herr Ober greeted him by name. They followed him the length of the old-fashioned dining room decorated in the opulent if heavy style of Franz Joseph. At a secluded table with a view of the river, they ordered with the help of the headwaiter, who went over each suggestion in great detail. Long before he finished, two waiters were there with special treats in the way of appetizers—all of them marvelous. Lewis ate little, glancing occasionally at a group of uniformed young men who sat at a long table a few yards to the right of them. Tascha, as usual unabashed, stared. At first, Jenny made nothing of this, then she lifted her eyes in their direction. She turned back to Lewis Miller. "What about them? Why are people paying more attention to them than to each other?"

"They're deadly filth," Tascha put in passionately. "They elbow pedestrians off the sidewalks; when drunk, they beat up the Jews; they're ready to overthrow the Socialists and hand Austria over to the German Nazis."

Lewis nodded several times. "They are Hakenkreuzlers, Jenny. That means they wear the swastika." Speaking quietly, almost whispering, he went on, "Nazism will liquidate psychoanalysis here and in Germany. The exodus of the European analyst to America is beginning. Persecution and the restriction of intellectual freedom shake loose the giants from their native soil. Professor Freud mourns Europe's loss, but he won't believe the danger he puts himself in. He insists that special laws against the Austrian Jews are out of the question. He puts faith in promises—in England and in France." Leaning toward Jenny, he asked, his voice shaking, "How can he be so blind?"

Jenny took another look and honestly had to concede that they were colorful. Bare-headed, mostly blond, built like burly athletes, they wore identical uniforms with the hooked cross banded on black to their arms. They drank beer, talked among themselves and looked as dangerous as a bunch of college football players. Gradually, one crew-cut youth became aware of Jenny's defiant eyes. *"Grüss Gott, gnädiges Fräulein"*—he flirted across the space. When she turned her head away, the young Austrian gave her a final glance. With a brief grin, he said to his comrades, "I don't trust American females; they're all teasers."

Lunch was brief and they were soon outside in the mild air. They spent the next hour or so moving slowly through sparse traffic, starting their partial tour of the city near the world-famed opera house in its strategic position on the Ring, now a broad thoroughfare circling the oldest section of the city, formerly a defensive system of solid city walls. It was Tascha who, with pleasure, identified the sprawling complex of buildings making up the Old Hofburg, the royal residence of the Hapsburgs dating back to the thirteenth century, its mixture of styles and courtyards witness to frequent reconstruction and royal whim. At one end of the complex stood the Albertina, housing some of the city's finest art; close by, near the innumerable gateways and grilled entrances, nestled St. Michael's, one of the oldest churches, the historic St. Augustine's where Napoleon wed Marie Louise, and the Spanish Riding School where royal tradition has ever held sway. On they drove past the formal expanse of the Volksgarten and the Burgtheater, then right into a section where small, shaded squares alternated with the handsomely decorated houses of Vienna's aristocracy and some of its musicians. This time it was Lewis who pointed out the massive hulk of the Schottenhof on its Romanesque foundations and the beauty of the late baroque church of St. Peter's. Then they were out in a large square and facing the magnificence of St. Stephen's Cathedral, its slender Gothic spire rising out of the very heart of Vienna.

Leaving old Vienna, they came eventually to streets lined with workers' cooperatives. Tascha pointed. "They're built like fortresses."

Jenny turned her head to look back at the housing units.

"This area used to be a horror, a real slum. People died like flies from tuberculosis." Tascha felt proud. Nudging Jenny, she said, "The Social Democrats took action—they're responsible for this housing."

Lewis Miller said with anger, "That damn housing is the reason why the workers refuse to take the Hakenkreuz Movement seriously. The Jews have learned nothing. The rich complain about taxes. The poor want more—soak the rich. Freud fighting the dragon of splinter-groups declares the bastards harmless. 'Children,' he calls them. 'They will surely grow up.' " Lewis Miller made an uncomfortable sound. "Why don't the leaders —men in high places—wake up before all is lost?"

There was silence until the Packard pulled to a stop in front of a dreary building where the Brotmans rented a room and the use of a community bathroom.

"This is where you live, isn't it?" Lewis asked, feeling that for one day he had put up enough with Tascha.

"Right," said Tascha, linking her arm in Jenny's.

But Jenny's eyes rested on him, innocently. With an effort to maintain his dignity, he said quietly, "Get your coat then, Tascha. It's turning cold."

With a faintly mischievous smile, Tascha answered, "I'll wrap myself up in something of Jenny's."

Lewis Miller shrugged his shoulders and turned on the ignition.

Bill Reilly invited Dan to a place where all the doctors met for lunch. It was comfortable and homely, just a stone's throw from the Café Edison and close to the Allgemeines Krankenhaus where Dan was to start his work. Before they reached their table, someone called to Bill. He stopped to greet the only occupant at a table for four. Turning toward Dan, Bill said, "Dan Gunther, this is Dr. Eva Bauer. Shake hands." Instead, Dan touched her hand. Very alluring, he thought. And obviously intelligent, with those sharp eyes and short hair curled over her ears. Cerebral beauty always appealed to him.

She liked what she saw, the way he touched her. It made her feel attractive as well as attracted. "Stop here and keep me company," Eva invited.

He met Eva Bauer's eyes with a steady smile. All through lunch, Eva scarcely looked at Bill—her gaze was on Dan. Bill knew many things about Eva, including the fact that she liked to mix pleasure with business. He felt a pang over Jenny. But deciding that Dan was well able to take care of himself, he left them to their third pot of coffee.

It was Eva Bauer who led Dan that afternoon to the research genius, Dr. Wagner von Jauregg, for whom she worked as a special assistant. And it was Dr. Wagner von Jauregg, recognizing the talent in the young American, who later decided that Dan could handle the special project on children's defects for him.

Before World War I the house had belonged to a rich merchant. Now it belonged to his daughter-in-law, and it provided her with a livelihood. A tall house with small iron balconies and a porticoed door, it suggested a grandeur not quite consistent with the rest of the street, where scruffy boys in boots and short trousers chased one another or played with the sharp-nosed dogs. A large double door gave onto a cool, flagged passageway and a wide ivy-covered courtyard beyond. One room was in constant demand. It was separated from the rest of the house by a private entrance, with access to the little courtyard. In addition to a white bathroom, it had a lavish dressing room that glittered with gold-framed mirrors; a tall, boxlike closet provided sufficient space for the contents of steamer trunks. Added to this, the house was within walking distance of the Café Edison.

Jenny hopped out of the car and stood looking up at the house. It gave her a chill. "It's because I'm tired," she told herself. But she knew that the old man with the vacant eyes leaning out of a second floor window had a lot to do with it.

Lewis Miller walked straight to the door. He inserted his key and turned the big brass knob, and as Tascha stood back, Jenny followed him in.

"Das Zimmer. Are you enchanted?"

"I don't know yet." Jenny walked over to the windows and pulled the draperies apart. Once more she stood looking. It was difficult to see because Das Zimmer was crowded. Its furnishings were entirely of mahogany. The sofa and chairs were ornamented in pretentious velvet. The huge bed looked up at a chandelier heavy with gilt. A faded carpet pressed against all four walls. But, in scale, the room was beautiful. A handsome stove decorated with an unusual pattern of tiles stood on one side. The windowpanes were clean. And in a wall niche was a handsome cut-glass vase filled with fresh flowers. Without speaking, Jenny took a look at the dressing room and, afterward, at the bathroom; then, facing Lewis Miller, she said, "It's really quite nice."

"It's appalling."

"I find suddenly that I give more importance to cleanness than to taste."

Tascha could only stare at them. Compared to her room, Das Zimmer was heaven.

The maid's steps could be heard along the corridor; the door opened and closed. A heavy, wide-hipped girl in workman's shoes and a black kerchief over her close-cut hair looked passively at Lewis Miller.

Lewis said, "Olga, I want you to help Frau Doktor Gunther."

Jenny smiled. "Hello, Olga. *Ich freue mich.*"

"Hello. OK." These two words constituted Olga's total English vocabulary.

As Jenny and Olga talked together in German, Lewis Miller went out. Some time later there was a knock on the door. Lewis had the New York *Times*, Paris edition, under his arm, and he was carrying a grocer's basket filled with fruit, more flowers, and wines. "It's lucky I left when I did. I met the landlady in the upstairs corridor, and I persuaded her—on my knees"—he chuckled—"to move in with Frau Katz and rent her room to me." Miller sat down on the nearest chair, crossed his legs, and took a cigarette. "Do you mind if I smoke?" Without waiting for an answer, he put the cigarette between his lips. Jenny held out the matches. Lewis Miller lit her cigarette. "We did have a bit of a row."

"You and the landlady?"

Lewis nodded. "Because there are two of you, she insists on double the rent."

"Oh!"

Smiling broadly, he said, "Don't worry about it. When Dan brings her your passports, he'll work it out after the customary haggling."

Tascha was still sitting on the bed. "Evidently you're sure Dan won't mind your moving in."

Jenny picked up an apple and bit into it.

For a moment Tascha wondered if Jenny understood. "This place costs plenty. With an increase—"

"Maybe," Jenny said, "Dan will consider having me settled as a kind of investment." She went back to her open suitcase.

Olga came in holding clean sheets and pillowcases. "Herr Doktor's—freshly laundered." The porter and another servant girl followed, went to the closet, got out suitcases, and the moving began. Lewis left. The girls worked side by side, with Tascha examining everything. As they were finishing, Tascha pressed Jenny's leopard coat against her body. "Someday, I'm going to have a real mink and a doorman with gold braid."

Jenny reached up and turned on the light. Then she lay down on the bed. "Want to wear my coat tonight or is the air still too warm for fur?"

"Oh, Jenny! Can I?"

"Sure."

"Listen, Jenny, we ought to get dressed. They'll be back soon."

Jenny was already listening for the sound of Dan's footsteps. She got up and slowly started to undress. She got her hairbrush, sat down on the edge of the bed, and started to brush her heavy hair.

From inside the open bathroom, Jenny heard, "What's your ambition—I mean—what do you want?"

Jenny waited a minute. "Children, after a while."

Tascha looked in. "That's not what I mean. I'm thinking more about the sort of things like a fabulous apartment and aisle seats on opening nights."

Jenny raised herself on her arms. "I want to be content."

"That," Tascha said, carefully, "is asking for an awful lot." Then she closed the door behind her.

Jenny finished toweling herself dry. She looked closely at herself in the mirror. Gradually she disappeared and she could distinguish Dan. She saw him asleep breathing evenly, his strong body stretched out beside her. She saw him over her and afterward when they lay peacefully resting. She saw the hundred various ways in which he showed her how much he loved her. And yet the future frightened Jenny, for she knew that in his climb for fame, Dan would grow beyond her unless she let him take her with him. A sound interrupted her thoughts and made her grab for her robe. A moment later Miller walked in, and the phone rang. Lewis made his way over to the telephone. He listened for a time, then his voice became full of emotion. "Lots of guys work with him. He never has them to dinner. You're sure as hell going!" He listened some more. "I'll stay with her. Frankly, I think you'll be home long before we are." And again he listened. "That's great, Dan. You tell her."

Jenny was watching his face intently. As he gave her the telephone, he said, "Here—you tell him. He'll feel less guilty."

"Hello, Dan."

"Sweetheart, I'm sorry about tonight. I won't be able to get back as I'm having dinner with Dr. Wagner von Jauregg, the Nobelist. I've just met him—and he may invite me to join him on a special project—part-time, that is, at the Allgemeines Krankenhaus."

Interested, almost forgetting her disappointment, Jenny asked, "Would that be good?"

"That, darling, would be very good!"

Quietly, Jenny said, "I guess he liked you."

"Listen, Lewis will take care of you. Have a good time."

"Dan—"

"I love you."

Jenny heard him jam the receiver back.

"All right. You can have the bathroom."

Lewis Miller took one look at Tascha wrapped in a bathtowel. "The arrangements for the evening are made, Jenny. I'll pick you up in one hour." He dropped his eyes and hurried away to dress.

Tascha looked at his retreating figure with scorn. The instant the door closed, her voice became indignant. "Rich bastards like Miller don't take into consideration all the hardships and poverty Abe and I endured, when they judge us. I know a thing or two about him. . . ."

"Don't say that!"

Tascha discovered that Jenny's eyes could get hard and she seemed to grow taller.

"Lewis Miller is Dan's friend. I like him. I intend to see a lot of him. What he does privately is *private*." Jenny studied Tascha a moment longer. "Clear enough?"

Inwardly, Tascha flinched. Outwardly, she managed a commendable degree of nonchalance. In a voice deliberately mild, she replied, "OK. Don't ever say I didn't try to warn you." Then she stood looking at the bathroom door for some moments.

Jenny lay back on the bed, content to be alone; Tascha appeared, a rather embarrassed little smile on her face. "May I wear this?" she asked. The turtleneck sheath of deep beige with its intricate pattern woven in lighter shades of cashmere threads was one of Dan's favorites.

"I guess so," Jenny said, reluctantly, and added, "Isn't it short for you?"

Tascha let the towel slip to the floor and looked at her own legs—nicely hard, nicely formed, with slender ankles. *Why shouldn't I show them*, she thought.

After a while, the girls were both sitting on the bed talking and Tascha learned about Dan's dinner date with Dr. Wagner von Jauregg. "Wow! That *is* swift work."

Jenny felt sure Tascha was glad for Dan.

"What else did he say?" asked Tascha, reaching for the dress.

"I'm to take courses in history of Western Europe and anthropology at the university, and if I complete the required reading and finish all the written assignments, I'm free to take the seminars too. That's rather nice, especially if Dan considers Lewis' suggestion. I so hope he does. I don't want to hang around this horrid place for the duration of an analysis."

Tascha was startled by what she heard: Das Zimmer—horrid? "Well, I must say—"

Then, with some surprise, Tascha asked, "Do you really want all that damn studying? It's such hard work."

Jenny looked at Tascha, who seemed doubtful. "If I don't study, what am I to do? I have the time. I need something of my own to do."

"Oh, Jenny—there are a multitude of fun things to do in Vienna—getting to know the city, concerts. If you ask, Miller will let you have his car." She went on rather fast. "Even his villa—you'd like that, wouldn't you?"

"I have a better idea," Jenny said. "You audit some of the lectures with me."

For an answer, Tascha only stared, her face intense. "Why?"

"Oh, the usual reasons. You know, learn something about your husband's profession—maybe a little about him, too—what he is, what made him that way."

"Jenny, I shouldn't say this. Give me your word you'll keep it to yourself."

"You'll have to trust my judgment," Jenny replied. "And if it's of no importance to Dan, I won't say anything."

Tascha walked up close to Jenny. "If anyone should ask me, I'd say analysis is useless. Miller knows that by now. He's been in therapy for years—here and in Berlin." Summoning her courage, she continued talking about Lewis Miller. "For all of his intelligence and polish, is he your idea of a man standing strong, on his own two feet?" Jenny's eyebrows rose an instant as she leaned forward, intrigued. Tascha continued, "I think he's still a child, a badly frightened one."

For moments Jenny said nothing. She seemed to be thinking things over as she slowly pulled on one silk stocking, then the other. She glanced at Tascha. "I'm curious. Do the men respect Lewis Miller?"

"You sat by him this morning. You saw."

"I mean—really? From a professional standpoint?"

Tascha's answer was honest. "Yes. The men say he is one hell of a technician—that he never mistreats a patient—that he never makes a mistake. Abe says that he is a genius—absolutely supreme."

Jenny did not answer. Presently she heard Lewis' footsteps. She was still only partially dressed.

By the time Dan finally got to Das Zimmer, it was late, very late even for him. Jenny was too angry to do anything—even look at him. Dan froze at the door and poked his head inside, one hand on the knob. Unsure what approach to take with Jenny—he had not reckoned on finding her up at 3:10 A.M.—he crossed the room. "I'm sorry; I didn't mean to be this late."

"Really?"

Dan leaned down to press his lips on hers, but Jenny twisted away to avoid the kiss.

Dan sat down on the edge of the bed, pulled off his shoes, and stretched. He was weary. "You're not to stay awake worrying about me. Don't do it, Jenny."

Indignant and fighting her sense of relief, Jenny answered, "I worried about me, *not* you. I'm too young to be a widow."

Then Dan made a mistake. He thought it was possible to tell her the facts in a natural way. "Bill Reilly introduced us at lunch. We stayed for a chat. For me it was a marvelous break, sheer luck. Professor Wagner von Jauregg was looking for someone with my particular background in pediatrics. Dr. Bauer said she'd be glad to recommend me, which obviously was no guarantee that he'd take me. So we met around five; he showed me around the hospital. I liked his approach; the man is tremendous, head and shoulders above most medical researchers. If I had to find one word for him, I'd call him a discoverer."

As he talked, Jenny listened in distant silence. Then she said, "Go on."

"He asked a lot of questions. Then hired me—part-time, that is. It's a completely new program, which makes it all the more exciting. We'll be observing the malarial treatment of syphilis of the nervous system and studying the effects of birth injuries on children. He absolutely insisted on taking us both out afterward. I couldn't refuse his hospitality, could I?"

"Liar!"

Dan knew Jenny was right. That made it difficult to register instant indignation. "Look," he said, assuming a moral tone, "Those are the facts."

Jenny was unmoved. "What has truth got to do with fact?"

"Jenny, you're being ridiculous. I had to take the damn female home, didn't I? How was I to know she lives all the way beyond Schönbrunn." Dan saw at a glance that Jenny was yielding. He started to undress.

"Is she beautiful?"

"I'll tell you tomorrow."

Jenny was determined. "Is she pretty?"

"No."

"Then why won't you tell me what she looks like?"

Dan eyed Jenny with a grin. "She looks as if she were dragged in from the rain—both damp and untidy. She's a sexless machine, all brains and efficiency."

Jenny brightened.

Dan put his arms around her. Jenny did not stir. Dan looked deep into her eyes and felt the same sense of wonder that began the first time he ever saw her—a slight, graceful sixteen-year-old freshman at Radcliffe who was passionately determined to attain the degree of scholarship her family expected of her.

Jenny was remembering, too. She remembered that she knew, at once, that the engaging senior at Harvard Medical School was her image of heroic man, and that she was determined to marry him. Jenny yielded her heart as easily and as naturally as a butterfly spreads its wings.

Dan had smiled a little. "I love you."

Jenny could sleep now.

It was the maid, holding a breakfast tray of coffee and a sweet roll, who woke her.

Dan was gone, but Jenny had heard nothing.

"Did Herr Doktor leave a message for me?"

"*Ja. Eines Briefchen.*"

The note read:

> SWEETHEART, I committed myself to a research briefing and lunch before I knew about Semmering. Go with Lewis. I'll join you later, probably with Bill. He has the use of a car for the weekend and nothing to do.
>
> All my love,
DAN

Jenny picked up the coffee cup and pondered the Dan she was seeing for the first time. Now she knew for sure that Eva Bauer was pretty. Jenny was not alarmed; she knew that as long as Dan stayed alive, he'd stay in love with her. But there was within her a sense of outrage and a sense of determination to be equal to any situation.

When Lewis Miller's knock came, she was ready and she knew what she would say.

"Jenny, for an auto ride, I suggest something less stunning and more travel-worthy."

"Do you mind very much if I explore the villa tomorrow?" Jenny stood with an apologetic look on her face. "I'm sorry. I have my reasons."

Lewis said, "Stop beating around the bush. What can you possibly want more than a drive in an open car through delightful country? Don't you want to look around without that insufferable Tascha poking her nose into everything?" Lewis Miller could see what Jenny was going to say, so he added, "I arranged for Bill to drive them. Dan promised to be on time."

"I want to talk to you. Please take me to lunch. Somewhere elegant."

"Does elegance make you feel safe?" Without waiting for her answer, he continued talking. "I'll be back as soon as I change."

Jenny picked up her coat, her purse, and a small traveling bag. "I'll wait in the car."

In exactly ten minutes the Packard was headed toward the Imperial Hotel. Lewis Miller talked of himself. In part, it was professional cunning—a sort of psychiatric *ruse de guerre*. He did not want Jenny to rush into confidences like a hurt child waiting for a grown-up to tell her what to do. He talked of his mother. "She's had four husbands, all of them rich. There was a time when I tormented myself over her lovers. I remember the torment, but my memory blocks at faces. Now, in her mid-fifties and still beautiful, she's involved with a handsome young drifter, who has reasons of his own for legitimatizing their affair."

Just as he expected, Jenny caught up in his tale, asked, "Have you met him?"

"Barely two months ago on the Riviera. I went there to disillusion her, but she was adamant. 'He is not in the least interested in my money. He gets more than he wants from his own family.' I confronted him. He embraced me. 'I love her. I need her.' My junior by several years, he called me son." Watching her, Lewis Miller concluded, "I fled."

"That is sad."

Jenny had planned to speak of her immediate worry. Instead, she began talking about her own mother, who—widowed at twenty-nine—had stayed together with Jenny's grandmother and never again committed herself to a man. With obvious interest, Lewis Miller said, "Your mother's relationship with her mother-in-law is rare. I can't help wondering—did they stay together for your sake?"

"Maybe, partly. But they have much better reasons. They love each other, and neither of them can get my father out of her mind. For them, he is not really dead."

"What about you, Jenny? Do you remember your father?"

"Oh, yes. I was almost nine when he came home on his last leave. He brought me a grown-up gift—a string of real pearls. I wore them for the first time on my wedding day."

Lewis Miller asked more questions.

"He was a lawyer with an appetite for public office. It is altogether possible that he also liked looking danger full in the face because he did not have to go to war.''

Lewis Miller gave Jenny an intense look. "Does Dan resemble your father?"

"No, not at all. My father was well over six feet tall and blond.''

"Well, that smashes one supposition, doesn't it?''

Jenny's eyes opened wider, but she said nothing.

Emerging from the smaller side streets, Lewis was adept at maneuvering the car onto the broad thoroughfare of the Ring. The trams surging forward on their appointed routes were part of a scene of unending movement—the street vendors quick to catch the least gesture from a pedestrian, elegant but somberly dressed men on official errands with the occasional flash of a uniform, older women from the country selling their fresh-cut flowers and scolding the impish children who darted everywhere, and old black horse-drawn fiacres, dim reminders of an imperial splendor long departed. Jenny's calm gaze absorbed the human activity against the façades of the stately buildings, visible on either side.

Finally Lewis Miller confronted her: "You wanted to tell me something. What was it?''

Jenny was surprised at her own candor. "I need help.''

The forcefulness of his piercing gaze hardened his face. "Are you placing yourself in therapy with me?''

Jenny could not hide her astonishment. "Therapy! Do you think me neurotic?''

"Let us start with the assumption that you are not!'' He looked at her. "What is it?''

"I have an odd feeling about Dan. Yesterday he met someone. Dr. Eva Bauer. I am sure he went to see her this morning.''

"Are you jealous?''

"Yes.''

Lewis did not care for Eva Bauer. To see Dan plunging headlong into a friendship with her— he patted Jenny's hand.

"It is dangerous for a doctor's wife to be jealous. And an analyst, in particular, must be able to rely upon his wife. How do you propose to handle your feelings about patients?''

Jenny looked right into his eyes. "I tell myself that Dan is incapable of violating the relationship between doctor and patient. But it nags me. However, it's the Marie Bonapartes, the Anna Freuds, the Melanie Kleins, with all their connections, whom I find far more threatening. Compared to them, patients are nothing.''

"That is an insult to three remarkably superior ladies. I should think you'd find it more—'' Lewis Miller did not complete that sentence. Instead, he continued; "Frau Professor Freud allowed her husband his relationship with both men and women. And several women played an important part in his life. Yet Freud is monogamous.''

Jenny remained unconvinced. "Do you know that his wife was content?''

Lewis Miller chuckled suddenly. "Damned if I know.'' Slowly he inhaled on his cigarette and became serious once more. "I gave Dan a lift this morning. The house he entered belongs jointly to two sisters, both of whom are neurologists engaged in research. Dan is, undoubtedly, involved in establishing his schedule and perhaps getting a few pointers. Were I you, I'd not let anything like this bother me. That's the sensible, the reasonable view. Now for the practical. You should be warned; women like Eva Bauer pay no heed to morals, to right and wrong. They flower on conquest.''

Jenny regarded Lewis Miller a long moment—the time it took to absorb his view of things. Then she asked, "Where does Eva Bauer live?''

"Practically next door to the hospital—just a walk from the Edison.''

"And the Professor?''

"Quite near. Why?''

Dan's lie hit her like a blast of thunder, and with great effort, she proceeded to confide her anxieties and muffled emotions to Dan's friend.

"Let me ask you, Jenny. What do you want out of marriage?''

"Everything. I want Dan to share his whole life with me. I want to be part of everything he does that is important to him. Right now, at the end of a long day, we meet and he makes love to me. That's wonderful—and I don't want that to change, but it takes more than that to make a true marriage. I'm also convinced that I have a contribution to make as a person. I've got to make myself more interesting and more interested so that he has no reason to make something special of an Eva Bauer or to seek her company.''

Lewis Miller had never come across anyone like Jenny. He looked down at the diamond-studded circle of platinum she wore. *Amazing,* he thought to himself, *how much it can mean to one woman and how little to another.*

"All right, Jenny. I'll help you. But if *I* decide personal analysis is indicated, are you prepared to go all the way?''

"I don't want to—very much, I don't want to. But if you have strong support for your opinion, I will. You have my word.''

Lewis Miller glanced at his wristwatch. After three. "I don't think we'll get to Semmering before Dan.''

"I don't want to.'' Jenny smiled. She did not feel it necessary to say to Lewis Miller, "You teach me what you know—psychiatry. I know about being a woman. And how I handle Dan is my concern.''

Lewis Miller told her that while the fog bothered him there was no reason for concern. He knew the roads up through the hills, and even though they seemed darkly mysterious, one could not miss the main route.

Motionless beside him, Jenny stared ahead. "Actually, I like fog. It reminds me of home." Jenny suddenly realized she was missing the foghorns. Soon she began thinking about San Francisco and its hills, and it was far more real to her than the Wienerwald.

Lewis Miller was finding it hard to keep his eyes open. The darkness, the silence. "Talk to me, Jenny."

"Sleepy?" she asked, lowering her window a little.

"I am a bit."

"It could be the wine."

"Tell me about Professor Freud. Tell me all the riddles. Why is he no longer identified as a human being?"

For moments Lewis Miller was preoccupied and silent, and then, without taking his eyes off the road, he started to talk. "In the spring of 1927, A. A. Brill, my then-analyst, terminated treatment. He said, 'Professor Freud is preoccupied with the problem of lay analysis; he is ill and plagued with pain; he leads a quiet life contenting himself with three patients a day. I am sending you to him. He needs a rich patient and you need him.'

"I sailed for Europe carrying with me an outspoken letter from Brill and an autobiographical sketch written in verse, which I called 'Black and White Judgments.' These, upon my arrival in Vienna, I sent to Freud by post, and in a few days I received his answer. He said that he was impressed by my poem and set the day and hour for our meeting. He received me in his drawing room as a guest. His critical gaze explored me beyond human vision. We spent an enchanting hour, during which we discussed Shakespeare and the comparative merits of Greek and Roman art. He conversed in excellent English; I, in German.

"Abruptly, his agreeableness ended. He made reference to my poem. His wit was barbed. In a few hours he knew my life history intimately. He said: 'You suffer from a displacement of dependency, and nurse on the penis as though it were a breast.' He refused to take me on as a patient but gave me his affable accessibility as a friend.

"Intrigued, I availed myself of every opportunity to be near the man who found his way into the unknown. I visited him, I followed him to meetings, I wrote to him, I read his every paper. His fame, his suffering, were mine." Lewis Miller paused. "Do you want to know more or have you heard enough?"

"Oh, much more. What kind of a man is Freud?"

Lewis Miller glanced at her. He continued talking. "Freud is a Jew. And were he not a Jew, Freud would not be Freud. He is arrogant, yet he has a strong sense of inferiority which dates back to a penurious youth. He is a pessimist with a huge capacity for fun. He is hostile, prejudiced, over-bearing, disagreeable, quarrelsome, and eccentric. He is also kind, polite, and amusing, as well as courageous, truthful, and compassionate. He stands for greater sexual freedom and is, in fact, a prude. It is said that he once told his friend Ferenczi, 'The overcoming of my own "homosexuality" brought me greater self-dependence.' "

Jenny gasped.

Lewis Miller turned slightly to look at her. "Homosexuality in parenthesis." His voice was gentle. "Freud used the word 'homosexuality' with purpose. He meant we each have two parents, male and female. It was his way of saying that he mastered his hostility to his father. Freud's sexual object was always a female. Does that sound crazy to you?"

Jenny said, "No. But what happens if a man does not master his hostility to his father?"

"Obviously, if a man has not mastered his hostility toward his father, he displays unbridled hatred toward authority figures, or he lives in abject fear of retaliation for his aggressive impulses."

Jenny was quietly reflecting on Dan and the harsh feelings he had shown toward his father ever since she had known him. But Dan surely did not hate authority, that she was certain of.

Lewis Miller guessed what was going through her mind.

"Simply because Dan does not show anything may be because he has fooled himself." When Jenny did not answer, he said, "It does not matter that you do not understand. These are the things I shall teach you." Still loquacious, his manner pedantic, he said, "There is a defense mechanism known as projection. In this way, a man disowns his own hostility and attributes it to another person. This is what Dan has done with his father. In general, the human organism prefers to feel danger as a menace from without rather than as a threat from within."

"Yes, Lewis, that I follow. One can protect one's self from the outside, but when fear is imprisoned within—"

"Good girl," Lewis Miller said heartily. "Now I quit. Your next les-son—" An incredulous look on his face, Lewis Miller said, "My God, we're here." The roadster braked to a stop. A familiar figure was framed in the rounded, ivycovered doorway.

The car door flew open and Dan cried, "Christ, where in hell have you two been? Even the mountain patrol claimed there was no way to find you in this blinding fog."

His worry was unmistakable. So was his relief. Jenny sat in silence, but

Lewis Miller said, with exasperation, "Don't stand there growling at us. Let us out of the car."

"Sorry." Dan stepped aside and tossed his cigarette away.

Lewis Miller got out of the car, but Jenny sat there without moving. "Go on in," Dan said to Lewis Miller. Then he took Jenny's hand. "Come. You must be cold and very tired."

"I'm neither," Jenny said and remained seated.

Dan slipped in beside her; then, fixing his eyes on her, he waited. Moments later he said, "We can't stay out here all night."

Tossing her head, Jenny said, "I can if I want to."

"No, you may not. Because the others are waiting dinner. Come now, you've had your revenge—you can be damn sure of that. I nearly went out of my mind with worry."

Jenny regarded him in the dark. "Do you blame me?"

"Be reasonable, Jenny. We'll have our chance to talk things over later."

"You're right. This is not fair to the others." She started to leave the car, but Dan stopped her. "I'd feel better if—"

Jenny turned and looked him full in the eyes. "Oh, Dan." Then she was in his arms. He held her close and she clung to him. After a time they saw through the darkness the small light of a flashlight. It was Bill Reilly calling them inside.

Lewis was, of course, absolutely right about Dan's feelings for his father.

It was well into the first year of Dan's analysis when he and Dr. Freitag had been talking about Dan's family.

DAN: "It was the summer between her junior and senior years and I hadn't seen Jenny for over two months, when her grandmother cabled from Cannes inviting me to join them in London. At dinner I informed my parents of the invitation. As I expected, Mother quickly said, 'You must go.' But Dad turned so that he faced her and said, 'I've a better idea, Miriam. My affairs are in fair shape here. I ought to be able to get away for a few weeks. What about you and I going along?' Dad looked extraordinarily pleased with himself.

"Mother answered in a voice so low she was hardly heard. 'I'm convinced, dear, it is only Dan and, perhaps, you, whom they want. Besides it would be difficult for me to leave just now.'

" 'Why difficult?' Dad sounded astounded.

" 'Haven't you guessed?' Mother answered. 'Marjorie is pregnant.'

" 'Why should I guess?' Dad asked with annoyance. 'Why wasn't I told?' Then he said, 'Marjorie is in good health. She has a perfectly capable husband. Please come with us, Miriam.'

" 'I'm afraid not' was the answer.

"With a shrug—"—Dan hesitated—"it was more than a shrug. It was a gesture of anguish, of sorrow—like a silent sob." The minutes passed. Then: "Dad strode away saying, 'Suit yourself.'

"I had, by this time, been used to Mother's refusals to go anywhere, so it was no shock to me. I accepted her decision without comment. A week later Dad and I were in London and a day or two after we were settled at Claridge's, we all drove out to Stratford-on-Avon, because Jenny wanted to see *Hamlet*.

"During the performance, I was thoroughly absorbed, overpowered. On the way back to London I was completely preoccupied." After a long pause: "I was tortured. Like Hamlet, my feelings toward my father were 'sicklied o'er with the pale cast of thought.' That night I couldn't fall asleep."

A: "This hyperreaction indicates that the playwright touched off something in your unconscious."

DAN: "I feel this is so."

A: "Can you put your finger on it?"

DAN: "*Hamlet* treats of the relationship of the son to his parents."

A: "As Freud explained: Hamlet is rooted in the soil of Oedipus Rex. And remember this. The drama of Hamlet was composed by Shakespeare when he was still mourning the death of his own father. Freud suggests the revival of his own childish feeling in respect to his father."

DAN: "I remember I felt threatened."

A: "It seemed to me, by the intensity of the emotion, that the tragedy of Hamlet must have touched off your own patricidal impulses."

DAN (at last speaking): "Claudius is not Hamlet's father."

A: "The hostility that Hamlet has for the queen's lover, his uncle, is the displacement of the hostility to his father in the original family triangle."

DAN: "This does not apply to me. It was my father who was unfaithful."

A: "You are distressed by both arms of the triangle—the resentment to father and the affinity to mother."

Dan becomes contemplative. He remains silent. As the hour draws to a close, Dan says, "I had a dream about my sister. I was in bed with her."

A: "We've run out of time. We'll talk about it tomorrow."

The next hour.

Dan avoids the dream. He talks trivia. He suddenly remembers a friend who collects African art, and this reminds Dan of a book on modern primitivism. "I rather enjoyed it. The idea that—"

Analyst interrupts.

A: "You've forgotten to mention your dream."

DAN: "What dream?"

A: "You said you had a dream about your sister."

DAN: "Er-er-it's vague—closed off."

Dr. Freitag allows Dan time to think, to remember.

DAN (his face tightened in concentration): "It comes back to me. The whole dream."

A (nodding): "I thought it would."

DAN: "I was in bed with my sister. We were just talking. My father opened the door, saw us, and, in a violent rage, accused me of crawling through the darkness to take pleasure with my sister. I told him he had the wrong idea.

" 'That's a laugh,' he said, still frenzied.

"Then he tried to chase me out of her room, but it was I who chased him out."

The analyst waits.

DAN: "That's all there is. That's the whole dream."

A: "Can you place the dream in time?"

DAN: "In the dream I was maybe twelve."

A: "Then your sister was about twenty-four."

DAN: "Yes." For a moment Dan was silent. "Strange that I should dream of my sister."

A: "Does the dream bear any relationship to an actual happening?"

DAN: "None. I was never close to my sister. My father—though he tried to repress his feelings or, at least, hide them—was completely indifferent to her."

A: "It is more likely that this dream is about your mother. Your sister is the dream distortion brought about by censorship."

DAN: "I certainly did not need to distort my father's rage."

Dan's voice sounded hostile.

A: "What this dream really indicates is your rage."

DAN (still denying his Oedipal situation): "I don't recall any such rage."

A: "The dream must satisfy something."

Dan does not challenge this assertion. "I agree. In some way, by some means, it is an endeavor to express something."

Dr. Freitag noted the significance of Dan's blind indefiniteness and called his attention to it. He concluded the hour with: "One of your defenses is your tendency to intellectualize. This enables you to talk about unconscious mechanism without really being in touch with your feelings. You have the words. The trouble is you don't have the music yet."

Dan's anger was rising as he got up from the couch. At the door he swung around. He studied the analyst's face. Then, with a polite nod, he turned away as though he thought it wiser not to speak.

Dan arrived at the Kinderklinik where he had been working for two months. It had all been arranged for him to listen to a case presentation by Dr. Emil Von Urban, a lecturer at the Allgemeines Krankenhaus and a distinguished physician. Dan was fortunate, as more and more students were making their way to his clinics. Everyone who could find chairs had been seated when Dan saw Dr. Von Urban approach. He had a kindly look and there was an air of dignity, of calm assurance, about him.

Emil von Urban started talking about Franz, a child of about six, who appeared alert and intelligent but who did not speak. His hearing was normal. At unexpected sounds made out of his line of visions, he blinked. And though he never responded to the spoken word, he seemed to understand.

In discussing the diagnosis, Von Urban dismissed the possibility of organic brain disease, either congenital or acquired. Rather he proposed that this was a case of bad learning from infancy.

"Franz never learned to talk," said Von Urban, "because no one ever spoke to him or because all of his wishes were anticipated and granted, and therefore he had no need to talk."

Von Urban termed this condition "audimutitas." "It means," he said, "mute because the technique of speech has not been mastered."

The young doctors and the medical students started asking questions then.

"Herr Dozent, could not this condition also have resulted from a single severe fright?"

"Nothing in the history suggests a severe trauma."

"What is the general attitude in the home?"

"As far as we know, the parents are intelligent, stable people. They seem devoted to the child. At this point they are desperately seeking help."

It seemed to Dan listening attentively, his eyes fixed on Von Urban, that there was an extreme contradiction in this case. He could not visualize this apparently old little boy, strangely isolated, the child of intelligent, stable parents. "Herr Dozent," said he, "did this child develop this condition because of a lack of stimulation or was he somehow overstimulated by a threatening environment?"

"My feeling is that Franz was understimulated and probably—at least in some degree—neglected in spite of what the parents claim. Strange how quickly parents repress things so that there's nothing to reproach themselves with."

There were no more questions.

Dr. Von Urban took off his glasses, wiped them with his handkerchief. He then replaced them. "I have told the parents I want Franz admitted as quickly as possible. He'll probably be with us this afternoon. I want him watched by a nurse who will maintain a warm, tender, friendly attitude. I want him placed in a totally empty room once a day for a two-hour session with an adult in constant attendance. If he wants a drink of water, if he wants a toy, if he wants to go to the bathroom, he must make his want known verbally. Only then is he to be given whatever he asks for. And he is to be given praise. The praise is very important.

"Questions?" asked Von Urban.

"Are you providing Franz with the complete attention of an adult for two consecutive hours?"

Von Urban nodded his head slowly. "But, of course."

"Herr Doktor Von Urban," said Dan, "must it be a nurse?"

Von Urban raised a brow and listened.

"May I have those two-hour sessions with Franz? Please."

"My dear young American," the Dozent protested, "you must not let your enthusiasm run away like that. You realize that reeducating Franz won't be easy. You might find the task you set for yourself quite tedious."

"I don't think I'll be bored, Herr Doktor."

"No harm in trying," said Von Urban pleasantly. "And I congratulate you on your enterprise."

They smiled at each other.

"Is it all right for me to start today?"

"It's your patient."

"Thank you."

"Keep me informed." Dr. Von Urban checked his watch. He dismissed the clinic. *"Auf Wiedersehen, meine Herren."*

Other than two chairs, a clock which hung on the wall, and a black telephone, the windowless isolation room was cleared of all paraphernalia.

Dan settled himself in the larger of the two chairs and looked at Franz. He saw a healthy-looking youngster smaller than average, clean and very neat in a dark blue suit and highly polished shoes.

"Hello, Franz. I'm Herr Doktor Gunther. If you wish, you may call me Dan."

Franz looked at Dan with no flicker of interest.

"You and I, Franz, will be spending part of each day alone with each other. I'll talk to you and I want you to talk to me."

Franz looked up at the clock.

"The adjoining lavatory is locked. If you want to use the facility, you must tell me. I have the key."

Franz continued to look up at the clock.

"When you get thirsty, let me know. There's a glass in there on the washbasin."

It was as if Franz heard nothing. He began to walk about, taking absolutely no notice of Dan. At the end of the first two-hour session, there was a puddle on the floor and his pants were wet.

Dan made no mention of it.

For four days Dan talked to Franz and ignored the puddle and the wet pants, and for four days Franz made no sound. On the fifth day Franz said, "Water."

"Good boy! That's fine." Dan took this normally ordinary occurrence of a boy asking for water and made Franz feel important. On that fifth day Franz stayed dry.

Progressively each day Franz added new words in his requests for objects, and each day Dan responded with praise and affection. He had a tolerance and liking for youngsters that matched his professional care. Improvement continued, and Dan began to bring Franz little presents. Well into the third week Franz began to talk in sentences. By then he had accumulated toys, and Dan observed him in spontaneous activity, taking note that his patterns of play were highly repetitive with little or no dramatic expression.

At the end of the month Dan invited the parents into the two-hour session. On that day the door opened inward and a handsome, well-dressed man with a plump, blond woman were there. Franz ran toward Dan, who placed his arm around the boy's shoulder and gently urged him forward. Franz hung back. Both his mother and his father were now talking to him, but he took no notice of them. He pulled away from Dan; he became mute and detached, and ignoring his toys and games, he stared at the wall clock; and he wet his pants.

Crushed, the mother said, "But, Herr Doktor, we were told he was making marvelous progress."

"He'll be all right."

After that the room filled with quietness. The parents walked slowly away. As the door shut behind them, Franz's eyes fell on Dan. Then he knelt down and touched his blocks.

Dan knelt down, too. "What shall we build?"

"A tall building."

As Franz carefully placed wood on wood, Dan talked to the boy. Then he observed the completed structure, and Franz gazed at him, entranced. "A present," he said.

"A present for whom, Franz?"

"Für meine Mutti."

Dan nodded.

"Will they come again?"

"When do you want them?"

"Soon."

Dan sighed deeply. After the nurse came for Franz, he went in and had a talk with Dr. Von Urban.

"He will be well very soon."

He was—and Dan was grateful for it.

The nine doctors who met together as comrades and colleagues, for evening sessions that fall of 1930, were all deeply concerned with how psychoanalysis could work best. In their meetings, they argued, complained, discussed, and theorized on all aspects of their chosen field—even to the mundane business of earning a living. As their skills sharpened, so their meetings became less superficial and they experienced real interaction, an exchange between personalities. "Fair exchange," eight of them called it. Lewis Miller named it group treatment.

This was not entirely true for Dan. He was not looking for therapy from the collective action of his contemporaries. He felt it inappropriate to discuss his father. For himself, he rejected the idea that mother meant a sexual affinity. He was thoroughly convinced that between him and Jenny everything was perfect. And Dan felt secure in the traditional belief that the healers are themselves wholly healed.

One wet Friday afternoon, late in November, Jenny rang him up at the hospital. "Are you planning another get-together tonight, Dan? Will it be here?"

"We were. Why?"

"It's the stale smell of cigarettes and beer, Dan. Das Zimmer is meant to sleep in."

"Jenny, you didn't say anything before. As a matter of fact, I thought you rather liked the idea. But if you feel you don't want the others around, we'll find another meeting place."

"No, Dan. That's not it. I finally figured out a way to put myself to bed in cool comfort and still listen to you talk when I want to by leaving open the connecting door. But I need two men to transfer the wardrobe into the bedroom and move the bed into the dressing room."

"I'll bring Bill back. We'll do it."

"Dan, do you want me to pick up some wurst and beer?"

"Don't go out in this weather. I can easily manage on the way home."

"Thanks, darling."

Some hours later they met. Jenny was settled now in the dressing room. Tascha was with her.

"I liked it better the other way."

Jenny sat up straighter in the bed. "Sorry about that."

"No, you're not."

Jenny looked at her with a smile.

"Want to play gin?" Tascha said.

"All right. Close the door."

"Oh, for heaven's sake—"

"The door, Tascha."

Not only did Tascha lose, but she missed an excellent session. It began dramatically with Lewis Miller's announcement. "As soon as Dan and Jenny decide they have had enough of Vienna, I'm off to associate myself with Magnus Hirschfeld in Berlin."

Abe's mouth started to open.

All his friends had made the immediate assumption that his reason for going was further therapy with the world's greatest authority on homosexuality. For the first time Dan felt consummate dismay for his friend. His action seemed to confirm what he knew the others were thinking.

Lewis Miller knew it was equivalent to a confession. He liked shocking them, mocking them, intriguing them with his arrogance. He then gave them his true reason for going to Berlin.

"I go like a knight-errant with a mission. The ideal society has, aside from its conformists, its dissenters. And the ideal society gives the dissenter his right to dissent. Our society's attitude toward the sexual deviate is wrong. If, as serious doctors, we conclude that homosexuality is a terrible affliction, then let us make some effort to understand the illness, its cause and course. Laws that forbid, moral rage that derides, prudery hampered by rumor, all reveal our own hostility and concealed cowardice.'' He turned his round, sharp-eyed face to Bill Reilly. ''You—the epitome of the masculine male—do uninvited dreams bring you fantastic imagery? Does the dream consist of a man running down the street being pursued by a much larger man and being unable to outdistance his pursuer? Is it not inevitable that the flee-er will be caught? And does that not mean that he who runs, wishes to be caught? And who is he who runs? The dreamer! Right?''

Abe spoke as if to himself. ''A kick in our collective balls.''

Bill didn't say anything. Lewis Miller, intent upon a response from him, persisted. Bill rocked his chair and stared at Miller a full thirty seconds before he said, ''The next time I dream, I'll draw the blinds.''

They all carefully thought that over.

Dan's quick mind recalled something from Freud's basic writings. He recited in German. ''What animals dream of I do not know. A proverb, for which I am indebted to one of my pupils, professes to tell us, for it asks the question, 'What does the goose dream of?' and answers, 'Maize.' The whole theory that the dream is the fulfillment of a wish is contained in these two sentences.''

Lewis Miller was shaking an angry finger at Dan. ''Jenny has learned more insight into fundamental psychiatry from me than you'll ever learn from memorizing Freud. Go back to America. Lie down on the couch. Experience what Freud proved. 'Man is man and nothing human is alien to him.' ''

''Right on the button.'' said Joe Sarofolo.

''Get lost,'' was Dan's reply.

''Let's be frank, Dan.'' Piotr Dubinsky finished his beer and put down his glass. ''If in your house, Papa loved Mama and Mama loved Papa and everyone loved Danny boy, like in an MGM movie, what in the hell are you doing here with us? Why aren't you a Park Avenue pill dispenser for the rich? Here we are living evidence of parental foul-ups. We're all neurotics in some way. We differ from others only because we admit to being neurotic and because we hope that by understanding ourselves we'll be able to help others.''

Peter Rice turned to Dan and spoke thoughtfully to him. ''I'd be interested to know more about you.''

Bill Reilly stretched his long legs. ''Me, too, Dan. Times when we recollected childhood traumata as clinical contributions, you hedged, offering us no idea of the influences in your life.''

Dan put a piece of cheese in his mouth. "I'm flattered by your interest. However, no melodrama lingers in my past. I had a normal sunny childhood. My mother didn't put me in dresses and call me 'beautiful baby.' And my Dad told me about the bees and the birds in fitting human terms."

Lewis Miller spoke for them all. "You betray the spirit of our meetings. You cannot be partially involved and still be one of us."

"OK, OK." Dan pulled loose his tie. He sighed. "My grandfather was a country doctor in upstate New York. His popularity secured my father sponsorship into West Point. A hell of a good athlete, he attracted considerable attention from the top brass. And his rugged good looks attracted considerable attention from the ladies. Four days after he was commissioned, he astonished everyone by marrying a girl from his hometown—a quiet girl with clear blue eyes and pale blond hair, whom none of his friends had ever seen. They were a strange couple." In a few verbal brushstrokes, Dan managed a description of their differences, paused an instant, and twice started before he could say, "My fourth sister lived. A lot older than I, she's plain, she's a prude and tormentedly attached to our father, who's crazy about her four kids but leaves the room if her husband enters. Well," Dan concluded, "that's it."

"Oh, come on—" Abe said and waited.

"What," Dan asked firmly, "do you specifically want to know?"

"Is your father a Jew?"

"He's an atheist."

Abe turned and pointed his remark to Jerry Blake. "A Jewish atheist is a guy without the guts to convert to Christianity." He turned back to Dan. "What sort of Jews did your mother come from—Ethical Culturists or Jewish Scientists?"

"She comes from Jewish Jews who converse in English and communicate in Yiddish. My mother is the daughter of an old-fashioned rabbi."

"That's lovely," Abe mocked. "You make me feel so damned good."

"How did your old man get rich in the Army?"

"None of your damn business. That has no bearing on my psyche." Dan's hostile reply was directed at all of them.

Piotr Dubinsky broke in before anyone could say another word. "I quarrel with that."

Lewis Miller said, "Don't hedge with us, Dan."

Abe said, "Think of the times you asked loaded questions."

"For Christ's sake—what *do* you want of me?"

"Isn't it clear, Dan? Talk about the money."

"Tell them," Lewis said, gently.

"My father owns an interest in a munitions concern—a damn lucrative business. Of course, he resigned his commission before he became a munitions manufacturer."

They were all quiet.

Dan pushed himself further. "My mother's gentle appeal vanishes in his presence. She is swamped by him. She just isn't his intellectual or physical equal. That's why, in my mind, I always keep them separate. Only so can I keep a channel of mental—even visual—communication open with my mother."

Dan misread their silence. Now, at last, they were satisfied. He was wrong. The group demanded more of him. Again, it was Bill Reilly. "It need not be a catastrophe, but it's a meaningful day—the day a boy finds out that his father cheats. How old were you, Dan, when you discovered your mother's loneliness?"

Cornered, Dan lit a cigarette.

In the silence Lewis Miller stared unseeing in Dan's direction and into the past.

It was in Paris and his mother was between husbands. Early one evening the maid opened the door of their apartment to a formidable, powerfully built man with fine, deepset, dark eyes. Beside him was a boy correctly dressed in a dark suit. The boy held a small leather bag. Lewis Miller's mother came hurrying toward them, smiling happily, the bright gleam of laughter in her eyes.

"So you're Dan. I've been curious about you." She gazed up at the man. "Andrew, he's beautiful."

"The lady admires you, son."

The boy seemed indifferent to the grown-ups. His eyes were on Lewis, who drifted over. *A neat operation,* Lewis thought to himself, *discreet and with the look of innocence—a friend making a call.*

Lewis Miller shook himself out of his reverie. As his eyes caught Dan's, he said with emotion, "You didn't know that time in Paris—did you, Dan?"

"I knew."

Lewis Miller nodded. "Which means you were about eleven. Sounds young, doesn't it?"

Dan rose. In a few long strides he was at the dressing room door. Opening it inward, he found Jenny and Tascha together in the middle of the bed sitting lotus fashion.

"The session is over," he said. "If you want something to eat, come and get it now."

Tascha's voice rose loud enough to be heard in the other room. "I want corned beef and cheese on sour rye." "I must admit it's nice being waited on," she added and slid off the bed.

Jenny got up, too. About a half hour after they were gone, Jenny looked around in relief. The room was aired and tidy.

The bathroom door opened and Dan stepped out. Bathed and shaved, he wore pajama bottoms. "Come," he said, catching Jenny's hand.

Jenny glanced up at him. "I thought I'd bathe."

"Not now."

"All right then. I'll just brush my teeth."

Dan followed her into the bathroom and sat down on the edge of the tub. "How much did you and Tascha hear?"

"We heard nothing—the door shuts out the sound of voices." Jenny drew her brows together in a frown. "Why are you bothered about it?"

Dan shrugged.

A few seconds later she was creaming her face. "What's the matter with you?"

"Jenny," Dan said cautiously, "you spent a lot of time with my father. Did he ever confide in you? I mean about personal matters."

"Y-yes"—Jenny turned around a second time—"but—"

"Did he tell you he was responsible for the accident that caused the death of two of my sisters?"

"Yes, but he didn't tell me how it happened; I don't think he could bring himself to talk about it. All he said was 'Dan's mother has a charitable nature. She never blighted my life with blame. For that I owe her much'."

Dan looked into Jenny's searching eyes. "What else?"

"Once he told me that he honestly loved your mother and thought her modest, gentle ways wonderful." Jenny looked away. She brought out a fresh towel and used it to wipe the cream off her face.

She did not speak again until after she threw back the covers of the bed and crawled in under the blankets. "What happened in there tonight?"

"I don't want to talk about it."

Jenny's smile was astonishingly warm. "I think I'm relieved."

Dan raised a brow.

Jenny nodded. "Because all day I've been looking forward to now."

Dan bent down and looked deep into her dark eyes. "So have I," he said very quietly.

Looking up at him, Jenny waited until his arms drew her to him, then her lips met his. Their last kiss was gentle, and then Jenny was asleep at once. Dan rested, thinking, watching the soft shadow cast by the one night bulb. A patient observer, he had an immense curiosity about the human mind. Dan was trying hard to formulate an idea he had into a theory. In later years he would explain it. But now he could not figure out why each person had his own pattern and that that pattern tended to repeat itself over and over. He wondered: *Is this what Freud described as the repetition compulsion, the attempt on the part of the organism to heal itself in the hope of arriving at a new solution?* Despite what he thought of Freud, Dan said to himself, *I cannot agree with this. I cannot see how healing takes place. If anything, the repetition compulsion must perpetuate old problems. Still, it must serve a purpose. A means of communication.* Stretched on his back looking up at the ceiling, Dan fell asleep.

He awoke with his face pushed into the pillow. Then Dan remembered the dream. A girl with soft pale hair was running after him; while he, looking over his shoulder toward her, ran as hard as he could until a stone tripped him and he fell into the tall grass. Only then did he see that her eyes were a pale blue. He lifted his head and glanced toward Jenny. In the dark he observed her coppery mass of hair—nothing like the girl in the dream. He brushed his lips against her cheek and went back to sleep. When he awoke for the second time, he had no recall of the dream. He climbed out of bed and, picking up his robe, tiptoed out of the dressing room. He got away from his friends, from conferences and arguments, and except for one light meal and two brisk walks in the snow, he spent the whole day in the library with books on dreams published in Germany. He was searching for a reason.

As they left for dinner, Jenny remarked, "The whole day?"

"Yes, Jenny. I went directly to the textbooks, secluded myself, and went through a pile of references."

I must ask Lewis his opinion, Jenny thought.

When Jenny had time to herself, she liked wearing her older slacks while she busied herself with reading or letter writing. This struck the landlady as unusual—so much so that she had to discuss it with her friends around the coffee table. They agreed that it was not altogether proper for a girl to dress like a boy. They sat in conference on other issues, too. "In all my years," the landlady said, "I never met anyone less impressed with the title 'Frau Doktor.' "

"A typical American attitude" was one comment.

"The penalty of democracy" was another.

Another habit of Jenny's, upon which the ladies sat in judgment, was her daily bath—fancy risking catching cold. Once a week was quite sufficient.

"I cannot prevent myself from thinking the Americans are basically a very dirty people." The landlady delivered a whole speech against the Americans to prove her point. Talking about Jenny never lost its novelty; she was the first wife to occupy Das Zimmer in all the years it had been rented to foreigners. Jenny, kept informed by the maid, maintained a cordial attitude, knowing the ladies suffered from a shortage of interests.

At the Café Edison, Julius, whose taste ran to ample breasts and broad thighs, also had his say. "American girls!" he would grumble. "Half-starved. Emaciated beanpoles. Bah!"

The Americans, however, saw nothing wrong with Jenny. They were proud of her. She and Tascha had formed a bridge group with some other American women attached to the university. Jenny played well. She divided her winnings. One half she gave to Julius to distribute equally among his waiters; the other half went into the poor box. When the mail arrived, there were a number of players at the Edison, partly for company, partly for warmth. Julius left his bar to deliver Jenny's letters to her personally. Jenny quickly played out her hand and said, "Let's make this the last rubber."

They played another forty minutes without stopping because their opponents kept overbidding and going down.

Finally, without apology, Jenny said, "All right. I've had enough."

Jenny made straight for an empty booth and lit a cigarette. One letter was addressed to her. Mailed from San Francisco, it was from her grandmother.

Dear heart, it started.

In these unsettled times of economic upheaval, there is financial ruin for many a house with only paper wealth. One way or another, almost everyone is affected. As always, the greatest casualties are among the poor. Men are bewildered; women, torn to pieces. There are numerous suicides, especially in the big cities. The government will have to intervene with assistance. Jobs for the men—food for the children, the real victims. Enough of this unhappy tale.

We, Jenny my child, are all right. Your mother and I look at each other and, without saying a word, are on the one hand grateful, on the other, a little guilty about our prosperity. The only profit your mother ever understood was the profit that came from real property. Consequently, her tall buildings here in the city, happily divided between offices and securely leased stores, bring in their monthly rentals.

But I, too, am fine. I do not exaggerate when I tell you that my land, tucked here and there in our state, will be worth a fortune. As for my stock certificates, my little pieces of America, let them rest in the bank vault. Like Sleeping Beauty, they will awake to a new era. Little Jenny, if God calls me, don't be frightened and sell. Have faith in America.

Your mother is a volunteer worker in a community kitchen. I have my hands full, providing a daily hot meal for schoolchildren. At night we look forward to your letters. Keep them coming.

Father Andrew telephoned and gave us the news. Dan must be absolutely devastated. Take care of him. Give him our love. I embrace you both.

Lovingly,
GRANDMOTHER

The second letter, which Jenny—in haste—ripped open, was addressed to her and to Dan. Mailed from downtown Manhattan, it was from Andrew Gunther.

DEAR DAN AND MY DEAREST JENNY,

I have to deliver a blow. Unfortunately, there is no way to spare you.

First, let me say that I am carrying out your mother's wish to the letter. I pledged my solemn oath.

One month ago today, Miriam suffered a heart attack. Within three hours I was by her hospital bedside. She pressed her hand into mine and said, "Once we were close. Somehow we lost each other. The sadness is that it really doesn't matter to either of us. Now, Andrew, I want your promise. Do exactly as I say."

I gave her my word. Here are hers.

"Bury me without fuss in true orthodox fashion. Keep my death secret from my son and his lovely bride for exactly thirty days. Tell Daniel not to weep. I am very tired and glad to go. Tell him, too, to be loyal to Jenny. Give them both my blessings."

Then Miriam closed her eyes. She left this earth quietly, just as she used to close doors. Your mother never did make noise—not in life, not in death.

Now I tell you the worst news possible, and before you have the chance to comprehend any grief, I must disclose the stupidities of your mother's will. At a time when I've taken a beating on the stock market and losses from holding too much paper in the form of second mortgages, your mother distributes the enormous fortune I gave her to charities. Miriam's legal declaration starts: "The law should forbid private gain from the sale of arms. I therefore, etc. etc." Dear, sweet Jenny, don't, as Dan's mother did, think of me as a King of Death. I'm just a businessman, dealing with other businessmen.

The house and furnishings are left to your sister, along with all personal possessions, with the exception of one gem diamond whose size and brilliance offended Miriam's modest tastes. This stone is yours, Jenny. Enjoy it; your luster outshines it. Not one thin dime is left to you, Dan. The will states: "My beloved Daniel begins a new life. His admirable profession frees him from the need of dirty money." So Dan, I have just deposited another ten thousand dollars to your account. You're my son, too.

I find the next sentences tough to write despite my determination to lay it on the line.

I have remarried. Your sister Marjorie rants and raves, 'You should have waited—at least a year.' I, however, find no respect in hypocrisy, no opiate in religion or public opinion.

Helen, my wife, is some eighteen years my junior. She has more than her fair share of good looks. She slams doors and loves a good time. She suits me. As a matter of truth, she has suited me for a number of years. In return for those years, I have given her my name and a decent settlement. She has signed away all claim to my estate. My will gives Marjorie her portion outright. Your money is in trust, Dan, for my grandchildren. That way you can't pull a stunt like your mother pulled. My deposit for Jenny is something very special.

Until I decide where Helen and I will live, we are in residence at the Sherry Netherland. I'd better draw an end to this letter by saying I am impatiently awaiting word from you both. I never could satisfy my father and we drew apart. I never could satisfy your dear, gentle mother, either. But you, Dan—we used to be pals. Remember? Your attitude *really* matters. And you, Jenny. I am counting heavily on your good sense.

My love,
DAD

February 12, 1931.

Jenny carefully put the letter back into its torn envelope and stuffed it into her purse. Walking past the wooden tables and chairs and into the clothes closet, she pulled on her overshoes and lifted her coat off its hanger. Lost in thought, she left the Café and walked slowly and thoughtfully through the dismal slush of the near-empty streets, past the dreary-looking apartment dwellings, trying to sort out her feelings and, more important, the images racing through her mind. There was a sense of shock in Andrew Gunther's legalized union with his mistress; it quickened her grief more than Miriam Gunther's death. Nearing Das Zimmer, Jenny was ready to admit to herself that she reproached her mother-in-law for dying and making way for her rival. "Let this be a lesson," she cautioned herself.

Through the courtyard entrance, Jenny came out of the early winter darkness into her quarters, also dark and silent. Like a stranger, she searched for the light. A look at the clock and she moved quickly for the telephone. Giving the operator Dan's number at the hospital, she continued to stare at the clock with considerable apprehension.

"Herr Doktor is already outside."

"Please run after him. Quickly."

"I don't think—"

"I am Frau Doktor Gunther. It is urgent. Try, please."

Dan returned on the run, taking the stairs in long leaps. "Jenny!"

"Please come home alone" was all she said.

"What's wrong with you?"

"Nothing is wrong with me, Dan. Why can't I ask for an evening all to ourselves? Maybe I want to—"

She got no further. "Good God, Jenny," Dan said irritably. "You scared the hell out of me."

"Dan, there's something else."

"I can't. I'll see you at the Golden Hirsch about nine."

"Dan, don't hang up."

With sharpness in his voice, Dan explained. "Anna Freud phoned. If I go right now, her father will receive me."

"Afterward, may we—?"

"Jenny, we must talk later."

The connection went dead.

Jenny's face went white. She burst into sobs. Her heart seemed to be breaking. Finally, when she understood that she was weeping for Dan's mother, her tears dried.

Lewis Miller arrived exactly at eight. He took a few steps into the room, bowed slightly, then looked at her curiously. "Something wrong? Why the black dress?"

"Don't you like it?"

"I prefer you in color."

"Shall we go, Lewis?"

Completely puzzled, Lewis Miller helped her with her coat and opened the door. They reached the restaurant well before Dan and chatted as the others arrived. The proprietor brought drinks for everyone. "Herr Doktor left the order," he said, looking happy.

Half an hour later, as the mood was becoming convivial and glasses were emptied, Dan danced through the entrance, his hands clasped in the air like a boxer, a broad smile on his face, his cheeks boyishly flushed. All ten faces stared up at him. Jenny's outfit immediately caught his eye. A soft black material with long full sleeves, it hugged her body like a glove. Taking a second to think about it, he realized he'd never seen the dress before, and that it made her look older, somewhat melancholy and remote, but lovelier. Dan drew a deep breath and said softly, "Hello, sweetheart." Jenny made the effort. She smiled a slow, little smile and lifted her face. Geared for a celebration, Dan made the kiss last.

Dan lifted his glass.

The questions they put to him came like shots from a pistol. "How did it go?" "Did his mind soar?" "What advice did he have to give?" "Did he feel tired?" "Is he weak?" "Did he give you tea?" At no point did they give him the chance to answer. "Tell us about the house. Is it grand?"

"It doesn't matter if it also suits his wife."

"It does matter. There's no need for. . . ."

"Shut up, Tascha. Let Dan talk."

"All right, all right."

"I have plenty to tell." Dan took his time and told it well, making every detail of the dark, old-fashioned room and the introduction to the Master come alive.

It was not a very imposing house that the father of modern psychiatry had lived in for the past thirty-five years. But it did not have to be. A not very large, somewhat shabby apartment situated over a grocery store in the ninth district, it suited him excellently. Dan had climbed up the first flight of stairs and knocked at the door. It opened and Anna Freud asked him to come in. She was short, almost dumpy, with clear blue eyes that said more than her outward appearance. The intelligent honesty of her face impressed him. Eager and somewhat hesitant, Dan followed her short figure down the hallway. She opened the door to her father's study.

"I can't believe I am here, Miss Freud. I wish I knew how to thank you."

His genuine gratitude made her smile. "Your interest in children is sufficient thanks. Come in, come in, come in."

Anna's smile widened and she waved him in. "Go quickly. Father is a very impatient man."

Sigmund Freud greeted Dan with a handshake. Dan noticed that the eyes that met his burned like a flame and that Freud's movements were light and quick, even though he looked frail and stooped. He moved forward, his heart pounding; it's a little like meeting God, thought Dan.

"Look around," Freud commanded in his good English, "and describe what you see."

Dan's thoughts raced. Unsure, he tried to mask his surprise as honesty versus nicety shot through his mind.

"Go on." The Professor sounded irritable.

"I see a room that is narrow, rectangular, high-ceilinged, and—though it faces a courtyard—quite dark. A white-tiled stove is to my left. A table covered with plush stands—"

"A table covered with worn, faded plush. Be accurate."

Dan saw that Dr. Freud's eyes had a twinkle and that his seeming annoyance had disappeared. "Yes, sir. A table covered with worn, faded plush stands in the middle of the room. The pictures all hang high on the walls. All the furniture is quite plain—"

"And ugly and shows wear," Freud told Dan, chuckling. "Come, let us sit down."

When they were seated on two straight chairs facing each other, Freud said, "Your friends will want to know if the appointments in Freud's reception room are suited to his prestige." Again he chuckled. This time with considerable force.

Dan had to laugh. The old man was enjoying himself.

Freud's quick eyes took in everything—the intelligence, the handsomeness, the pleasing personality. He decided he liked the young American. He stood up and moved his chair at the head of the couch in the corner. Switching from English, which he spoke well, to German, he began to talk to Dan on the level of teacher to a young colleague. First, he spoke of training, telling Dan that the purpose of the analysis of every analyst is to increase his clinical proficiency. Cautioning Dan never to forget his physiology and biology, he suddenly mentioned his own compulsion to work. And then—all in the same breath or so it seemed—he said, "A patient under analysis should be seen six days a week—a decrease in hours is an undesirable concession."

All the while he spoke, Dan looked into his face, concentrating completely on every word. Suddenly Freud lapsed into deep thought.

Dan sat there wondering what to do. Anna had warned him. "Limit your visit." His conflict was obvious to the old man's prying eyes. "What is it?" he asked. "Did my daughter instruct you to leave as soon as possible?"

"Well, sir—she—"

"I know, I know. Always now the same caution. It makes me feel centuries old." He paused to pour a chocolate drink out of a porcelain pitcher. "The hot chocolate becomes cold chocolate. Drink it anyway."

Dan sensed a deep tiredness in the old man. He raised the cup to his lips and drank slowly. When he finished, he said, "That was delicious. Thank you."

Freud's energy rallied. He studied Dan and said, "Don't let yourself become anxious about my tiredness—it comes and it goes. I pay it no mind."

Dan nodded slightly.

"I have things, important things, to say to you, Daniel Gunther. You have committed yourself to the study and practice of psychoanalysis. You will pass your knowledge on. My American friends I prize, and I consider their full support urgently necessary to the growth of psychoanalysis. There was my time—a time of revolution and discovery. Now, in collaboration with your contemporaries, is your time. You must all be made free to contribute. You must look closer into people's thoughts and their problems. Be both tenacious and sagacious. And be courageous. Mistakes will be made. Don't worry about them. Learn from them. The most striking, the most advanced diagnostic procedures, the truest scientific methods, the perfect understanding, and, perhaps, even the perfect treatment will, for obvious reasons, not come until the time of your sons. If psychoanalysts lose sight of the fact that science is a continuous open end, and if they stifle new ideas and increments of knowledge, they will bear the burden of turning psychoanalysis into a stagnant discipline."

For a moment Freud rested. He put his feet up on the hassock, picked up a half-smoked cigar from the ashtray, struck a match, and after a puff or two he began to talk about people. He spoke of A. A. Brill's enthusiasm and intellectual curiosity; he praised Ernest Jones' talent; he mentioned, among others, Franz Alexander and Siegfried Bernfeld, calling the latter a brilliant lay analyst.

Dan sat very still, listening and waiting.

All at once Professor Freud put out his hand. Not quite touching Dan, he said, "I shall now make another little speech—on therapy this time. The whole trick in therapy is to break down defenses and defeat resistance. There are more ways to disarm a patient than there are legal juggleries to outwit the executioner. The ultimate strategy of breaking through the resistance is to get to and dissect the infantile neurosis. This can be done only through the establishment and working through of the transference.'' Professor Freud cleared his throat and drew in more cigar smoke. Dan understood now why Princess Bonaparte made so much of his passion for tobacco. Dan could almost feel the old man's enjoyment. However, before he could collect his thoughts, Professor Freud was again talking. "When you return to your friends later this evening, tell them that I told you an amusing episode that happens to be important."

"I am anticipating tonight, sir. You have a pupil with a good memory."

Professor Freud acknowledged Dan's remark with a knowing nod. "A few years back I took into therapy a young American doctor—personable, remarkably bright, and the son of a famous physician. Our first interview was perfect. I did the talking. However, before I gave my usual speech, which prepares the patient for free association, I introduced my dog, a magnificent Alsatian. I indicated the attachment that existed between my animal and me and advised my patient to regard the dog as fellow explorer into the depths of stored memories and buried emotions. At the conclusion of the hour, I gave the patient an appointment for the next day and dismissed him.

"My patient came regularly and promptly for months. He spoke, without conviction and without feeling, of current trivialities. My intelligent canine friend refused to tolerate such dribble. To escape boredom, he used the excuse of nature's call quite often during the hour. And I, like a good master, did my proper duty. I opened the door to let him out. Soon afterward I opened the door to let him in. The constant going and coming—coming and going—created in my patient a growing resentment.

"Finally he found the courage to speak out. 'This has got to stop. I can't stand it. Do you think, Professor Freud, that you can go on collecting money from a patient who means nothing to you or to your damn dog?' He elaborated on the theme of our rejection but put special emphasis on the dog's journeys in and out of the study rather than on my movements.

"I replied: 'My unusual dog fully comprehends your intellectualization. And he perceives the degree of your resistance. He requests my permission to leave only because you are doing nothing in your analysis. Once outside, he feels such compassion that he decides to come back and give you another chance. I know, for certain, that when your resistance is no longer a block in therapy, my dog will identify himself with you and will respond with acceptance to your unconscious.'

"My patient then remained silent for weeks.

"I, without hesitation, opened and closed the door. At last the day came.

My dog, back in the study at the time, was almost asleep at my feet when my patient burst into weeping. Whereupon my huge Alsatian leaped upon my patient, frightening him half to death. My patient's sobs became a heart-rending wail. The scale of my dog's pity for the man is beyond description. He pressed himself closer and moved his tongue over my patient's face, all the while caressing him with his paw. The only thing to do, I did. I left them to their mother-child union. It was to the good of both parties.''

Dan burst into hearty laughter. He could not help himself.

Professor Freud went on soberly: "Daniel Gunther—of course, I know that you've not even scratched the surface of the dynamics of psychoanalytic theory. But I'd like you to remember—so that you can go back to it, perhaps in a couple of years—that this vignette illustrates three of the basic principles of psychoanalysis. One and two—resistance in the service of defense against emotion. In this case, depression, which expressed itself as transference to the dog—really me—as the rejecting parent. And, finally, the triumph of the reality principle when the patient could permit himself to be accepted by the dog. Again me.''

Dan stood up, nodding his head firmly and shook hands with Professor Freud.

Dan, meanwhile, was caught up recounting his first impressions of the shabby surroundings which Freud's perceptiveness had pinpointed in his mind; he told of the shifts in mood, as the Master had moved from serious warning about psychiatry's future and the need to search for new ideas, new treatments, to the warm evaluation of his American colleagues. Finally, with a smile on his face, Dan stressed what seemed significant in the anecdote about the Alsatian, pausing to repeat the underlying therapeutic themes. The others, listening, bursting with their own stories about Freud, were caught up in Dan's tremendous elation and bombarded him with unending questions in their enthusiasm.

For Dan it was hard to believe that dessert had come and gone. He refused coffee and poured himself more wine. Lifting his glass, he said, "To Dr. Sigmund Freud.'' He was only dimly conscious of the fact that Jenny did not raise her glass to her lips. He looked around at the friendly, interested faces and said, "Jenny, no one wants to leave.'' Then he beckoned the waiter and ordered more wine. "Keep it coming.''

Jenny could hear their uttered words: Abe's, about his analyst of five months; Lewis' critical interjections. Her mind preoccupied, she paid no attention to them. Lighting one cigarette after another and with a feeling of blackness, she surrendered herself to the struggle going on in her mind.

She could see Dan's face in shock absorbing the enormity of his father's transgression. Her eyes welling full of tears, Jenny excused herself and, pulling her coat along, made for the ladies' room.

It was Lewis Miller who broke up the party. He turned to Dan. "Jenny is ill. Take her home."

Lewis Miller could not help but observe the pride of Dan's face. "Ridiculous! Jenny had whooping cough in fourth grade. She's never had a sick day since." He slid the wine bottle to Miller. "Here, Mother Hen, have another drink."

Tascha sounded as if she were trying to persuade herself. "Can't a girl have the blues—or cramps—without—"

The light touch of a man's hand to her thigh silenced Tascha. It was meant to. In an instant, the hand was gone. Tascha turned to look at Bill and found him eyeing Dan. Highly bewildered, Tascha quickly experienced a rush of pleasure.

In the short silence Lewis Miller's eyes flashed in anger. "Because the Old Man let you across his threshold, Dan, you can't pull yourself out of your emotional orgasm. Well, it was I who paved the way with Anna, don't forget. You are beholden to me. You'd better start after Jenny at once."

Dan did not stop to argue. He moved swiftly. Lewis Miller was at his heels. They found Jenny at the door waiting. Dan caught her roughly. "Tell him."

"What shall I tell him?"

"Are you or are you not ill?"

"No need." Lewis Miller smiled at her and held out his hand. "I'll drive you home."

Leaning against Dan, Jenny looked up. "Please, darling, I'm tired."

A glance passed between the men, and Lewis Miller repeated his offer. Jenny felt herself being lifted. "Let's go," said Dan, taking the lead.

At the door of Das Zimmer, Jenny waited while Dan unlocked the door. Then she gave Lewis a warm smile and touched his lips lightly with hers. He left them without speaking, moving silently.

As Dan made ready for bed, his thoughts were on Jenny—her telephone call—her complete withdrawal—she had scarcely uttered a single sentence all evening. Something pretty decisive had happened. That he knew. But what? Pregnant? Not likely. Bad news from California? Dan was confident that was not so, or else they'd be on their way home by now. Meanwhile, his certainty that illness was not the problem doubled.

When Dan entered the bedroom, he found Jenny in flannel pajamas—high-necked, long-sleeved, and tight-fitting. He looked at her somewhat surprised. *Why the pajamas,* he wondered fleetingly. *Armor?*

Lowering himself atop the covers, he faced Jenny, who sat cross-legged looking boyishly prim and extremely young with her hair brushed back over her ears, gripping a letter and watching him with something like dread.

"Here," she said, "I don't know how to tell you."

He accepted the letter without comment. Although he kept his head down, Jenny, watching, could see his face tighten, could hear his wild curse, see him struggling to comprehend the fact of Miriam's death.

Dan sprang to his feet. He crossed to the carved sideboard and drew out a bottle of brandy. He took a single tumbler and poured with measured care. He looked over the rim of his glass at Jenny.

She was brimming over with love and compassion, and her voice grew husky. "I can't sleep without you, darling. I'm too upset."

For an answer Dan turned abruptly and sipped his brandy, his hand trembling.

As Jenny lay awake trying to adjust to Dan's first reaction of anger, she came to the disturbing conclusion that Dan was not free to express his heart's ache. Finally, worn out, she dozed, knowing that for the moment, she could not help him. A few hours later, when she opened her eyes, Dan's arms were around her and a bitter cold wind was blowing in through the open window. Jenny found herself longing for another blanket and a hot drink, but realizing it would be difficult to manage either without disturbing Dan, she limited herself to snuggling up to Dan.

Dan said, his voice flat, "It's still dark."

She took his face into her hands. "Speak to me now," she begged.

Dan remained remote. "I don't feel a thing. I'm numb. Maybe I'm just hardhearted."

Jenny looked at him wide-eyed. "Wouldn't you cry if I died?"

He kissed her warmly and ruffled her hair. "Bear with me, Jenny," Dan said very quietly.

He climbed out of bed, crossed to the window and lowered it. Then he switched on the light—the morning was dark—and built up the fire. "Shall I see if the landlady can supply us with breakfast?"

Jenny shook her head. "Dan, come here."

He came to the bedside.

"Please, let's get away from here for a few days."

"I'd rather work, I think."

Jenny simply stared.

"I have a luncheon appointment tomorrow. I see no sense in canceling."

"With whom?"

Dan thought about that as Jenny watched him intently. "With—a—with Professor Wagner von Jauregg."

"Do you mean to tell me that—?"

Dan intervened. "I have a research idea. I got my cue from watching children at play. I want to try it out on the Professor—see if it interests him."

"It will keep," Jenny said emphatically.

Dan did not want to refuse her point-blank. He wanted Jenny to understand him. Weighing his words, he said, "Why does it astonish you that I resort neither to hysterics nor to flight?"

Hiding her real thoughts, Jenny answered, "Remember that once your professor asked me if I enjoy your work? Remember he told you to include me in some of your luncheon meetings? Perhaps this is the time for me to go along. I'll sit as quiet as a mouse. We could leave from the restaurant. That's reasonable, isn't it?"

"What a girl!" Dan was almost ready to laugh at himself, and at the same time he felt a kind of relief. The noon meeting was intended chiefly to give himself an hour or so alone with Eva Bauer to talk over his conjecture that the disturbed child can be reached through play. She had sound judgment along research lines. He had no illusions about Eva Bauer or her amorous glances. He knew quite well that were he to make a serious sexual advance, she'd approve, and that her heart would have nothing to do with it. Eva Bauer was brazenly unsentimental and had a constant need to go to bed with handsome, virile men. He let his eyes wander back to Jenny. She looked clean and cool; there was something virginal about her. Dan felt a strong mixture of desire and tenderness and began to picture himself making love to her. Her voice startled him out of his musing.

"What time is it?"

Glancing up at the plain wall clock, Dan said, "Almost seven."

"I might as well get up. I'm starved."

"Stay where you are."

Washed and shaved and wearing a dressing gown, Dan came back with a bottle of Rhine wine and a tin of English biscuits. He settled himself comfortably alongside Jenny.

"I just remembered something. There are apples and cheese in the outside window box."

Dan smiled. "I can't get up again. I'm too comfortable."

It was seldom that Dan ate more than Jenny, but he was very hungry. And he drank almost all of the wine. It delighted Jenny to see him eating. Gradually, she realized that sleep was stealing over Dan and felt her own eyelids getting heavy. It was an agreeable feeling. They slept soundly until two o'clock.

Jenny never imagined that Dan would awake alive with desire. And she could never have believed her own mounting passion. She allowed him to take off her pajamas and caress her smooth body. She let herself be led into violent lovemaking. Afterward, both lay in silence, Jenny with her eyes closed, deeply mortified by her own disrespectfulness; Dan, with no fleeting shame, had his eyes wide open. After a time, he stretched luxuriously and rose on one elbow. "Where do you want to go, sweetheart?"

In agreeable surprise, Jenny suddenly sat up in bed.

"The Imperial. Is that all right with you?"

Dan merely nodded, got out of bed, and went to the bathroom.

Jenny hugged herself happily and felt guilty for the second time. She reached out for the pad and pencil she kept by the bed. The note, which Dan later taped onto the outside door, still later both annoyed and hurt Lewis Miller. But he blamed Dan because Dan knew how much he counted on being with them over the weekend. How easy it would have been for Dan to divulge their whereabouts. And yet, while these thoughts ran in his mind, he worried about them and Jenny's strange behavior of the night before still upset him. He read over again what she had written.

DEAR LEWIS,

Please do not wait dinner. We thought we'd drop out of sight —possibly through Monday. And don't worry about us—we're finé.

Our love,
JENNY

All that night and for the next two and one-half days, Lewis Miller mulled over countless theories and added melancholy verse to his countless stanzas.

During their stay at the Imperial, Dan and Jenny had a serious disagreement about Andrew Gunther, and finally Jenny, cut to the heart, raised her voice fiercely in temper. She could not see him in the same black light as Dan did.

Late Saturday afternoon Jenny followed Dan into the bathroom, and while he shaved, she got into her bath.

"What shall I wear?"

"Anything."

"That's no help. At least, tell me where you're taking me. A dark place where I'll hardly be noticed? A glamorous, expensive, splendid place where I'll be received magnificently, like a princess?"

Dan wiped his face dry. "Jenny, you've got to realize you're married to a doctor with no private income. This disgustingly expensive suite is our last fling at luxury for some time to come."

"What, Daniel Gunther, do you imagine we're going to do with my money? Bury it—while you luxuriate in perverted emphasis on his—mine—hers. Really," Jenny said, shaking her head, "there's some excuse for Tascha, but your attitude toward money is not only trying—it's ridiculous."

Half in jest, Dan said, "OK, if you want to make a kept man out of me, indulge me in luxury."

"While you stick to principle—not one cent from father."

Annoyed, Dan had to struggle with himself to keep from exploding. He said, almost harshly, "Jenny, don't let me hear you refer to that bastard as Father *ever* again."

Jenny could see in Dan's face that his hostility toward his father was no simple matter. What was the term Lewis had used—projection mechanism? Determined to speak, she did not allow herself to be diverted. First, however, she climbed out of the tub, and grabbing a towel, she said, "Here."

Later in the evening, when they sat down to dinner in the crowded dining room, Jenny said, "There are things we have to talk about—and you had better listen because what I have to say is mighty important to us and to our future."

Taken aback, his heart beating a little faster, Dan said, speaking calmly, "Don't spoil the evening, Jenny."

"I simply must talk. Please, Dan."

Jenny's sincerity impressed him.

"All right. If it means that much to you, I can't ignore it. Speak. I'll listen."

In her heart she ached for Dan, but she felt she was right, and so she spoke her mind. Dan listened attentively and, at times, dumbfoundedly.

"I shall continue to take money from your father, Dan, because I have come to the conclusion that—for the time being—it is the only way to keep open a channel of communication between him and us."

Dan shook his head several times in gloom. He fixed his eyes even more intently on Jenny and passed a hand over his face. "He married her—a *fait accompli*. It's done, Jenny. Consider him dead."

"No, darling—that's no marriage. Andrew Gunther belongs to your mother and to us. He'll remember Miriam as she used to be, and in time he'll not be able to bear Helen. She will embarrass him, exhaust him. He'll feel compelled to rid himself of her because he'll want his children—not a shabby substitute for the woman he really loved.

"I feel this, Dan. I feel it deeply."

Dan thought: *How little I know about this girl I married.*

"Well?"

"You do as you wish, Jenny."

"And you?"

Dan greeted her plea noncommittally. "When your prognostication comes to pass, I may feel impelled to relent somewhat."

Wisely, Jenny stayed silent until Dan, regaining his good spirits, turned to her and said, "Let's dance." They had one dance, an orange brandy, and then retired to their elegant sitting room. Dan got a book to read. Jenny wrote letters. On Sunday they were up early.

After coffee, they braved a bitter wind to walk for miles through the winding streets of old Vienna, the small alleys and elaborate shopfronts alternating with medieval churches whose stained glass bore witness to the city's heritage of master craftsmen for centuries past. Crossing the Danube Canal close to the city's ancient beginnings, they made their way to the Prater, playground of many generations. Its long walkways and open grass were in direct contrast to the cramped atmosphere of the older quarters. Jenny loved the feeling of space, the sense of natural growth alongside the long, formal malls. "Let's look at the funfair now," she suggested. So back they went to the more populous section; they even rode the big ferris wheel and came back down to earth to happily munch wurst from a small stand and talk with some children. On their way back, Jenny said, "I've been trying to remember something all day and I can't."

"Don't strain. It'll come to you."

Vexed at herself, Jenny said, "It's important. I know."

Dan's thoughts were already elsewhere.

When they got into the hotel room, Jenny kicked off one shoe, then the other, and pulled her dress over her head—all the while telling herself, "A fine idiot I am." It might have been around midnight. She was unhooking her brassiere when her voice rang out. "Professor Wagner von Jauregg. Did you telephone him?"

Dan was having trouble with a knotted shoelace. "No. Why?"

"What if he waited?"

Dan was still listening with only half an ear. Belting his robe, he said, "The old boy is on a lecture tour."

Jenny's reactions were irrational—primitive rage that Dan had lied so casually, so easily to her, then shame. She quickly dressed herself in a robe, immobilized by the conflicting emotions within her, then gave vent to her fury. "You bastard. How dare you judge your father?"

Dan's heart sank. *Christ, what have I let myself in for?*

Her voice was still violent. "He didn't cheat right away—only after. . . ."

"Good God, Jenny." Dan interrupted in honest resentment. "You don't think. . . . All I ever wanted from Eva Bauer is what's in her head."

"Shut up." Jenny whirled on him. "You may be like your father, only not as good, but I'm not like your angelic, long-suffering mother. Do you understand?"

Dan gazed at her helplessly, loving her.

Jenny seized a pillow and flung it at him. "Get out. I don't want to hear a goddamn thing from you about her."

"OK, you little idiot." Dan pulled a blanket off the bed and turned to go. Again, she took him by surprise and almost succeeded in getting the key—but, not quite.

Dan stared moodily out of the window, seeing nothing in the darkness and not even hearing the wind's howl. He was deep in thought. He loved Jenny—adored her—worshiped her. That was certain. He did not care about Eva Bauer any more than he cared for the numerous women he had known. All that was definitely at an end. Then what was the purpose of his intentional excuses, arranged meetings, lying to Jenny? Why? His own strong need to attract physically appealing women? A hostility he could not discern? His mind couldn't find the answers. All at once, tiredness enveloped him and he said aloud, "The hell with it." Two hours later he was lying on the sofa, highly dissatisfied and still wide awake. He decided to go to Jenny, hoping that meanwhile she had fallen asleep—or maybe was waiting for him to come to her.

Jenny was sitting in comfort, smoking. Her eyes still blazed alarmingly, but she said nothing. And when he got into his side of the bed, she crushed out her cigarette. Dan grinned to himself, but the face he showed Jenny was composed. Slowly, he took her into his arms.

"Tell me."

"I love you, Jenny."

"I'll always be jealous."

Dan smiled at her. "I'm stuck with you. I took you for better or for worse."

Jenny could not bear to be angry with him any longer. She cradled her head on his shoulder, and soon they were both asleep.

At the sound of the buzzer, Dan opened his eyes.

Jenny looked down at him and said, "Our coffee, our omelette. Also, our hot rolls with wild gooseberry jam."

"What time is it?"

"Eleven fifteen."

"My God!" Dan got hold of his robe and went to the door.

"Dan," Jenny said, looking down at the carpet, "I dreamed of Eva Bauer. She had thick ankles and a nose that twitched."

Dan wanted to laugh. After he put down his coffee cup, he said, "You must have seen her somewhere."

"Yes, I suppose so."

Dan came around to Jenny and gave her a long kiss. "Get dressed, sweetheart. We have to go."

By Monday evening the group all knew. By Tuesday morning word had gotten around: "The less said, the better." During their usual breakfast of raisin schnecken and coffee, no one spoke words framed in his mind. Only Tascha yielded to her feelings. And as they were buttoning overcoats and pulling on galoshes, Bill lingered a moment. "About tonight, Dan, do we meet?"

"Of course."

Lewis Miller responded to Dan's pressure on his arm and waited. When the others were out of sight, he offered again the usual words sharing a friend's sorrow.

Dan gave him a grateful look and touched his arm. "Give me a lift."

"Sure."

As they set off in the car, Dan asked, "Do you suppose you could drink one more cup of coffee?"

"No, but I'll watch you."

The closest restaurant was the one near the hospital.

"Not here," said Dan, and he suggested one some distance away. "I have no stomach for Eva Bauer today."

Lewis Miller's round eyes grew larger as he looked at Dan in amazement. "Watch the road."

Lewis Miller drove on, his eyes on the road, his attention obviously on Dan.

"Did you buy new chains?"

Lewis Miller's scowl deepened. "Yes, but what the hell have chains—"

Dan cut in. "Would you take Jenny out of the city for the day?"

"Any particular place?"

"No."

"Any particular reason?"

There were so many things Dan wanted to say—so much to tell in confidence to a friend—but he decided it would be better to leave that to Jenny.

"Dan Gunther, don't sit there like a Buddha. What are you really saying? Explain it to me."

"I thwarted Jenny's tears, and to her, death and mourning are equated. She needs to talk."

Lewis Miller felt very near to Dan for entrusting Jenny to him. Nevertheless, he entered the restaurant with a grim face. After a few moments of ordering coffee for two, he asked, "What was that about Eva Bauer?"

Dan's first impulse was to admit to the truth. He contemplated Lewis as he sat there watchful, and rejected the idea. Why bother repeating the honest mistake he had made with Jenny, just to receive the same sort of abuse. He gulped down his coffee. "There's nothing to tell. However, should Jenny ask, it is in my interest for you to know that aside from her brain, I find her about as desirable as the broad-beamed porters at the railroad station."

"Oh c-l-e-v-e-r!" Dan saw in Lewis' face what he thought. "Don't play games with me, Dan. Your flirtation is at an end? Definitely at an end?"

"Yes," said Dan in a controlled voice.

"Congratulations on your narrow escape. Without reference to Jenny—what about Bill? I believe it is the custom, among gentlemen, to respect each other's claim."

"What?" Dan asked, trying to recall a single hint of interest in either Bill or Eva toward the other. He could not. But the face confronting him unquizzically was the face of truth.

Lewis Miller cleared his throat. "Bill has been sleeping with Eva for almost a year."

"Thanks, pal," Dan said dryly.

"I assumed you knew."

After Dan had lit a cigarette for himself, he got to his feet. "Let's get out of here."

When they drew up in front of the hospital, Lewis Miller said slowly, "Look here, Dan, let me give you some advice. While Dr. Bauer thought her chances bright, she assigned you some fairly interesting work to do. Once she senses—"

With a friendly smile, Dan cut in. "Ease your mind, Mother Hen. I'm going in for the last time. I can't quit my service without thanking the Professor and offering him some explanation."

Lewis Miller stretched out his hand. "You're certain. You're completely committed to Jenny."

Dan took Lewis Miller's hand and pressed it. "The complete truth is I love Jenny."

When Lewis Miller entered, Jenny had a blazing fire going. Snuggly wrapped in Dan's long robe, her hair tousled, her lips free of lipstick, she was curled up in the big armchair, wading through some lecture notes. She welcomed him. "I am glad you've come."

As Lewis removed his overcoat, he said, "I'm taking you to the villa, to Semmering. We'll have the whole day to talk. Dress warmly—it's cold and windy. There'll be much more snow up in the mountains."

"I can't afford the whole day. I have to study."

"Don't be concerned."

"I'd just as soon stay here. Later, you can take me out to a late lunch. Tascha was here. I sent her away until evening."

"That proves you do have some sense," he said, suddenly smiling as he pulled up a chair and seated himself directly in front of Jenny. "Jenny, oh, Jenny—why torment yourself all those hours? Why didn't you allow me to share in your anguish?"

"It didn't seem right for you to know before Dan knew."

"Now, Jenny, you know perfectly well that would not have been Dan's view. I'm sure you realize I wouldn't dream of keeping secrets from you."

"Wait until you have a wife—you'll see all the secrets you'll be compelled to keep."

Lewis Miller flushed. "Me—a wife?"

"I don't see why not."

His eyes never leaving hers, Lewis Miller said, "Let's leave that for now and talk about you."

"There's only one person I want to talk about—"

"Dan?"

"Yes." With a deep sigh, she added, "His behavior confuses me."

"There was no outburst, no show of sorrow, no great sadness?"

"That's right."

"No external manifestation at all?"

"There was anger. That was very pronounced."

"Did you quarrel?"

"We certainly did."

"The anger was directed against you?"

"Oh, no—against his father."

Lewis Miller continued to look into her bright eyes. "Dan disappointed you. How?"

Jenny's eyes filled with tears. "I wanted him to weep for his mother. When I have sons, I want them to cry for me."

Lewis Miller handed her his handkerchief. "Here," he said in a quiet voice. He waited. "Now listen. Don't you realize that this is how Dan maintains his tie to his lost love object? By postponing his mourning he *is* keeping his mother alive. A defense mechanism."

Jenny opened her eyes wide.

"Remember the timing—it's part of the explanation. At a time when he is full of supreme exultation, comes the tragic letter. His experience with Freud is still vibrating through every fiber. He is full of ideas, full of importance. What else? Father Freud has chosen him. That single point, Jenny, is important. Father *gave* him. *He* is content. Too content to go back to the Oedipal situation. Understand?"

"No."

"Look at it this way, Jenny. Mother gave father the babies instead of giving them to him. These intense unconscious connections between gratification, rivalry, sexuality, and death flooded Dan with so much affect that nothing registered. But Dan is a careful man. He doesn't let it show. In addition, his very large streak of ego strength knows when and how to mobilize. Because you, his mature love object, wanted it, he hurried you off to an expensive escape, and he went through all the motions of living."

Jenny was more confused than she'd ever been. "That part about wanting his mother to give *him* the babies baffles me."

"I don't expect you to grasp all of this at once."

Jenny had to say it. "As a matter of fact, I can't."

"In time you will. Meanwhile, remember this—it's natural and there's no shame in it." Lewis Miller felt compelled to tell Jenny one more thing.

"The emotions, the delayed mourning, will come later. In his analysis there will be rage, despair, detachment. And finally, there will be resolution."

There was.

Dan was developing an increasing antagonism to his analyst.

A: "You are testing my memory."

DAN (losing his temper): "What's the matter—are you jealous? Do you have a wife with not one stretchmark on her belly? Was your wife both campus queen and Phi Beta Kappa? I seem to have everything you want. I must ask you to fill my hours."

No reaction came from the analyst.

The next hour.

DAN (intense): "I cannot accept your amoral, lax attitudes. You left your true wife to form an alliance with a much younger woman. Didn't you consider your son—what this would do to him?"

A. (calmly interprets): "Just like your father."

It hits Dan. The flood of resentment comes.

DAN: "That son of a bitch—when I found out he had other women—when I realized the suffering he caused my mother—I wanted to put him where the fire burns eternally. The one thing I've decided—there is no trace of doubt left in me—that bastard murdered and wanted my mother dead. It left him free to marry the other woman and protect his reputation. The hypocrite always represented himself as a devoted family man."

A: "You must also have been very angry with your father when you were a little boy."

DAN: "No, that's not true. When I was little, we were pals. I have hundreds of separate memories to prove it. He was proud when I looked like I might become an athlete. He took me to football games and prizefights. I saw him as a great guy when I was a kid. At night he would tiptoe into my dark room and stand close to my bed. And when he moved away, I could hear his breathing. No one else, not even Mother, made me feel so secure.

Dan resisted for months.

A: "You have a strong need to maintain an ideal father image in your childhood."

DAN: "Apparently, Doctor, there is only one way to please you. OK! As a mere child, I had destructive tendencies. All my hostile strivings were toward my father. My first image was sexual intercourse between my parents. Well, is that enough for you? Are you satisfied?"

A: "This mockery betokens a great deal of resentment toward someone."

In these sessions, the analyst had addressed himself mainly to Dan's unconscious resistance, thereby stirring many buried memories. Dan began to report dreams whose pictorial representations were quite new.

One hour.

Dan tensed his muscles and clenched his fists. "I have a memory."

Reassured that his doctor was there, Dan resumed his normal position on the couch and reported the memory.

"I was three years old. My mother was truly lovely then. And then, she allowed herself to play and to be happy. We were cracking nuts meant for a fruitcake. My mother's cakes were culinary creations. I remember the kitchen was warm and full of good smells, and that there was laughter between us. All at once father stormed into the room. Mother rose and stood quite still. But her laughter was gone and her eyes filled with tears. Father said, 'Miriam, I'll have your answer now.' His voice was hard and it frightened me. There was more conversation, with my father giving my mother orders. I remember that she refused. And he, with a show of great strength, grabbed her hands and dragged her out of the kitchen, leaving me all alone. I cried and cried and no one came."

"I remember thinking he is going to kill Mother and I'll never see her again. After that I was really petrified."

A pensive silence, then DAN: "Maybe my anger started then."

Another hour, another denial, followed by a long pause, then the discharge of a memory called to consciousness.

DAN: "I never thought about my parents' sexual life. I never observed any of their sexual activities."

Pause.

"I did, as a very young child, experience primal fantasy and traumatic pain. I heard talking and other sounds, late at night, when they were together in their room. I feared. So many times, I thought: He is hurting her; he is taking away all of her body warmth. There will be none left for me. I cried and took refuge, hiding my head underneath my blankets."

A: "Dan, this *is* the classical Oedipal situation."

Shortly after this session, Dan came in depressed. He talked about his feeling of being the luckiest guy on earth, and yet somehow, it didn't all add up. Suddenly, Dan burst into tears.

A: "One cries for a reason."

Dan sobs: "I never mourned my mother. I wouldn't listen to Jenny. I shut my eyes to her sense of shame to my reaction. All my striving was to avoid pain. To complete the picture, I fornicated as an adulterer, making Jenny my courtesan."

Dan swallowed his sobs.

A: "There is unfinished business here."

The flood of memories came, one after the other.

DAN: "My mother had gentle hands. Her face was soft and

her smile was tender. She watched over me. I have a thousand memories of her kindness, of her virtues.''

Dan mopped his face.

"When I brought Jenny home, Mother took my girl in her arms. She looked into those deep, dark brown eyes, and with no word spoken, she made Jenny her daughter. I was wild with happiness that night.

"The next morning, my mother paled in importance. Maybe importance is the wrong word. Maybe it's more accurate to say: 'The next morning, Mother changed in my eyes—became part of the house—someone upon whom to depend for meals or a clean shirt.' Oh, hell!''

A: "What happened the next morning?''

DAN: "There was a call from the station. An hour later my father was home. And he flipped over Jenny.

"With me, he made a bargain. 'By all means, take every opportunity to be with your girl. But—be selfish—you have internship, residencies. Finish your training. Be generous; at least, be smart —don't interfere with Jenny's education. Particularly, give her time to grow up.'

"He laid one hand around my shoulders, the other in my palm. 'Sow your wild oats, son.' ''

The analyst nodded.

DAN (eyes wide open and looking at the analyst): "I never saw her in her coffin. I have never seen her grave.''

A: "This is your unfinished business.

Dan was crying at the memory of his mother, his tears those of a child who had a glimpse of utter aloneness.

He was remembering: Little and pressed close to her breasts; warmth and food and encouragement. Her proud smile, the time he said, "I haven't said anything to Dad yet. This time I wanted you to be the first to know. I've been accepted at all three medical schools to which I applied. I've decided to stick with Harvard.''

Dan stood up from the couch. He stood a second longer. "I used to take my mother for granted. Now she's gone. And now I know I really lost something when I lost her.'' Dan turned and left the doctor's study.

Several weeks later.

DAN: "What do you want of me now? I looked death square

in its ugly face. Jenny and I visited her grave. I mourned as an admirable son should mourn. I cried until Jenny cried: 'Please, you're breaking my heart'; until she seized and shook me. 'Dan, you still have me and your career.'

"What more can I do or say to please you?"

A: "I do not want anything of you for my sake. I do want you to understand your feelings for your sake."

DAN: "Stop torturing me."

A week later.

A: "You have been arriving late these last four hours."

DAN: "Sorry. I'm very busy."

A: "Busy?"

DAN: "Christ, you bug me. The universe is tailored to meet your schedule. If I saw a man lying wounded at your doorstep, you'd expect me to step over him and jump down on your worn-out couch and start free associating. You recognize no value in my work—only in yours. If I'm with a patient who needs my help, what am I supposed to do? Say: 'Sorry, old boy, I've got to hurry. My analyst sits on his fat fanny and refuses to be kept waiting. On the hour I hit that couch—not a minute before, not a minute after.' "

A. greets this outburst with silence.

DAN: "I resent your silence. It represents criticism. When my father was critical of me, he was solemnly silent. I remember. I'd take myself to my room and lock my door. I'd pretend that he beat me, and that soon he'd come and beg my forgiveness. But I'd find a way, a clever way to punish him.

"Later, when I was much older, I still resented censorious silence. I think he knew how much his silent treatment outraged me."

A: "You reacted with defiance."

DAN: "I was defiant. And I found the way to punish him. He wanted me in his firm. I told him that I detested the idea.

"He said, 'Son, don't let anyone fill your mind with imagined horror. My business is like any other business—supply and demand. I want you beside me. I've wanted that since you were born.'

" 'To me,' I answered, 'the munitions business is like saying: "Welcome death." Like saying: "I spit on everything decent in man." Like everything vile.'

"My father's reply was silence. He tried again—before I

entered medical school. 'Join me for one year. If, after that, you still see through your mother's eyes, I'll never mention my business again. What you will lose, in that time, will amount to nothing. What you will gain will be the kind of sophistication which will prepare you better for being your own man.' "

A: "Being a doctor makes restitution for many of your old feelings sublimates your hostile impulses. And also, by reaction formation, you do good, proving that only father was bad. You say, 'I heal. I save lives. Don't blame me.' "

DAN: "Being a doctor makes me feel a union with my mother."

A: "And this permits you to do actively what you have experienced passively."

By the end of the second year, Dan's rage and despair were gone. Later, detachment came. Eventually, there was restitution. When this evidenced itself, Dan's therapist viewed their therapeutic success with pride.

At dinner they were alone with Lewis, and afterward they went straight back to Das Zimmer. At their door, Lewis nodded, leaving them with a brief good night.

Dan set the alarm for six thirty. Jenny undressed and took the spread off the bed. She opened the cupboard and got all the pillows and piled them against the headboard. She wanted to read awhile. Soon she decided to take a long hot bath before going to sleep. "Will you wash my back?"

A big smile spread across Dan's face as he replied, "With the greatest of pleasure." His smile stayed as he lifted Jenny and carried her into the bathroom. Putting her down, he said, "It might be extremely economical if we bathe together."

Jenny stepped closer to him. "That's true." Dan turned his head and eyed her slim body and firm young breasts. Acutely aware that he wanted to make love first, he raised his brows questioningly. And Jenny, her wide eyes smiling, beamed at him. "Why not postpone our bath?"

Dan took hold of her hand and led her toward the door. He lifted her and cradled her against his own naked body. That night they loved each other completely. Afterward, Dan rolled over on his back, counting the wild beating of his heart. When he opened his eyes and looked at Jenny, her eyes were closed. She was asleep. Smiling again, he settled the covers around her and put out the light. Then he lay awake, thinking: *Jenny is probably pregnant. I have nothing more to learn here. It's time to go home.* And so they moved into the lease of a fresh spring.

Professor Aichhorn stepped into the room precisely on the hour and seated himself in his leather armchair. As he greeted his students, his eye fell on Jenny and Tascha sitting there quietly. "I see we have visitors. Entirely proper."

With this acknowledgment, they started in on the discussion.

Erma Schmidt coughed. This particular trainee, whenever she wanted to attract attention to herself, coughed, as everyone knew. No one liked it. Professor Aichhorn did not care for it either. Nor did he care for the way she smoked, with the cigarette hanging from the corner of her mouth. But no one could have suspected his feelings from the tone of his voice. "Frau Doktor Schmidt," he said softly. "You want to say something?"

"You have said that the aim of psychoanalysis is to reduce judgmental valuations of persons. Right?"

The professor nodded. "Or on cultures."

"Suppose a neighbor tells me her husband steals from his employer or she confides that he cheats at cards, am I to remember that, because I am a psychiatrist in psychoanalytic training, I must come to no conclusion about the man? I am, in fact, not allowed a personal opinion."

Lewis Miller muttered something about stupid female under his breath.

Part of the professor's mind was annoyed. He had made this point abundantly clear twice before. Now, he shook his head, as he said, "My dear Fräulein, you know better. Naturally, each of us has personal value judgments. We do not, however, allow them to intrude into the therapeutic relationship between us and our patients. In the therapeutic transaction, the physician deals with the neurosis. He does not stress: Good, bad; ought, ought not; moral, immoral. He is loyal to the thesis that all behavior is a matter for study. He does not arrive at conclusions without supporting facts. He does not attack. He does not reprove. He does, when he has valid reason to, make suggestions he considers fitting and relevant."

Professor Aichhorn looked at his students and waited for a comment. It came from Dan. "I have given some thought, sir, to the weight and value of guidance in working with disturbed children. I think it is important to prepare the child for living."

"You are quite right. But remember, the root of the matter is the relationship between you and your young patient. Everything depends upon that."

"Herr Professor." On hearing Bill Reilly's voice, the professor turned his attention to him. "Please, sir, could you elaborate on the concept of reeducation in therapy?"

Professor Aichhorn lit a cigarette. He drew on it and blew out smoke. After that, he answered. "Sometimes, especially with young people, it works. The personality and attitude of the patient are large factors. The severity of the disturbance and its duration are also factors. It is well to teach the young patient to attempt only those things possible within his limitations. A boy of average intelligence must be taught not to strive for a career beyond his educational capacity. Obviously, it is well that we, as physicians—as far as possible—impart to our patients the concept that misguided effort increases stress. Our repertoire of therapeutic techniques most certainly should include persuasion and suggestion. Both are pedagogic tools.''

Someone in the back of the room stirred. He raised his hand. The professor nodded quickly at him.

''If one's conduct is thoroughly conscious and goal-directed, does this, by definition, make it nonneurotic behavior?''

Professor Aichhorn tapped the long ash of his cigarette with his finger. Then he ground out the cigarette. ''Generally speaking,'' he said, ''yes. However, let us not lose sight of the fact that the behavior of the psychopath—though he may lack restraint and though he responds to his impulses without thought or consideration for others—is often both conscious and goal-oriented.'' The professor paused. He took another cigarette from his pocket. He did not light it. He studied it. Then, he said, raising his eyes, ''I want to emphasize *this*. In dealing with the psychopath, it is up to the analyst to set limits expected by society. I mean: If a man commits a criminal act, he must know that, as the result of this, he will be removed—for the safety of society—from the community and put into prison. You see,'' the professor concluded with earnestness, ''though the psychopath never thinks twice about consequences, we must.'' As he was reminded of the cigarette still in his hand, he decided not to light it, and, quickly glancing at the clock, he said, ''We have time for one more question.''

''I'd like to know, Herr Professor, if you think the wife of an analyst must be analyzed?''

Professor Aichhorn was partial to pretty girls. ''That, dear child, is a good question, the plain answer to which is: No. The neurotic wife needs analysis. The nonneurotic wife does not.''

It was time for the pause.

During the short recess, the windows were opened to let fresh air and rays of sunlight into the lecture room. When they reassembled, someone closed the windows to shut out the street's clatter. Always, as the professor reached his chair, he blew a smoke ring and crushed out his cigarette. This was the signal—the seminar continued for the remaining two hours. At this time, the presentations and the discussions were more formal.

Today, as they expected, the professor, in a few sentences, reviewed the case concerned with transvestism. The professor noticed that not much was imprinting itself on Miller's mind; his attention had slipped away somewhere. Lewis Miller was daydreaming about Berlin, and, at the same time, he was suffering. At the thought of parting with Jenny and Dan, his world grew cold. He needed their companionship; he needed Jenny. With her, he was at peace. Completely absorbed, he did not hear his name, but he felt the strong nudge of Jenny's elbow. He looked up and saw the professor watching him closely.

"You, Dr. Miller, are the longest in training. It is fitting you start. From what you know of the case we reviewed earlier, reconstruct Hans' history."

Lewis gave a brilliant and exact estimate of the young transvestite's background and his identification with his mother, to the wearing of her clothes during puberty. As always, his insights were incredibly astute and accurate. The professor felt a sense of gratification in having guided such a mind. It made the teaching aspect of his profession so much more worthwhile.

In about thirty minutes the sterile discussion of other perversions quieted down, leaving the final minutes to Professor Aichhorn.

"So much for the patient Hans. In a few days you'll be getting your Zeugnis. You Americans are a European people continuously struggling for pieces of paper, the print of which establishes an identity, gives permission, gives power. For decades now, you bright young people come, you take a peek into your own unconscious, and the future of psychoanalysis rests with you—my intense geniuses. Some of you will be ruthless, some fiercely ambitious, some militant. Some will violate the entire spirit of psychoanalysis and, by their own insecurities, will foster rigidities. Some of you will even prove Adler's theory that all human behavior is the striving for power. But most of you will be good doctors and most of you will show impressive skills with patients. A few of you will attain greatness. At this early point of your professional development, it is not exactly easy to separate the lambs from the goats. So—go forth into your communities, develop your techniques, allow yourselves to be good human beings, like your patients—it is permitted." His voice a bit hoarse, the professor consulted his watch.

For a moment or two it was quiet and then, all at once, the applause started. It went on until Jenny left her seat and approached the professor. Handing him a beautifully ribboned package, she said, "It's a gold cigarette case. It's from all of us."

Genuinely surprised, Professor Aichhorn thanked them warmly, then departed without wasting time. He went straight to his consultation room, where a patient was waiting.

The final party turned out to be a disaster. The whole group had gone to a special restaurant up on the hills to the north of the city. Around them was the sweet scent of pine forest; below, the lights tracing the Danube's outline as it flowed past the cliffs and into the heart of Vienna. The wine couldn't have been better and everyone, including Jenny, drank more than usual. Then Tascha, for once less than her usual confident self, made her announcement. Daisy, Joe Garafalo's "model" friend, dominated the immediate hubbub with a flood of unexpected tears: "A baby—oh, how wonderful." And Abe received his first and only kiss from a prostitute.

Jenny, quietly smiling, was warm in her congratulations and her eyes showed her genuine pleasure for Tascha. But she kept her own peace.

It must have been the feeling of uncertainty of new beginnings as each of the doctors looked back on his training, in the city of the Master with all his traditions, and forward to uncharted fields of psychiatry. There was certainly a false cheerfulness as they all promised to keep in touch and meet regularly back in the States. And then the unsettling emotion of good-byes to close colleagues; the girls clung to each other miserably. Dan finally drew them apart and kissed Tascha firmly. Bill drew Jenny aside, then slipped an arm around Tascha's waist. Finally, spent, they parted in twos and threes as a gray light appeared on the eastern horizon.

Jenny and Dan went off with Lewis, who inquired why Jenny chose to remain silent about her own pregnancy.

Recalling Tascha's face, Jenny said, "I just didn't want to spoil Tascha's moment. It meant so much to her."

Lewis Miller shrugged. "It doesn't matter."

Dan frowned. He was trying to hide his mixed feelings about the baby. Fortunately, they were not watching him.

The three of them were scheduled to meet again at eight in the morning. Dan had difficulty in getting Jenny out of bed. She gave him a faint smile but, almost at once, closed her eyes again. The low-cut nightgown displayed a beautiful bare shoulder; the chestnut hair fell in two short braids framing her face. "Jenny," he said, "you'll rest in the car."

Slowly, Jenny's hand came up to his face. "All right, darling."

Dan smiled at her, and as his lips touched her gently, he whispered, "I love you."

Jenny whispered back, "And I love you."

Dan put his arms around her and pulled her out of bed. "Get ready before Lewis gets here." He watched her go slowly, gathering up clothes for the outdoors. When Dan opened the door to the expressmen, Lewis Miller was already there, bossing them around in his usual fashion, exhilarated. "We'll do all sorts of things one can't do in the city. I can't think why we didn't do this before. Semmering was great, but we were seldom alone." It was amusing and touching to see his excitement.

The men staggered under the weight of Jenny's steamer trunks, which were to be checked through to London. They gave Dan a hand with the suitcases jammed into the Packard's rumble seat. Then Dan locked the door to Das Zimmer for the last time. At the outside gate, they spent at least ten minutes with the landlady and her tenants, all of whom had come out to say *Auf Wiedersehen* to the young Americans, *their* Americans. Jenny was kissed and kissed and made to promise to write and send pictures from home. Then both men put on caps and Jenny tied a kerchief over her hair and they rode off. The Austrians watched them go. *"Lebewohl."*

The last few days went by in a country inn in a picturesque village lying in green-clad foothills of the Austrian Alps. There was a lake nearby, and a cluster of balconied and painted houses surrounded the inn. The village was famous for its ancient church, the inn for its cuisine. Their bedrooms, with their pleasing wood furnishings, were connecting—each with its own bathroom and both looking out over the gardens and toward the mountains.

The days passed in peace. The weather stayed magnificent. Dan and Jenny would start out early carrying a picnic lunch and a blanket to spread on the ground. They went up the mountain, climbing the narrow winding paths, avoiding the munching cows, yet pleased to come across them. Jenny gathered armfuls of wild flowers and handfuls of wild strawberries to bring back to Lewis. He never went along. He had neither their passion for climbing nor their stamina. Nor could he tolerate the thin air. The days slipped by pleasantly enough for him, writing poetry on his balcony overlooking the garden scented with honeysuckle and roses. Dan and Jenny left the mountain at least an hour before the sun dipped over the peaks. That gave them plenty of time to bathe and dress. At night the inn was lively. Dinner was served in a room softly lit with wax candles in old brass candelabra, and decorated with huge bowls of roses. Every night Dan and Jenny danced, and Lewis, who considered himself inept, watched, adoring them. He never spoke to the other guests. Around eleven he suggested bed drowsily. And Jenny fell into the habit of saying, "Yes. I suppose we should." Night after night they went upstairs together. At his door, Lewis said, "Good night. Sleep well."

Dan, his hand on the doorknob, said, "Good night," and went in. Jenny always kissed Lewis lightly, and then followed Dan. Their door closed, Dan sank into a chair and opened his arms. "Come here." Or it was Jenny who, running her fingers through his hair, made the suggestion with a look or with a smile. It was always right and it was good, and in the morning they got up happy in belonging to each other.

Part II

THE STATE HOSPITAL YEARS

FACTORIES closed down. The cheap restaurants were empty. The air was filled with the smell of fear. The homeless, the hungry, the miserable, gathered aimlessly on sidewalks or waited in bread lines. And children begged. New York was full of need and suffering.

But Jenny did not see this. Fifth Avenue was bright and thronged. Bergdorf Goodman's was crowded with elegant merchandise. Tiffany's windows sparkled. Men filled the Sherry Netherland bar. And well-dressed crowds passed through theater lobbies each evening. Nor was she aware that professional men in shiny suits and worn shoes were supplementing their incomes in workman's jobs, thereby robbing the workmen; that young doctors announced themselves in favor of socialized medicine; and that state civil service jobs at mental hospitals represented the epitome of security.

Jenny was sitting in their hotel bedroom, a corned beef on rye in one hand, a dill pickle in the other. It was her custom, now, to send a bellboy down to Reubens toward the end of the afternoon. Just as she began to speculate on what was keeping him, the door was flung open and Dan came in soaked, his hair dripping.

Jenny came over and looked up at him, smiling. "Hello." Jenny came closer, ready for his embrace.

"Don't. You'll get wet. It's pouring out there."

"I don't care."

Jenny stared after him intently. Intuition told her that something was wrong. She turned and sat down in the most comfortable chair.

Dan undressed and bathed in a hurry. He put on a dressing gown, released the draperies, shutting out the best of the rain, and drew up a chair. He touched his fingers to Jenny's face and said quietly, "You're absolutely radiant—even more beautiful. Softer."

Jenny smiled at him. "Liar."

"No. Fact."

Pleased, she gave him a grateful look and, after a pause, said, "I do want babies, you know that. But I hate pregnancy. There should be some improved way to carry a child."

Dan removed his hand and sat down.

A puzzled look came into her eyes. "What did you do today?"

Dan said, his face becoming very serious, "I came to a decision."

"I knew." As she watched him, her face took on the expression of apprehension.

This disconcerted him. Putting his hand on hers, he said, "Jenny, I had a talk with Doctor Stevenson."

"And he agrees with the others?"

"Yes. An intimate knowledge of psychotic patients is essential for a well-rounded training. Besides, the most desired residencies are contingent upon a minimum of one year in-residence training at an accredited mental hospital."

Jenny nodded. "In that case, I think you should follow the seasoned advice of American psychiatrists with whom you've talked. But can you get a first-rate placement this late?"

"Yes. A good hospital wants me, providing I don't seek civil service status."

Jenny bit her lip. Desperately wanting him to return to California, she knew that her native state had not, as yet, pushed ahead with psychiatry; in fact it had hardly moved west of Topeka. "Where will you go?"

"Long Island. On the north shore."

Jenny wondered about his analysis. Certainly, he could not commute into New York five times a week from the north shore. Surprisingly, he gave her the answer before she managed to ask the question.

"It means postponement of my personal analysis."

How strange, Jenny thought. *I am profoundly relieved.*

Dan sensed nothing of her feeling of deliverance. He was still wrestling with his own decision. Was it the best way ahead?

"Darling."

Dan became attentive.

"We won't be producing a true son of California. I am rather disappointed, aren't you?"

Jenny wondered why her remark aroused so strong a reaction in him. Dan struggled. On the defense, he thought to himself, *I am thinking of her. It will work out all right.*

Jenny was watching him with troubled attention, as he looked up. He was amazed to see her eyes moist. *Good God,* he reflected, *it's almost as though she knows.* Her hand clinging to his reminded him of a small child in an alien place, in need of protection. By the time he spoke, his heart was beating fast, though the tone of his voice was tranquil ("his matter-of-fact doctor's voice," Jenny called it.). "Sweetheart, I have a request. Hear me out. No interruption, OK? It's important for us both."

Jenny tried to smile. "How about afterward?"

"I know how much you were counting on having the baby in San Francisco. And you shall. You go back to the West Coast and be with your mother and grandmother while I complete the internship here. I'll come out and visit you. New Year's especially we'll be together." Dan repudiated his feelings of guilt in a low voice. "I don't want to part with you, Jenny. Yet it seems the only way. A year will be nothing really."

He talked and talked, using arguments he felt would convince Jenny. Yet his words hit her like an icy blast, and not a murmur escaped her lips until he finished with: "Please, Jenny, take the sensible view."

Then she cried out, "Why, Dan? Why are you sending me home?"

Almost hoarse, Dan sighed. "I've explained. To get the training I need now, I must go in as a psychiatric intern, with no civil service status. I'm not entitled to a wife. This is the only solution I see. It must be done. I want you where I know you'll be safe and cared for."

"That, Dan, is a very unsatisfactory answer, not at all convincing. What have you got against my renting a small place near the hospital? You won't be on duty twenty-four hours a day, seven days a week. In any case, I'll be near you. Don't refuse me, Dan. Please!"

Jenny's mind turned to San Francisco. The stately town house—the high-ceilinged rooms with the gleam of brass and the sparkle of silver and crystal. The trees that faced the street and the tranquil garden in the back, its high brick wall vivid with color the year round—lush green in winter; a riot of red, yellow, white, and purple from spring on. And a spectacular view of a maze of rooftops sloping down to the Golden Gate. The empty feeling possessed her. Dan soon discovered, however, that Jenny's silent withdrawal was no ground for hope. The emptiness was replaced by anger. She pulled away her hand and lashed out in fierce indignation. "Be honest with yourself. The real truth is you don't want to be answerable to a wife, especially a pregnant one.''

Dan had already dealt with his conscience, and all he could say was "Christ!" He rose and walked toward the bedside table where Jenny had placed the cigarettes. He felt Jenny rush past him, turned, and caught a sight of her in the closet. Dan's impulse was to laugh. She looked funny in her terry-cloth robe, with her shiny hair falling down her back, enthusiastically attacking her suitcases.

"Now what?" Dan asked, mastering his impulse to laugh.

Jenny looked up. She started with, "If you had one ounce of real character, you'd have gotten rid of me last week while Mama and Grandma were still here.''

Dan leaned his head against the door. Again, he had an overwhelming urge to laugh. But, as before, he did not. "Stop it, Jenny. You'll exhaust yourself.''

"Go to hell.''

Coming closer to her, Dan bent forward and lifted her. "Stop struggling, little idiot. You'll hurt the baby.''

"Put me down.''

Dan let her down on the bed and reached for the phone. "Room service, please.''

The sheer stupidity of wandering about in the storm made no difference to Jenny. "I want to go out. I've been cooped up here all day.''

Dan ignored her. "Green salad for two, club sandwiches, fresh strawberries, coffee.'' He then remembered she was eating something on bread when he came in and changed her order to steak. "Have it ready in about a half hour.''

"I want a fudge sundae.''

Dan was waiting for that; Jenny loved fudge sundaes. He ordered one, telling the girl to send it up later with more coffee. He sank down on the big bed and watched Jenny watching him for a moment, and then said, "I couldn't tell you sooner because I was not altogether sure about my staff appointment until today. But Mother and Grandma both know—I discussed it with them. They were overjoyed. Although, I must say, they did warn me you'd not take kindly to any such plan.''

Jenny's reply was quick. "Why should I?''

Dan inched closer until their shoulders were touching. "Don't be unhappy. I'll be with you when the baby is born. And we'll see the New Year in together, too. Believe me, sweetheart, time will go a hell of a lot slower for me than it will for you.''

Jenny had serious doubts about his last statement, but she did not mention them. She could never forget that he always proceeded exactly as he pleased, often without one word to her until after his decision was made. "And now, Dan, I don't want to talk about it anymore. I'd like to leave as soon as possible. Please make a reservation for tomorrow. If you're busy, I can take care of it myself."

Dan was surprised. Nor did he care for her determined resentment. He reached for her hand and cupped it between his. She tried to pull away. "Don't."

Jenny stopped pulling then.

"You're not going anywhere until I check in, and that's not until the end of the month. My internship starts on the first of July."

Jenny said, "All right. It makes no difference to me."

Dan was not satisfied; she had never stayed mad this long before. Dan decided to come up with the last thing he had to say on the subject. "I'll be earning two hundred and sixty dollars a month, Jenny. I'll send you one hundred and sixty of that, and if I can pick up a little extra taking night calls for the local doctors, I'll send you that, too."

Jenny did not answer. Did he really think she could possibly care about how much money he sent her each month? Dan wasn't thinking about money. That had to be said, and once said, it was over. He was thinking about how wildly in love he was with Jenny, how much he wanted to touch her, to kiss her enchanting mouth. He did neither. A few minutes later the man from room service wheeled in their supper.

All during the meal over which she lingered, Jenny was subdued. Finally, she put down her napkin. "One thing—we ate better in Vienna."

Early in the morning Dan awoke remembering he had been dreaming about Jenny. He let his eyes open and gaze at her curled on her side of the bed. He looked at her a long time and wondered if she ever dreamed of him. Even in her sleep, Jenny sensed his gaze. She adjusted her position and pulled the sheet over her head. His eyes smiling down at her, Dan swung his feet to the floor, realizing suddenly he had no one to see and nothing in particular to do, and that Jenny would not be getting up for hours. It seemed a shame to waste part of the day—one of their last together. He went to the window and raised it. The summer storm was over. Except for the faint sounds of running cars, the avenue was quiet, the air clear in the early morning sun. He stared across the trees and beyond them to the grass of Central Park and, for a moment, felt lonely. It was a strange sensation, and gradually he became aware how lonely it would be without Jenny—going to bed and waking up alone. He turned around. Jenny was silently watching him.

Rushing over to her, he took her in his arms and she felt the touch of his lips. And then his hand went to her abdomen, and he let it stay until he felt his child stir. "My darling Jenny," his voice was husky. Jenny wanted to press her hand over his. She wanted to fling herself back into his arms. It was, however, apparent that Dan was touched with misgivings, perhaps with regret, and she stopped herself, determined to go home to have her baby. Even he could not stop her now. That was to be his punishment.

Dan was expecting that, at any moment, Jenny would make some loving gesture toward him, at least say something. She did not. "Let's take a long walk before breakfast. Afterward, we'll do whatever you say. Hire a car and ride out into the country. Picnic in the woods. Would you like that? Or would you rather be near water?"

"Either would be nice, Dan, but if Dad is free, I'd like to spend part of my day with him." Dan straightened in surprise. "I'll make it another day, if you prefer."

The warmth of feeling went out of him. "Make your call."

Jenny saw that he did mind. "We can still have our walk," she said softly.

"Yeah, sure." He rose. "Order coffee. I'll get dressed.

Jenny delayed until he shut the bathroom door.

She met Andrew Gunther in the Oak Room at noon. For a long time Andrew Gunther said nothing; he just studied her with pride—the reddish hair, the large dark eyes, the soft complexion, the few freckles on her pretty nose. What he liked most was her mouth. *Yes,* he said to himself, feeling a strong love, *Jenny is my kind of girl—lovely, warm, self-assured.* He reached out and took hold of her hands. "How's Dan? I caught a glimpse of him at the club. It seems he drops in for a workout and a swim."

"Yes, I know. No matter how busy, he stays in shape."

Andrew Gunther wondered uneasily if Jenny had tried to bring him along. Then he caught her expression.

"This time, Dad, it's my fault. I didn't ask him."

Andrew Gunther grinned Dan's grin. "In a way, I'm not sorry." He released her hands and beckoned the waiter. "What would my grandson like to eat?"

Jenny smiled. "He's too young to make a decision. You choose."

They shared a clear, cold borscht served with sour cream, a salad, and, for dessert, Tarte Tatin. And when they emerged from the Plaza lobby, Andrew Gunther hailed an open cab. Soon they were settled behind a brisk-stepping horse heading into the park. Clusters of people of all ages could be seen—some idling on benches or seated in the grass under the shade of trees, couples strolling, children playing, adolescents jostling with the hint of violence, and the very old sitting still, faces downcast.

Andrew Gunther's brown eyes under thick brows looked with sagacity at Jenny. He felt her need to unburden a problem.

"Dad, I have to talk to you in complete confidence."

Andrew Gunther looked down at her again. She looked so young and fragile in her thin yellow cotton dress piped in navy, her bare toes exquisitely groomed showing from open sandals. His heart went out to her. "Dan?"

Wetting her lips, Jenny said, "Yes."

Andrew Gunther responded by putting his arm around her shoulder. She leaned very close. When she had finished telling her story, they looked into each other's eyes. After a while, Andrew Gunther said, "That's a hell of a situation. I don't like it. Besides which, Dan deceives himself. He's essentially my son, not gentle Miriam's—with my vitality and my appetites. Jenny, my love, a year is a long time." Andrew Gunther's strong face now looked carved in granite, inexorable and unbending.

Shaken, Jenny pressed closer to Dan's father. She sighed deeply. "Dan is not altogether to blame. It is I who wanted a child instantly. I felt it necessary to have something of importance for myself—a baby to care for. Dan was in no hurry. He'd have waited until all his training was out of the way. But because I wanted it so much, he let it happen. Now he is sending me away for my sake—so he says—and for no other reasons."

Cursing his son for a fool, Andrew Gunther said, "What if you were to move in with me? Dan could eat his cake and have it too—a pleasant, uncomplicated bachelor life out at the hospital and a beautiful, ardent wife nearby at all times."

Oh, how I wish I could! flashed through her mind. She answered. "Dan is not ready. He still longs for his mother and doesn't know it."

"Is that a psychiatric theory?" he inquired, deeply unsympathetic.

Jenny knew from personal experience that it is hard to conquer doubt. And with her father-in-law, it was more than a matter of doubt. It was distaste for psychiatry. She was sorry she had chosen to mention it. But he was looking hard at her, wanting an answer. "Dan calls out for his mother in his sleep. Sometimes, he talks. He is a small child, and always he is somewhere with mother Miriam. Hand in hand, they are together."

Andrew further considered her confidence carefully. "What does he say about it? Doesn't he remember anything?"

"He doesn't remember a thing. But Lewis told me that in his analysis, when he needs it, it will be ready to surface from his subconscious."

Andrew further found himself thinking: *Christ, it's terrifying.* "Well, Jenny my love, the baby will be here before you know it. After that, Dan won't be such a fool as to let you go a second time, especially after he has seen you enchantingly slim again."

She began to cry.

Andrew Gunther gave her his handkerchief and kissed her. "Silly little goose."

Well over an hour had slipped by while they were talking, and Jenny felt she had left Dan alone long enough, but Andrew Gunther had more to say.

"Expect Dan to become unraveled around fifty. Most of us do."

As she concentrated on what he was saying, her dark eyes looked gravely into his.

"Surprised? Or weighted down with apprehensions?"

A moment later Jenny answered, "Uneasy."

He went on. "Dan will never be a philanderer in the ordinary sense—he's too utterly disciplined. But at fifty a man is faced with new anxieties. By then his success or nonsuccess has been established. He has conquered women—his romantic exploits are seemingly over—a chilly reminder that time itself is now the enemy. A sense of despair envelops him. Often in a futile attempt to defy fate he will marry a beautiful, demanding young woman—just as I married Helen when Dan's mother died. And I quickly learned what a mistake I had made. Helen and I grated on each other. I found myself recoiling from her sexual demands, which had initially made me feel like a young buck. I'm glad I had the sense to divorce her. Otherwise I think something within me would have been destroyed; I've seen other men my age who tried to meet demands like that, and their manhood completely collapsed. They were dead. Finished. I was lucky to escape. With your devotion, Jenny, Dan won't have to go through that."

Jenny pushed back her hair, moved by this unexpected revelation. She finally said, faintly, "I won't forget."

Andrew Gunther took a quick look at her. Then, with a smile, he said, "Sweet Jenny, stay as you are. Keep Dan's love alive. That will protect him from any age. Other women will only make him love you more." After this, he told the cabbie to take them back to the hotel.

They found Dan waiting. To Jenny's intense relief, he said, "Hello, Dad."

His father's voice answered clear and firm. "Good to see you, son."

Dan walked into the hospital's Residence Hall a little after three. Reaching into his pocket, he pulled out the key the housekeeper had given him.

Up a short flight of stairs, he came to number eleven. Dull-colored, medium-sized, a room that had nothing to distinguish its ordinariness. There was the usual bed, chairs, writing table, and an odd-shaped chest of drawers. Away in one corner on a wooden stand was a telephone. Obviously, it had been put there by mistake. It belonged next to the bed. Behind one door was a closet where a fairly large mirror hung on the wall. Another door opened into the bathroom. Dan assumed it was for his private use. Aside from the telephone, his eye was caught by a huge basket ornamented with blue tissue paper and gilt ribbon and full of delicacies. The attached note read: "To Dan from Jenny—to brighten a lonely evening."

Only hours before, he had taken possession of a new Buick coupe. Also a present, according to the note, from Jenny's grandmother. Dan could not face unpacking. Nor could he push away the pictures racing through his mind. He decided to sit down and think things over. There was time enough ahead of him.

He and Jenny had taken a taxi to the train, just after breakfast. His father met them at Penn Station. From the light in his eye and the broad grin, Dan could see he was especially happy. Dan supposed it was because he was going to California with Jenny. Andrew certainly liked taking care of her, but there was a bonus of added excitement.

"I have a surprise for you," he said to Jenny, as they entered her drawing room. Turning, he addressed Dan. "This will please you, too." The next thing, his eyes were on Jenny. "I approached the Armstrong Moores."

Instantly, Jenny cried out: "Lake Tahoe! Their wonderful house!"

Andrew Gunther smiled. "It's all settled. We have the big cottage adjoining the main house and the use of their pier."

Jenny sighed, delighted and eager.

Dan's reception of this piece of news was polite but reserved. Partly, it was because he saw how admirable his persuasive, charming father looked in Jenny's eyes. He jumped up from his chair, thinking that being jealous of his father was absurd. He *was* pleased that Jenny was not going to travel all that distance alone. It *was* good that Jenny's family would now leave the summer fog for the summer sun. And yet! Dan still could not unpack. He went back to his chair. Pleasant scenes floated before his eyes. There was the well-equipped cottage on a knoll surrounded by pines and some cedar, with its panoramic view of lake and towering mountains. He had spent part of one summer vacation there with Jenny, her mother, and grandmother. He saw himself and Jenny following the old Indian trails up the mountain; he saw the horses they rode on the slopes above the lake, the shelter they built of pine branches. He could see clearly the picnic parties in the meadows of wild flowers. He recalled Jenny, lovely in clinging chiffon belted at the waist, dancing at the tavern. Suddenly, he thought of his father again—what a fine mountain man he was, what a crack shot.

Dan came out of his reverie to the sound of his door opening a little. "I'm number nine. May I come in?" The voice was female, slightly throaty.

Dan instantly raised himself to his feet. "Come on in."

"Hi." There was a laugh. A tall, athletic-looking girl entered. He noticed her regular features, the even teeth.

Dan answered quickly. "Hi."

She swept across the room to where the bed was. "Shall I sit here?"

"If you like."

For some time, they observed each other in silence.

Sprawled on the bed in breeches and riding boots, she looked like a man, good-looking and competent.

"You look in good shape. How do you work under pressure?"

"I avoid it," said Dan.

"Nope," said she. "Not here you don't. We're understaffed and over-populated."

"In that case, I thrive on it."

"If we're to visit, you must sit." Then she added, "I'm Sue Palmer—we share the bathroom." And then, with no change in tone: "Do you bathe or shower?"

After some consideration, Dan answered. "I shower. However, I think my wife will take a dim view of—"

"I think you're right," Sue cut in, laughing. "I'll use John Tevis' bathroom. He's our neighbor across the hall—and divorced."

"Nonsense, I'll—"

Sue broke in. "Don't be silly. But you won't mind if I happen to use your toilet at night, will you?"

Dan said, "No, of course not." He suddenly felt uncomfortable; he couldn't help wondering why this arrangement. Why wasn't he put—? Before he could complete his thought, Sue was explaining. "Ours were the only unassigned rooms left when I arrived. It's astonishing, but except for Helen Rose, who is married and lives in one of the cottages, I'm the only female resident here. And now let me tell you about supper. Later, I'll show you around. If you like. . . ."

"I didn't notice. What time is supper served?"

"I regret to tell you the hospital food is terrible. As a result, we eat here only when we must. But down the road a few miles is a diner that serves the most scrumptious hamburgers, crispy French fries, homemade pies that are heavenly, and clam chowder that is out of this world."

Dan nodded his head slowly, a bit bewildered, and asked her how long she'd be getting ready.

"Oh, I am ready." It was an offhand comment.

Dan shrugged his shoulders. "Then I'll wash up."

"I'll wait," Sue replied, her eyes on Jenny's basket. "You're well-provisioned, I see. From your wife?"

Dan nodded. His hand halted with the doorknob half turned as Sue asked with open interest, "What's she look like?"

Suddenly he realized that Sue's breezy manner reminded him uncannily of Tascha. What hurt, he wondered, are all that swagger and bluff hiding?

It was as if she could read his mind. "It took years of therapy to drag me out of my shell. Have I come out too far?"

Dan hesitated.

"Well?"

"As a matter of fact, I like people willing to reveal themselves. I find them interesting."

Sue chuckled. "Now, that's what I call a graceful dodge." She let him go into the bathroom, saying, "I put fresh towels out for you. The toiletries are a present."

Thinking: *My day for presents,* Dan said, "That's most considerate. Thank you."

Ten minutes later they were on their way out. The hospital grounds were silent; patients no longer huddled around the flower bed. The white-uniformed attendants were gone, too. The Buick, parked nearby in the doctors' parking area, was the newest and best-looking car there. Sue hurried over to it, her swinging stride like that of an athlete. "Dan," she said, her eyes level with his, "for five dollars a month you can get a patient with ground privileges to wash, polish, and keep your car waxed."

Opening the door for her, Dan said, "Really."

Taking a cigarette pack from her pocket and offering one to Dan, she said, "I have just the man for you."

"Good."

Presently, they were on a narrow road with just a trickle of traffic, driving through pretty wooded country, long lanes twisting out of sight amid centuries-old trees. Dan noticed the well-kept farms, the horses grazing the pastures. A short drive and they were near a main highway.

Inside the diner, Sue steered him to the counter. Perched on the high stool, she greeted a group of truck drivers. "Hello there." Dan felt they were regulars. A few minutes later the counterman came over. Well over six feet in height and almost as wide, the giant beamed at Sue. "Hi, Doc. How goes it?"

"Pete, meet my friend, Doctor Dan Gunther."

Pete looked at Dan a long time before he put out his great big hand. "Glad to make your acquaintance, Doc."

"Thanks, Pete. Same here." Dan winced from the handshake.

"Pete used to be a boxer. He still tears the Manhattan telephone directory in half," said Sue.

Dan grinned. "I believe it. All at once, I'm hungry."

Pete went for coffee. When he came back, Sue ordered. "The usual, for two." It seemed strange to Dan that he was not consulted. Later, as they dipped into huge steaming mugs, he supposed it was because of the home brew Pete served. Sue started talking about herself, drinking plenty.

Looking at Sue seriously, Dan asked, "What motivated your choice of profession?"

"My height had a lot to do with it—five foot ten in stockinged feet. And I wanted to get away from a dull marriage, a country house, and conversations revolving around diapers, formulas, and maids."

"I mean the real reason. Whom are you revolting against? Your mother?"

Sue raised the mug to her lips and emptied it. "To my mother—the unfeeling bitch."

Dan drained his coffee. "I'm sorry. I didn't particularly want to pry. Reasons interest me."

"Forget it, *mon ami*." Her face lifted. "Why are you a doctor?"

"I can't remember a time when I didn't want to be one."

Sue cast an astute glance at Dan. "And you wanted to please your mother?"

"Well, yes. That's part of it."

They sat there talking seriously. It suddenly struck Dan he was doing most of the talking about his wife and his goals. He slid a hand into his pocket to pull out his wallet. "Do you mind my going on about Jenny? The snapshot's in there. Take a look."

Sue's lips smiled at him. Her cool gray eyes teased. "How can I mind a girl with soft hair, perfect lips, and dark eyes fringed with long lashes?"

Dan laughed. "I suppose you're right. You can't possibly mind. We'd better get going."

"Oh, no," said Sue. "We go dutch."

Dan gave Pete a twenty-dollar bill without answering. Pete looked at him across the counter and smiled.

Dan felt grateful to Sue that she was quiet as they drove back. But at her door, when he assumed the evening was at its conclusion, she said, "The night is young. Come in. I'll enlighten you about admissions."

Dan did not accept her offer. "Tomorrow, Sue. I want to write to Jenny. And I still haven't opened my suitcases or put anything away."

"I'll help."

"No, thanks."

"Well, good night."

"Good night," Dan answered, smiling.

The next morning he did not linger over breakfast, although the coffee was unexpectedly good. Sue joined him, and they walked outside in a mood to enjoy the refreshing gusts of wind that blew up from the sound. It was hazy and hot under the huge old trees scattered near the hospital. They walked slowly now because Sue was pointing out the various buildings, some in clearings, some between the trees. Rich green lawns extended to the edges of the well-kept flower beds laid out in circles. Sounds of birds made it hard to think that people were walled in behind bars and locked doors in bare rooms. Nearing Female Admissions, where Dan had been assigned, they quickened their pace. The "Building," two-storied and of plain red brick, was divided into four wards, each consisting of a dayroom and dormitories. The ward given over to paroled patients was an open-door ward smelling more of sunshine than of paraldehyde. In the intermediate ward the patients were passive: some emerging from the darkness of depression, some from a more violent manic state. Here the phonograph player went on and on. The patients listened in silence—some aware of the continuing sound, some staring fixedly at nothing. Trying to think? Trying not to think? But compared to the disturbed ward, this was a place of peace. The depressed ward was coffin darkness. Aside from the ward, the sunless corridors, the wide stairs, the cold concrete ramps, there was a large dining hall—an ugly room, bare, with long wooden tables and wooden benches. At one end a door led into an institutional kitchen. At the other, another door—this one a double door—led into the occupational therapy area. One whole wing of the building was given over to offices and to the hydrotherapy unit. And everywhere the prevailing sound was that of the metallic clang of keys.

Sue left Dan at the office room prepared for him. It was small, musty, and the one tightly sealed window looked out on an alleyway littered with garbage cans. Its space was crowded with a desk, three chairs, and a couch. There was nothing for him to do until after his interview with Dr. Larry Stein, who headed Female Admissions. He slouched at his desk, in the peculiar quiet, feeling closed in. He straightened up at the sound of footsteps. A nurse stared into the room. "I am Miss Graham, Doctor. I am to take you to Dr. Stein."

Dan quickly got up from his chair and went toward the door, wondering why he could not go alone across the corridor.

"Lock your door, Doctor," Miss Graham reminded him. "It's very important."

"I have no keys."

Miss Graham turned in surprise. "How did you get in?"

"Dr. Palmer let me in."

Nurse Graham lifted a key from her ring and locked the door behind them. Dr. Larry Stein's door was locked, too. As he stood waiting, Dan thought all the locking and unlocking unnecessary. Again, he watched the key lift. The door opened.

Dan found Larry Stein immersed in a stack of records. A moment later he looked up and waved Dan in, energetically pushing aside the papers. He seemed vibrant, in tune with his work.

Larry was a research-oriented, fast-talking, faster-thinking man. Five-foot-nine and kind-looking, casually dressed in a tweed jacket, he regularly maintained a seventeen- to eighteen-hour a day work schedule five days a week. His wife, Betsy, a slightly plump, dimpled social worker, had gone from Cornell to Columbia for her professional training and had met Larry there. She was honest, affectionate, and brainy. She loved a variety of things, ranging from popcorn to her Jewish husband.

"Hello," Larry Stein said as Dan reached his desk. Still sitting, he gave Dan his hand. "It's nice to have you here. Pull up a chair." Another moment passed. "Something wrong?"

Dan laughed out loud. "Yes. You're holding my hand."

Larry Stein said happily, "Now, that's interesting. I wish I knew what I meant by that."

Presently Dan was seated. Larry sounded the buzzer for Nurse Graham. The door unlocked again. "I don't want to be disturbed. Dr. Gunther will be lunching with me. I'll be back at my desk by one." The door locked. Larry saw the faint grin on Dan's face and immediately guessed what was on his mind. It wasn't so long ago that he, too, had been made aware of the constant security. "One of the tasks that faces us here is to see that no one gets hurt. We are thirty-five doctors responsible for five thousand and seven hundred and some-odd patients—the great majority violently disturbed—housed in a plant whose maximum capacity is three thousand. Our nursing corps is way understaffed. Our attendants—the dregs." Dr. Stein stopped. He saw that Dan was beginning to understand. He smiled. "At first, it's difficult. I asked Dr. Palmer to take you under her wing since she has unique knowledge of mental hospitals. Before she came to us, and before her analysis, she was a patient. She is a most competent doctor. She insisted I tell you this. It was six o'clock when she called me this morning.''

Dan's eyes were openly puzzled. ''Why me?''

''I don't know. It's out of character. She keeps it a secret. Only the superintendent and I were supposed to know.''

Larry Stein realized that Dan found the conversation vaguely disturbing and didn't know what to say. He ruminated over this, and then, glancing across at Dan, he spoke. ''Anyone who tends to belittle Sue as a physician is wrong. She's a good doctor. And with patients she knows what she's doing.''

Dan wondered: *Why the verbal fretting and fussing?* He found it odd.

''When Sue's dependency needs are gratified, she has the ego strength to assert a protective attitude toward her patients. In fact, she identifies herself with their suffering, but her instability does not come across to them.''

Dan felt a momentary sympathy at Larry's loyalty to a member of his staff.

''Well,'' said Dan, ''that's understandable. Her exposure to personal therapy probably gives her insights into the dynamics of psychopathology that are far deeper than those many of us have.''

''Exactly! You should have seen her with our bird lady, Heloise.'' Larry Stein retold the story briefly but in a manner that made the transaction between doctor and crude manic patient come vividly alive.

''It would take too long to give you even a small idea of what Heloise was like. She was smart and she had full knowledge of mythology. So when she decided to transform herself into a bestial shape with a bird's head, she had more than her own imagination to go on. Intent on producing pain, she had the other patients on the ward paralyzed with fear. The things she invented! Even the attendants and the nurses were terrified of her. But not Sue. She was able to go into Heloise's world and share in a parallel way what she was experiencing. She could live the mad woman's fantasy.

''On more than one occasion the bird lady tested Sue. Less afraid for herself than of failure, Sue endured more than anyone has the right to expect from a doctor, and each time she gave more and more understanding—more and more support.''

Larry let Dan think about it. Then he went on. ''Heloise is now a woman of normal sexual habits. On Sue's counsel she did not conceal her past from her husband. They are marvelously happy in spite of it.''

Dan nodded.

Larry peered at him through his glasses. "Nearly three years ago, Sue came as an intern. She's now a junior physician. So far she has not tried to bother with the civil service exams."

"Is she working toward accreditation?"

"I really don't know what her plans are in that regard. Talk of the Boards just hasn't come up between us. But if she is content to stay in her present status, we're more than content. We're thankful to have her."

Dan thought that natural enough. A good doctor at a bargain rate.

"Well," said Larry, after a time, giving Dan an encouraging smile, "what do you know about institutional care for the mentally ill?"

"Nothing."

"You'll learn a tremendous lot here." Larry Stein thought it fitting to start with the admitting procedures. "We get our patients from Bellevue and from King's County. Some sign themselves in. Most patients are committed by some member of their family by legal process, which means that two certified physicians have to decide. Sadly, the doctors are political appointees and don't know a goddamn thing about mental illness. Once committed, the patient loses all civil rights. You'll find that the alcoholics, as soon as they sober up, are the best patients. And that the women patients are the sickest."

"Really?" said Dan, surprised.

"That's right. That's why, around here, always be on the alert for trouble—expect anything. What I am trying to tell you is that anything and everything can happen. Things you can't believe. Take Lizzy, for example—catatonic for years and years, and for all those years she stands mute, her left arm extended, her right hand on her left wrist. About nine months ago, another woman, Mathilda, was brought into the disturbed ward from Bellevue. She instantly grabbed a high stool and placed it in front of Lizzy. Each day she'd play with her stool, and no one paid any particular attention to the constant moving about. Then one day she dragged her stool and a sheet into the darkest corner of the dayroom and hung herself. But for Lizzy, she'd be dead. With speed that bore no relation to her catatonic state, Lizzy rushed to Mathilda, held her up, and screamed for help. After the rescue, she froze back into her catatonia."

Dan took in the story of Lizzy, but his thoughts kept returning to Sue; what possible reason could she have to single him out? With an effort, he forced his attention back to Larry Stein. "That's amazing."

"It's more than amazing; it's wonderful. Think about it."

"I shall."

"Another thing about catatonic patients"—Larry Stein grinned sheepishly at Dan—"when I get wound up—"

"Please go on." It was exactly what Larry Stein wanted most to hear. He went on, with barely a pause. "The memory of the catatonic is uncanny. There isn't a thing that happens on the ward that they don't recall once they are well."

"I'll remember that."

"And now I'd better get on with how we do things around here. You'll be working with Sue as a team, normally on the saner wards. You're both responsible to me. Should you blunder—" Larry Stein stopped speaking for a moment. He fixed his eyes more intently on Dan. "I've got a better idea. Ask questions. I haven't scheduled anything for myself until our staff conference at one fifteen. There's plenty of time for an interpersonal, two-way transaction between us."

Dan knew Larry Stein was doing more than establishing an intimate professional relationship; he was testing. He said immediately, "Sullivan?" It was the right response.

"Ah—" Larry Stein was delighted. "So you *are* conversant with him. Most of the doctors we get here are weighted down with *Esquire* and *The Police Gazette*."

This evoked a smile from Dan.

"Well, I can hardly wait. What do you think of him?"

"A good friend credits Harry Stack Sullivan with providing psychiatry with some of the most brilliant, advanced thinking. He says that Sullivan has widened our horizons, freed us from some of the rigidity, in the European manner."

"That's true," Larry exclaimed. "I'm an omnivorous reader. When I discovered his early articles, I forgot to come home. Since then I've spent countless hours reading Sullivan."

Dan nodded. "I know what you mean. Since Lewis Miller introduced me to—"

"Lewis Miller!" Larry Stein looked at Dan, grinning happily. "So he's your friend. Tell me, if you invited him, would he come here? Would he talk to us?"

"Yes," Dan replied, "he'd come." There was a pause as Dan thought. "How do you happen to know about Lewis Miller? In contrast to most psychiatrists, he doesn't write articles. He refuses to publish. Speech is his contribution."

"My analyst, Clara Thompson, is most explicit as to whom she considers the most brilliant, the most intellectually unrestrained among the younger men today. I got interested in Lewis Miller through her. She told me the most amazing story about him.

"Since my student days I considered the maligning of one physician by another a most serious offense. It seems there are times when a reputation is of no importance because one's first loyalty belongs to the patient.''

Dan realized that he was to hear once more how Lewis Miller finished off a transference for all time and brought a man back to good health.

"A late colleague had done an atrocious thing. He betrayed a trust. He wanted the patient dependent. He needed the patient. Then he acted with complete disregard for the patient. Suddenly the doctor died. Alone and afraid, the patient contemplated suicide. But there was something that drove him to seek help. He asked Lewis Miller for an appointment.

"Lewis listened to him. He did not interrupt. Then he said, 'Now, you listen to me. I knew Jacob Keyes. He was a wretched excuse for a human being because he shit all over his patients, and they shit all over him and between them there was an awful stink. I cannot help you. You must help yourself. Go home and *live*.'

"Lewis Miller waited. The patient's face grayed. Lewis Miller continued to wait. The patient forced himself out of the chair. Lewis Miller braced himself.

'' 'You do understand,' the patient said. 'I am well out of the mess.' He started out. 'Thank you, doctor.' ''

Dan decided to let Larry think the story new to him. After a comfortable pause, he said, coming back to Clara Thompson, "I suppose you see your analyst five times a week. Isn't it a problem—the responsibilities of this job, a wife, the commuting?''

"My analysis will go on for more years than ordinarily necessary. Betsy, my wife, is on her analyst's couch five times a week. I go twice. Each Tuesday and Thursday, I catch the four seventeen to New York; the six forty-five back. How about you? I suppose you got started in Vienna?''

"No.''

Larry Stein's brows went up.

"In spite of all you hear, no one wants to get involved with therapy in Vienna anymore. They know there won't be time to finish. They go to Ernest Jones in London. Or, like me, they wait till they get back here.''

"If you like, I'll ask my analyst if she has time. I know you couldn't do better.'' It wasn't until after he had spoken that Larry Stein realized what an extraordinary thing he had done. He saw Dan looking at him with a very curious expression.

"Thank you, no. I must work with a father figure.''

"The therapist changes roles.''

"I know.''

"Dan,'' Larry said, "we could talk all day. Come to supper on Saturday.

Come around six. Just you, our good friend George Atlas, Betsy, and me. We'll have a fine time."

"George Atlas the All-American?"

"The same," Larry replied proudly.

"Of all people! On the staff here?"

"No," said Larry, thoroughly amused at the idea. "George has no use for psychiatrists. He thinks we're all nuts. We grew up together in the same town—Chevy Chase, Maryland. His father was our family doctor. George, when he winds up his residency in the city in January, is going back home to be a general practitioner. A shame. With his personality and his charm, he'd make an outstanding therapist."

A quiet moment passed and again Larry spoke. "A new patient is assigned to a doctor, then goes directly into the disturbed ward for about three weeks for detailed observation. Then, at an open staff meeting, the patient is discussed, a diagnosis made, and a deposition planned. And that's about it."

Dan nodded without answering.

"Of course," Larry said, as if his next remark made everything all right, "we don't use quieting restraints here."

Dan restrained himself from saying something about straitjackets because he recognized in Larry Stein a decent man and a dedicated doctor who wanted to be proud of his service and was not. Instead, he asked questions about wet-packs and tubs. Sue had just explained the techniques, but he listened attentively.

"One more thing," said Larry firmly. "Never lay down your keys."

"All right."

When Larry was opening the door into the corridor, Dan said, "You understand, don't you, that I'll not be here for about four weeks? I want to leave around the twentieth of September."

"Yes, Dr. Flood mentioned it." Larry Stein glanced at Dan as he was speaking. "That's something incredible. I've never known our superintendent to be that generous. How did you get him to agree?"

Their eyes met. "I forget."

That made Larry laugh. "Come along. I'll introduce you to Lizzy."

Dan could not believe his eyes when he saw what awaited him in the various wards—the overcrowding, the stench, the pervading despair, the arbitrary rules, the vague supervision, the tacit acceptance of physical cruelty on the part of the attendants because they—the attendants—were responsible for keeping the wards quiet and the more passive patients safe from attack by the violent ones.

"Well, what do you think?"

Dan shuddered, stopped, and looked over at Larry. "Christ!"

"I'm afraid the chronic wards are worse. Would you like to see one?"
Intent upon what he was feeling, Dan merely nodded.

They went silently out of Female Admissions and up the road toward
the older buildings, passing parole patients, some of whom spoke to Larry.
Occasionally someone glanced at Dan and nodded. Dan offered his nod
in return. They walked a considerable distance, turned a corner, and found
themselves at Building C. Larry pushed a button. "This is not my service.
I don't have the keys."

The door was opened by a brisk-looking nurse and they went in.

The patients were segregated according to sexes—walled off from one
another by solid doors locked shut. Dan suspected that some attempt was
made to separate patients according to age. Dan had now had his first contact with the senile old, discarded by their families, and sent here to die.
He was astonished to find how many there were. Larry explained. "Sadly,
most of them do have relatives. They don't even visit."

Further observation followed, with further questions. When finally Larry
said, "Seen all you want to see?" Dan answered, "I didn't begin to imagine
this horror." His voice was bitter.

"What did you expect?"

"I don't know," Dan admitted. Hardly pausing, he said, "I can't understand one thing. How does a man spend years of his professional life here?"
A series of images was building up in his mind—the fixed staring, the senseless screaming, the ugly obscenities, the pain, the waste, the endless darkness. It was depressingly inhuman, something he had not known his fel-
lowman capable of before.

Larry considered him, speculatively. "Some never get used to it. Some
don't give a damn; it's a job—sign in at nine, quit at four, with lunch
providing a pleasant interlude." A pause ensued, after which Larry said,
"Get personal. I don't mind."

"Am I that transparent?" Dan asked somberly.

Larry smiled at Dan. "I know a lot about you. It's only fair you know
a little about me. I came here intending to stay one year. I met Betsy and
wanted to marry her. She persuaded me to reconsider something I had
already rejected—to take the civil service exams on the ground that we'd
always have some security. The stock market crash proved her right. Now,
until the conclusion of our therapies, it's quite impossible for me to quit
the State Hospital system. But I, personally, am not unhappy here. I like
what I'm doing here. I find challenges. I single out the men I want to
teach, the patients I want to treat. If any of us are interested in research,

there's an awful lot of freedom here. In numbers alone, we're provided with unusual opportunity. However"—slightly raising his voice, Larry concluded—"I have not abandoned the idea of one day leaving all this behind me."

"Thank you for taking me into your confidence," Dan said.

Again, Larry took Dan's elbow. "Hadn't we better get moving?"

They started out, but Larry paused, wondering if he had any right to reveal something else to Dan. "Things have a way of getting around. Maybe you'd better hear about Warren Ryan from me. He's fastidious, immaculate, and he has blond curling hair. He wears monogrammed shirts, flamboyant sport jackets, and his nails are manicured. My head nurse, who keeps track of such things, tells me he's all man. He comes from the south—a large Catholic family. Some months ago, he transferred his attention from student nurses to Sue. She was willing enough. Lately, she's been acting wounded. I keep wishing nothing had happened between them. I'd feel awfully sorry if Sue were hurt again."

"Again?"

Larry nodded. "That's right. She always needs someone to go to bed with."

"Sex or solace?"

After a long moment, Larry shrugged his shoulders and started down the last three steps to the dining room.

The exodus from the dining room began around one. They reached the conference room close to one fifteen. That the psychologist and several of the social workers were there was not at all surprising. That the superintendent of nurses came was not out of the ordinary. The dietician was a surprise. Larry Stein purposely waited until everyone was seated. Then he introduced Dan: "Dr. Daniel Gunther is not to be regarded as an intern. He'll not act in any kind of subordinate capacity. He is Board-qualified in two branches of medicine, yet he decided to start all over again in the specialty of psychiatry. Soon after he made that decision, he went first to Dr. Jones in London, then to Paris where he worked with Princess Marie Bonaparte, and then to Vienna where he stayed more than a year. Upon his return here, some of our great teachers recommended exposure to psychotic patients. He chose us over a prestigious university appointment. He's here at the expense of his own analysis." While talking about Dan, Larry looked at his audience. Now he turned his eyes on Dan with a grin. "We're delighted to have you here. I am turning the conference over to you since you are the attraction. Ordinarily we don't find ourselves honored with so many visitors."

Dan rose from the chair and stood close to Larry. He looked at his audience quietly for a moment, then said, "It's hard to begin. Perhaps if we start with questions, I'll do my best to answer."

Dan had been talking for more than an hour when someone said, "You've said nothing about Freud. Did you meet him? Did you discuss psychoanalysis with him?"

Dan was loath to get involved in a detailed account. Besides, he wanted to talk about an idea he had been nursing awhile. "Yes," he replied, "I did meet Professor Freud once." He stressed the once. "We did not discuss anything that would be relevant here. May we talk about it another time?"

From the back of the room, one young student nurse called out: "Dr. Stein, when the talk on Freud comes up, will there be notices on the bulletin boards? I should hate to miss it."

"That's a good idea. I'll see to it." Then, after a moment's thought, Larry addressed Dan. "You're concerned with therapy and its effects. Obviously, intensive psychotherapy for each and every patient is impossible in our setup. Did you gain anything from your detailed observation in Vienna that might serve as a meaningful substitute here?"

It's almost as if he were telepathic, Dan thought. Then he continued, "I do have an idea. It's vague and formless, but I'm willing to talk about it." His eyes wandered around the room. He had their attention. Sue Palmer, among others, had her pencil out, ready to take notes. Dr. Dunbar had an anticipatory look on his face as Dan began to speak.

"In Vienna, the doctors tended to separate themselves by specialty—not that we weren't all friendly, even sociable—but the more intense relationships were established within fixed groups. Most of the psychiatric group, unlike myself, were not beginners. We met at least two evenings a week, at first, simply for the pleasure of exchanging ideas. Gradually, something happened in the group, something I can scarcely describe. But it was a therapeutic experience in peer relationships. We learned we could, we wanted, in fact, to support one another. We expressed reactions to one another, we overcame inhibitions; there was collective effort and collective cooperation in an atmosphere of democracy. And our group sessions gave an increased pace to those in personal analysis. It all started with Dr. Aichhorn, who was no ordinary teacher—there was brilliant sense behind his method. His classes were not oriented exclusively to case presentation. He emphasized and expected active participation from us all. He exposed us to hostility, to the overt expression of interpersonal conflict. At various sessions, he even rated the hostility—its presence or absence—to the peers or to the professor. And so on." Dan stopped. It was apparent that they understood what he was getting at, the setting up of groups for interaction among the hospital's patients.

Dr. Dunbar greeted the idea coldly. "That group business may be dandy as an exercise among ourselves, but can you just see my bunch letting off steam? They'd kill each other."

Another doctor, Leo Russnick, felt it would be completely wrong to chance it. At best, dangerous.

"It's a disturbing idea," said a blond man whom Dan recognized as Warren Ryan. "But I like it. Maybe schizophrenics can help one another."

"That's not even remotely possible."

"May one ask why, Dr. Everett?"

"Because, Miss Graham, I don't believe it."

Miss Graham had run up against his preconceptions before. "I find, Doctor, that reasoning and suggestion, even with the most disturbed patient, often help. I tell my girls to disperse the patient's fears. It does increase faith in the possibility of recovery."

The same thoughts were passing through Sue Palmer's mind. She produced a cigarette from a pocket and struck a match against her shoe.

"No smoking," someone reminded her.

"Damn!" Sue protested with a glare.

Larry Stein glanced at her and smiled. "Aside from a cigarette, what's on your mind, Dr. Palmer?"

"Since we've practically abandoned individual therapy here, it makes sense to try it. And some therapy in small groups can't hurt, can it?"

The resultant noisy discussion reflected a variety of opinions. Dan, in answer to a direct challenge, had to admit that those of whom he spoke were drawn together by common interest. "But," he added, making a direct parallel between doctors and patients, "the situation is somewhat the same here—not exactly, but similar. Everyone here is in conflict with himself and with society. That unites them. Loss of freedom unites them. Earnest desire for health unites them. What is more poignant—suffering unites them. I'd say there are enough common interests here to carry through the program. So far there has been nothing said about leadership. The first thing to establish, it seems to me, is the services of a wise and good therapist."

Larry, Sue, Warren Ryan, and others instantly sided with this. And then Larry mentioned a friend of his in the New Jersey penal system.

"He contends that therapy in groups is not incompatible with individual therapy. He works with prisoners, and those of us who work with large numbers of people must look to a diversity of approaches to mental health."

Larry glanced at the clock—close to three. "I can't list all the arguments he advanced now. We'll talk again." He now looked in Dan's direction. He was going to pay him a compliment but decided against it.

The exodus began. The student nurses filed out first. Sue Palmer chose to walk out with Dan and Larry.

Dan started to express some of the nagging doubts in his mind. "I get the impression that the doctors here are custodians of chloral and hyoscine. What's our function as therapists? What are our treatment goals? Surely there should be some insistence on therapy?"

Larry then explained with difficulty that of the thirty-five doctors on staff, only about eight really cared. The others lacked proper training, accepted routine, and spent more hours playing bridge than in study.

"It's a real problem. I always encourage the staff in clinical research and hope some new ideas will evolve. Yet you can see from this afternoon's conference that the general reaction to therapy is one of apathy. However, there's one other thing I want to say, Dan. If I were you, I'd start analysis now. Don't waste a whole year. Please let me talk to Clara Thompson. With what I have to say to her, she'll decide to take you."

"I can't. In other words, I can't go to a woman analyst. Jenny won't stand for it."

Sue looked stunned. "God Almighty!"

Larry looked puzzled for a minute. Then he chuckled. "Run along you two. I need to get to work."

That evening, when Sue was ready to start out for rounds, she found Dan reading in the doctors' lounge. She called from the door, "Still up?"

Dan glanced at his wristwatch—ten thirty. "Why not? It's early."

"I know you've had a full day, but I'm on my way to check on our girls and I wonder whether you'd come along."

"I'm glad to have the chance," Dan said, getting up.

The nurse on duty, her white uniform gleaming in the dark, met them when they came in. She was carrying a flashlight.

"Good evening, Dr. Palmer."

"Good evening, Mrs. James. Have you met Dr. Gunther?"

"Not yet." Her glance leaped to Dan. "I believe I saw you walking with Dr. Stein around noon."

Dan smiled at her. "Yes, Mrs. James, we were together then."

Mrs. James led them to the nurses' station. Sue signed the sleeping orders for the night. "Any incidents of importance?" Sue asked.

"Dora Davis fell out of bed. It's all written up in the report book."

"Is she still here?"

"Yes, Doctor."

"Dora is suffering from a senile psychosis," Sue said to Dan. "She was to have been transferred to a chronic ward. I wonder why she was left here." Sue turned back to Mrs. James. "How is she?"

"She seems all right."

"Let's have a look at her."

Walking softly, they went over to the patient's bed and found her awake, clutching the covers.

"Hello, Dora. How do you feel?"

"I guess better."

Dan stared at the old woman. She looked starved. "Are you in pain?"

"Who's he?" Dora showed some excitement.

"He's a doctor," Sue said, taking the flashlight from the nurse.

"Does he want to slit my belly?"

"No, dear. He's a friend."

The patient seemed confused.

Sue lowered the blankets. "Let us take a look at you, Dora."

"He can look, but he can't touch."

Sue saw that the patient held her right leg in an extremely awkward position. She turned to Dan. "What do you see?"

As Dan looked down, he said, "The same thing you see. A fractured femur."

"Don't move, Dora." Lightly, Sue pressed the area around the right hip. "Does it hurt?"

"Not much. When he reaches in with his dagger, it'll hurt a lot more."

"Dora, I'm sending for an ambulance to take you to the infirmary. A specialist will put you in a hip-cast."

Dora looked at Dan. "You're a nice kid."

"Thank you, Dora. You're nice, too."

As they went out of the ward, Sue said to Mrs. James, "I'll write an order for a fourth of a grain of morphine. That should keep her comfortable."

In the corridor, on their way to the next ward, Dan said, "I'm impressed, Sue. You made that diagnosis on a minimum degree of complaint—made it on pure observation."

"The positioning of the limb was typical."

Dan observed Sue's sense of pleasure and realized how quick her response to compliments was.

The next ward was quiet. So was the disturbed ward. "No difficulties at all," said the charge nurse.

It was well after eleven when Sue unlocked the door to the depressed ward. The sound of sobs came to them clearly.

"I'm glad you came, Doctor," said the nurse in charge. "We're having a problem with Cecile. You'll find her in the lavatory sitting on a stool. I had to put her there because her crying was preventing the others from sleeping."

"Is she safe?"

"Oh, yes, Doctor. She can't hurt herself there. Besides, I left the light on and the door open."

"We'll be along in a moment."

After Nurse Kramer left, Sue said, "Cecile is suffering from a postpartum psychosis. With no history of any mental symptoms, she developed hallucinations and delusions of a persecutory nature a couple of weeks after her delivery. She became completely detached from reality and had to be committed. In the three months that she's been here, I just haven't been able to reach her. She's not receptive to any insight therapy."

"How old is she?"

"Mid to late twenties."

They walked over to the open door of the toilet, discussing possible theories.

Dan remained in the open doorway, watching Sue.

Sue put her hand gently on the patient's shoulder. She said, "What troubles you, Cecile?"

The patient turned her body and lifted her head. She swallowed her sobs and drew in air before she found the breath to say, "I want my baby."

It was clear even to Dan still in the doorway that the woman was no longer isolated in her own strange world. Something good was about to happen. Sue herself was inwardly excited; she had made some contact. At last, she existed for Cecile. She said to her, "How old is your baby?"

"Almost four months old by now."

"Where is she?"

"I think my husband's mother is taking care of her."

Sue thought: *She's ready to spill.* She continued asking questions about her pregnancy and delivery.

Cautiously at first, Cecile slowly talked about her devoted but unattractive husband, of being pregnant and feeling good, and of the sudden sadness and trapped feeling. Then Cecile buried her head into the crook of her arm and began to cry.

Sue contemplated her next suggestion a long time. "Would you like your baby to come visit you here?" Sue looked and saw Dan's unmasked astonishment.

In a sudden rush of joy, Cecile lifted her head. "Then I'll be able to hold her?"

"Of course you may."

Cecile's elation soon turned to a cold dismal feeling and then to an aching pain. "I don't want my baby to see me in a locked ward."

"I'll arrange a more suitable place. I'll see you tomorrow, and we'll discuss your transfer to an open ward."

"Oh, God!" Cecile wiped her eyes. She was unable to thank Sue.

The nurse unlocked the door for them.

Dan led Sue off. After moments of silence he said, "I'm enormously impressed."

Sue accepted his praise again with a smile.

"All in a night's work." Seconds later, she glanced at Dan and said, "I don't normally take a drink on duty, but would you consider one beer anything worth reporting?"

As they stepped out of the building, Dan said, "I was just about to make the same suggestion to you."

Sue came right to the point as they walked on. "What did you think when Larry told you I had suffered a serious breakdown?"

Dan looked straight ahead. "Now that you mention it, I guess I was surprised."

"Do you think I shouldn't be doing what I'm doing?"

Selecting his words with care, Dan replied, "From what I saw tonight, I'd say you're probably a better doctor because of it."

"I hope so. All the same, I worry. I never know for certain. Am I recovered or am I in an extended remission?"

"That's morbid, Sue."

Sue laughed. "I agree."

Friday night was hot and muggy. Dan could not sleep. He kept envisioning Jenny—with her hair coiled on top of her head—in bed waiting for him, waking, her arms still around him. He switched on the light and looked at the clock. It was three hours earlier in California. He reached for the telephone. "I'm calling Lake Tahoe, California. I don't know the number. My guess is it will be listed under Andrew Gunther."

Dan counted the rings.

"There's no answer, sir."

Dan's disappointment was complete. "All right. I'll try them again tomorrow."

After his unsuccessful attempt to reach Jenny, Dan shifted his position and watched his toes for a while. He tried to read but found it difficult to get interested. He considered getting dressed, getting into the Buick for a fast drive. "Christ!" he said, pounding his pillows. "One week and I'm ready to climb walls."

It was nearly light when he finally fell into a deep sleep. The alarm went off at seven. The bathroom was still littered with Sue's things.

Dan came into the hour experiencing a feeling of hurt and anger—a sense of loss of closeness. Without even a perfunctory hello, he took the couch.

A: "You seem disturbed."

DAN: "I am. I'm so damned mad at Jenny, I can hardly talk."

A: "That's unusual."

DAN: "Jenny has the capacity to release her deepest feelings. I've never known anyone less locked up inside. That's okay, I guess. But she sure is quick with value judgments."

A: "What offends you so?"

DAN: "I can't even remember how it started. I made some off-hand remark about Dad, and Jenny exploded in a tirade, accusing my mother of all sorts of Machiavellian cunning. According to her, Mother lived for herself, enjoying martyrdom. She told me bluntly that Mother destroyed my relationship with Dad. Then she said a frightening thing. She said Mother was full of repressed rage against men, and some of it came my way especially when she placed me in a position of dependence by scornfully dispersing the inheritance, which, by right, was mine."

A: "How do you see your mother?"

DAN: "Christ, I've been telling you for three years how I see her."

A: "For a moment, let us discuss your mother as Jenny sees her."

DAN: "Were I to do that, I'd have to see her as a sado-masochistic individual, as a passive-aggressive person, as a woman who used her withholding as a weapon."

A: "Did your father see her that way?"

DAN: "If he ever thought it, he never said it to me. Quite the opposite. "Warmhearted," "gentle," are words he always used. Once, in the middle of our few heart-to-heart talks, he said to me, 'In spite of my bitterness, my love for Miriam persists.' "

A: "Did this seem strange to you?"

DAN: "Not really."

A: "Do you think what you heard from Jenny came from him?"

DAN: "That may very well be. And I resent it."

A: "To whom do you address your anger?"

DAN: "To both of them."

A: "Perhaps more to father."

DAN: "Yes, more to father."

A: "It often happens that when a truth is revealed, the first reaction is anger or protest."

In the ensuing silence, Dan drifted back into his childhood and retraced scene after scene.

It was an important day for Andrew. He had not expected the promotion to major. At the same time he knew he well deserved it.

At supper that night Andrew said, "Miriam, my love, we're celebrating. I'm taking you to the Officers' Club. We're going to laugh and dance and drink champagne."

"Oh, Andrew, I can't."

"What's wrong?"

"I've got things to do. Besides, you know champagne gives me a headache."

Andrew got himself up from his chair and, without a word, walked out of the room.

Another occasion when Dan was about eight or nine. It was New Year's Eve.. Andrew asked patiently more than once, "Miriam, don't you think it's time to get ready?" Then: "Rose is perfectly capable of looking after Dan. That's why we employ her." Then: "We are expected for dinner."

Finally, Miriam gave him her answer. "I'll tell you what. Why don't you go on alone? And you needn't worry about me, dear. New Year's Eve is merely another evening."

"No, Miriam. This time you are coming along."

Even now Dan could see her face, its delicate resignation. He could remember her tender smile, when she kissed him good night. "Poor baby. To think I'm leaving you for an evening with all those dreadful people."

For a time, Dan sorted and pondered aloud, giving Dr. Freitag the memories he had kept so long concealed.

"Before we were rich, Danny, life was lovely."

"Were God to work a miracle, Danny, he'd send your father back to the good and simple life."

"You must not be angry at your father and you must always show him love. Perhaps his sins are God's way of testing me."

A: "How do you feel now?"

DAN: "Like a death in the family."

A: "Does this put your mother in a new light?"

DAN: "More to the point. It puts Dad in a new light."

A: "In what way?"

DAN: "I guess he wasn't a total bastard."

A: "How do you feel now about Jenny?"

DAN: "I'm never angry at her very long."

A: "Because you feel there's validity to her statements."

DAN (his hands covering his eyes): "I always knew about Mother's hidden aggressiveness. But I couldn't admit it to myself. I had to remember father hard as iron and maintain an idealized primary love object."

The analyst remained silent.

Not at all upset, Dan said just as his hour ended: "I'm grateful for this insight. It permits me to love my father."

The analyst's reply came back quickly. "You always have loved your father."

At the door Dan turned. "Now I see my parents, side by side, as people. I think I no longer have the need to create Mother into a perfect goddess, and Dad into a human god, powerful and dangerous."

Reluctantly, Dan stepped out of the shower. He secured the bath towel around his flat abdomen and walked back into his room. Standing by the window, glancing out at the sunshine, he reached for an apple from Jenny's basket. Munching in an absentminded way, he was startled out of his reverie. A quick look toward the door and he made a grab for his silk dressing gown. "Christ! Don't you ever knock on doors?"

Sue laughed. "That's so commonplace. Besides, what have you got I haven't seen before?"

"A jealous wife. Who is expecting a baby at the end of September."

"Does that bother you?"

"It would bother me a hell of a lot more if she were not jealous."

Sue's face showed surprise. "Do you equate jealousy with love?"

Dan belted his robe. "I don't. Jenny does," he answered.

Sue picked up the apple Dan had put down and bit into it. "How would you like to share a bottle of Château Lafit over prosciutto, melon, and curried chicken? And, for dessert, mocha ice cream. My treat."

"That's very decent of you, Sue. I'll take a rain check."

"What's the matter with now? What I mean is—next Saturday night you're on call."

"I'm invited to dinner at the Steins." Dan glanced toward the windup clock on the night table beside the bed. "I've got to dress."

Dan had the impression that she was not listening. "Sue," said Dan sharply, "the visit's over."

Sue deliberately moved herself over to the bed and sat down. "If you believe in being modest, dress in the closet. I thought I'd go with you to the Steins."

"Sue, why don't you split that bottle of Chateau Lafite with Ryan?"

Sue shook her head. "That lanky Romeo with the sexy look in his big blue eyes? No, thanks."

"I think you had better," said Dan, grinning. "I also think you had better start losing at tennis."

Sue, who had started to light a cigarette, stopped.

Dan's grin widened. "I've decided to give you more expert advice. Go talk to a priest. See about converting to Catholicism. It's probably simple."

The match still burning singed her finger. "Ouch!"

Dan opened the door. "Get out."

Sue lifted herself off the bed and walked toward Dan. "What did that Ryan," she demanded, "tell you about me? It's untrue, most of it."

"Nothing," said Dan, opening the door wider.

Looking baffled and defiant, Sue left the room.

Dan stripped off his robe, wishing he could work up enough energy for a few pushups. Instead, he took Jenny's letter mailed from Chicago and read it again. Then he lit a cigarette and stared dreamily at her photograph. He sighed, wishing she were with him and not pregnant. Then he flipped a coin to decide whether to exercise.

The telephone bell sounded. Thinking it might be Jenny, Dan moved swiftly. "Hello."

"I had a talk with Larry. I'm invited to dinner," Sue said breathlessly.

"Change, I'll be—"

"I'm ready."

"And comb your hair. I'll be in the hall outside in twenty minutes."

As plump as he had expected but decidedly more merry-looking, Betsy Stein answered the door. "Hello, Sue."

"Betsy, this is—"

"I know. Larry gave me a full description and then added, 'He's going to be our second best friend.' " Betsy closed the door. "Well, Dan Gunther, aren't you going to kiss me?"

"I most certainly am," said Dan. He did.

"That," Sue broke in, "is more of a welcome than I got."

Betsy giggled. "From me or Dan?"

"I refuse to say."

Dan was smiling at Betsy.

"Larry and George are in the study playing chess." She pointed. "It's the end door. Just follow your nose. Come into the kitchen, Sue. I need help."

Sue stared at her. "Me in the kitchen! You've got to be kidding."

Betsy sighed and looked at Dan. "Tell Larry his next move is to dinner. I haven't done a thing."

Dan nodded and went into the study, thinking: *I don't believe it. Two women and neither can prepare a meal.* The room was a mess, but Larry apparently didn't mind. He greeted Dan smiling and relaxed. Dan smiled too. He moved toward the tall, broad-shouldered man, holding out his hand. "I've watched you play football. Man, you move!"

George Atlas was instantly on his feet. His handshake was firm, immediate. His smile was warm and appealing, showing fine white teeth. Dan had the impression that he was instantaneously judged and found passing. Faintly amused, Dan realized he was doing much the same thing. For a moment longer, brown eyes stared into gray, then George said, "I'm glad you're here. Larry can certainly use someone like you."

"Dan," said Larry, "sit down. I'll fetch drinks. Rye all right?"

"You're wanted in the kitchen."

George sighed. "What sort of a cook are you?"

"No kind, I'm afraid. First I had a mother who was a divine cook. Now I have a wife who"—Dan grinned at George—"among other things is good, really good."

George took two long strides toward the door. They went down the hall to the low kitchen and found it completely cluttered with everything imaginable, including a chopping block on legs, a huge maple rocker, a barometer on one wall, and, on another, a shelf shaky beneath the weight of potted plants.

Dan turned to Betsy. "Mind if I use the phone? I want the operator to know where I am in case Jenny phones."

When they were in the library together, Betsy sat down and beckoned Dan to sit beside her. Dan went over and looked at her intently, instantly conscious of the serious look on her face. "There is something on your mind."

"I got you out of there because Larry and I have a thought. It seems a shame that Jenny can't share your life here when we have an extra room here, empty. You'd have no need to worry about her. With us, she'll be well looked after."

Dan smiled at her gratefully. "That's a nice thought."

In a faint voice Betsy confided. "I'm in analysis because I can't get pregnant, yet there's nothing wrong with me or with Larry. It would be so wonderful to have a baby in the house, especially the baby of special friends."

For a few minutes Dan did not speak. Then he took Betsy's hands in his. "I thought I made the best possible arrangement. Jenny has always lived in luxury. I was afraid that she had no real idea of how demanding a baby can be, how lonely she'd be looking after herself. I wanted her home under her mother's and grandmother's watchful love. My plan met with violent reaction from Jenny. Now I'm not sure it was the right thing." Dan paused. With a heavy heart, he remembered that Jenny rushed off to his father. "But I let her go. Jenny is proud. She has a strange wisdom and a rare strength. I don't believe that I can persuade her to come back now."

Betsy sat absorbed for a time. She looked into Dan's face, then said softly and very gravely, "Be careful of Sue."

Dan drew Betsy's hands to his lips and kissed them. Then his grin appeared. "If Sue likes me, it's because I'm no threat to her masculine pride." Slowly, he let go of her hands.

It was a relaxed meal they sat down to finally at the wide table, the centerpiece a bouquet of fresh flowers in a Steuben bowl. The wooden chairs painted white (Betsy later told him, "I painted them myself") were in sharp contrast to the sterling flatware, the Lenox china, the sparkling white tablecloth of handmade lace. ("All wedding presents." This, too, Betsy told him.)

Dinner started with a salad of lettuce, tomatoes, and avocadoes. They drank Italian wine, supplied by George, with the spaghetti and meatballs.

"The sauce is so good it's shameful," said Sue.

"I'll make some cuddly little girl one hell of a husband." George began to sing: "Five foot two. Eyes of brown—" His booming voice was meant to add cheer but angered Sue, all too conscious of her height. "Sweet Jesus! A big ox like you, and consistently you emphasize 'little.' Why?"

"He's just teasing." Betsy felt a bit uneasy.

To her words Sue replied hotly, "My foot, he's teasing."

Dan observed that Larry was concerned now. Larry lighted a cigarette and handed it to her. "You're tired, Sue."

"And now for dessert," George said calmly. He hastened out to the kitchen and came back with a platter piled high with giant strawberries sprinkled with brown sugar. A small bowl of sour cream was in the center of the platter. "First choice," said George, "goes to Sue. I'm fickle-minded about girls." He offered her the platter. "Fall to."

Sue was feeling sorry for herself. "I don't want your damn dessert."

"Please."

They were all relieved when Sue smiled. "All right."

George was the first to rise and pick up his plate.

"Leave them," said Betsy. "The maid comes in the morning."

"We'll clear the table. Then, I'll get the coffee."

"Jenny," said Dan, rising, "simply can't leave dishes. She's a very orderly person. Has a mania for neatness."

Sue studiously refrained from making any comment.

Betsy laughed aloud. "Then make her come live with me. That way we'll both change a little. I'm a slob."

"Nothing of the kind," Larry said to Dan. "Wait until you see the living room. Betsy takes responsibility there." He waited a minute, chuckled, and went on. "I get to go into it each Saturday night or Sunday afternoon—*if* we have company."

Betsy was the last to put down her coffee cup. Sue finished her cigarette. When Betsy stood up, she did, too. Larry guided Dan through the narrow hall, and as they entered the living room, Dan saw magnificent bowls of roses, chrysanthemums, and other flowers. For fully two minutes he stood enjoying the sight. "Do these come from the hospital greenhouses?"

"Indeed they do. The head gardener keeps us constantly supplied."

"I can't understand why the wards are not periodically serviced. It would be such an easy way to bring color and a little cheer into places with hardly anything but ugly bare walls to look at."

George from the door said, "Now Larry, why didn't you think of that?"

"Because I'm stupid."

Betsy plumped herself into the armchair and looked earnestly at Dan. "The head gardener is a special friend of mine. I'll talk to him immediately."

Larry smiled at her. "I advise waiting for morning."

"Ask him if I can have a few in my room. I miss flowers."

"I shall," Betsy promised.

Sue glanced at her wristwatch. "Do you suppose there's time for a couple of rubbers of bridge?"

Betsy considered.

Larry stood waiting.

"I've eaten too much," said Dan. "I need to walk some of it off."

"I feel energetic," said Sue. But George was determined that he was through with Sue for the evening. At most they'd take her as far as the Residence Hall. Before he could make the offer, Larry cut in. "Take your walk. Sue will remain here a few minutes longer."

She looked at him reproachfully but held her tongue.

"I'll see you home."

Bending down to kiss her, Dan said, "Thank you, Betsy."

She beamed at him. "We loved having you. Come back soon."

George gave Betsy a special glance. "Don't wait up. Dan and I are going gallivanting." He turned to Sue. "Be good and I'll let you beat me at tennis tomorrow."

Sue was suddenly happy. "About ten."

"Make it noon."

Dan's leave-taking of Sue was guarded.

There was no need to talk. Neither Dan nor George was overwhelmed by silence or made uncomfortable by it. Furthermore, the pace they set for themselves was not conducive to chatter. In the meantime, however, something was happening between them. Both sensed the affinity between them. It was almost as though they had known each other for many long years, had grown up together, and made similar discoveries.

"Like it or not, you and I are going to be thrown together quite a lot." George did not say it as though he were handing Dan a handful of diamonds.

Dan considered this. "Yes," he said.

George's gray eyes narrowed. "You don't sound ecstatic."

Dan eyed George with a grin. "You can set your mind at rest. I like it."

George slowly relaxed.

"Let's go back. I'd like to ask you in for a nightcap. Instead, may I offer you an apple?"

George let out a laugh. "My favorite fruit."

Dan had more to offer in the way of hospitality than he had anticipated. On the table where he kept Jenny's basket stood a brand-new replacement brimful. He understood then that Jenny had left a standing order. The basket made no impression on George. He did not even see it. He stood gaping at Jenny's photograph. Then he heard Dan's voice. "Five foot two and eyes of brown—dark, dark brown."

It astounded him that Dan remembered like that. "I've just seen my dream girl."

Dan accepted this. At his nod George extricated himself. "Has she got a sister?"

"She has a widowed mother whom she does not resemble and a widowed grandmother whom she does."

"I'll take grandma."

A short time after this, George, speaking softly, said to Dan, "You're puzzled by Sue, aren't you? By her fits and starts. Let me explain some of her sad background."

Acutely aware of the thin wall separating his room from Sue's, Dan spoke barely above a whisper. "Tell me from the beginning."

"That's a vast request. I don't know the beginning. Maybe Larry does. I was the one who brought Sue to him. The story starts with our freshman year in medical school, where Sue and I were classmates. I dropped out for a time to play pro-ball and lost track of Sue. Then our dean asked a favor. He told me that it was in regard to Sue Palmer. 'Things crowded in on her. Too much happened at once. She's had a nervous breakdown. Her psychiatrist has been obliged to hospitalize her. Sue is in need of a friend.'

"I agreed, of course, and mentioned that I'd be in Chicago for weeks.

" 'That's splendid,' he answered and gave me the name and telephone number of her psychiatrist. 'Ask him first.' "

"Do you remember his name?"

"Leo Butler. Know him?"

"I recognize the name."

"Well, that's how I got involved. We both reappeared at Columbia at the same time. No one, except the dean and I, knew where or why Sue disappeared for two years.

"One dawn, only days before graduation, she was in my apartment. I supposed she had been let in by the janitor, but it seems she managed to open the door with a hairpin. I finally sensed someone standing over me.

" 'I haven't had any sleep, real sleep for days,' she said finally. 'I am so tired. Will you help me?'

"I understood she was verging on another nervous breakdown. I took her into my bed. She cradled her head on my shoulder. An avalanche of distorted thoughts poured out of her. She was out of control, ranting about sex, from homosexuality to promiscuity. Someone must have hurt her, and badly. I held her—the wilder she talked, the closer I held her. Finally, in utter exhaustion she fell into a deep sleep. And I slept. We both slept for a long time. I've forgotten what woke us. I suppose it was the telephone.

"Over coffee came this, 'By this time tomorrow, I'll be dead.'

"Her air of detachment scared the hell out of me. 'Look, Sue,' I said, 'don't joke like that.'

" 'It seems the right thing to do,' she said. 'My hold on reality is tenuous. I'd much rather be dead than committed to a hospital for the insane.'

"Well, I had a different idea. Larry knew precisely what to do. 'Work and love,' said he. 'Good health depends upon it.' Then he said this to her: 'Go back with George. After graduation you'll have a job waiting for you here. As for love—well—we'll think about it.' "

George was silent for a time. He understood that Dan was wondering: Who did what to her and why? What early unhappy experiences, what emotional frustrations, were behind her maladjustment. Dan restrained his curiosity and asked no more questions. George was relieved. Because Larry and Betsy had asked it of him, he had revealed far more than was characteristic of him, far less than he knew.

When George stood up to leave, he moved toward the basket, his gaze again on Jenny's picture.

Dan was looking at him in a strange way, as though he were trying to make a decision. "Something wrong?"

"Not necessarily. What made Larry ask you to tell me about Sue?"

George gave Dan a keen glance. He seemed, however, unwilling to make additional disclosure. Just as Dan was ready to accept his reticence, George said suddenly, "Love and hate are emotions to be reckoned with—and closely related."

"I miss the point."

"I think not," George answered thoughtfully.

"But that's absurd."

"Look, Dan, Larry likes you without reservation. I'm going to tell you exactly what I think. Because Sue can't relax long enough to enjoy sex with any man, she despises all men. There's a good chance she thinks you're different. Watch out! Or you'll be damned if you do and damned if you don't." George waited, his eyes speculative.

Conceding the truth in George's warning, Dan nodded.

"Under the circumstances, your warning is appropriate. Thank you."

With a grateful glance, George held out his hand. They shook hands. Dan watched him go down the dimly lit corridor to the stairway.

Once more back in his room Dan lay fully dressed on the bed gazing at the ceiling, trying to sort out his thoughts. Sue's weakness made them all afraid. That angered him. Then there rose before his eyes a vision of Jenny. She was undressed and her figure was slim. Locking his doors, he went to the writing desk and took paper and an envelope out of the drawer. He started his nightly letter to Jenny. A half hour later he folded the papers, sealed the envelope, and put aside his pen. He remained seated looking at Jenny in the picture frame; she looked straight back at him. Finally, he stretched and slowly rose. When he came back from the bathroom, he again locked the door. He went to bed and, after a while, he slept. He had a terrible dream. His heart gave a jump of relief as he opened his eyes. He clutched the sheet and wiped the beads of sweat on his forehead. Saying to himself, "Christ, I've got to get out of here," Dan followed his first impulse.

In spite of Dan's tendency to repress dreams, this one he remembered and it came up early in his analysis.

DAN (fingering his collar): "I was in bed with Sue trying desperately to ignore her proximity, but Sue pressed closer, pushing her body against mine and fingering my thigh, her hand crept upwards. I was hating myself, but I could no longer hold back. At length, I felt Sue shivering in the spasm of climax. I lay panting in the bed when I heard a sound, and there, in the doorway, was my mother. I was sure she had seen everything. She seemed stunned, shocked. Sadly, she said, 'I suppose it was inevitable that you should imitate your father.' I finally got rid of Sue, but not until after Mother said, 'I shall never again speak to you.' The door closed. She was gone."

A: "Give me your associations."

DAN: "The struggle in my dream was with myself—the conflict between my impulses and my conscience. When my mother appeared, my guilt and shame were unbearable."

A: "I notice your mother appeared rather than your father."

DAN: "Perhaps because my father might have condoned my behavior."

A: "Your mother's appearance in the dream was in part your wish to bring her back to life."

DAN: "I think that's true."

A: "Secondly, she came to punish you for your disloyalty to her. After all, she had forbidden you to be like your father."

DAN: "There was no force stronger than my mother's loyalty to me. I, therefore, owed supreme loyalty to her."

A: "This mutual loyalty between your mother and you is, in fact, the basis for your fidelity to your wife."

DAN: "Is it also part of my conscience?"

A: "Yes, it is part of the structure of your superego. Ordinarily, one thinks of the punishing father as the symbol of the inhibitive force—the castration threat—but your dream illustrates the ego ideal of loyalty to your love object is a strong side of your nature."

Dan turned and looked his analyst full in the face. "Jenny, in relation to mother, is sometimes disrespectful. She decided that mother harped upon the munitions business because it was the lesser crime. Father's unfaithfulness was what she could not resign herself to."

A: "How is this disrespectful?"

DAN: "Jenny has never bothered to disguise the fact that she shared none of my feelings about father." Dan began to be irritated. "Well, I see my time's up."

Dan finished dressing in Western jeans, an old jersey, and a dark-blue overshirt. He stuck his feet into open-toed sandals, extracted his wallet from his trousers and thrust it into his slit-pocket. The car keys in his hand, he tiptoed out of his room, shutting the door gently.

The house was in darkness. That did not worry him. He was sure he'd find them all sleeping. He picked up a handful of pebbles and started pitching. He could remember exactly where George's room was. George heard the first spray and got up. Marveling at his speed, Dan was relieved to see George at the open window. George peered out, then disappeared. Soon, he reappeared in khaki pants and a gold turtleneck sweater carrying two pairs of swimming trunks in one hand. He opened the window wider and lowered himself, landing as lightly as a dancer on the gravel.

Dan said nothing—merely started walking rapidly toward the doctors' parking lot. George followed down the gravel path, his eyes regarding Dan steadily. Dan turned the key and opened the car door. They both climbed in without a word. Dan backed the automobile toward the main road, swung it around and roared forward. Holding the wheel with both hands, concentrating on driving, Dan asked, "How far to the ocean?"

George's heart warmed to Dan. "Miles away. Go east, then north. You'll have no difficulty finding it, even in heavy mist. You'll hear its roar."

"Mind the speed?"

George studied Dan's handling of the car with admiration. He settled back. "No. I'm enjoying it."

Dan turned his head away and stared straight ahead.

George was rather liking the quiet—the companionable isolation—still, after a time, he said, "Now, that I think of it, has Jenny got a cousin?"

Remaining grave and aloof, Dan seemed oblivious.

George leaned his blond head on the back of the seat and said no more.

Finally, Dan pulled up alongside a wide stretch of beach and braked the car. "If you don't care much for a wild surf in thick fog, there's no need for you to come in. I'm a strong swimmer. I'll be all right alone."

George's grin reassured Dan. "You can't get rid of me so easily."

They took off their clothes and started for the water. Until the fog cleared, George stayed very close to Dan, ready at any moment to reach for him. Finally, when he was shivering cold, he put a hand on Dan's arm. Dan made a turn; George gestured him to follow him out of the water. Dan did, his mind free of his dream.

"I'm an absolute fool," George said. "Why didn't I grab towels?"

"I have a couple in the trunk," answered Dan. "Ever since I've known Jenny, she has provided me with emergency supplies. From thread and needle to an extra spare tire, practically everything has found its way into the trunk of my car."

"Do you recall hot coffee in there? Maybe a melted cheese sandwich?"

"Let's find an all-night lunch wagon. There must be a town near here."

"Great," said George. "Let's."

They found a place that served excellent coffee and massive cheeseburgers. Dan finished his and watched George eat another. "You know, Jenny is going to admire you the moment I tell her about your appetite."

"That's terrific. I deserve a little admiration." George drained his coffee and ordered milk and fresh peach pie.

As soon as the waitress left, Dan said, "You had your choice of at least a dozen colleges. Why did you choose Notre Dame?"

Stroking the golden fuzz on his face, George settled back, and, narrowing his eyes, he said, "My mother died at my birth. I grew up without my father most of the time. The only parent I ever knew was my father's office nurse, Maggie. She raised me. I felt I owed it to her to play for the fighting Irish."

Dan looked at George in thoughtful silence.

"Right. She was his mistress and he made her miserable. All the good I can say about him is that he loved my mother. After she died, he lived the rest of his days with a broken heart. Only his concern for his patients sustained him."

In the silence that followed, Dan took the time to digest this. He felt it was inevitable that he and George should meet and gravitate toward each other. He did not doubt that George felt it too. "Yeah," said Dan finally. He sounded sad.

George nodded, understanding the compassion.

Dan smiled then. A little later he said, "Remember, you've got a tennis date."

"What a memory!"

"That's my trouble," Dan said and grinned.

"Let's make it a foursome. We'll get Ryan to join us."

"All right."

As they waited for the check, George said, "Christ! Do we wash dishes?"

"I have money."

In a moment, George was on his feet. When they were seated in the car, George said, "I'll buy you a lobster for supper."

"Good. I'd like to get away from the hospital."

In the late afternoon they drove into the city. Dan was back shortly before eleven. He was particularly glad that no one was around to greet him.

"Where would you begin?"

"Hell, Larry. I don't know. With the chronic wards, I guess."

"You won't find it easy there. Schizophrenics are not approachable. The split with reality is complete, so nothing works."

Dan was evaluating his idea of treating some of the patients in groups. He knew—from his Vienna days—that there was a therapeutic force inherent in the group process. He was also convinced, and was trying to convince Larry likewise, that it could serve to broaden the scope of the mental hygiene movement. It could and it might reach more patients, thus making the doctor more effective. If anything, Larry was not exactly a follow-the-rules type of doctor. Still— Now Dan was turning over a suggestion that chronic schizophrenia had an organic cause.

"You mean the cures might be found in physiological chemistry? How?" Larry asked challengingly. "It's never been proved by the pathologist. The schizophrenic brain looks the same microscopically as any normal brain."

"True. And yet, I do wonder."

"You surprise me, Dan" was Larry's rejoinder. "I thought all you guys trained in Vienna considered psychogenic causes to be the root of mental illness."

"Acute cases, yes," agreed Dan. "No question. But chronic schizophrenia may be entirely different, and its organic nature cannot be ruled out. But—to get back to my group idea—I'd very much like to try working with a small group of ladies from the chronic ward. Patients might learn from one another by being reassured that other people have similar problems. It would be supportive for them."

"OK, Dan. That sounds reasonable. But let's confine it to an experimental group. I suppose patients might be less frightened once they see and recognize similar problems in other people."

"Exactly," said Dan quickly. "Patients are encouraged too by the improvement in others; they even imitate, sometimes quite quickly, the 'coping' devices." His mind was already leaping ahead to which patients might benefit from the interaction process and when he could set up the first session in his office.

Dr. Dan's ladies, as they came to be called, were all in good contact with reality, ranging in age from twenty to forty-five. Most of them, however, were in their thirties. They met with Dan biweekly, and each session lasted a full hour. Dan always rose to greet them and remained standing until chairs were moved and arranged—more or less—in a circle. He sat down only after his ladies were settled.

Dan waited a moment before saying, "Thanks, Larry. Well, I guess I'll be getting back to work."

But Larry stopped Dan with an unexpected question. "How's Sue behaving?"

"Beautifully," Dan answered, not really wanting to go into it.

"I imagine Ryan is the reason."

Dan thought: *He's certainly the reason there's no need for me to lock my doors.* Aloud, he said, "Yes, of course."

Looking greatly distressed, Larry eyed Dan. "Betsy says: 'Poor Sue. If she thinks he'll marry her, then she doesn't know Ryan.' " He paused to let Dan voice his opinion. Finally, he said, "A penny for your thoughts, Dan."

"Christ, I don't know."

"Either way I'm in a difficult position." Larry then explained. "I owe Warren Ryan some loyalty. He should, at least, know the facts. But I've been instructed by Sue to remain silent. I'm honor-bound to do so."

Dan's eyes regarded Larry with feeling, but he remained silent.

"I can understand your reticence, Dan. I am, however, asking for advice. It's not as if Sue were a stranger to you. I've often heard her say that you are, in ways, the most congenial friend she's ever had. You never pry, and yet she feels that her welfare means a lot to you."

Dan had realized for some time now that Larry was faced with a unique problem. One word from him could ruin Sue's chances with Warren Ryan.

"All right," Dan said after a long pause. "The situation does call for comment. I'm very much afraid that George and I are largely responsible for Ryan's renewed interest in Sue. And we did it in my interest. Nice, isn't it?"

"It's understandable. After all, what chance did Sue have with you? Besides, she's calm now—behaving beautifully. You yourself said so."

"I now regret it," Dan said in a more heated tone. "In fact, I worry about it. I feel certain in my own mind that Sue's is a surface calm that could collapse at any time."

"What ought we to do?"

"God knows."

"Well, if He does, I pray for Sue's sake, He sends us a message. Meanwhile, I think it rather up to us."

"Yes," Dan said reflectively, "I guess it is."

Prompting, Larry said, "I'm listening."

"Admittedly, we're all devoted to Sue, but the more we explore objectively what we know about her the less sure I am that she should marry."

"You mean anyone. Not just Ryan."

"Yes."

"How does this deliver me from my dilemma? I think it deepens it."

"Look, Larry, I can't help knowing what goes on between them. The walls are paper-thin." Dan paused. "That doesn't necessarily mean that it's more than a night's entertainment for either of them. Much of the time they're gloriously soused."

Larry's look sharpened. "Uh-huh. Go on."

"On Friday morning Ryan starts his vacation. Let's see what happens in his absence."

Larry smiled a little. "You know, Dan, once one gets past your evasions, your ideas are sound. Without Ryan around, perhaps I can persuade Sue to go to Detroit and see her analyst again and be guided by him."

"And in two weeks Lewis Miller will be here. I have the feeling that once he makes Sue's acquaintance, he'll know how to deal with her. At least, he'll give us a correct prognostic comment."

"Good," Larry declared, much relieved.

Dan prepared to go, but before he left, Larry said, "It's very gratifying to me that you and George have become such great friends."

"I'm hoping," Dan said, opening the door, "that he'll eventually settle in California. He'll be happier out there away from all the memories of Maggie and his father."

Larry gave Dan an appreciative look and a concurring nod. "Poor Maggie. She came to grief and George can't reconcile himself to it."

Through the hot summer the wards were stifling and smelled of cabbage and urine. The barred windows kept locked shut out sun as well as air, and in the dismal corridors the pale bluish night-light barely lightened the dark passages. Patients lay around insensible and numb—neither weeping, nor the fury of obscenity, nor the rabid screams fuel to their deadness. Practically all work halted; no one really cared. Dan, in spite of his will to work, longed for Jenny with a new agony, aware that his wish to get to her was barely greater than his wish to get away. He found himself a refuge—the ocean. Off-duty weekends he and George spent together, dashing off to one of the numerous sandy beaches. They talked for hours, eager in their exchange of memories.

The doctors in residence woke up early to make rounds through endless doors before the sun burned. Sue and Dan were standing around idly. Others were playing bridge or drinking iced tea.

"Here it comes." Dan grinned.

"I've never waited for his letter before," Sue replied.

The housekeeper gave them their letters at once.

Dan looked at the envelope in her hand. "From Ryan?"

"Yes." Sue smiled. "I guess I'll go to my room. I'll read it there."

Dan followed. He walked into his room, she into hers.

Dan opened Jenny's letter first and read. Once again it struck him that Jenny wrote delightful letters—newsy, amusing, and loving. She was able to make him share with her and laugh with her. He then read the letter from Tascha Brotman, happy to know that she was in the mountains away from the suffocating heat and that Abe remained in the city because he wanted to—his practice was growing. Dan glanced hastily at a picture postcard from Bill Reilly, put it aside, and ripped open the letter he was waiting for from Lewis Miller. It was long.

P.O. Box S
Chicago, Ill.
August 21, 1932

DEAR DAN,

First and foremost—leave things alone until I get there.

I have carefully examined all that you have reported. Don't feel safe because Sue has quieted down. It's a temporary calm. The girl is sizzling with suppressed rage. What passes as sensitive is masked paranoia. I don't know what was done to her because Leo Butler, whom I have contacted in Detroit, has not told me her whole story; nevertheless, *she* is telling us that life is unbearable. Now, if her anger turns inward to deny her homicidal impulses —watch out! She'll suicide.

I don't like this Warren Ryan business at all. Frankly, I think it's a mess. And I don't accept your explanation as justification. Dan, the reason that nothing is really right for you at the hospital is that you were not right from the start. God damn it, Jenny did not marry you to be protected from life but to live it. This time you made a bad mistake. Put an end to it. Get on your knees to Jenny.

I want to tell you about Leo Butler. Too bad you never met him. But when you were in Chicago visiting me, he was in Vienna visiting Anna Freud. They are good friends. And Anna, as you know, does not have much time for personal friendships.

Leo is certainly first-rate. He is a Catholic. He is an analyst —Freudian but close to Sullivan. In my opinion, he is slated to become an international figure. One day he'll be called upon to head up the American International. He is a fine gentle man who knows when to be tough. You'll learn more about him. And you'll be meeting him soon.

I'm catching the night train to New York on Friday. I'm having lunch with Bill on the day of arrival. He wanted to bring along the Brotmans, but I protested. I'll see big-bellied Tascha later at their apartment, where I understand you're to pick me up. Bring along your friend, George Atlas.

Tell Dr. Stein it's pointless to program my time. We'll talk over all manner of things at leisure, and the devil take the student nurses. Who needs them?

Jenny writes regularly. She tells me she's simply wonderful. Bless her. How I miss her!

My love to you, Dan. Take care.

LEWIS

In her room, Sue was tearing open Ryan's letter.

I've known Mary all of her life. I used to call her "my infant." But she's grown up all of a sudden. There can be no doubt of that. We have gotten to know each other afresh. Mary is pretty—not the kind of looks that create a sensation, but pretty enough. She is very intelligent. And fortunately, she's to get a trust fund from her grandparents. A great help to us, for, as you know, I do like to live well. Mary's Catholic; that plus all her other qualities suits me fine. We plan to be married before Christmas.

As for us, Sue, let's be honest. I never made you any promises. Nor do I think what I stirred in you was love. We both had a clear notion of what we were doing.

Ryan attempted to soften the blow by concluding, "My friendship and my affection for you have in no way changed."

With a trembling hand, Sue reached for the bottle of 140-proof alcohol.

Welcome fire ran down her throat. While she tilted the bottle, time passed in drear remembrances.

Seven years old and Jane was what? Eight? They were in the small cozy room that once belonged to a live-in maid. The game—mummy and daddy. They had played it other times. This time Jane used a cardboard roll freed from tissue paper.

Bruised, Sue cries out in pain.

Jane's hand tightens its hold deeper and deeper.

More abuse.

Pain and pleasure hopelessly confused.

JANE: "That's enough for now. Cover yourself up."

Jane gone. The loneliness, the fear.

Memory flung back to a later time.

A boarding school. A lonely girl among other lonely girls. Another Jane. Another and another met in want, actively and passively. A measureless milestone—her first love affair.

Surely this time it was real and binding. The student nurse came to her willingly and freely. The desperate night she said: "It's over, Sue. I'm getting married."

Dan's door opened wide and Sue's voice, thick, said, "God, I'm a fool. I'm unworthy of love. My mother was right to reject me." She tossed Ryan's letter at Dan's feet.

She stumbled, then sat down, her face haggard.

Dan pulled up another chair where he could keep an eye on her as he read. "Well," he said, with a deep sigh, "so much for Ryan."

"Pour me some whiskey."

"You're going to wash your face, get yourself into bed, and sleep off the whiskey you've already had. Later I'll take you out for a bite. And after we've finished supper, you're going back to bed. You're exhausted, Sue."

"God damn it to hell," Sue swore. "May I *please* have a drink?"

Dan went over to the telephone. "Connect me with Dr. Stein, please."

While he waited, holding the receiver in his hand, Sue seized his hand and pulled. There was nothing he could do but hang up. He did not want the operator to hear a scuffle.

"All right, Sue. Let's talk."

But Sue, standing now, went on pulling. "Kiss me."

"No, Sue."

"Why not? I'm not drunk."

Gently, Dan freed himself.

Sue continued to urge him. "How long can you live chaste as a monk?"

"As long as I have to."

But Sue went on. "Like hell—it's only a matter of time. I hear you tossing after you're settled in bed. I hear you taking cold showers, too." Seized with a jealous rage, envious of his stability and equanimity, the tortured soul stormed on. "You can pay for my favors. I haven't done that before. You'll be the first."

"I want you to stop, Sue." Dan spoke sharply.

"Why don't you throw me out? Why don't you tell me to go to hell?"

"Because I like you." He meant it.

Dan turned and stared at the ringing phone. In a low voice he said, "Sue, I'm going to answer. Please behave yourself because I don't want you to end our usefulness as physicians. There are people here who need us."

"Oh, sweet Jesus." Sue began to cry.

After saying hello to Dan, Larry asked, "Did you try to get me?"

"Yes—I want you to come right over. If Betsy is home, bring her along. I need phenobarbital—two-grain tablets."

"We're on our way," Larry turned to Betsy. "It never rains but it pours. Get Ryan's letter."

Nine minutes later they were in Residence Hall.

Her tears checked, Sue regarded them and said, with an attempt at gallantry, "Ryan has got himself engaged. My heart's intact, but my pride has taken a tumble."

"We know what happened. I wish—"

Sue interrupted Larry with, "I want to be away from here." Her voice rising, she added, "I don't want to be laughed at when he returns."

"But, Sue—"

"Larry, please, let me go."

"You're tired and upset. You're being foolish and. . . ."

Dan handed Sue a lighted cigarette. "You can't leave because I need you. You have to be here so that I can be with Jenny when our baby is born."

"I only wish I could." Sue looked up at him wretchedly, an earnest look on her face. "I'm sorry, Dan."

Opening Ryan's letter, Larry said, "Listen." His eyes searched and found the paragraph he wanted. " 'I never meant to hurt Sue. Perhaps, if I don't return, it would make it easier all around. Sue deserves to be spared the embarrassment of seeing me again. It'll be uncomfortable for me, too. Surely, you can replace me. Fire me if you have to.' "

The room was silent.

"I rushed off a letter. In essence, I told him to consider himself fired."

Dan thought it over. It seemed hardly fair; Ryan had not forced himself on Sue.

Sue's reaction was a responsible one. "Ryan is a good doctor. I don't want him hurt professionally."

Larry kissed her on the cheek, heartened by her sense. "I'll handle it with the front office. His record will stay clean."

And Betsy said, "Come, Sue, I'll help you undress." She put an arm around Sue's shoulder.

Dan brought her a glass of water for her pill. Sue held out both hands.

They heard the click of the door and the tub filling with water, and both men started to speak at once.

"Excuse me."

Larry said, "Staying?"

"No. I've got to earn my wages."

"I think," said Larry, "you've more than earned them today."

"I'm not sure."

"You mean that?" Larry watched him.

Dan nodded.

Larry sighed, then held his breath. His feet moved forward and he opened the door. The men cut across the grass and headed for Female Admissions. In a flat voice, Dan said. "There's a soft breeze."

"It feels good," answered Larry, moving slowly.

Lewis Miller moved into Ryan's room. Four days had gone by since his arrival, and except for informal seminars he held for the staff, he stayed on the wards with Dan and Sue. There he could study Sue—her every gesture, every expression, and try to piece together the jigsaw. This was not easy because Sue felt sure she was being observed. She confided to Larry. "He watches my every move. I think he hates me."

Larry dismissed this as nonsense; for Sue, in fact, was getting on nicely and regaining some of her spirit.

"You know, Larry, it might be better if I were to die."

Absorbed in other thoughts, Larry replied, "Oh, for God's sake, Sue."

Then Lewis spoke to Dan privately. "I am convinced Sue is a sick girl. She still has enough intact ego to handle most of reality, but the schizophrenic process is going on. Don't underestimate, Dan. Remember, suicide occurs after there has been a remission of illness."

Dan still hesitated to accept the probability of Sue's total collapse. His eyes were shut in friendship and affection. Because Sue had a special way with the sick—she made them feel they mattered. So he began to offer excuses. "It's natural to be mildly depressed following personal loss. I feel she's handling it well. She *was* prepared to marry Ryan. More important —she was prepared to love him."

"You're telling me she can't control loneliness."

"Well, yes, that's part of it."

"You're pigheaded blind, Dan. You delude yourself."

Dan sighed resignedly. "What do you propose?"

Lewis' immediate reaction was "When it happens, don't be here."

All Dan did was shake his head.

"At least, don't live in a room that communicates with hers through a bathroom. You know what Jenny will think of that."

"Jenny will simply have to understand that."

"What have you told Jenny about Sue?"

"Nothing, virtually."

Lewis answered. "Listen, Dan, you've got to be watchful. Sue is on her way to a fully developed depression. Look out for weight loss, sweat, insomnia, irritability, delusional thinking, a feeling of worthlessness. Above all, look for an upsurge of her suicidal impulse."

That same day Dan brought back from the ward several capsules of chloral hydrate and tranquilizers and hid them among his socks.

On Friday Lewis Miller gave his lecture on dreams, and, on Dan's invitation, Abe Brotman and Bill Reilly were in the overflow audience crowded against the wall. Lewis was brilliant. He spoke with authority. He supported his thesis with skill and wit. His listeners found even his arrogance, an area in which he was without peer, fascinating. He delved into every part of his subject, presenting case material. Dry ideas assumed flesh and blood in his words.

He devoted much of the hour to summing up Freud's thinking.

" 'The dream is the royal road to the unconscious.' This is true. However, while the dream is the peephole through which we see what is going on in the unconscious, the very same dream can also hide from us the material which—in a way—it is so loudly expressing. Furthermore, the dream may be a mask. A mask used by the patient to conceal his accumulated feelings from himself or from his analyst. In the latter instance, the dream is in the service of the resistance. The dreamer is denying his secrets. When the concealment is from oneself, it is in the interest of survival."

Miller talked on: "We agree that the dream is expressive—a leakage of one's inner desires—the desire being unfulfilled wishes, hidden impulses like lust, incest, and other forms of raw, unwanted sexual hungers. On the aggressive side, rape, retaliation, revenge, and murderous impulses."

So it went for another thirty minutes. A glance at his watch reminded Lewis Miller that there was not much time left. He cut short his summary. "As therapists, we must welcome the dreams of our patients as the tools by which we interpret the signals and decode the messages. Whatever the patient's most private wishes—and conflicts—might be, the dream reveals. We need them. We must never discount them."

For five minutes after Lewis Miller had stopped speaking, the sound of applause filled the room. It was an ovation. Finally, the professional staff began to file out of the auditorium. It was only after the superintendent of the hospital and the clinical director turned away that Lewis fell on Abe and Bill. It pleased him that they were there, and with a pleasant nod and a gesture, he beckoned them forward. They were quickly joined by Dan and Larry. It was the first time that Bill had met Larry Stein. With nothing that he could really put his finger on, Bill Reilly reminded Larry of Ryan. He decided not to invite Sue. "How about coming over to our house for a spot of lunch? There's always ham and cheese. Betsy will be delighted."

The conversation which took place during lunch was dominated by Abe. Lewis Miller steeled himself for the interminable bragging. Abe needed his colleagues to believe in him as a leader.

Bill Reilly concealed his judgment of Abe, and for once Lewis' manner was so cordial the Steins remained completely unaware of the contempt he held for Abe whom he considered—among other things—an analyst of limited capability. As a result, Abe, on his return to New York, actually poured out words of praise for Lewis when he reviewed the day's events to Tascha.

Unbelievingly Tascha lifted her head to study Abe. *Yes,* she thought, *he is telling the truth. How nice that Bill was there, too.* Then she slipped into partial bewilderment. Why did Bill Reilly's presence always intensify her feelings? The absurdity of it!

Tascha emerged from her thoughts and rose from her chair. She said to Abe, "Let's give a party for Lewis. I'll bet he'll come if we invite Bill and the Steins.

If it had not been for Sue, Lewis Miller doubted if he would have stayed on to be taken advantage of professionally. However, his staying was not an act of charity. He had developed a feeling of aversion toward Sue, mostly because of her increasing dependency upon Dan. If Jenny had been there, and if her relationship with Sue were good, he would not have worried himself. At least, not to the same degree. For he knew much was not right.

Dan, in his turn, was not insensible of Lewis' feelings.

"I'll tell you frankly," he admitted to George, "I'm grateful. I need a rest from Sue's problems."

"Is Miller really hanging around for your sake?" George waited for Dan's answer.

"What in particular do you mean by that?"

George's eyes looked back at Dan. "I believe his interest is elsewhere."

"Go on."

But George gave no explanation.

As the silence stretched out, Dan realized that George would not make a concrete statement. He took off his robe, dropped it on the floor, and started to dress. Putting on socks, then sneakers, he talked. "I know that you're not willing to understand Lewis. In fact, you made up your mind about him immediately after your first meeting. You don't like him because you think he doesn't like you."

George got up and went over to Jenny's basket. He spotted a big ripe peach. He took it and slowly bit into it. "I think it's just the opposite," he said calmly. "I don't mind being liked, and, on the whole, I accept Miller's attitude toward me with complete calmness. It's just that I find myself remembering that I am someone Sue trusts." George frowned at Dan. "Hell, man! I nourished hope on Miller. Because of his reputation, I succeeded in selling myself a bill of goods—he'll have the answers. I did not dream his attitude would be so one-sided, and, for some reason or other, I don't feel that his concern is for you. All the antagonism Sue arouses in him is in some way tied to Jenny."

"And that stirs jealous feelings in you?"

George gave Dan a hard stare. "Quite." Then he turned. His eyes found Jenny's picture and his face changed.

"Isn't she marvelous?"

George saw that Dan was smiling. Without looking at him, he asked, "Weren't we going for a swim?"

Dan nodded his head. "It sure as hell beats a cold shower."

It was getting late in the afternoon and the discussion was still going on.

Dan ran his fingers through his hair absently. "They're building Pilgrim Hospital. Seventeen thousand beds! It's appalling."

George Atlas excused himself and withdrew from the doctors' lounge.

"You know, Dan, I pushed for those beds."

Dan turned around and said to Larry, "More and more money for more and more buildings. Asylums! Would you want someone near and dear to you confined in one of them?''

"To be quite frank—no. But that doesn't alter a thing.''

"Life does not have to be harsh, and isolated, and monotonous for the mentally ill. Why can't we send them back into their communities after the acute phase is over?''

"Because, my friend, no one wants them.''

"That's right, Dan. Even the family wants only to wash its hands of the burden, the shame.''

"What about educating both the family and the community to the basic wrongs of the institutional system? Someone ought, at least, to set our legislators straight about the harm of bigness.''

Lewis Miller cleared his throat. "You have Geel in mind?''

"Well, now that you mention it, yes.''

"Belgium is a small country. We'd need hundreds and hundreds of towns like Geel.''

"I passed through Geel once,'' said John Tevis. "At nightfall. Wherever we went through the whole town from end to end, we met the insane on their way home. What impressed me most was that behavior—and some of it was mighty bizarre—was received matter-of-factly, even indifferently. What might have been horrible was thereby reduced to the ordinary. We reached an inn and stopped for supper. The innkeeper was talkative, and he related facts about Geel that were fascinating. He told us: 'In this town, hundreds of years ago, there lived a nobleman. He had a niece, his sister's child, and she was lovely. The girl—she was only fifteen—was intended for the son of another great man of the region. But the uncle—one moonless night—reached her room full of drink. Afterward, he left the whimpering child, cursing himself. The next day she was found roaming about completely mad. By winter she was dead—a sordid death by her own hand.'

"Guilt and remorse fell heavily on the nobleman. That is why he turned his town into a sanctuary for the mad.

" 'Knock on any door. We shall let you in.' ''

George Atlas waited motionless in the doorway until the story was concluded. Dan's glance went to the door, and in an instant he sensed something in the sudden total silence. His eyes turned slowly back to his colleagues in the room. Even Sue was all smiles.

Betsy approached to where Dan sat, and she smiled as she handed him a beautifully wrapped package. "From all of us to Jenny.''

In the moment it took him to think, Lewis was at his side, and in his hand he held an envelope. "Your railroad ticket and a Pullman berth. You can exchange it for a bedroom on the train. We're sending you back to

Gorgeous because we don't want her coming down from that mountain into an empty house.''

Even then, Dan considered his duty. "God knows I want to go, but—''

Lewis Miller cut in. "I, my boy, am taking your place.''

Dan could then only stare at Larry, who explained, "The clinical director approves. We had a talk with him. His reply was 'When I tell the superintendent I have Lewis Miller pinch-hitting for our intern, he won't believe me.' ''

"Look, Lewis, what about your own commitments?''

Lewis Miller gave a loud hoot. "I need more training.''

"I don't know what to say.'' Dan got up and embraced Lewis. "Thanks.'' His voice came out choked.

"We've got to leave right away.''

Dan nodded at George. "As soon as I throw a few things into a suitcase.''

"You're packed and ready to go.''

They cut the good-byes short. Dan kissed both girls. He extended his hand only to Larry and swiftly followed George. Now he was in a hurry to get going.

George took the wheel immediately. They drove for a time in reflective silence. Then George looked in Dan's direction. "That round little bastard is quite a guy.''

Dan cast him a sidelong glance. "So are you.''

After that, neither of them had much to say; nevertheless, the ride into the city—though it was still hot and muggy—was extremely pleasant.

George stayed with Dan until the porter announced, "We're pulling out in minutes, sir.''

George smiled half sadly. "I'll miss you, Dan.''

"I'll be back—maybe sooner than you think.''

"Why?''

"Because Lewis is not up to the strain of routine hospital duty.''

"Ooh!''

"Tell Larry to look after him.''

"He'll be all right. We'll see to it.''

"Thanks.'' Dan extended a hand, which George took into his two powerful ones. "Give my love to Jenny.''

Dan smiled, nodded, and said, "I'll call the minute the baby is born.''

George spent that night with a woman. But just as he was dropping off to sleep, he saw Jenny's face.

Ellen, the maid, was at a window facing the street, thinking that it was time to go back into the kitchen and prepare some food. She could imagine how upset her two mistresses were when the doctor's father had to rush Miss Jenny to the hospital because the bag of water burst and the labor pains started before the right time. It was then that she caught sight of Dan's taxi. Suddenly her heart skipped a beat. Who but the good Lord could have sent him? She ran, and as she reached the street, her voice called out, "Don't send the taxi away, Doctor."

Taken aback, Dan halted in the cab's open doorway. His heart beating wildly, Dan had to force himself to speak. "For God's sake, Ellen—"

"She's all right. You see, the baby started coming early. Your father got a police escort and got her down in record time. At the hospital Dr. Kelly was waiting; everything was ready." Ellen addressed him proudly. "You have a fine, healthy son—eight pounds, twelve ounces."

Dan gave a deep sigh of sudden relief and settled back on the seat.

Ellen went on talking. "When they got to the pass, the sheriff was there. He held up all traffic to let them through. You can imagine what a job that must have been on Labor Day." Ellen beamed at him. "Your father, sir, is a born driver. When the policeman rang me up, he said, 'That man can put pros half his age to shame.' "

Dan said, "Good." This time he really felt it.

Ellen kept on talking and smiling. Dan had to cut in. "Are they all at Mount Zion Hospital?"

"No, Doctor. Miss Jenny's mother felt they simply had to close the house. Mr. Gunther agreed; there was nothing they could do here. They called from Sacramento almost two hours ago. I am expecting them any minute. I'll tell them—"

Ellen was still talking when Dan murmured his thanks and then said to the taxi driver, "Let's go. Mount Zion, please. Don't spare the horses."

The curtains were drawn; this put the room in semidarkness. Jenny was lying there in soft crepe de chine, her arms bare, her eyes closed, her chestnut hair spread across the pillow. Dan approached the bed quietly and contemplated his wife. Tears welled up in his eyes as emotion overwhelmed him for a moment. *God! She's more beautiful than ever.*

When Jenny began to stir, Dan knelt by the bed. He slowly wiped away a tear with his finger, then pressed his lips lightly upon hers.

Jenny opened her eyes and gazed at Dan intently. "I think I am dreaming," she murmured softly.

Dan took her in his arms and covered her face with kisses. Pausing only to tell her that he loved her, he heard her whisper, "Hello, Dan."

Smiling down at her, he replied, "Hello, Jenny, baby."

"Come into bed with me."

Dan made no move. "What will the lady in white say?"

Jenny extended her hand. "Please. I want you to."

Dan took her hand, brought it to his lips and slowly let it go. "I guess I had better take off my shoes."

They lay side by side holding hands, utterly silent. After a long while, Jenny said, "He was born at dawn." Releasing Dan's hand, Jenny slid closer and leaned her head against his shoulder. "I want to call him Paul Adamson after my father."

Dan discovered that he was both surprised and relieved. He met her eyes saying, "Don't you *really* want to name him Andrew?"

Jenny giggled. "I explained to your father that I intend to have at least three sons, which is why he can afford to be sporting about this one."

Dan smiled at her a moment. "All right, I agree. Paul Adamson Gunther he is." Then, all at once, Dan saw her eyes fixed on him earnestly. "What's the matter?" he asked.

Jenny raised her face. "Tell me the truth, Dan. Go look at our son. Is he, as father and Dr. Kelly said, 'Perfect'? You know I was too active and he came early and—"

Dan tightened his arms around her. "He's not premature at all. We must have miscalculated." Dan hesitated a moment before he completed his thought. "He's the spitting image of my old man."

"Yes," Jenny said softly.

Presently, Jenny leaned back against her pillows.

"Tired?"

"I'm hungry."

"They'll be bringing your tray soon."

Jenny insisted. "I want something now."

"All right, sweetheart. I'll go down to the coffee shop." Dan rose just as Andrew Gunther opened the door. "May we come in?"

Dan walked across the room in his stockinged feet. He spoke almost shyly. "Thank you, Dad. He's a grandson to be proud of."

Andrew Gunther accepted his son's thanks with a grin; a sixth sense told him to keep it light. "Congratulations, Dan."

They had no chance to talk further because Dorothy and Sara, Jenny's mother and grandmother, entered the room—laughing, kissing Dan with affection, asking questions, eager to greet Jenny.

Dorothy said softly, "We're so glad you got here, Dan. The family is complete now."

The telephone began to ring. Dan lifted the receiver. It was Lewis Miller calling. "We heard the good news because your father was trying to reach you here. Tell Jenny—"

"Wait. She insists you talk to her."

Mostly Jenny said, "Fine, fine. Yes. I guess so." And she laughed out loud. "Don't be silly." Then: "I'm not in the least tired. Honest." And, finally: "I'll ask." Jenny smiled at her mother and grandmother. "Lewis wants to know what you lovely ladies think of his heir, meaning his inheritor."

Dan interrupted with "For Christ's sake!"

Andrew Gunther chuckled.

Jenny's mother said, "Really! He can't do that."

Sara Adamson said, "Tell Lewis we just saw my great-grandson, and we think he is beautiful. And then, Jenny, you must rest."

But Jenny's brow was now wrinkled in thought. Presently, she said, "Hello, George Atlas." She stared into the telephone. "Thank you." She listened and answered in a small voice. "I really think I am a little. I'll turn you over to Dan. Good-bye, George."

"Jenny, darling, I think we should leave."

Jenny nodded and closed her eyes. Ten hours later she opened them. "Hello, Dan. I dreamed about a big juicy steak and a hot fudge sundae. It's not too late, is it?"

It was still hot in San Francisco, but in the clean, quiet, expensive street of mansions, it was pleasant. The scent in the air was of salt spray and roses.

Dr. Kelly had agreed to allow Jenny and Paul to come home because Jenny had begged and pleaded there was so little time of Dan's stay left. The doctor laid a hand on Dan's arm. "Mind you," he bellowed, "she stays off her feet."

"Sure," Dan promised lightly, wondering why a healthy young female needed two full weeks in a hospital and, at least, another week of bed rest at home.

Dan carried Jenny cautiously into the spacious entrance hall with its rare Oriental screen and two strategically placed elegant Georgian chairs. Ellen and the other maid were waiting near the foot of the long mahogany staircase, their primness belying their curiosity about the newborn. Jenny's grandmother held Paul, and Andrew Gunther followed with the suitcase. He kept seeing the day he brought Miriam home with Dan. He was also thinking about tomorrow, when he would drive Sara north, up the rugged Sonoma Coast, in his rakish custom-built two-door roadster. They both loved that area and its wild vistas: the ocean—sometimes terrible, with fog hanging on the horizon—and sometimes clear and calm under a blue sky; the boulders; the slate ledges; the hills of spruce and dark green pine.

They all dined at seven in the high-ceilinged room with its superb architectural detailing. The table setting included Georgian silver candle-sticks that belonged to Sara's grandmother, and the chairs around the antique walnut table were Louis XVI. The French mirror was a gift from Andrew Gunther.

Ellen and Hilda, dressed in black with aprons stiffly white, waited on them: onion soup followed by roast veal, served with eggplant and leeks vinaigrette. They sat at the table for the better part of an hour, sipping wine and savoring Sara's compote of fresh fruits, which Jenny ate with fudge squares. And because she was already as slim as she had been before she had a child, no one made a fuss about calories.

Andrew, smiling at Sara, said, "She's like you—there's no possibility she'll ever have to fight weight."

Then Dan was doing the talking. Mostly about the hospital and especially about the ladies who were in his newly formed sessions of group interaction. He had high hopes for the plan, Jenny thought as she watched him explain with enthusiasm. From time to time someone would ask a question or make a comment.

When Ellen came in with the coffee, she put the silver pot down in front of Sara. "Please ma'am, am I permitted to sit in the nursery?"

"You mean at this moment?"

"Yes, ma'am."

"There's no need to, Ellen. However, you may if you wish."

"Oh, thank you, ma'am," said Ellen, hurrying out.

Sara laid down her napkin. Addressing Andrew, she said, "I'm looking forward to tomorrow."

Andrew smiled at her.

Dorothy wanted to know how early they planned to get started and added, "Ellen could prepare a picnic lunch."

Andrew looked pleased. "Wonderful."

Dorothy turned to her mother-in-law. "I've an idea. Why don't you stay overnight—you know the new inn? It's about midway between Fort Ross and the cove."

Sara and Andrew remained silent. Dan raised his eyes. Jenny lowered hers.

Dan sensed everyone was sitting there waiting. Mystified, he asked, "What's going on?"

Jenny whirled toward him. "Nothing!"

Amazed, Sara and Andrew exchanged a glance.

Afterward, when they were alone, Jenny said irritably, "Why are you constantly and chronically suspicious of Dad? Must he offer a reason for going fishing?"

Reasonably, Dan said, "I only asked a question. The puzzle is that I seemed to have stepped into a secret." Whereupon Jenny replied, "They are going up the coast. That's all there is to it."

His eyes still puzzled, Dan left the room.

In the library Andrew Gunther poured himself a stiff drink.

Jenny, meanwhile, settled herself with a yellow writing pad. The first letter was to Tascha, whose child was just about due. The other was to Lewis. Mostly, she commented upon the advice he continuously gave. And then, on impulse, she penned a note to George Atlas, thanking him for his many kindnesses to Dan and telling him how much Dan missed his companionship. By the time she had finished, it was after eleven.

Dan loved Jenny's room with its sheer white curtains and velvet draperies. Her collection of dolls—some exquisite, some antique—intrigued him. He got into bed and drew her to him. "We've got to talk," he said.

Jenny could see in Dan's face an expression of mingled hope and sadness. "I know what you're going to ask, and I've made up my mind, Dan. I won't take my baby to that dreadful place, and I won't leave him—not for nine months.

"Please, Jenny. I'm no good without you."

Jenny raised her head and placed both of her hands on Dan's face. "I'm glad, my darling."

Watching her face, the outline of her brows, Dan knew he was defeated. After a long time he said, "Know what I missed most?"

"What?"

"This. Just holding you in my arms."

Her gaze lingered upon his face. "I wish I were ready."

Holding her tightly against him, Dan felt her body tremble. With a fast beating heart, he whispered, "I love you, Jenny, darling," and brushed her lips.

The south wing of the house was Sara Adamson's. It was her private world of serenity and separateness. At midnight she opened the door of a small hallway leading into her rooms, and Andrew Gunther, elegantly robed in brocaded silk, stepped in. The door closed softly behind them, and he took her into his arms. Hand in hand, they passed into the morning room.

Like a devoted couple, they settled themselves on her sofa and talked, and Andrew was enchanted with her—the still slim body, the high full bosom, the rounded shoulders pleasingly visible underneath her stunning negligee. But about the time Andrew began to feel pleasantly weary and ready for bed, Sara said, "Jenny knows."

"Yes," Andrew answered soberly.

"The miracle is that she approves."

Again, Andrew said, "Yes."

"I'm frightened to death about Dan."

"Frightened, darling? Or ashamed?"

Sara pressed her head against his shoulder, lowered her eyes, and did not reply.

Andrew was annoyed that his son had the power to make Sara unhappy. "Dan won't know. There's nothing to worry about."

"All the same, Andrew—" Sara did not finish her sentence because Andrew again took her in his arms and kissed her. "The solution to our problem is simple. We're getting married and honeymooning in the Orient. I hadn't expected to tell you until tomorrow."

Sara freed herself from his embrace and slowly shook her head.

"Listen, my darling, you've got some pretty silly notions. I concede you a year or two of seniority, but you're still the most sensuously beautiful woman I have ever known."

Sara laughingly replied, "That's almost half true."

Andrew touched her lustrous white hair tenderly. "Let's put it up to Dorothy."

"Never!" Sara declared, grasping his arm. "On no account, Andrew, are you to disturb my daughter's equanimity. Are you out of your senses?"

Andrew's face darkened. "No wonder Jenny has her stubborn side," he swore. "She gets her streak of iron from you."

"My dear, listen. Be patient. When Paul's father died, I was young. I lived alone most of the time because I sent Paul to school and to places where there were men and boys. I thought it better. He got interested in Dorothy in college. Soon they fell wildly, madly, in love. They decided they did not want to wait. I said, 'Bring her home, son.' She's been with me ever since. And, mind you, Andrew, it wasn't for the lack of chances that she has remained a widow."

Andrew's eyes hardened. "In my whole life, I've loved only two women. Miriam, who never wanted the things I wanted. And now—you. All the women in between were nothing, but they were the ones who were willing to do anything for me—the money was only part of it."

Sara watched him with an anxious expression, while Andrew was bitterly reviewing their situation. Then with subdued rage, he demanded that she forget Dorothy, forget Dan. "Marry me. I don't want to get along without you."

There was a moment of tense silence after Andrew paused and waited. Then he jumped from the sofa. "Does this then boil down to an affair?" His voice cracked with emotion.

"Please, Andrew, don't spoil everything. Be patient."

Andrew reined in his anger and his disappointment. What could he possibly do but woo her all over again. He let himself sink down beside her. "Do you love me?"

"Yes, I do."

"Say it." Their eyes met. With the quiet dignity of a wife, Sara said, "Let's go to bed, dear."

Proudly, Andrew Gunther rose. In the ticking of a second, Sara was happily aware that she was in his powerful arms, crushed against his chest. In bed, as Andrew stretched out beside her, Sara abandoned herself to the bliss of his hands. Later, when she was asleep, he kept himself awake to listen to the soft rhythm of her regular breathing. When the sun came up, he left. His own bed felt empty—the only sounds the songs of birds.

On the whole, the patients on the ward reacted to Dan's return with indifference. Some did not give him so much as a glance; others took his presence for granted. But he got a big welcome from Sue, who took his hands and, pulling, dragged him into an empty conference room off the ward. Her manner intimate, she asked, "Why didn't you send word—or call me from the station? You know I'd have come to get you."

Dan was making an effort to focus his attention on Sue, but his thoughts were elsewhere. Sue saw his eyes go in the direction of his wristwatch. "OK, Dan. I know you want to read Lewis' progress reports. We'll get together later."

Dan's eyes narrowed, as she waited anxiously for his reply. "Some other time, Sue. After my visit with Larry and Betsy, I've got to settle down at my desk."

"What about tomorrow night?"

"I've got a date with George. I'm staying overnight because I want to see the Brotmans on Sunday."

"Monday, then? I do want to talk with you, Dan."

Dan hated to put Sue in the position of begging. "Monday is fine, Sue. Are you willing to settle for the lunch wagon?"

"My favorite place with my favorite man."

Dan groaned inwardly. Then he turned to Sue and said, "Would you mind sending my ladies in?'' Sue turned and left Dan. After a grueling session with his group, Dan got into his car and drove out to the lunch wagon alone. Placing a bottle of prescription liquor on the counter, he heard Pete's friendly greeting.

"Hi there, Doc! Congratulations. And welcome back.''

"Thank you.''

As Dan climbed on the stool, he said, "Feed me, Pete. I'm starved.''

"What'll it be?''

"Anything, Pete. I can't be bothered deciding.''

Turning on his heel, Pete filled up a mug with good strong coffee and a plate with French fries.

"Nibble on these, Doc. I'll put a steak on the grill.''

Doing his best to unwind, Dan bit into a hot crisp potato and listened to the radio. Soon, Pete eased over to him. "I wrote you a few lines saying that I sure was glad you got home in time, but I forgot to give it to Dr. Sue to address until a few days ago. I bet you never got to see it.''

"No, but thank you for writing.''

"That's OK.'' Pete went back to preparing Dan's meal.

Dan absently watched some high school students at the far end of the counter. He was thinking how much he wanted to call Jenny. Christ, he would have three months more to wait. Finally, Pete brought over the steak and a big salad. "Would you like some ketchup?''

"No, thanks.''

Pete watched him eat. Then he took his prescription bottle and, thanking Dan, put it away. After a while he turned the music up loud, filled two mugs with fresh coffee, and came around to Dan's side of the counter leaving everything to his helper.

Dan observed him fidgeting uncomfortably. "What's on your mind, Pete?''

"Something that's strictly none of my business.''

Dan turned slowly and met Pete's eyes. "If you want to talk about it, I don't mind.''

"It's Dr. Sue,'' said Pete as he was lighting a cigarette. "You missed her by maybe ten minutes. I wish I'd known you were on your way. I'd have stalled them.''

Dan gave Pete a quizzical look and Pete, in turn, gave Dan a nod. "Yeah, them. He started coming in a few weeks ago. He's on a big construction job around here.''

Dan interceded with, "Pilgrim Hospital?''

"That's it. As a matter of fact, the night they got acquainted he was still wearing his workclothes. Now mind you, Doc, I got nothin' against a decent hard-working pick and shovel man, but this guy is no damn good. And he treats Dr. Sue like she was some kind of broad.''

It was a long time before Dan said anything. Was Lewis right when he indicated volcanic emotions seething beneath the surface of her present calm? Then he asked, ''How long have you known Sue?''

''Got you. Like a chicken scratchin' for food, Dr. Sue is scratchin' for love.''

For some time neither of them said anything. They just sat silently looking at each other. Finally Dan spoke. ''Frankly, I don't know what I can do to change the situation but I'll give it thought.''

Pete moved away to bring over hot apple pie and more coffee.

Dan finished his meal and got up to go. ''Thanks, Pete.''

''So long, Doc. Don't take any wooden nickels.''

Dan grinned but did not answer him. He was leaving Sue and her problems in the lap of the gods. He reached his room and shut the door behind him. On his desk was a neatly addressed large manila envelope. In it were several unopened letters and a note from Jenny. On a sudden impulse he picked up the telephone receiver. ''Operator. Get me Mrs. Gunther in San Francisco. The number is JO-7-2274.''

As he spoke to her, Dan gradually became aware that his anger was gone. ''What are you wearing, sweetheart?''

''Why do you ask?''

''I'm lying on my bed and imagining you're with me.''

''In that case''—Jenny laughed—''I'm wearing something indecent with nothing underneath.''

On Sunday Dan stopped at the Brotmans. He walked into the living room and looked around. Abe apparently hadn't heard him close the door, so he yelled, ''Anyone home?''

Abe called out from the bathroom. ''Hold your horses. I'll be right out.''

Dan sighed resignedly and sat down, remembering with amusement that Abe always used a dull blade, dragging it over his face. Then, scrubbing it, he carefully replaced it in a cardboard box among the other used blades.

At last Abe came in. Dan rose. Embracing Abe, he offered his congratulations.

Nodding, Abe said, ''I wanted a son. Tascha wanted a daughter. So''—Abe suddenly smiled—''naturally, we have a daughter.''

They talked for a time before Abe asked Dan to lunch. ''Then we'll visit Tascha.''

Dan agreed. "After that I'll probably leave. I keep thinking about all the paperwork facing me without doing anything about it."

The days ticked off, and the weeks, and Christmas approached. Dan was both busy and unhappy. When he took an occasional day off, he usually met George, and they went somewhere. One freezing night they got drunk together. They were in George's apartment around the corner from Presbyterian Hospital in the city. In the next apartment a radio was going full blast. They were discussing the relative merits of boxer shorts versus jockey shorts.

"Take jockey shorts," said George.

"Look here. Can't you get your neighbors to pipe down?"

George laughed. "One kind word from me and those two dollies will be in here suggesting something downright bawdy."

"Think you can handle them both, because I'll be leaving?"

George laughed with good humor. "It won't be the first time."

For a half hour more the noise and the drinking continued.

With the sudden quiet Dan's eyes brightened and he spoke fast. "Now that I can be heard, I have an announcement to make. Jenny will be here on the twenty-eighth." He took her letter out of his wallet and waved it. "It says so right here."

George started up from his chair. "Let me see for myself."

Dan watched attentively. "Does it meet your expectations?"

George looked ready to cry. He admitted it was a beautiful letter, very beautiful—as far as he was concerned, the most beautiful ever.

"As your friend," said Dan, "I'm going to tell you you're drunk."

"What makes you think a thing like that?"

"Curious," said Dan. "I may even be tight myself. Whatcha think?"

"Naturally." George waited a moment and laid a heavy hand on Dan's shoulder. "You can't leave this apartment. 'Woe unto him who steers drowned in strong libation.' Wait until tomorrow."

Without one word more, Dan got up and began to prepare for bed. He pulled the bed out from the wall and flung a blanket across it.

Dan woke early. George was like Jenny—slow about getting up. Dan took a shower, shaved, and made coffee; he made it strong, as he had come to enjoy it in Vienna. Then he came back to wake George.

"Good Lord, my head."

Dan gave him a smile. "Here."

George put his hand around the coffee mug. "Thanks." After he finished his coffee, he asked, "How do you feel?"

Dan grinned. "I don't want to answer that."

"I've got bread. Fix us some toast."

"We're going out for food. I want orange juice and grapefruit. The waiter can bring the toast with the eggs."

"Good—only I've got to get up to go."

"Hurry."

"What's the weather like?"

"Shivering cold."

George half rose. He held out a hand to Dan. "Help me."

Dan laughed and turned away.

Shaking hands, they parted after breakfast.

"Until New Year's Eve," said Dan. "See you at the Steins."

A smile touched George's lips. "So long, Dan. Give my love to Jenny." He moved briskly away toward Presbyterian, wondering what it was going to be like knowing her.

Two days after Christmas it dawned windy and wild. A heavy snowstorm had hit the Northeast on Christmas Eve, blanketing out communications, forcing families into the security of their homes. They said Vermont was completely snowbound. There was snow aplenty on New York's sidewalks. Out on Long Island Dan was growing increasingly alarmed, afraid that Jenny's train from Chicago would never get through. He looked out of his office window onto a flat white world intersected by the dark streaks where paths had been swept. Even as he looked, the wind blew another spurt of snow into a wild eddy. Dan felt gloomy and wished the day would pass. He tried to relax—to fix his mind on work. That was useless. Then he tried to kill the evening and invited Larry and Betsy out for supper. They could just make the Italian restaurant in the next town. He thought of inviting Sue but couldn't find her anywhere. Around ten he dropped the Steins off at their home, parked his car, and trudged back through crunchy snow to the quiet of his room. He was almost ready to put out his light when Sue appeared. His heart missed a beat; she was stark naked. In one hand, she held a half-filled bottle of whiskey. In the other, a package of contraceptives.

"Take me, Dan. For God's sake, take me." There was plaintive despair in her voice.

Looking at her across the room, Dan stood rooted. His doctor's eye was seeing her just as if she were a lesson in surface anatomy. She had no female distribution of hair—no curly triangle. Sue's was a masculine pelvis and the contour of her biceps was distinct and visible. And yet there was an appealing quality that stirred him.

"Dan, please," she repeated.

Dan had his silk robe over his pajamas. He took it off and put it around her, tying the belt. "I don't want you to catch cold."

"Good, kind Dan." Sue's voice wavered, and she trembled.

Dan put his arm around her waist and, leading her over to the bed, told her to sit down. He was grateful that she did. He drew a chair close to the bed and said, pushing down the panic that rose in him, "Let's begin with a drink."

Sue laid her head back on the pillow. "Kiss me."

Dan sensed her feverish excitement, the taut fragility of her mood. She looked capable of anything—screaming, weeping, creating an uproar. He kissed her.

"That was satisfactory," she said. "Now, make me purr."

Dan forced himself to laugh softly. "What's the hurry?"

"Sure," said Sue. "We've got all night." She let him have the bottle. "Here, take these, we'll need them." She said it with such sudden calm that Dan was terrified. He uncorked the bottle and put it down. Then he tore off the wrapper around the contraceptives, and taking out a couple, he handed them to Sue. "Put these in your pocket. I want to hide the rest. All I need is to forget and have the maid find them."

Sue accepted this, giving Dan the opportunity to reach his dresser drawer and palm a capsule of chloral hydrate. With his back still turned to her, he said, "Get the glasses, Sue. In the bathroom."

Suddenly, she was suspicious. "You're trying to trick me. The second I step out, you'll lock all the doors."

Dan again detected rising excitement and his heart began to pound violently. "If that's what you think, I'll go."

Sue was seized with a passionate fear. "No! You won't come back. We'll drink from the bottle."

He turned and, almost irritable yet still nervous, said, "Where in hell would I go in my pajamas?" He instantly made for the bathroom. Once inside, he opened the capsule and poured the full seven and a half grains of the sleeping drug into Sue's glass, figuring that the ten or twelve hours of sleep was something she could use. At least, it would get them both through the rest of the night.

Sue moved over and made a space for him. "Come sit by me."

Dan held out her glass. "Later." He lowered himself into the chair. "What are we waiting for?"

Sue drained her glass. Quite confident now, Sue asked conversationally, "Afterward, you won't be sorry, will you?"

Dan only smiled.

Misunderstanding, Sue smiled, too. "And, we'll still be friends?"

"The best of pals," said Dan, biding his time, waiting only for the drug to take effect.

Sue seized his hand. Forcing a calm air, Dan placed himself on the bed beside her.

The minutes passed slowly until she dropped off. Dan waited several more minutes. She did not stir. Then he rose and, tensing his muscles, lifted her bodily and carried her into her room. He put her down gently, freeing his arms of their unwelcome burden. He then went to her closet and took out her fur coat. Covering her like a child, he stared down at her, thinking why do we all bother so with this distraught, unstable woman? Is she worth our gamble? Can she ever be a useful doctor? What will happen to her under the normal stress of hospital life? He found no answers. Turning, he left her. Conscious of a sudden, overpowering weariness, he got into bed, moving deliberately away from the lingering scent of Sue's body cologne.

By six fifteen it was dark and gloomy. The snowcovered platform of the Long Island Railroad was piercingly cold and strangely silent. Up the road as far as Jenny could see, there was no sign of life. It was a bleak prospect. She went back to her suitcases to watch and wonder. Gradually, Jenny made out a figure in dark pants and a fur parka approaching on foot. All at once her eyes blinked in the beam of a strong flashlight.

"Hi there," said a throaty voice, "I'm Sue Palmer. I think you're the Jenny I'm looking for."

"Yes, I am. You must be Dan's colleague. Is he. . . ."

Lowering the flashlight, Sue asked, "Have you had any supper?"

"No."

"Come along—my car's around the corner. I'm taking you to our favorite eatery and feeding you. They've got great apple pie."

"Where is Dan?"

"He waited at the station for you until it was time for him to go on duty. They told him your train was eight hours late."

"We made up time after they cleared the tracks of snow."

"Look, Jenny, your telegram from Chicago came only two hours ago. The telephone operator read it to me. I immediately tried to reach Dan. It took a while before he answered his page. He's heading back now."

"How long will it take him?"

"Hard to say in this weather. The roads are hell, icy near the sound."

"Could you give me some idea?"

Sue said, looking around, "An hour and forty-five minutes."

Motionless, Jenny looked at her. She needed a minute to recover from her disappointment.

Sue continued to scrutinize Jenny's luggage. She stepped over to the valises and got two of them. "I can manage the night-kit, too, if you put it under my arm. You take the flashlight."

"I can carry the rest," Jenny replied.

Conscious of Jenny's appearance, her petiteness, her expensive furs, the high boots, Sue set a snail's pace guiding her through the misty darkness of dense fog. Jenny was thoroughly upset by Sue's apparent judgment of her as a hothouse flower. Finally, she said, "Sue, I'm a hell of a lot tougher and stronger than I may look. Now let's get moving before we both freeze to death."

Sue took that as censure from Jenny. Turning slowly, her voice cool and remote, she said, "I am instructed to take good care of you. I am trying."

Jenny eyed her with surprise and immediately apologized.

"That's all right," Sue said stiffly.

Sue's car was roomier than it looked and easily took all of Jenny's suitcases; this was a great relief to Jenny. Sue drove with detached expertness, and Jenny sat at her side of the seat, trying to see. "Are we going toward the hospital?"

"No, away from it."

Jenny said, politely, "It seems to me Dan is imposing on you. If you have plans, I don't mind waiting alone."

"I may have a date later. I never quite know." While she spoke, Sue's eyes left the road and met Jenny's. They gazed at each other in silence. It was Sue who began to feel uncomfortable. Then after she turned her face away from Jenny, she asked tersely, "Anything you'd like to discuss while we're alone?"

"No," Jenny answered, surprised. "Nothing special."

"Anyone?"

"Whom do *you* have in mind?"

"I suppose we could talk about George Atlas."

"Why?" She waited, but no reason came from Sue.

"How about me?" Sue suddenly said.

"That I should appreciate. I'd like to know you."

"What if I were to tell you that even as a little girl I envied boys. Later I wanted only to humiliate them. Now my attitude toward men is the typical ambivalent attitude of the nymphomaniac."

Jenny felt she was being tested but had no inkling as to Sue's purpose. She kept her own counsel, noting her companion's mood, and remained quiet.

"What if I were to tell you I have fantasies of being a prostitute. That—in psychiatric language—is my incestuous longing for my father."

After that, conversation lagged. Finally, Sue said, "Have a cigarette. They're in the glove compartment."

Jenny leaned back and smiled. "It makes Dan happy when I don't smoke."

"Light one for me then."

Jenny did.

"Thank you." Sue took a deep drag. "See those lights?"

"The diner?"

"Yes."

Jenny smiled up at Sue. "I'm hungry. We ran out of food about ten in the morning."

Pete gazed at her across the counter and smiled. "Pleased to make your acquaintance."

"And it's nice to make yours, Pete. Thank you very much for the boxing gloves you sent for my son Paul."

"How is he?"

Her eyes shining, Jenny responded with maternal pride. "He's wonderful." She gazed at Sue a moment. "He really is."

Sue grinned. "Yes, of course he is."

Jenny pictured Paul in her mother's capable hands and her grandmother smiling at his struggling movements. Sue said, "Mrs. Gunther has had nothing to eat all day. Hand her a cup of coffee. I'll take the usual. Then you decide what we're to eat."

"Hot soup, then steak," said Pete and he returned to the grill.

Sue sipped her whiskey and examined Jenny—the twin sweater set in bottle green, hugging her figure, the low pleated skirt, the coppery hair, not cut short, the arch of her brows. The rich scent of the perfume she wore. Sue knew the twinges of jealousy. Jenny possessed everything that her own mother regarded as provocatively feminine. She could still hear her mother's voice, "But, dear, Sue is at least a head taller than the boys." And she could hear her mother responding when her father spoke up. "She may be all right on a tennis court, but it's a different story on a dance floor. God—she's awkward."

The realization that her father, whether for the sake of expediency or because he was in actual agreement, came back with: "If only she had been born a boy!"—haunted her. She decided to have another drink.

Dan came into the diner at a half run. Jenny spun around on her high stool. Then she was on her toes, and Dan was kissing her on the lips. Sue took a deep swallow of her drink. The men sitting up and down the counter cast warm glances at them, and Pete exchanged a smile with Willie, the counter boy.

Sue moved over one seat. "Come sit between us," she invited.

Dan removed his overcoat and his galoshes and accepted Sue's stool. Pete set a fresh cup of coffee in front of him. He turned to her, but before he could thank her for meeting Jenny safely, he noted the question in her troubled gray eyes and shook his head slightly in reassurance. Sue gave him a glance of infinite gratitude.

Jenny marked the exchange. In the warmth of the diner she experienced a feeling of sudden cold. She turned her head toward the door, but it was shut; no freezing breeze blew through it. Her eyes went back to Dan and he looked at her, and then, with a smile, he put out a hand and brushed the hair away from her cheek. Jenny felt her heart pounding, the blood rushing to her cheeks.

Sue took a cigarette from her pack and lighted it. Standing up abruptly, she said, "So long, you two." She pressed her hand on Dan's shoulder. "See you tomorrow?"

"At breakfast. I've an idea for an objective test to measure emotions quantitatively. I want your reaction to its possibilities." It was Dan's way of telling Sue, "Forget the night before last. Don't hate yourself."

Sue took her kerchief, put it about her head, and tied it. She put on her overshoes and then her parka. She glanced at Jenny, who evaded her eyes. Sue turned about and started out of the diner. "So long, Pete."

"So long, Dr. Sue."

Jenny let her go without saying a word.

In a low voice Dan asked, "What happened?"

"Do me a favor, Dan. Drink your coffee and let's go."

Dan lowered his eyes to the counter. His fingers curled around his mug of black coffee.

Dan closed the car door after Jenny climbed inside. Then he walked around and got in beside her. And when he took her into his arms and murmured that he loved her, loved the feel of her, the smell of her, Jenny forgot Sue and was happy. She raised her face. "Oh, Dan. I am so happy to be here at last."

Moments later they were both breathless. Jenny freed herself. Dan reached into his pocket for cigarettes. He lighted two. "How's Paul, sweetheart?"

Jenny laughed. "I was scared to death you'd never ask."

Dan put the car in motion. Jenny sat close and talked to him about their son, his activity, his constant curiosity about what was going on around him, his recognition of his grandmother and great-grandmother, and his impish quality when Jenny picked him up.

Dan said, pausing to think about it, "I never imagined an infant could be so intensely sensitive to his environment. When I visualize Paul, I see him just eating and sleeping."

Jenny smiled at Dan, studying his face intently. Then she looked away—nothing to be seen but darkness and fog, nothing to be heard but the roar of the wind. Suddenly, she said, "Don't drive so fast. We'll skid."

Dan said, "Don't worry." And he drove on. After a few moments he said, "The drugstore closes at ten. It's nearly quarter of."

"Dan, I have toothpaste and soap, and I even brought your favorite—"

Dan looked down at her in astonishment, then laughed aloud. "Brushing my teeth is not exactly my idea of a palliative on a chilly evening."

Jenny felt all hot and shaky inside. She looked out so that Dan should not see. From the window she caught a glimpse of lights. "Is that the village?"

Dan nodded.

When they reached it, Dan drove to the end of Main Street and stopped the car in front of the drugstore. "Hurrah! I expected to find it closed."

"Dan, I want another baby."

There was shock in Dan's voice as he repeated, "Another baby!"

All at once everything was too much for Jenny—the months of loneliness, the tiring trip, the sense of strangeness about Sue Palmer. Why should Dan refuse her a baby since children did not interfere with anything he wanted and planned for? He was never around to look after them. Jenny burst into tears.

Dan tried to think. He had to get into the store while there was still time, but for the moment he could not. "Jenny, baby," Dan whispered, "you're cold and tired."

"I'm not," Jenny snapped.

Dan's urge was to reason with her, but by no means did he want to upset Jenny further. This was not the moment to announce, "You're not going back. We'll find a house and send for Paul." And so he found nothing to say.

It did not matter because Jenny continued, "It's for Paul's sake, mostly. Three women hovering over him—a doting grandfather to indulge him. It's too much for one little boy. Jenny held out her hand to him and added gravely. "There's another reason. It's easier to wait for you pregnant than not pregnant."

Dan felt he could not say what he wanted to say because now, and for the following few days, he wanted only to make love to her. "Very well, sweetheart," he replied, lifting her cold hands to his lips.

Jenny was astonished at her easy victory. In gladness and in certain anticipation, she sank down in the soft leather.

Dan turned the key. Soon afterward, his headlights picked up lights that came out of the darkness.

"The hospital?"

"Uh-huh. That's it."

Dan put away the car and they ran across the snow together. Jenny's spirits renewed as the cold air met her face. Perhaps she had been harsh on Dan.

The room was warm. The lamp was burning. Flowering hothouse greens were arranged in a bowl. Her nightgown lay on the turned-down bed, and her clothes hung in the closet. Sue had arranged everything for her.

Jenny held herself tense and looked around slowly.

Watching her all the while, Dan asked, "Pleased?"

"Not really."

"I can't understand why you seem antagonistic to Sue. She's an extremely generous person. A great help to us all."

"I don't doubt it."

Dan looked down at Jenny with tenderness. "We're both on edge. Take your bath, Jenny dear. I'll show you where. I'll borrow a bathroom."

"All right, Dan." Dan went to her with his hand held out, but Jenny hung back. "You get started. I've got a couple of things to unwrap."

She looked at him curiously. "Do two bedrooms attach to one bathroom?"

"Yes."

"Does Sue live next door?"

Dan put his arms around her and drew her to him firmly. "She does."

Jenny dropped her eyes. "Oh."

"Look at me."

Her refusal betrayed her sense of anger.

Dan spoke with infinite gentleness. "For months I've hungered for you, only you."

Then Jenny looked up. The change was startling. "Honest?"

"Honest," Dan said and kissed her.

Jenny clung to him, then laughing she told him to shave. "Because you feel scratchy."

"Yes," said Dan and he went out.

Jenny turned to get her purse; while he was absent was a good time to hide the present Dan's father had picked out. "The most handsome cuff links I've ever come across. They'll go well with anything." She glanced around and remembered that Dan liked a drawer full of socks, at least half of which he never wore. Smiling to herself and feeling relaxed, she opened the drawer she felt to be the right one. It was. Her hand reached in for a good hiding place and discovered the contraceptives between pairs of socks balled together. With dread, her eyes went to the familiar trademark—Trojans. Of the twelve, two were missing. Angry, confused, tormented by questions, Jenny hurled them back among the socks. After closing the drawer, she paused only to return the cuff links to her purse. Then she flew about picking up her robe and slippers, and finally, with tears streaming down her face, she stumbled into the bathroom and snapped on the light. Her hands obeyed automatically. They turned on faucets, took off clothes, creamed her face—did everything swiftly. Her eyes alternately closed or gazing at the white ceiling, Jenny lay in the hot water, searching her mind for some course of action. Ultimately, she knew she would do nothing, express none of the mounting anger within her. She stepped out of the tub and wrapped herself in the terry-cloth robe.

Dan greeted her with a wide smile, expectant, and reached out for her. At his touch Jenny became rigid. His gaze steady and intent, his tone gentle, Dan said, "Darling, you're as frightened as you were the first time. Don't be. Let yourself go."

Jenny lay down carefully. Dan spent the next minutes fondling her, kissing her throat, her eyes, and softly he whispered his love for her. After what seemed a long time to him, he felt her body respond. Huskily he murmured, "Jenny."

She put her arms around him, and soon Dan became conscious of the fact that there was a wantonness in her ardor. He could only understand it as a full ripening. Nothing could have made him happier. The pleasure she gave was almost more than a man could endure. Ages passed. Dan kissed her again and turned over on his back. He was asleep at once.

Weeping softly, Jenny lay listening to his breathing, thinking. He touched her. She touched him. She kept seeing them together, and for the first time she understood hatred. And she knew, too, the fury that gives vent to a desperate act.

"Good God, I've got to stop thinking about it. He loves me. That's what counts." Exhausted, she got out of bed and tiptoed into the bathroom to wash her face. She shut the door noiselessly, without its creaking. The light on, she stared at herself in the mirror. She looked exactly the same. Was it possible?

Sue opened the other door quietly, huddling Dan's silk dressing gown around her. "Can't you sleep either? Would you like to come into my room and have a whiskey with me?"

Jenny could not believe it possible that anyone could be as bitchy as Sue—to come in with proof of their intimacy and. . . . Jenny struggled to pick the right words.

Her failure to speak puzzled Sue. Looking down at the robe, Sue realized what was wrong. "You're upsetting yourself about nothing."

Jenny was pale. Her dark eyes were filled with disbelief. Still she said nothing.

"That's true, Jenny. But I do have a confession to make. I think of this robe as my father's arms around me." She sighed. "But if you don't want me to wear it, I'll give it back. It was only on loan anyway."

Unhappily for Sue, Jenny did not believe her, and her face revealed the depth of her hostility. Her eyes flashed. "Neither my husband nor I ever want to see that robe again."

Sue responded calmly and sadly. "When I was a little girl—only I was never little, only young—my mother turned every childish prank into something dirty—evil. When I reached out to her begging for affection, she would leave me. And, on top of that, she told my father, exaggerating everything until he ended up doing just what she wanted him to. It seems unbelievable, doesn't it, that a woman could hate her own child so?"

As Jenny watched Sue, she began to feel pity for her. She made herself think about the things Sue had hinted at in the car—about her attitudes toward men and how she liked to humiliate them. Maybe that's what she was trying to do to Dan. Tight-lipped, Jenny nearly gave vent to her own sense of insult to Sue, but she considered it far better to say nothing. She did the cruelest thing possible. She left.

Sue heard a voice, far off in the darkness. It came directly to her. "Die. That's for you." Her heart began pounding hard. She started out of the bathroom in a daze, the words ringing in her ears. "You still alive?" At that moment she knew what her next action would be. She picked up her car keys and walked out into the night.

Dan shut off the alarm before it rang. Without making a sound, he stood looking down at Jenny. His contentment was so complete, he again almost forgot Sue's indelicate donation. As he got rid of them one by one in a neighboring bathroom, he felt a deep thankfulness that Jenny had not yet asked for drawer space.

Jenny was awakened by a winter storm of snow, hail, and hard-driving wind. She got out of bed and made her way to the window only to find that it was fixed so that it could not be pushed open. It gave her a queer feeling, especially after she discovered that Dan locked her in the room. She called him and there was quite a wait before she heard his voice.

"Dan, what time is it? I forgot to wind my watch."

"Almost noon, Jenny, baby."

"No wonder I'm starved."

"Get dressed, sweetheart. We'll go to lunch as soon as I can get away."

In an effort to pass the time Jenny picked up a magazine. With no intention of going back to the sock drawer, she started to read. But a compulsion seized her. Part of her said, "You don't want to see them again." Part said, "Uh-huh, but you will." She closed the magazine and moved to Dan's dresser. "They're gone," she said quietly to herself. Then she began looking in earnest. After a while she closed the drawer. Jenny was barely back in her chair, when a knock came. An unfamiliar voice said, "Turn the knob twice, Jenny, counterclockwise and the door will open."

For a few minutes she stood staring at him. He was even more handsome than she supposed—fair skin and bright hair, his mouth wide over strong teeth. And he was bigger somehow.

His gray eyes took her in with pleasure.

Before he could speak, she smiled and her eyes sparkled. "Hello, George. Will you come in?"

He stepped inside and dropped his coat and muffler on a chair. He wanted to kiss her. "Take your hat off, Jenny. We aren't going out yet. Let your braids fall."

Jenny's hands moved to obey.

He touched her hair and stroked it.

Jenny could not understand why she felt so completely at ease. It was as if she had always known him. "It used to be cut short as a boy's," she said. "Dan made me grow it out."

"Dan knew what he was doing. Such lovely hair." At Jenny's answering smile he removed his hand. And then he was saying, "I brought delicatessen and other things to eat from New York. Betsy is making coffee for us over at her house. I think you had better dress warmly; the temperature is still falling."

"But I'm waiting for Dan."

"I know. It'll be difficult, however, for Dan to leave the ward just now. He asked me to take good care of you," he added smilingly.

A look of apprehension flickered across Jenny's face.

"Don't be frightened. Let's go over to Larry and Betsy, and we'll talk together."

Jenny already guessed that something was wrong and that it had to do with Sue. "I'll get my things."

Even for George, the icy, windy walk was a struggle. For Jenny it was impossible. He lifted her simply into his arms. "Rest your head on my shoulder, Jenny." She put her arms around his neck and pillowed her head, hiding her face. His head down against the flurries of dry, hard snow, he carried her all the way.

The Steins' front door was locked. But Betsy was watching for them near a window. George put Jenny down and she thanked him.

"My pleasure," George answered gently.

Betsy stood in the doorway, her dimpled face alight. She looked rather like a small Teddy bear standing there in a shapeless blue dress. But her welcome to Jenny was as warm and direct as anyone could wish. Subterfuge in emotion or action was completely alien to Betsy. She put her arms around Jenny, embracing her, then helped her off with her coat and scarf. Without taking her eyes off Jenny, Betsy launched into a monologue that had Jenny perplexed. "Larry called, too. He won't be home for lunch. Miss Graham is bringing them in sandwiches from the nurses' kitchen. Everything is under control, but they have to be there. Dan sent word that he'd like Jenny to come over around three."

George dropped his overcoat, and thinking Betsy had talked enough, he moved them inside to the living room. "Come on. Let's eat."

"Everything is ready. We can go into the kitchen. It's warm there."

Jenny allowed herself to be pulled. George followed, pleased that Jenny and Betsy obviously liked each other. A cigarette between her lips, Betsy served really good coffee and brought out rye bread and a salad to eat with the cold meats.

George and Betsy watched Jenny eat with approval. With her second helping, George emptied his wineglass and said in carefully measured words, "Jenny, Sue Palmer has disappeared. And her disappearance makes no sense because not one single article of clothing is gone."

"Tell me something," Jenny asked, frowning. "Is her car missing?"

"Yes."

"And you think that—" Jenny did not complete the sentence.

George shrugged. "Maybe."

Continuing to look full at George, Jenny sat quietly thinking.

Betsy left her chair and refilled the coffee cups. As she reseated herself, she spoke. "Couldn't it be suicide? She's threatened it often enough."

Jenny looked at her thoughtfully. "What does Larry plan to do now?"

"Wait." Betsy looked at George and, smiling a little, said, "What is your objection to Jenny lifting her cup?"

Releasing Jenny's hands, George answered with an easy grin, "None."

* * *

When they got to Dan's door, he was there to meet them. He kissed Jenny (George stood by, genuinely astonished that he envied Dan the right to do so), and they moved inside. There was hardly time for them to talk before Larry joined them. As he shut the door, he said, "The police rang a few minutes ago." Some seconds passed in which he greeted Jenny, admiring her V-neck sweater and classic skirt. Then, prompted by Dan, he told them all he knew. The police had started their search, beginning in the small town, then widening out in the surrounding area. New tracks in the snow across farmland were investigated, abandoned cars searched. It added up to nothing.

Then Dan was saying, "In a sense, I'm more worried now."

"Because we can't rule out the suicide angle?"

Dan nodded slowly. "Exactly. We had a better chance faced with the possibility of the other alternative. I am completely confident that—unless she were taken by surprise—Sue would be able to handle any physical danger."

"That," said Larry, "is exactly my thought. So there's no use in delaying. I'd better inform the front office."

"Before you do that, let me check out one thing."

"All right, Dan. A few hours more won't matter now."

George, who was watching Jenny, became aware that something was bothering her. "You look puzzled."

"I am. How do you all know that nothing of Sue's is missing."

"We searched."

"Who searched, Dan?"

Dan gave her a long look. "Does it matter?"

Jenny gave a shrug. "Maybe. Betsy and I—"

George interrupted. "It wasn't hard to establish, Jenny. Whenever possible, Sue wore pants. She had a very limited wardrobe."

After a slight pause Jenny said, "In that case, I have a suggestion to make. Maybe Sue took clothes that don't belong to her. She had enough opportunity; there must be a number of unlocked rooms."

They all stared at her, and George saw a gleam of hope in an otherwise disturbing situation.

Larry got out of his chair. "Now, Jenny, you and Dan will be having an early supper with us before the party tonight. If you want, dress at our house. That way you won't be windblown."

"Thank you, Larry. We might do that."

"Well," Larry said, rising, "I'd better go back to give Betsy a hand."

He smiled at Jenny. "Her once-a-year, big, splashy party. We always do it for New Year."

"It won't be much of a party for those of us who know," Dan answered.

After George and Larry had gone, Dan leaned back in his chair. "Like them?"

"Very, very much. George, especially."

Dan pushed his cigarettes across the desk.

For once Jenny said, "No, thanks. What makes you offer me a cigarette? Do you think I'll have need of a crutch? Or are you trying to get your own courage up?"

With an exasperated sigh Dan said, "My sweet Jenny, sometimes I can't help wishing—though I have not earned it to the same degree—that you trusted me as much as I trust you."

That was almost impossible for Jenny to ignore, and her expression did soften.

With Jenny in a more friendly mood Dan began to question her, maybe she might know something useful, though she herself saw no relationship nor would she shed light on Sue's mood the day she met her. Dan felt he had to cover as many of those last hours as possible—any clue might point the way forward; every clue was a signpost to her possible state of mind.

"Tell me, Jenny—and please try to remember—did anything strange or unpleasant or unusual happen between you? You see"—he held her hand—"Sue was traumatized by her mother's rejection of her. Every subsequent rejection, which she herself engineered, shattered her."

"Sue sounds more like a patient than a doctor."

It sounded like criticism, but Dan did not argue Sue's cause.

"When you first entered Pete's wagon, did you by chance notice anything significant? Or did she glance at or talk to some man in a way that said they knew each other fairly well?"

"A man other than Pete?"

Dan nodded. "*Other* than."

"What kind of man?"

"Oh, for Christ's sake. How should I know? A man."

"Why are you cross-examining me?"

Dan gazed at her measuredly. It was on his tongue to say, "Why are you so evasive?" But he recalled her remark about connecting rooms. And that was not quite all. He had discovered during the morning that his silk dressing gown was missing from Sue's closet.

And Jenny was thinking unhappily, "You keep your secrets, Dan Gunther. Let me keep mine."

"Sorry, Jenny, I didn't mean to badger you. It's just that I'm kicking myself more than you'll ever know for stringing along with Larry instead of taking the strong stand Lewis wanted me to."

"Lewis?" Jenny asked sharply.

Dan nodded sadly. "I didn't tell you because I didn't want to worry you. As an undergraduate, Sue was put in a psychiatric hospital. It's possible she's ill again; she's been under great emotional strain. Lewis felt she again required hospitalization. Larry, George, and I talked about it. We felt, however, as friends and colleagues, we could help her lead a useful life. At least, we felt obliged to make the effort, thinking there'd be ample opportunity to read the danger signals, if any."

Jenny said, "Oh, my God," and lapsed into silence.

Dan was patient and smart enough to wait.

"In the car, Dan, when she picked me up at the station, she began to talk pretty wild. I kept thinking she was being outspoken about sexuality because, in some weird way, she was either ambivalent about me or, in a crude way, groping to see if I would pass muster."

"Jenny, I'd like to know why you delayed telling me this."

In sudden fierceness, Jenny said, "Why should I?"

Dan rose and walked slowly over to Jenny. "Get up," he said, giving her his outstretched hand.

When she stood facing him, he said, "Do you suspect me of an affair?"

"No, I don't."

"Of yielding to—" Suddenly, he leaned toward her and kissed her passionately. All he said was "Just the opposite, Jenny, baby. You're the only one who means a thing to me."

Jenny accepted this. "I believe you, Dan. I *really* do."

Dan put away some papers in his desk and they left, Jenny clutching his arm.

The blizzard was especially bad over the North Shore of Long Island. Roads were closed. Cars were left abandoned. Even with chains Dan's car skidded from right to left, crossing and recrossing the highway. There was hardly anyone else braving the elements.

It took them longer than they expected to reach the Steins'. But Betsy was there to pull them in from the bitter chill outside and greet them, cigarette in one hand and a glass in the other.

Smiling back at her, Jenny said, "I'm sorry we're late."

"That's all right," Betsy answered cheerily. "There's a bar and eats set up in the dining room—food for Larry's kin, booze to keep mine happy. The party can start without us. We've made up our minds to enjoy supper. George got hold of some real French champagne." Then she took Jenny's elbow. "Let's go up and put your fur coat safely out of the way."

As soon as they sat down around the kitchen table, the telephone rang. Larry got up to answer it. He came back saying, "Jenny, that was your friend Tascha. They won't be here either. She wants you to call her tomorrow."

Betsy said, "Oh, no!"

Larry said, "I told you, dear, not to count on anyone. You heard the eight o'clock news."

Jenny's heart had jumped at the mention of the evening news.

It was George who noticed. "It's all right, Jenny. The news was very commonplace—disrupted commuter service, stranded motorists." Lifting his empty glass, he touched hers and said in a lighter tone, "To you, Jenny. Next we'll drink to Paul and then to your grandmother, and then to. . . ."

A merry twinkle in her eyes, Betsy said, "Shut up, you ass, and pour."

Jenny changed quickly into her body-hugging pink shirt and long matching skirt, called Tascha, and by the time the first few couples had arrived, she and Betsy were downstairs talking.

Larry took the coats. George gave them drinks, and Dan proudly presented Jenny to many of his hospital friends. The guests were mostly doctors, their dates mostly nurses, and from the start of the evening, it was pretty clear who was sleeping with whom. For Jenny it was easy to mix, to be nice to everyone, to enjoy the party with her customary enthusiasm. She was meeting strange faces for the first time, and with Dan beside her it was no effort.

Larry tried to be a good host and move around, but it was not easy for him. Engrossed in thoughts of Sue, he was in no mood to celebrate. Betsy's charm and her infectious giggle did much to enliven the evening. Dan made up his mind to enjoy himself and leave the problem of Sue's disappearance to the future. George was of the same mind as Dan, but whereas Dan made himself entertaining and mixed in the crowd, George tended bar and did not waste as much as a glance on any woman other than Jenny. Several of the unattached girls, obviously taken by his rugged looks and roguish grin, hoped in vain that he'd get more friendly as the evening wore on.

By eleven thirty, coats and ties were off and the dancing was becoming wild. George walked in the half-darkened living room to wind the phonograph. Rug up, it was, except for the radio and the phonograph, empty of furniture. He watched Jenny and Dan in step with the music and with each other. Then he tapped Dan's shoulder. "My dance. You tend bar. It's only fair."

Dan glanced at his watch. "Not much time left."

"Time to spare." George laughed. "I got a station that picks up California."

"Nice of you," Dan answered with a grin. As he walked toward the dining room Betsy placed herself in front of him. She laughingly said, "Compromise me."

With a quick movement Dan caught her around the waist. "I'd love to." He held her very close and they reached the dining room dancing. At the bar he poured two drinks. Betsy remained beside him.

George towered over Jenny. They danced beautifully together—completely relaxed and happy. Neither of them spoke; neither took notice of anyone else. From time to time George smiled down at her and she smiled up at him. There was a difference between them, however. Jenny was dancing for the sheer joy of dancing. The fact that she felt warmly toward George and that she knew Dan liked him very much made it all the more pleasurable. George was dumbfounded, perhaps even a little unnerved, by his feelings. Her soft body, warm against him, made his heart pound in a way that rather terrified him. The last thing he wanted was to fall in love with his friend's wife. Meanwhile, he decided: It's New Year's Eve and I've had a lot to drink. He pulled her close, and, bending, he rubbed his cheek lightly against hers.

Jenny's eyes sparkled. Otherwise, she remained composed.

"It's almost time," he whispered in her ear.

They left the room and found Dan, his back to Larry, relating to Betsy a slightly edited version of the octogenarian whose doctor ordered breast-feeding.

Betsy giggled and Dan smiled down at her. Then his eyes went to George. "So you're back."

"Been back for hours."

"No! Just think," he added, turning to Betsy, "we spent—"

Cries of "Happy New Year" rang out, and everyone was shouting or kissing. Noisemakers were twirled, toy trumpets tooted, and glasses were raised. It was as if a large flock of starlings had raised their heads together and were trying to outdo one another in eloquence. But Dan and Jenny were on their own island of calm. He put his arms around her, and Jenny rose on tiptoe to receive his prolonged, caressing kisses.

And George stood by waiting until Dan released Jenny and she lifted her face to his.

George allowed himself to be pulled away. "I'm your hostess. Remember?"

"Sorry, sweetheart. I guess I forgot to remember." He kissed Betsy competently and, in fun, she let out a big sigh. Then she leaned against Dan and met his lips. But Larry forgot to kiss Jenny. Later, when they had a few minutes alone, he apologized to Betsy. "I know. I ought to have. But my mind was on Sue. Remember last year when she got high and had such a good time?"

"She got drunk. And it was hardly fun for that Harvard boy."

Betsy could have spared herself the trouble of speaking. Larry hardly heard her. "I wish she were here. Or that we at least knew where she was."

Betsy went to him and rested her head on his shoulder. "So do I, dear."

Larry took off his glasses and wiped them. "In your heart you never liked her, did you?"

"No, it's true. I did not."

Larry took something from his pocket. It was an engraved medallion the size of a silver dollar on a heavy gold chain. "Happy New Year, which means—I love you," he said. Then he drew back.

For a moment Betsy stayed where she was, reflecting. "My poor darling. How good you are."

The party broke up about two, as everyone struggled out to the calm of a snowbound world. Betsy prevailed upon Dan and Jenny to stay on though Dan kept insisting that Larry must be beat. Larry protested.

"I've got the solution. Larry goes to bed. Jenny takes her call here. After that, I'll prepare cinnamon toast and scrambled eggs. The girls can make the coffee." He grinned at Dan. "No job for you. You can sit and admire your Dad's cuff links from Shanghai."

Dan's eyes came slowly around to Jenny. He said, "I suppose you somehow managed to speak to him."

Her eyes meeting his, Jenny said, "We'll both be speaking to him soon."

"Again?" Dan almost gasped.

"What's strange, Dan?" said Jenny. "It's good for Paul; he needs a man in his life."

Dan was still looking at her. "Why didn't you tell me that Dad was back in San Francisco?"

"Because," Jenny answered truthfully, "I have not had much of a chance to tell you *anything* yet."

Betsy mumbled under her breath. "And we all know who's responsible for that."

The telephone bell sounded promptly at three A.M.

Jenny said, "I'll go," and got up quickly. Dan was on her heels, and they reached the phone at the same time. The operator said, "Mrs. Gunther, I have your party on the line." Though weary, Jenny talked and laughed and asked questions. Talking with the family revitalized her. Finally, she began to feel guilty. "Dan's beside me," she said. "He wants to talk to you all. And, Dad, he's just mad for the cuff links."

Later, when they were sitting comfortably around the kitchen, George asked, "Is Paul behaving himself?"

Dan jumped up, still sleepy, and grabbed the receiver. Larry was calling to say that the police had called. The body of a woman found about noon could be Sue. They were coming to the house. Would it be convenient for—?

Before he could finish, Dan cut in. "Yes, right away."

"Dan, they want to see Jenny, too."

"OK."

Dan hurried back to wake Jenny.

She opened her eyes slowly. "It's your day off. You promised me we'd sleep in."

Dan said, "We did, Jenny baby."

"Are you sure?"

Dan nodded slowly. "I looked at my watch." Then he repeated Larry's alarming information.

"My God—what a way to start the New Year!"

Dan kissed her, went to the window, and pulled up the blind. It was clear—no hint of wind, but hard and frosty white everywhere.

"I wish I had coffee."

"All right, Jenny. I'll get us some. The dining room is still open." He had already begun to dress.

Jenny spent several moments in thought before she stepped out of bed.

To the officer in charge, Lieutenant Detective Hank Chapman, this was an important case—his name in newspapers, his voice on radio. That was the way to move up. But these were important, well-to-do people, professionals all. He would have to be tactful. And so, at the start, he was a bit nervous. He pointedly ignored the remaining evidence of a boisterous New Year's Eve party. He accepted coffee, which Betsy poured, using her sterling pot. Then he relaxed a little.

"I am here to gather pertinent information and make my official report. When there is reasonable ground to suspect that death was due to violence or other unlawful means, and if the coroner and the medical examiner have reason to suspect that murder or manslaughter has been committed, the coroner is bound to hold an inquest and summon a coroner's jury. This, however, is merely a routine preliminary investigation.''

"Who's coroner here?'' Dan asked.

"In Nassau County it's a justice of the peace who acts as coroner. In this instance, when the body that lies dead was found, he was notified. He immediately called the physician designated to make the postmortem examination and ascertain the truth concerning the cause of death. Together they went at once to the place and jointly took charge.''

Remembering what Sue really was like and what her potential was, the many beautiful and generous things of which she was capable, Larry could not conceive of the "body that lies dead.'' It was too brutal.

Jenny had withdrawn herself.

George was silent because he was thinking about two people—Jenny and Dan, who now meant more to him than anyone on earth—and how it just might affect them.

Betsy was thinking: Dammit, why do those guys refuse to see her as she really was? And why did George have to bring her here and hand her over to Larry?

That left Dan. He looked somberly at the police officer. "Do you have any sound reason to suspect that the woman you found is Dr. Palmer?''

"I didn't find her, doctor. A stalled motorist seeking help found the body in a cabin on a deserted road off the main highway.'' Lieutenant Hank Chapman consulted his notebook. Reading from it, he gave them the detailed description—height, weight, age, hair color, and so on. That was a description of Dr. Susan Palmer reported missing by Dr. Larry Stein on December 31, 1932, at six twenty P.M. Then he read the description of the woman found. Every detail matched identically except one. Larry described her as a superb athlete, whereas the medical examiner wrote super-excellent physical specimen in his introductory report. The Lieutenant looked around. "Convinced? We would, of course, like one of you gentlemen to come down to the coroner's office later to give positive identification.''

"I will,'' said George. "These gentlemen have more pressing duties here.'' Betsy accepted this without question. The loyalty in his offer remained concealed from Jenny, but Dan gripped the arm of his chair in profound relief. Larry straightened up and squared his shoulders. Speaking softly, he said, "The duty is mine. I was her boss and her closest friend.''

Officer Chapman nodded in approval. Then, looking around the room, he said, "I have a few questions to put to you people.''

Breathing heavily, his face drawn with despair, Larry said, "We are prepared to answer."

"Are you in full charge here?"

"Only in the absence of the superintendent and the clinical director. And then, only of my service."

"Am I to understand that your superiors are absent?"

"They both return tomorrow."

"When did you last see Dr. Palmer?"

"The afternoon of December 28. She dropped into my office to tell me that the Gunthers got their signals crossed. He was on his way to New York to meet her, and she was on her way out here."

The police officer wrote all that down. Then he turned his head to Dan.

"The evening of December 28, at Pete's diner."

George was next.

"I don't remember exactly. A couple of weeks ago."

The lieutenant looked up from his notebook. His shrewd eyes curious, he asked, "How's that?"

"I'm not on staff here."

"Uh-huh. Then you are not really part of Dr. Palmer's company of friends."

"On the contrary, Sue and I go back a number of years. We were classmates—Columbia Medical School."

The lieutenant cleared his throat. "I have to ask you this. You are under no obligation to answer." He pushed on. "Were you romantically involved with the deceased?"

Jenny's eyes widened and she held her breath. Her knees crossed, Betsy swung her foot vigorously.

"Not my type," George answered.

It was Jenny's turn. They, all but Dan, turned and looked at her. He—his strong wish to shelter Jenny apparent, regarded the police officer and spoke with some irritation. "My wife knows nothing of the situation here."

"I find that interesting."

There followed an uncomfortable silence. Dan broke it with: "The mere fact that Sue Palmer lies dead is no reason to assume she was murdered. She talked a lot about suicide. But during that time she functioned well; we gradually forgot the times she was overstrung."

Hastily Lieutenant Chapman put that all down.

Betsy watched with interest and then, without a single glance toward Larry, she said, "I have something to say." To which the policeman replied, "Please do."

"There were times when I thought Sue Palmer used the threat of suicide to lord it over us. Furthermore, I fail to see why we must continue to protect Sue. It wasn't her nature to sleep in a solitary bed." Betsy suddenly stopped. Hastily, she lit a cigarette, realizing too late that she had revealed too much.

Braced and ready, Jenny waited for his attack. But he did not start by firing questions at her. There was no need for him to hurry.

"Tell me," he said, addressing her with the voice of solace, "all you know."

"Sue Palmer met me at the railroad station. On instructions from my husband, she drove me to Pete's Diner, where we ate and waited. Shortly after Dan arrived, she left. I never saw her again."

The police officer showed some surprise. "You say you never saw her again?"

Unfazed, Jenny stared into his face and repeated, "I *never* saw her again."

The policeman's eyebrows lifted. "Think carefully, Mrs. Gunther."

"Hold on, " George said. He looked ready to throttle the detective.

"What are you getting at?" Dan asked angrily.

"A material circumstance."

Betsy lit another cigarette with a hand that shook. Nervously, she offered them more coffee.

No one paid any attention to her because the police officer was saying, "While you were on your way here, Dr. Gunther, we had a talk with the housekeeper and with the room maid. We saw your quarters. Quite a setup. A connecting bathroom. Doors unlocked."

"Do you have some tangible thought in mind?"

"Nothing firm, Doctor. Just an idea. Two girls change clothes. Maybe they have a little talk in the bathroom."

"Had that been so, my wife would most certainly have told you so."

All the time they talked, Jenny was having an imaginary fight with Dan. And it was lively. *Because it might have been a nuisance having me and a baby around, you made a liar out of me. And if there's an inquest, I'll be a perjurer, too.*

"Mrs. Gunther, do you deny seeing and speaking to Sue Palmer again the night of December 28?"

Jenny straightened up and said quietly, sounding entirely sincere and truthful. "I do."

The police officer spent the next minutes being exceedingly placative toward Jenny. He was impressed by her sincerity. Jenny gave him her very special wooden smile, the one she used when she did not dare to stick out her tongue.

George wanted to hug her. So did Betsy. Dan almost laughed aloud. His anger overcome, Dan made a reasonable suggestion. "Tell us what you know and we, who knew Sue and understood her, may stumble onto something helpful."

"Sue Palmer's body was found wearing a man's dressing gown. The silk cord was drawn tightly around her neck." Turning a little to Jenny and glancing at Betsy, he said, "Sorry, ladies," and went on. "Two unused safeties were in the right pocket of the robe."

George tilted his head back. "I'll be—"

Betsy moved closer to Larry, her hand touching his briefly. He took notice and his eyes smiled at her a little. Then he said, "At last, we have something."

The lieutenant nodded. "The silk cord. The questions are: Did she kill herself? Did she invite murder? Or did she arrange it? According to the deputies there is, at this time, no evidence of foul play. Nothing around her was disturbed. An autopsy is scheduled for tomorrow."

Jenny's eyes studied the policeman's face. He knows, she thought. That robe has a San Francisco label. Frowning a little, giving every indication of being artlessly reflective, Jenny said, addressing Dan, "Remember darling, I told you your silk dressing gown is missing."

The policeman's eyes brightened as he turned to Dan. "Are you admitting the robe might be yours?"

She was so convincing, Dan himself almost believed her. He grasped her purpose immediately. Overwhelmed by her enormous loyalty, he checked his strong temptation to show it. Instead, he took an attitude less gallant and far more sensible, one that suited the game of parrying suspicion in which he found himself. He answered, at ease now. "It's possible. My wife bought me a new silk dressing gown last Christmas."

"And how did Sue Palmer come in possession of it?"

Dan shrugged. "I haven't the slightest idea."

"Look," George said to the lieutenant. "You yourself gave us the answer in the information volunteered by the day maid. The doors were never locked. Sue helped herself, thinking nothing of it."

"And the safeties?"

"How the hell would I know," George said.

"I'm asking Dr. Gunther."

Dan shrugged noncommittally. "I didn't put them there."

The police officer looked rather dubious. Then speaking from the doorway, he thanked them for their time and added, "You may be subpoenaed. Please hold yourselves in readiness."

For moments each of them watched another. "I'm furious," Jenny said suddenly. "If Sue Palmer wanted to kill herself, why did she have to make it so ugly and so vicious. What kind of person leads the police to her friends?"

Only Larry wanted to defend her. "Sue was a splendid person who, in fear of becoming hopelessly regressed, ran from the terror of madness."

"She abused your friendship—yours and Dan's. She knew what a hospital is like—a small ingrown community—that secrecy is impossible."

"Look, Jenny," Dan said, reaching her side in easy strides, "for all her instability, Sue Palmer was not a corrupting person. She couldn't see where she was going. But this is the last we'll talk of her until we hear from the coroner's office."

Stubbornly determined, Jenny stayed angry.

Softly, on the balls of his feet, George walked out of the living room. As he went through the door, he said, "I'll fix food. It won't be ten minutes."

"Come along," said Betsy. "Our friend in the kitchen needs help." Larry pulled the door shut behind him.

Left alone with Jenny, Dan said, "To begin with, I love you. OK?"

"I like that for a beginning."

He was still kissing her eyes, her throat, when George brought them orange juice.

Although Jenny did not relish the prospect, she went around the hospital facilities with Dan as planned. On the way there, she kept him busy answering questions; he told her that, in the less disturbed wards, there was a camaraderie among the patients, but their talk was not about the important things.

"What about the doctors and nurses?" Jenny asked. "Do they gossip about them?"

Dan glanced at her with a grin. "Nothing strange about that. Doesn't everyone?"

"Don't be silly. You know what I mean."

"Actually, they do. Jenny. Sometimes, I am very much afraid that they know more about us than we do about them."

Jenny asked in mild surprise, "How do they get to know?"

"The grapevine," Dan said to Jenny very seriously.

Dan took her first to a small examining room that lay off the depressed ward. It had no window, just an examining table, two white enamel chairs, a metal wastebasket, and a standing medicine cabinet stuffed with supplies. "You see, we don't treat anything out of the ordinary here. There's a fairly respectable infirmary about a half a mile away."

"It's a pity this is so unfixed-looking."

"I know. But that's the way things are in a state hospital."

He watched her and saw the same sense of disdain that he felt flicker across her features. After a long pause he indicated one of the chairs. "Sit there, Jenny. I have to change a dressing. We won't be here long."

As they waited, Jenny had another look around. "Where do you wash your hands?"

"The nurse will bring a basin of bichloride."

"Wouldn't it be simpler to have a sink?"

A smile flickered across Dan's eyes.

"What—?" Jenny asked. She did not have to finish the sentence. Dan told her. "A self-inflicted wound, cut with a single-edged blade across the flexor surface at her left wrist. Fortunately, the radical artery was not severed, nor were the tendons injured."

"Oh, dear, why did she try suicide?"

"Depressed."

"I know. But what precipitated it?"

"Her husband. The sly bastard told her that she had to give him a divorce because, having developed a repulsion toward the marital state, he had to live his life his own way. This led her to believe that there was something the matter with him. After a talk with the family doctor, she was convinced that, unless she gave her husband his freedom, he'd definitely suffer a serious breakdown. She let him go."

"And that's all there is to it?" Jenny asked quickly.

"Not quite. The minute the divorce was final—and things seemed easier for her, by then—he married his secretary. They're honeymooning in Mexico."

"A damn shame she didn't cut his—ah—his wrist."

Dan grinned, thinking to himself, "Just what Nurse Romm said—only in plainer language."

A glance at his watch reminded Dan it was late. But as he started across the floor to telephone, a trim young nurse appeared. "Mrs. Romm sent me. She is on her way. The floor is quiet now."

"What happened?"

Guarded, the girl glanced in Jenny's direction.

When Dan saw her hesitation, he said, "I'd better introduce my wife." He smiled. "I'm sorry, Nurse, I don't know your name."

"I'm Claire Benson, Doctor."

As he introduced the girls, Dan said, "Now, what happened?"

It took Nurse Benson an appreciable time to recount the new episode of a free-for-all in the wards, and Dan, because of Jenny's curiosity, let her go on.

Then in a crackle of starch, Mrs. Romm and her charge walked in.

The tall elderly nurse went over to Jenny. "Doctor's picture of you doesn't capture your coloring at all."

Jenny smiled at this and returned the pressure of the older woman's hand. Behind her hovered a sad-looking woman in her forties, the lines etched in her face making her seem older. She avoided Jenny's not unsympathetic glance.

Dan called her Marie and, while soaking off the dressing with hydrogen peroxide, remarked, "You're pulling out of it. Good girl."

The patient dropped her eyes to the two-and-a-half-inch wound on her wrist. "It's infected, isn't it, Doctor?" It was Marie's first expression of interest.

Dan looked up with a smile. "Slightly." He went on speaking to her as he deftly removed the black silk sutures from the uninfected area with the forceps. He left the dry boric acid dressing in Mrs. Romm's capable hands and then led Jenny out into the corridor. "Remember," he said, "no handshaking."

Miss Graham was sitting at her station. Jenny was struck at once by her importance. With a smile, she said, "I'm pleased to meet you finally, Miss Graham." She remained there in silence as the head nurse looked at Dan and lowered her voice a little. "I'm awfully sorry about Dr. Sue. What in heaven's name impelled her to do a horrible thing like that?" Before he could say anything, Miss Graham excused herself to answer the telephone. And for a few seconds, he had a feeling of deliverance—until her startled but crisp "Oh, no!" brought him up sharp.

Jenny looked at Dan, who shrugged.

Miss Graham cradled the receiver and shifted her position slightly. "There's simply no end to it." After an interval, she added, "That was Pat in pathology. She's the gal who types out the autopsy reports. The forced feeding passed into the breathing passages rather than the esophagus. Dr. Day's patient."

Dan sighed heavily. When he saw the look in Jenny's eyes, he said, "It sometimes happens, Jenny. The tube may be inserted inexpertly."

"Dan, I hate to ask you . . . is the doctor responsible?"

"It's always the doctor's responsibility but not necessarily his fault, particularly with a catatonic patient. That makes it extra hard."

"My God. I don't know how you stand it."

Miss Graham looked at Dan, who said after a reflective pause, "Because someone has to keep on trying."

There was another pause, then Miss Graham got up, took a key from her large ring of keys, and unlocked the massive wooden door to the disturbed ward. Dan and Jenny went through.

"Don't be afraid," Dan said.

"Stay with me."

The ward nurse, an open sweater caped over her snow-white uniform, walked along beside them as Dan led Jenny among the persecuted, the paranoiac, the delusional, the mentally battered. She saw things she thought impossible, heard inhuman sounds, as she became aware of humanity's darker side. A syphilitic—her nose was missing—screamed out obscenities. A patient did a dance around her, singing out: "Drop dead. Drop dead." Jenny tried hard to give no sign of noticing. Then a wild-eyed girl of about eighteen ran up to them. "Did you do it to her, Doc?" She gave Dan a lecherous wink and, pulling up her skirts, screeched, "Look, no pants."

Jenny wanted to put her hands over her eyes and ears at the same time, to shut out a reality she had never before experienced. Soon a dark-haired attendant led the girl away. She went like a disappointed child. A jovial fat old woman, who had stabbed and killed her son, approached Jenny. "Be happy," she said to her. "Time will pass."

At this point Dan gave the nurse his nod. It was her signal to unlock the door. "Come see us again, Mrs. Gunther."

That's the last thing I will ever do, Jenny thought, but smiled. "Thank you. I'll try."

They made another stop at Miss Graham's desk en route to Dan's office, where they were able to have time alone to talk. Soon a phone call from Larry interrupted them. "My note catch up with you?"

"It did."

"It's official. Tell Jenny."

"OK."

"See you later."

Dan put the telephone receiver back on its cradle and turned to Jenny as she turned her eyes to him.

"That was about Sue, wasn't it?"

A grave-faced Dan answered. "Suicide. No inquest."

They sat in silence that was as long as it was troubled. There were too many thoughts linked to Sue. Dan was wondering: Will Jenny finally reveal what is in her mind? He knew there was more to be said—sometime. Meanwhile, he peered cautiously into his own feelings. Unwilling to deal harshly with himself or go too deep, he felt for the moment untouched. In astonishment, he thought, *Am I hardened? Dead is dead. She no longer exists.*

The silence ended as Jenny began thinking aloud. "To the casual observer, she had everything."

Dan listened attentively to Jenny talk about Sue. She paused for a time and then continued. "What did she really want, Dan? What was so far beyond her reach that it could lead to her death?"

Dan stared into Jenny's eyes, noting their deep watchfulness. "She longed to be a woman."

Jenny's look softened as she put out a hand. Dan took it and caressed it gently. Impulsively he spoke out. "There's one thing I'll always be grateful for—the autopsy report. An inquest would have been a sticky thing for us."

Trembling with rage, Jenny said, "I don't want to know why she was wearing your robe."

His heart jumped. "No mystery, Jenny. Obviously she borrowed it."

"You've an answer for everything, haven't you, Dan?"

Helplessly he shook his head. After a brief interval, he said, "There is something I'd like to know."

Immediately, Jenny's eyes were guarded. Her voice anything but friendly, Jenny said, "Go on."

Dan realized for the first time that her restraint matched his own. His thoughts swung away from Sue. "Let's turn the conversation toward us."

"What about us?"

"Do we get a house here in town? Or would you prefer to stay at Dad's place in Manhattan. In which case, I'll come in as often as I can."

Dan had been watching her attentively. He saw that he had chosen the worst possible moment to bring up the subject. "OK," said he, "we'll leave it for another time."

Giving him a grateful glance, Jenny accepted the cigarette he offered. With a surge of friendliness, she said, "You never did finish telling me about the men's ward. Do they suffer as much as the women patients? Are they as apathetic, or are they as enmeshed in themselves?"

Dan plunged into an account of the apparent normalcy of many men patients, but the dangers of their actions if they once turned hostile. Jenny rested her chin on her palm and regarded Dan thoughtfully. "Tell me more. Where do they come from? Why are they like they are?"

"Do you really want to dwell on this? Or are you making talk to pass the time?" Dan asked, giving her a lingering glance.

"I want to know," Jenny answered briefly, her knees touching his as she waited for him to continue.

"I don't know, Jenny. It's hard to say. Many come from tainted heredity. In the predisposed individual the point of stress can be of a minor nature. Many are the victims of environmental forces—terribly low standards of living, racial discrimination, vice, no steady jobs—all the pathological aspects of our present-day society."

Jenny had another question she wanted answered. "Will many leave this place and places like it?"

Dan was hurt by what he had to say. "No. The number of mentally ill we return to the communities is no higher than the number who came out of the eighteenth-century snake pits."

"Then what you have here isn't the answer."

"I never thought it was."

"Are you wasting your time?"

"God, no! I'm learning. I really believe I am."

After a glance at her wristwatch, Jenny said, "Almost four. Quitting time."

"OK. I'll call George from here and then we'll go."

"Dan," Jenny asked. "Won't George be leaving now that. . . ?" She paused to frame the rest of her sentence.

Dan, however, knew well enough, and he was as unwilling as she to mention Sue again. He spoke quickly. "George is on sort of a vacation until he opens his office. As far as I know, he plans to spend time in observation here and his apartment in the city until he visits a teammate in Chicago."

Jenny moved for the door and waited. Dan's call pleased her because she heard him tell George that they were headed for a hot bath and a nap. "He'll come to supper with us," Dan told her, opening the door. "Afterward, he'll take you to a movie. That's just what you need, sweetheart. It'll take your mind off things." He took her by the shoulders and kissed her.

"Won't you be coming with us?"

Looking into Jenny's face, Dan grinned. "The trouble with movies is that the love scenes are make-believe. No, I have to finish a long report on some preliminary cases."

Jenny's dark eyes flashed, but she made no comment. Dan locked the door as they left. It was still miserably cold, without any sun, but bedeviled by snow, as they walked back to the doctors' quarters.

Jenny kicked off her shoes and, sitting high against both pillows, started to arrange her dress.

"Take it off," Dan said, unbuttoning his shirt.

Jenny stood up and began to take off all her clothes. Dan whistled softly and smiled. He loved watching her undress. His smile slowly faded as she wrapped herself in a robe of red wool. She made herself elaborately comfortable on the bed. Watching, Dan laughed aloud. "Kitten."

To his surprise, Jenny narrowed her eyes at him. "There is no resemblance between me and a cat. If there were, this would not be question and answer time. I'd simply delight in feel and smell."

Slightly taken aback by this pronouncement, Dan said, "Jenny baby. What in hell are you talking about?" Their eyes met for a long moment, and he said, "Begin again."

Regarding him levelly, Jenny asked, "Dan, something strange happened my first day here—to do with George."

"Go on, Jenny."

Jenny smoothed back her thick mass of hair. "It's really very strange," she said with emotion. "I always thought that because Grandma and Mama are so adoring and caring, I never really missed anything by not having a father."

Dan put his arm around her and drew her to him.

"I was wrong. When you sent George for me the first day here, the shrieking wind very nearly blew me off my feet. So George picked me up and carried me. And the most incredible thing—I had a flash memory.

"We were in Boston. It was the end of December and the weather was awful. I remember the fierce wind whirling white snow. I remember sinking into a drift and my father lifting me high. I pushed my face against his, and I gathered such safety, such warmth from his strength. I remember his wonderful fresh smell."

Jenny lifted her eyes to Dan, imploring him to understand. "When George, with the same powerful arms, lifted me and I put my face close to his ear, I felt gloriously safe just as I'd felt with Papa." After a brief unbroken silence, Jenny resumed. "He even looks like Papa—the same size, the same reddish-blond hair, the same hazel-gray eyes."

Dan pulled her closer and stroked her gently. "Jenny, my love, the reason you made this transference is because of your childhood. Your father lost his life before your Oedipal investment in him was fully resolved. George is only a transference symbol. He represents a pertinent male figure. Don't be perturbed by it. You are safe with him."

"But, Dan, I am not a child."

"To some extent you are."

"For goodness sake, Dan. You sound as if I were your patient."

Dan grinned. "I'll put it in writing that you're not."

With a thoughtful gaze, Jenny said, "Don't joke, Dan. I'm serious. I'm certain George is attracted to me—maybe excessively."

Dan glanced down at her, his face now thoughtful. "I want you to under-stand," he said. "George plays the field. But, with you, because you are already married—a taboo object—he can savor enchantment without the commitment physical passion carries—without intrusion. Completely free."

Jenny's eyes filled with astonishment. "Do you really believe that?"

"I do."

"All right, Dan. I hope you're right, but I do not think George trusts himself as much as you trust him."

"Jenny, baby, leave the worrying to me. George is restrained by a strong streak of Puritanism. He is also a romanticist. You represent to him his idealized goddess."

"Mythology is full of stories about goddesses who erupted like volcanoes when encircled by a Titan of great size and incredible strength."

Dan's answer was quick and sure. "The goddess of whom we speak is wife to Saturn. Until his sons ascend to his throne, he rules supreme."

Even Jenny was stunned by Dan's colossal conceit. When she did not immediately reply, he decided to finish undressing. Within seconds he stepped back into bed. Jenny touched his face. He took her hand and guided it downward as he kissed her with passion.

Toward the end of an hour.

DAN: "With one of my young clinic patients, I'm experiment-ing with a doll representing the therapist. I'm learning in effigy the child's feelings toward me."

A: "Good idea. Sounds productive."

DAN: "I want to review the literature. I asked Jenny for a free weekend, and she arranged it with George. They're taking the boys to Annapolis tomorrow and to the Washington Zoo on Sun-day."

A: "What are your feelings about these excursions?"

DAN: "Pleased. I'd hate to cheat them out of fun because I'm doing what I like doing."

A: "You are indeed smug about the relationship between your wife and your friend."

DAN (with a laugh): "I have absolute confidence, that's all."

A: "Your self-assurance is noteworthy."

Dan swore.

The analyst sat back in his chair.

DAN: "Maybe George doesn't worry me because I feel triumphant over my father."

A: "That remains to be seen."

Dan found himself thinking: *What in hell does he mean? Does he think I'm overconfident—I don't care a damn if he does. Does he think I am deceiving myself?* Dan had the feeling that his analyst was too relaxed and that his associations meant nothing to the man. With a conscious effort to impress his anger upon the analyst, Dan said, "Your attitude is negative, completely negative."

A. remains silent.

DAN: "You've the idea I'm cocky. Arrogant."

A: "Possibly. I think we should consider if this is a reaction formation to your feeling of inferiority—a striving to be big, to be powerful like Father."

DAN: "That sounds clever, Doctor. And I suppose it is. But I know what you're trying to do. You're throwing stones, trying to cut me down."

A: "If you fear that, then you are reliving an old feeling."

DAN: "I don't *fear*."

A. (ignoring the steel in Dan's voice): "Then the prevailing feelings must be those of competitiveness and the desire to prevail over another male."

DAN: "Adlerian theory. I'm familiar with it, Doctor. Mondays and Thursays, we listened. Always at his overcrowded flat. Ten dollars an hour and we never forgot to leave something for the maid."

A: "We do not dispute some of Adler's contributions." The analyst laid down his pad with the fountain pen. He had some teaching to do. "Remember, you are a candidate in training. I am calling your attention to my interpretation, which was similar to Adler's thinking, because it is on an ego level; we are dealing with social relationships. Later, on a much deeper level, we'll deal with id material—the instincts and the bodily representations of those instincts."

' Dan stayed silent for a few moments and then said, "I shall always trust George because I know that in some areas he represents an idealized extension of myself—which, in a sense, gives me the embodiment of my wished-for brother."

A: "We shall speak of this again."

The next three days were exasperating for Jenny. There was not much to read, and there was no one to talk to. Dan and Larry were busy, and, the holidays over, Betsy went on with her job and her analysis. It gave her little time to entertain Jenny. Even the few rubbers of bridge (which Dan avoided), played between twelve and two in the afternoon, gave her no pleasure because the conversation always got around to Sue. And what was said became increasingly unkind. Nor did they spare Warren Ryan. For the first time in her life, she found herself looking over her shoulder in expectation whenever she walked alone. Jenny took to staying in the room for long hours, writing letters as if they were a running diary, and calling Tascha.

During one prolonged telephone conversation, she suddenly realized that there was something she had given little thought to. She said to Tascha, "It has just occurred to me that we had better put the phones back into their cradles and leave them there. Abe must be infuriated with us."

There was a moment's silence. Then Tascha's voice came back with a chuckle. "I've been trying to convince Abe I need a phone all of my own." Tascha waited a second. "Jenny, before I hang up, I have a suggestion. What's to prevent you from spending the rest of your stay in the city? From what you've just said, it's obvious to me that you'll be seeing Dan no less here than there." After a second Tascha said, "Well, what's your answer?"

"I can't, Tascha. Dan puts in so many hours, it's incredible. I don't want to cut in on the little time he has to relax by dragging him into town every night."

"He'll get used to it. Some men commute every day of their lives."

"No, Tascha. I'd have a terrible sense of unease about it."

"Well, then, for goodness sake, get on the twelve twenty-five and get here for a late lunch. I'll take a taxi and meet you at Penn Station."

The phone clicked dead without giving Jenny the chance to decline.

Dan was hard to track down, but the operator finally located him in the pathology laboratory, discussing a biopsy on one of his patients.

He said to the operator, "I'll take the call here."

Without a moment's hesitation, Dan said, "You do that, Jenny. Take the car and leave it at the station. I'll pick it up later."

"But you have the keys."

Dan very nearly said, "There's a spare in the drawer of the night table." But fortunately he remembered in time her dislike of driving. "That's right, Jenny. I forgot. I'll see that you get a lift."

"Thank you, darling. I'll call you and let you know what train to meet. Early, so that we can have dinner together."

"No, sweetheart, I'll pick you up at Tascha's. Expect me around seven."

By the time Jenny reached the arranged meeting place, Tascha, all dressed up, was standing with her back to Jenny, her face to a good-looking, cigarette-smoking stranger. Finally Tascha turned her head slowly and looked at Jenny. The man stared and he kept on staring. He said incredulously, "Well—hèllo!" He added, "You will have a bite with us, won't you?"

Jenny found Tascha watching. She felt something. A hint? A plea? A warning? She stayed uncomfortably silent. Suddenly a new thought came to her. Tascha did not know him either. "No, thank you," she said. "I'm afraid we can't." Jenny felt the reluctance with which Tascha accepted this. Then she said pointedly, "It's kind of you, but we'll be with our husbands by then."

The word "husbands" caught his attention. "That's always the way. Meet a pretty girl and she's bound to have a husband."

Unabashed, Tascha said, "Anyway, it was nice visiting with you."

"Well"—the man hesitated—"well—" He was fumbling for something appropriate to say.

Jenny moved closer to Tascha. "We really must go." Tascha agreed.

The man nodded his head. "Well, maybe another time."

The girls began to move away.

He grinned and walked on.

They took a taxi and told the driver they'd get off at Fifth Avenue and Fifty-ninth Street. On the ride uptown Tascha said, "Wasn't he dreamy?"

"I didn't find him exactly irresistible."

Clearly intended as scoffing, Tascha said, "Listen to Queen Victoria."

"But surely, Tascha, you could see the man was stupid?"

Torn between her extravagant admiration for Jenny and her frustration, Tascha said, "That's a quick judgment. Tell me why he's stupid. Because he had the good taste to find us attractive?"

"Because he did not possess expertise in extricating himself from an awkward situation."

Tascha remained quiet a long time, wondering if a girl had to be a born lady to know that.

At the Plaza, where they decided to eat, they ran into the wives of two analysts—acquaintances of the Brotmans, who at once surmised that she was with her well-to-do friend from California. They immediately arranged for a table for four. They spent at least an hour longer than they intended over an amicable lunch, which left Jenny with less time for some feverish present shopping. Afterward, having to choose between a very crowded bus and a fairly long walk, Jenny persuaded a grumbling Tascha to agree to the latter.

"You'd think," said Tascha, "with things as they are, you could find a taxi in this town—even in the rush hour."

Turning her head from the icy wind, Jenny said, "New Yorkers don't walk enough."

"It's exhausting."

Jenny's face broke into a laugh.

They reached the Brotman apartment chilled through and went into the bedroom, the only room in the house that was private. Tascha's part-time housekeeper did not allow visiting in her kitchen. The room looked both cluttered and disarranged. Newspapers and magazines on the floor. A huge open box of sweets on the dresser. Tascha's ideas about managing a home were utterly lax. Now and again she went around picking up things she had flung down. But, on the whole, she could hardly care less. One of the truly genuine pleasures she had was that, a few times a week, a cleaning woman came in.

The girls sat, side by side, a long time, talking and occasionally eating a piece of candy.

"You know," said Tascha. "In a way, we're both in the same boat. Dan, at least, is sexy."

Tascha's remark did not fit in with any part of their previous conversation. Jenny looked at her with uncomprehending eyes.

Tascha saw her perplexity and said quickly, "Abe is so busy politicizing, it's like living alone. You know. The old story. Ambitious husband; lonely wife."

"Tell me, Tascha. Is it because you're restless that you spoke to that strange man at the station?"

For a brief second Tascha considered taking Jenny into her confidence: *Restless and empty and hungry.* But now that Jenny was here, she did not want Jenny's pity. "Of course not," she scoffed. "He came up and started talking to me. I really didn't care because I knew you'd be along."

Jenny thought: *My poor Tascha. Such despair in your bluff.*

On Friday morning George arrived from the city.

Jenny gave a start on hearing his voice. She unlocked the door. "George!" She smiled at him. "Come in." And she was thinking: *I am so glad to see you I could throw myself into your arms.*

George took in the hair falling below her shoulders and the soft mouth. He laid his huge hand gently on her shoulder. "Shall we go downstairs?"

"I practically freeze in that drafty lounge. Let's wait for Dan here. He ought to be back by noon." Jenny seated herself in one of the chairs and invited George to make himself at home. For George the next hour passed all too pleasantly. Relaxed, he found himself telling her all sorts of personal anecdotes, revealing more of himself than he had done for a long time. Then Jenny asked, "Will you tell me about Maggie?"

"Yes, Jenny, but not now because—" George paused in thought: *How very odd. Of all the girls and all the women I have encountered, Jenny is the one in whom I see the qualities that made Maggie the person she was. The one with whom I feel the same sense of belonging.* He raised his glance to Jenny, found, under the long lashes, her eyes on him and knew she was pondering his last words. "When there is more time," he said, "I want to make you see her warm and alive. She was the only mother I ever knew."

Jenny nodded. There was a long comfortable pause.

"What are you thinking about?"

"On the one hand, Jenny, I am hoping against hope that I'll be able to take you to Chicago and then onto California. I want to look around out there. On the other, I don't see how it is possible for you to leave. These past months were hell for Dan, you know. He was about ready to climb the walls."

Now it was Jenny who sat lost in contemplation, her forthright way of thinking was becoming confused. She was on her way to wisdom and was already far wiser than she was given credit for. That Dan loved her was certain. She had absolute trust in that. Her disquiet was strictly something else. Husbands remain human. It was George who disturbed her now. Every movement of his body told her of the thumping in his heart. Yet his concern for Dan was no hollow pretense.

"You're trying to decide, aren't you?"

Jenny could not answer right away. She got up and went to the fruit bowl. She took an apple and brought him one. George proceeded to eat it. "I am leaving next week," Jenny said. "I must. I hardly see Dan during the day. I didn't see him last night at all. I stayed locked in here alone because Betsy was too tired for company. I miss Paul dreadfully. I was unable to sleep because I was scared to death."

"For God's sake, Jenny. You had only to pick up the phone."

An amused expression came over Jenny's face. "I doubt that you are afraid to sleep alone."

George gazed at her for a long moment, his heart in his eyes. Then he leaned back in his chair, passed his hand over his face, and did not speak.

All at once Jenny sprang to her feet. Her skirt swirling, her eyes alight, she said, "I hear Dan."

George knew he was forgotten.

Saturday was much warmer. The rain fell steadily. Jenny stared out of the car window, and as Dan rounded a slushy curve, she leaned toward him, her hand on his arm. "I'm glad you decided you'd take your own car."

Dan glanced sideways at her.

"I'm sick of people. We're hardly ever alone."

Dan frowned. "Don't you want to drive in tomorrow to see Tascha and Abe? Because if we're not going, I'd better switch Sundays."

Jenny looked up quickly. "Of course, I want to see them. Especially the baby." Her voice changed. "I wish we had Paul. It'd be fun to take him along to meet their Annie."

"I have an idea," Dan answered. "Let's send for him."

Tears stinging her eyes, Jenny withdrew, and Dan, concentrating on driving, never realized it. "We'll be home in about twenty minutes. With you here, it *is* home."

The Residence Hall seemed totally empty. They climbed the stairs and went into Dan's room. Dan put his arms around her waist and leaned forward to kiss her. "Let's go to bed, Jenny."

"I want a bath," Jenny pulled herself free. "Then I want to talk."

"So do I." Dan took off his coat, jacket, loosened his tie, and stepped lightly away. He paused at the door. "I'll call Tascha in the morning and tell her to expect us."

Jenny heard her bath running. She kicked off her shoes, unfastened her dress and let it fall. In the bathroom, still for her filled with the memory of Sue, she stepped into the filled tub visualizing Dan letting himself sink into water across the hall.

The moment Dan was in bed, his tousled head resting comfortably beside hers, Jenny said, without preamble, though she had been planning a soft approach for days, "I'm going home, Dan."

Disappointed and somewhat taken aback, Dan recognized that he had been expecting this from the beginning; nevertheless, he was not giving up without a struggle. "Jenny," he said softly as he moved closer, "that's unthinkable."

Dan was not exactly cheered by her answer. "I suppose deserting Paul is thinkable. Well, I have the old-fashioned idea that my mother should not be doing *my* job."

Dan thought: *It may be that she thinks I'm not doing my job. Maybe I should be with them. But I know Paul is in good hands.* As he inwardly accepted her point of view, his verbal skirmish took on a deeper note. "Keep in mind, Jenny, that right now I belong here. And you belong with me. When we've made suitable arrangements—"

Jenny interrupted with: "I thought you'd say that."

Dan was greatly annoyed. "That's no answer."

Jenny eyed him. "That's not what you said last June."

"I'm not holding myself blameless. But if all you're doing is getting back at me, let's stop that. It's childish."

Sitting quietly, Jenny delayed over her answer. "At first," she said, giving Dan a long honest look, "I wanted only to hurt you. And, at first, I put all the blame on you. Maybe, a little, I still do." Jenny paused and Dan sensed she was about to say something important. Their eyes met and held. "The months I have been alone have taught me to look at things differently. I came to realize you needed this separation. It was hard for you to accept the oneness of marriage—but you are as chained to me as I am to you. Together we form a whole.

"And something else became completely clear to me. I shall never again—no matter how much pressure—go along with anything I know to be wrong."

Dan was deeply touched by this old-fashioned strength in Jenny, and his gaze, which became loving and understanding, rested on her hair lying loosely against the white of the pillow. He leaned forward and whispered quietly, "Delay your return."

Jenny made a quick movement and her arms were around his neck pulling him to her. "Oh, Dan, I hate this place. I stay awake listening for sounds."

His fingers caressing gently, he said, "Yes, Jenny, I know."

"And after I leave, I'll never, never walk into a hospital of this sort again."

It was bleak and windy as Lewis Miller met Jenny's train. He was completely unprepared to see George too, for whom the trip to Chicago was as much pleasure as it was duty. Savagely he glared at George, who had to smile at this display of possessiveness toward Jenny. Jenny immediately did what she could to ease the situation. Showing no sign that she'd noticed Lewis' unblinking fury, she said, embracing him, "Dear, dear Lewis," and murmured how good it was to see him. Then she put her hand on Lewis' arm, silently urging him to invite George along.

The force of his jealousy staggered Lewis, but he made himself turn away from Jenny and extend a hand that trembled. "Consider my home your home."

George held the hand firmly, gazed at Lewis, and nodded. "Thank you, I accept." Grinning to himself, he picked up the remaining suitcases and followed the chauffeur as they set off for the Duesenberg.

They made their way through Chicago ankle-deep in slush and eventually got to a handsome building with a distinctive Georgian air, where a uniformed doorman admitted them and whisked them through to a penthouse apartment in Lewis' private elevator. Jenny gasped involuntarily as she walked into the living room with its two Chinese screens, the long sideboard, and the lovely Postimpressionist paintings. A molded archway led into a spacious dining room simply furnished with an oval table, seating twenty, and covered with antique mirrors. Next they went into the kitchen—all white cedar and alive with some gay Portuguese pottery—then through the sitting area off the master bedroom to a balcony poised above the lake. It was like a backdrop for a sumptuous stage set, and yet it all reflected Lewis' faultless taste and flair for truly fine things. When they entered Jenny's room with its fireplace and view, she quickly recognized the four or five rare figures from his Chinese art collection. Then her eyes fell on a carefully wrapped package lying on the rose silk spread. Lewis watched her with a quizzical smile as she unwrapped it and found the exquisite snuffboxes.

"Why, Lewis, what a marvelous surprise! They must be priceless—and I love their shape" was her delighted reaction. She realized quickly that his delight lay in spoiling her.

"You are getting too old for dolls, my dear."

Lewis stood up as Jenny came into his library later that afternoon, pleased with what he saw. Against the dark paneling and the rows of rare, morocco-bound volumes, she looked as pretty as a picture and yet had that special elegance he so rarely found in other women.

Jenny came forward. "Oh, Lewis, all those lovely presents. And the beautiful flowers in my room. Thank you."

"There's no need to thank me, Jenny. You know that."

Jenny smiled at him, her genuine affection quite apparent.

"Jenny, I have a request—one I do not cherish. As you may know, my old friend, Leo Butler, of whom I spoke this afternoon, was Sue Palmer's analyst. He drove in from Detroit a good hour early—especially because he wants a chance for a private talk with you. Can you manage that?"

She nodded her head.

"He's a major prophet in the psychiatric field—someone I would rank with Amos, Hosea, and Isaiah. *And* a very dear friend. Allow yourself twenty minutes, my dear. That'll give Leo time to freshen up. And cook is prepared to delay dinner, if necessary."

Jenny—elegantly dressed in a sheer wool gown, high-necked and long-sleeved, that fell to the floor in classic folds—stepped into the library to join Leo Butler. Then Lewis gave orders that no one was to disturb them.

"Hello, Dr. Butler," she said as she held out her hand to the big, shambling man with the beetle brows over steady, gray eyes.

"Jenny," he said and pressed her hand. Because she was inwardly tense, she held herself very still. *Strange,* thought Leo, *how little emotion her face shows. The eyes are alive, yet there is undeniable strength in the mouth's lines. Nor does her body betray her, as she sits with her legs tucked under her on the ottoman.* He felt it was time to get to the point. "Shall we begin? Why did Sue Palmer die?"

"I should think, Doctor, that you'd know better than anyone."

"Maybe I do. But the precipitating cause, Jenny?"

Jenny shrugged.

"I implore you, Jenny. Tell me what you learned of Sue Palmer. What happened between you? She was kind to you, yet you let her leave that diner without so much as a nod or a good-bye. Why?"

"She wrote you!"

"It must have been while she was unpacking your pretty things. She called. 'Such lovely colors,' she said, 'so delicately female.' There was outrage in her voice. 'Jenny hates me. And she has not one speck of proof that Dan and I indulged in sexual intimacies.' "

"That's a big lie," Jenny said, concealing her pain. "Why would she think that?"

"Did you fight with Dan, or take him to task in any way, because their professional relationship quickly ripened into a friendship?"

"Fight with him! That would have been stupid—turned nothing into something."

"You're angry, still angry. Why?"

Jenny inclined her head, unsure how to react.

Gazing somberly at Jenny, he said, "Give me one reason."

"All right. I quote, 'And she has not one speck of proof—.' That's a nice thing to say! The implication is: Maybe they *did* indulge in sexual intimacies. She did the same damn thing to me in the diner. The minute Dan stood between us, she let go with a series of small signs barely perceptible. I did not like her then and I liked her far less later. Betsy Stein, who is no busybody scandalmonger, told me—among other things—that it was not unusual for Sue to go out of her way to befriend the wives of men she hoped to use in some way."

"Jenny—I put this to you bluntly—do you trust your husband?"

"That's a curious question."

"Yes, but you don't resent it. Why? Because you have been exposed to some psychoanalytic training. You know there is nothing casual about this conversation." Leo got a cigarette and snapped his lighter.

Jenny gave a little sigh. "I don't know. I am more inclined to think I just don't trust men—generally."

Leo's mind came back to Sue. "I feel bitter about Sue's suicide and I feel guilty, too," he said with a profound sadness. "I ask myself: 'What did I do wrong? What could I have done that I did not do?' "

"Please don't blame yourself."

"I was blind, Jenny. Lewis knew. I did not, and I was her analyst. Like Larry Stein, I had greater confidence than I had the right to have."

Jenny wished to help. "I don't think you failed her. Besides, how could you know—you were no longer her doctor."

"My dear Jenny," he said, "it is the fine judgment of a clinician to determine when to be truly alarmed and take action. The telephone was the cue. She was in extreme distress." Leo rose carefully and put his hand out to Jenny. Because of Lewis, he said, "You and Dan are already dear to me. Sue fell into darkness because her mother was cruel to her. I don't want her to pull you down. Unburden yourself, Jenny, and be finished with it."

"I tried to hurt her. I decided I had the right. Actually, it was she herself who showed me how." Jenny was speaking softly, so softly that Leo had to strain to hear her. Then, while he still held her hand, Jenny sobbed without tears. "She wanted my understanding, my sympathy. I refused. I walked out and left her alone. I'll never forgive myself for that."

Leo waited for her to finish. Then he took her into his arms and held her. When he saw she was again calm, he led out, saying, "Everything is going to be all right, Jenny. Take my word for it."

Lewis, meanwhile, sat in the quiet comfort of his study, which was handsomely furnished in fine period pieces. His eye took in the handcarving of each piece, the objects carefully arranged among his rare books, and the French candlesticks on their stands. While he waited for Jenny, he took up a pen to write to Dan.

January 21, 1933

DEAR DAN,

I'll be frank. I have regretfully come to the opinion that you are out of your mind. Consult a physician.

I see you, Dan, and you are amused. Well, wipe the grin off your handsome face, because mixed with respect and protectiveness is Desire, even Lust. That six-foot-three, two-hundred-and-nineteen-pound footballer is playing a waiting game.

And since you are such a damn fool and Jenny is so trusting, I'd say patience is far smarter than passionate pursuit.

I fear for you because you persistently refuse to look your truth squarely in the face. That the blond Adonis is your soul brother is rank bunk—hokum—hogwash.

Let me do some plain speaking. You are reckless with Jenny, not because (as you tell yourself) you can rely on her, but because you are instinctively afraid that—without a rival, without contest —Jenny will lose some of her appeal. Do some thinking yourself before the filly bolts.

Sighing deeply, Lewis concluded the letter with, "I believe I hear Jenny. . . . Your unhappy friend, Lewis

On the day the three of them were to leave for San Francisco, he sent a telegram.

DEAR DAN,
MY FOREBODING INCREASES. THE MAN IS DEEPLY, HONESTLY, AND HOPELESSLY IN LOVE.
LEWIS

There came an immediate reply.

RIGHT! HOPELESSLY. CALM DOWN, MOTHER HEN. NO REASON FOR ALARM.
LOVE,
DAN

The dinner party broke up late, and after everyone had gone, Lewis gently drew Jenny into his study.

"Just for a few minutes," he promised. "I have something important to say to you. Have you any idea why Dan wanted George to come out here with you?"

"He wanted to make sure there was someone to take care of me, I think," said Jenny simply.

"And how do you feel about it?"

"I was glad to have George's company; he's become such a close friend. I like him a lot, you know."

"Oh, Jenny, yes. I see that very clearly." Then Lewis asked her many searching questions about her feelings, and it was obvious that the closeness between George and her disturbed him deeply. Finally he drew a breath and shifted his position. "Jenny, Jenny, can you really be so blind? It is not you I worry about—but Dan. He is in reality fooling himself. He has, it is true, complete faith in you and complete confidence in George, his friend. His reason, subconscious probably, for throwing you two together is to prove to himself and to George that you—an extraordinarily beautiful girl—will always cling to him.

"This is displacement, as Dan will discover in analysis. He is seeking the ultimate triumph, you see—he never had it over his father. Therefore, he wants it over a rival.

"Dan's analysis will not be for the relief of symptoms but for the dissection of character traits. The road to maturity is a jagged, rocky road."

Jenny shivered and gazed into the fire, listening to the clock's tick. "I see," she said, "although I'm not sure I really understand the dynamics."

"But you are an apt pupil, Jenny, my dear. And now it is time for bed."

Jenny slipped gratefully between the cool sheets in her bedroom with many thoughts on her mind. She turned over again what Leo Butler had spoken to her about earlier; and she realized perhaps intuitively Lewis' concern for Dan. Unable to sleep, she kept saying to herself, *Stop thinking.* Finally she relit her bedlamp and got up. With her robe on, her feet tucked into fur-lined slippers, she sat down and wrote to Dan.

January 22, 1933, 3:48 A.M.

MY DEAREST,

Your call, which came just as dinner was over—perfect timing—was such a wonderful surprise. I can't say that I'm sorry your room has become a gloomy monastic cell without me. It's good you miss me.

The dinner party was a great success. George's dinner partner, who graciously accepted a last-minute invitation, proved to be a poised woman with a charming smile. Her décolleté was quite daring and—all through dinner—George made no effort to keep his eyes from wandering. They left early—about eleven thirty. All in all, an evening you would have enjoyed—sumptuous food, a delightful assortment of amusing and interesting guests, and dazzling conversation.

Darling, I met Leo Butler. He's a wonderful man, someone I would implicitly trust, he's surprisingly gentle and soft-spoken for one of such size. At first those fierce brows do not impress, then one catches the steady eyes. I managed to learn that he is a devout Catholic. He is staying on as the third houseguest because he is participating in a symposium on suicide and homicide at Michael Reese.

I am sitting here looking at the paper, trying to put this delicately. Lewis and I had a long talk, darling, and he is not given to abstract ramblings. He said your reason for throwing George and me together is to prove something to yourself.

He used a strange phrase—he said you were "seeking the ultimate triumph," something you never had with your father. So you need it with a rival.

My dearest, I don't want to give up George's friendship, or even his companionship. But, more important, let's not hurt anyone. You understand these dynamics better than I do.

I love you. I miss you. The next six months will be endless.

All yours,
JENNY

"Christ Almighty!" came his answer. "Don't let Lewis upset you. You are my wife. George is my friend. Mother Hen doesn't know everything."

His next letter to Lewis determinedly made no mention of George but caused Lewis to exclaim, "Fantastic! Brilliant! He's onto something and he's quite right."

Lewis, I made an observation. One characteristic that runs true to form in many of my patients, regardless of the diagnosis, is the phenomenon of distance. At first I thought this to be something missing—the inability to establish channels of communication. Now I am beginning to look upon it as something positive. It's a real force that keeps the patient away from other people.

I have begun the study of the dynamics of distance, with a seventeen-year-old dementia praecox patient. What purpose does distance serve? What does it mean? Is distance fear? Fear of what —fear of being hurt? Or fear of hurting someone else? How do we break through distance?

I can't answer my own questions yet, but answer them I will. What are your thoughts on the riddle of distance? Anything in the literature you know of? Put that brain of yours to work. If you have some unformulated ideas, crystallize them. I'm convinced I am on the right track.

Yours,

Dan

For San Franciscans, San Francisco is a place apart. As the train approached the Bay area, George was awakened from a deep sleep by Jenny knocking lustily at his door. "Come. Be dazzled by the ugliness of the Oakland Mole."

George came to the door with a grin.

"I know breakfast won't be served until six thirty, but I was awake by five." Her eyes, more than her words, told him that she was brimming with anticipation to be home once more and see her child.

George touched her cheek. "Give me fifteen minutes."

Jenny seemed to know that he understood her feelings. She returned to her own room and gazed out of the window across the tracks to fields of green and distant hills.

It was not long after they emerged from the dining car that the train pulled into the station. Minutes later Jenny was held fast in her father-in-law's arms and was kissing him. When they started for home, George could see, by the way Andrew Gunther drove the car onto the ferryboat, from whom Dan had learned his skill at the wheel.

Jenny's mother met them at the door and, taking a long look at George, cried out, "Oh, no!" She almost fainted. Sara, holding Paul, was as surprised as Dorothy. She managed to say: "Jenny, darling."

Jenny held out her arms for Paul, as if she were about to receive the treasure from the high priestess. They all went into the living room, where, sinking down into a chair, Sara turned her beautiful face to George. "You are the living image of my son. The same build—the same coloring—the same hair and mouth. Even the bone structure is identical. Except for my own eyes, I would not have believed it possible."

Jenny had informed George that he strongly resembled her father. Nevertheless, he was confused now. On the one hand, he was enormously pleased and conscious of a feeling of belonging. On the other, faced with possible disapproval from Dan's father, he thought it might be better to go to a hotel. Andrew Gunther's inquiring eyes disturbed him. He looked to Jenny for guidance, but, though she sat close beside him, her face was averted, her eyes on her bubbling baby, and she seemed oblivious of all else around her.

But the matter was soon settled. The white-coated Chinese houseboy was called to take Dr. George's suitcases to his room; and George was persuaded to stay mainly because of Andrew Gunther's insistence. "Where I can keep an eye on him." It angered him that it was in his son's nature to entrust Jenny to another man. He was sorely tempted to telephone and give Dan a tongue-lashing. Instead, he wired.

SON, YOUR STRONG EGOTISM BORDERS ON INSANITY. YOU NEED HELP.

DAD

In hours he had his answer.

DAD, I HAVE HELP. I HAVE YOU. LOOK AFTER JENNY.

LOVE,

DAN

DEAR DAN,

Your old man won't let Jenny go anywhere unless it is with him. She won't go anywhere during the day without Paul. And since his favorite joy in life is passive motion through space, it's good I came equipped with a pair of stout walking shoes. I've been from the Embarcadero piers to the ocean. I've been up and down every crazy golden hill in town. Thank God for the flatness of Chinatown. At day's end I limp homeward. Jenny and your dad, walking strong, take turns with Paul. For me, it's home to dinner and hopefully—bed. For them, it's looking forward to evening when they both *really* come alive. And around midnight, Jenny gets hungry again.

Seriously, Pal, why didn't you tell me that your dad is sweet on Jenny's grandmother? Or didn't you know? Walking arm in arm, they're a compelling-looking couple. I can see Jenny at Sara's age with Sara's grace and Sara's charm. You lucky stiff, you're missing a hell of a lot in your drive for fame.

Your dad and I had a night on the town by ourselves. We walked down to Fisherman's Wharf, sat at a window table with a view of the Bay, watched the fog roll in, gorged ourselves on sour-dough bread and abalone steaks, and talked football. Then on to a few joints in the old Tenderloin. The clientele wasn't much, but the potted geraniums were beautiful.

I think, Dan, that your father is now reasonably satisfied that Jenny will not be taken from you. He has suggested, since we're going back together, that I give up my place and stay with him until I make my move. And while I'd like to, I wonder how you feel about it? Think about it. No hurry. I'll see you a week from Sunday. I expect I'll be wretchedly lonesome for the new women in my life. As for Paul—I'm hopelessly in love. He's very blasé about me, but he's nuts about your wife.

So long, Pal. I want to dash off a hurried note to Betsy.

Yours,
GEORGE

February 16, 1933

MY DARLING,

Dad and George have taken enormously to each other. Dad has offered to let him stay in his place, until he makes a final decision where to work. You know, it will be like having one more in the family. I really mean that. They leave tomorrow, then there will be weeks and weeks of waiting. I am not a patient waiter.

I am not sure who will be missed most. Dad, who invited himself to accompany George, or George, who has given Mama so much pleasure. He has been utterly wonderful to her—indeed to all of us.

Dan, my darling, I am sure. Tomorrow, I'll tell the family. I don't want Dad to leave without knowing. I hope the new baby is as lovely, as sweet, and as smart as Paul. I know I should go on and tell you all the things I feel, but for some reason I'm not in a letter-writing mood just now. Will you settle for:

I love you very much,
JENNY

For four weeks Dan was studying his patient almost daily. She had dementia praecox with the characteristic row of acne across the forehead and inappropriate emotional responses. Except for the fact that she now looked toward him, there had been scarcely a change. She remained the same crushed little spirit with the measured gait and the withdrawn look, who, if she answered at all, answered in monosyllables. Dan meditated on his observation. Plainly the girl put distance between them, and somehow—if she were to be helped—he had to find the way to bridge that, break the silence and establish the rapproachement necessary between patient and physician.

He sent for her parents.

The mother came into Dan's office hesitantly.

"Won't you sit down, please?" Dan said, rising.

She seated herself nervously in the chair and said, "I came alone. My husband can't leave the restaurant. But, believe me, Doctor, he is plenty worried about our daughter." As an afterthought, she added, "He's a good man."

"I'm sure he is." Dan paused. "Mrs. Taropian, you have answered the questions put to you by the social worker. I have been studying her report. I'm not satisfied."

Mrs. Taropian's eyes went to the papers on his desk. She was frightened. "Everything is true."

"I know it is," Dan said soothingly. "But it tells me nothing." Conscious of the woman's relief, he regarded her thoughtfully. "I want to help Maria get well. In order to do that, I must know everything—her entire history, starting with you. What brought you to the United States? How did you learn to speak English as well as you do? How did you, a newcomer, meet and marry Philip Taropian just two days after your arrival? Was Maria's birth planned? Or was it an accident? Were you resentful? Were you terribly overworked, helping in the restaurant, caring for two youngsters? Was America a big disappointment? Was Maria's being a girl a disappointment?"

A glimmer of understanding showed on the woman's face.

Dan smiled. "Between us, we'll have Maria out of here by June. But I need your help, too."

Sophia Taropian burst into sobs. Dan let her cry, and when she was calmer, he said, "Anything that comes into your head—say it. From time to time, if there's something special I want you to pursue, I'll interrupt. All right?"

Sophia Taropian told what she knew of her husband's history. "If he had not stowed away penniless for America, he would have been conscripted into the Turkish army. His own mother said, 'Better dead.' By the time he sent for a bride, he had his own little business."

Dan regarded her gravely.

"I was scared." She let it go at that and Dan did not probe.

"We both worked very hard. We lived on practically nothing to lay away money to buy a little house in a nice neighborhood. Jamaica we wanted. That was the most important to me."

"Were your expectations then realized?"

Her lips moved but no sound came.

Dan knew from the case history that by then, Maria was irritatingly neat, overly obedient, annoyingly prim, and that she made a fetish of hiding her mop of pretty, almost curly, sunny-colored hair. Himself disturbed at the woman's acute distress, he urged her to go on. "At what age did strangeness start to evidence itself? Do you know exactly when she began to blame her hair for causing all her trouble?"

Sweat broke out on Sophia Taropian's forehead and on her upper lip. She dropped her head.

"How old was she? Please try to remember."

"Oh, Doctor, I remember all right. Because my son was run over that afternoon. He was in Bellevue. I had to take Maria with me. But would she go? Of course not. She looked up at me with those big blue eyes and said, "You've got to brush my hair.""

Now Mrs. Taropian could hardly bear the violence of her feelings. It frightened her now as it had frightened her before. "I acted crazy, Doctor. I ran to my sewing box and grabbed my scissors. After all her beautiful hair was on the floor, she reached down and picked up one curl. Very quietly, she said, 'You know, Mama, I'm not pretty anymore.' I think my heart broke." Long moments passed. "Will it help, Doctor?"

Dan smiled gently at her. "Your peace of mind, yes. Maria—you may have—I don't know—given me the key with which to unlock her silence. Now," Dan said, rising, "suppose I drive you to the station. We'll have a cup of coffee along the way."

Dan turned in at the diner. He paused at the counter to talk to Pete, leaving Mrs. Taropian to take off her coat. When she was seated in a booth, he brought over two mugs of steaming hot coffee and two servings of green-apple pie. They ate in silence. When she had finished, she said, "That was good. Especially the coffee. I love good coffee."

He took the hint and got up. Pete refilled the mugs and Dan brought them back. He saw that Mrs. Taropian looked less white and less strained. And she looked across at him. "I'm all right now, Doctor. Thank you."

Dan nodded. "Mrs. Taropian, the social worker's report says that Maria developed delusions of persecution and ideas of reference when you and your husband insisted that she invite a boy to her class prom. In view of her extreme reaction, can you tell me anything beyond what you have already reported?"

Mrs. Taropian wiped her lips on her napkin. "You mean about the man coming to rape her or about the noises?"

"I was thinking more about your anxiety. Why—if she was not ready for dating—were you pushing her?"

The woman looked at him. "I thought it was the right thing to do."

"And your husband?"

"He thought what I thought. We both made a mistake."

With a slight smile Dan thanked her. "You've been very obliging, Mrs. Taropian. As for making a mistake—that goes for all of us."

There was a nod and a look of deep gratitude on her face in reply.

He said good-bye to Pete, and they walked out to the car. On the way back from the railroad station he stopped at the local five and dime and bought a couple of yards of blue silk ribbon. Back at the hospital he gave the ribbon to Maria, wondering if she liked it; if she wore it, then his efforts so far were not completely negative.

The next day Dan stopped by the ward to have a one-way chat with her. The next he spent time in the occupational therapy room where he helped her with her ashtray. The next he took her for a walk. On Saturday he went looking for her at the patients' dance. The nurses were somewhat surprised at the formality with which he requested a dance. She told him that she wanted to but that she did not know how. He spent a rather long time teaching her. And then she told him that the other patients were envious of her. Dan felt a slight shock of warning, but he chanced it. She was talking to him. And her blue eyes laughed up at him a little. At last, fragile as it was, an interchange between two individuals was taking place.

Monday morning at ten o'clock the charge nurse came in. "May I speak to you, Doctor?"

Dan looked at her and nodded.

"Maria is telling everyone on the ward that she is Mrs. Gunther. Her old delusions have been replaced by these new ones, Doctor. She seems very happy."

Dan saw that the charge nurse was obviously not happy.

"Please bring her in and stand by."

A new, animated Maria came through the door. Slender legs peeked out beneath the freshly pressed grayish-brown hospital sack she wore as a dress. Her hair was combed and ribboned. And she carried herself well. Dan sat back, taking careful notice of her skin; her forehead was clear and healthy-looking. "You look very nice," he said politely.

"Naturally," Maria replied gravely, walking to him. "As your wife, I should look nice. The others expect it of me."

"Maybe you had better sit down, Maria."

She took her chair and held up her left hand, inspecting it. "It's beautiful. Don't you agree?" A length of blue ribbon was fastened on her third finger, wedding-band fashion.

Dan lifted his gaze from her finger. Carefully, in a friendly voice, he explained: "You grew up sure you were unloved, unwanted, and unimportant. That made you watchful and suspicious of people. The idea came to you that you were different from other girls. That frightened you. You did good work in school because you wanted to hide, to keep yourself safe. But your parents wanted you to have friends, to go out, even to find yourself a boyfriend. This was too painful. You became more frightened. Something else happened. You became angry. When your fright and your anger were more than your parents could handle, they brought you here.

"As your doctor, I made you feel that you are not alone, and for the most understandable reason you developed a fantasy about me."

Maria looked at him in disbelief. "Why are you making a fool of yourself with lies like that?"

"Maria, because your father—"

She jumped up angrily. "Don't mention him to me. He never did pay any attention to me."

"That is true. And because I did pay attention to you, I became important."

Maria was trembling, and her face had gone white. "But I'm also important to you."

"Of course you are. All my patients are important to me."

Maria caught at Dan's sleeve. "Don't say that. I can't bear it. You know you're in love with me."

"I'm your doctor, Maria. I want you well."

"There's nothing wrong with me. Take me home." Her eyes had an odd stare in them.

Dan waved a finger, summoning the nurse. "Maria, you go with Miss Jones. We'll talk again."

Shouting crazily, "He's my husband," Maria fought the nurse, who held her tight to her bosom. Sobbing, Maria tried to claw at the nurse's face. Two attendants advanced, and Dan watched them forcibly remove the slim crazed girl. The door closed behind them.

Dan shook his head unhappily. He reached into his drawer, brought out Maria's file, and recorded the interview. Then he called Larry.

"Well," Larry asked, "does this change everything?"

"I don't think so," Dan answered. He stayed at his desk thinking about his theory—the breaking of distance by the therapist. *Perhaps I should have been more cautious in my approach. Maybe it just doesn't work with psychotic patients.* Dan sighed. After a while he told them to bring in the next patient, a woman who called herself the Virgin Mary.

Back in his empty room, Dan picked up his telephone and said into the mouthpiece, "Operator, get me Doctor Miller, person to person. You have his number." He sat back and waited. Twenty minutes went by before it rang.

"Hello, Dan?"

"Yes, Lewis. How are you?"

"Scandalously lonesome."

"Me, too."

"What's the good word?"

When, at last, Dan finished his story of Maria, there was a long silence. And then Dan said, "Well?"

"First things first, Dan. Before I say one word about the patient, I want to talk about you. Whose needs were you meeting—yours or the girl's?"

"I want her well."

"Why? Because her eyes were an unexpected blue? Or to satisfy your own narcissism?"

"Oh, come on, Lewis. Almost everyone here takes the hopeless approach. What's wrong with wanting at least one happy ending?"

"Nothing unless—as in your case—a seduction went on. You found a dainty, delicate girl. You thought her manageable and yielding, and you tried to make her feel that you were indispensable to her. With her concrete thinking, that's not surprising. Her delusion gave you a shock, and abashed, you confronted it directly. That meant everything was gone for her and she blew."

In the pause that followed Dan realized what was passing through Lewis' mind. *He is wondering what effect his disclosures will have upon me.* Going over it all, Dan knew Lewis was right. He said, "Thank you, Lewis. You have made everything clear."

"Good!" Gently now Lewis asked, "Shall we talk about Maria?"

"I'm satisfied that I know what to do." After a moment he said, "I am going to start all over again. Next time I'll make no mistake. I'll get Maria well for Maria's sake."

Dan waited four days. He then visited Maria in the wet-pack room. Sedated, she was mummied peacefully in the sheets. She was friendly and affable. He sent her back to the ward. A week later he resumed the interviews.

The nurse led her in and left her. Maria turned her very blue eyes to Dan's face. "I don't exactly remember what happened. Are you angry with me?"

In an easy tone, with no trace of emphasis, Dan replied in the negative.

A little of her uneasiness went with his reply. "I am much better," Maria said eagerly, giving him a gift.

Dan did not commit the sin of accepting, thereby shifting the burden of seduction onto her. There was no immediate answer from him.

Maria's face flushed.

"What is it, Maria?" Dan asked.

Half lowering her eyes, she said, "Nothing."

"Are you bothered by something? Is there something you recollect?"

"Mother!" Maria said suddenly. Then conscious of Dan's scrutiny, she fell silent.

"Your brother came again today."

"I don't want ever to see him. It's all on his account that I hate my mother."

The talks went on day after day. Together and slowly, they relived Maria's past, with Dan guiding carefully and gently and watching intently for change, which did come. Maria moved from fear, to anger, and, finally, to acceptance.

By mid-June, Maria knew she was well. One day she presented herself to Dan on rounds. "Did you hear?" she said. "My brother has been helping me with geometry. And you know, Doctor, it isn't hard at all. It's fun." Almost immediately she ran off.

Dan neglected to send for her for two days. On the third he did send for her and he explained to her his reason.

After a while she said to him, "I have been thinking about it and I do understand. Because I could not distinguish between a father, who was always working to support his family, and a stranger, who was nonexistent. I therefore thought I did not exist in his life."

Dan was out of his chair with a smile, and he walked with her to the door. She had come to realize that she had set a distance between herself and her family, an unreal distance. She was ready to leave the hospital. On the following Monday Dan presented Maria's case at staff meeting, with the recommendation that she be discharged.

On Sunday both parents came and Dan had the feeling that the father was taking his first holiday. Maria took her leave, politely accepting Dan's good wishes with a shy smile. Maria's mother wept. And she thanked God that there were men like Dan.

Dan waved them off and then ran over to Larry's house to have lunch with them.

Larry gave him a curious glance. "What makes you so happy?"

Dan laughed. "Goddamn, I finally sent—not one but two—home. Let's celebrate."

Betsy said nothing.

Dan bent and kissed her. "We'll be seeing each other a lot."

She picked up her shoes.

Part III

DAN and Jenny were spending a few days in New York City that summer. Lewis Miller was pleased to go and it made logistics easier for Leo Butler to get there. The rest of the family were staying in the ocean-front house at Atlantic Beach, which Andrew Gunther rented for the summer for them. He was living there, too, thus spending the best part of the year near Sara.

At the knock on their hotel suite door, Dan said, "It's open. Please come in." He smiled at Leo as he embraced Lewis and then took Leo's extended hand. "I'd know you anywhere." Offering them chairs, he brought out drinks and cigarettes.

Sounding slighted, Lewis said, taking a chair, "I thought Jenny was with you."

"She went out to buy fruit. She'll be here soon."

Only seconds elapsed before Jenny walked in, looking young and fresh, her pregnancy almost hidden under a skillfully designed dress. She ran to Lewis. Dan and Leo, who stood up, watched her as she kissed him and said, "I'm sorry. I didn't mean to be late." Lewis acknowledged her apology with a smile. "I suppose, Jenny, you bought out the store."

Jenny laughed. "You'll have to help eat it all." She turned quickly to Leo. "Hello, I've been looking forward to this. Thank you for coming." And she kissed him, too.

"Jenny," he said, "it is so good to see you."

189

Jenny excused herself and made her way to the bedroom, intentionally leaving the connecting door slightly open.

"Dan," Leo said, "your Jenny is good with people."

Dan nodded. "I know it."

They accepted the drinks Dan made for them and sat down.

"Well," said Lewis, "you know why we're here."

"It's all settled, Lewis. I've made up my mind. I want to go to Baltimore."

"Everyone in the world wants Boston or Chicago, and you choose Baltimore. Why? Because of that footballer who went back to Chevy Chase?"

Dan grinned. "I thought you'd say that. Why don't you like Baltimore?"

"I don't have anything against it. Some of the dominant figures in American psychiatry are in the Baltimore-Washington area—Sullivan, Hill, Frieda Fromm-Reichmann. It's just that I half expected we'd be together."

"I know," Dan said, "and I'm sorry. But there'll be frequent visits."

Lewis Miller could have wept, he was so unhappy. But he displayed restraint for Dan's sake. "Sure, sure," he said, "of course there will."

Dan was grateful. And Leo understood.

"You realize this conference is going to be long," said Lewis. "Please ask Jenny to join us. I want her to hear our views."

Dan called to her.

"Yes, dear. In a few minutes." Her hair swept up, her shoulders bare, Jenny reentered the sitting room in something long and cool. She said, "I've ordered dinner. Does seven suit everyone?"

His legs astride the back of his chair, Dan said, "Perfect. Thanks."

Jenny took ice from the bowl and freshened their drinks. Then Lewis motioned her to the sofa and took his place by her side. "We were talking of Baltimore," he said to her. "Sheppard and Enoch Pratt should round out Dan's training nicely."

"I don't think Dan is thinking about Sheppard or Enoch Pratt, Lewis."

"What?" Lewis demanded sharply.

Leo Butler picked up a cheesestick and, nibbling with relish, half-smiled—Lewis Miller behaving like an overparticipating parent despite all his wisdom and all his experience.

Dan sipped his drink, then put it down. Another moment or two went by and then he said, "I know it's going to sound awful to you, but I'm going to Johns Hopkins to be with Adolph Meyer. My residency which includes—"

"My God, I can't stand it," Lewis cut in. "That little goat of a man, untrained in psychiatry, who asks himself stupid little questions and mumbles stupid little answers into his beard. Commonsense psychiatry: psychobiology. Baa!''

Dan grinned. ''Yes, that's the one.''

Leo smiled at him, unperturbed. ''You were saying?''

''I'll be teaching fourth-year medical students and supervising psychiatric interns at Johns Hopkins. My residence is split between outpatient psychiatry at Phipps and child psychiatry at Harriet Lane.''

''That seems sensible to me,'' Leo said and helped himself to more whiskey.

Lewis turned on him. ''You're wrong! Wrong! Dan belongs in an analytically oriented training center among the 'Chosen.' ''

Leo laughed. ''I am amazed at you as I so often am. Only last week you were demanding that Adolph Meyer be given his due.''

''So—I doled out a little praise in admitting the great contributions made by the old goat in changing psychiatry into a dynamic therapy. Is that a reason to hand over Dan?''

Leo lit a cigarette. While smoking, he looked at Dan with interest. ''Why did you commit yourself to Adolph Meyer?''

''I'm not committed to him. I *am* intrigued by his method, and I'd like to know more about his pluralistic concepts because I want to remain open to biological and physiological study, as well as psychological. I believe that—above all—as I move forward, my involvement must be without hampering and constricting controls. I am a physician first, interested in my fellow human beings. I don't want to be just a specialist interested only in specific cases.''

Leo reached out and put his hand on Dan's shoulder. ''Open-mindedness and a willingness to commit oneself. These are the concerns of a physician.''

Jenny silently prayed that Dan would continue to maintain his concern for his patients as human beings. She had no doubt about his technical skills. To her, people and their welfare were far more important than the mastery of objects.

Lewis was already reconciled, but because of his fierce protectiveness, he withheld full approval and, to compensate himself for Dan's independence, he quoted pointedly. ''As Freud taught, 'The antagonism of the son is deeply rooted in the unconscious.' You think your refusal to bow to a parental figure is manly, adult, and mature. It is defiance. You will be among the most difficult of candidates to analyze because you have already experienced some degree of success in your profession. You're already in the parental role, Dan, and this means you will be reluctant to regress to an infantile state. And because you are not suffering, because you have no anxiety or depression, you are going to resist all effort to disturb the inner balance.''

Dan answered good-naturedly. "I'll straighten that out on the couch."

He did. After a long time.

It was the first interview.

Assured and relaxed, Dr. Bernard Freitag, the analyst recommended to Dan, sat in his high-ceilinged study. Paneled in walnut, it was, except for the old-fashioned rolltop desk, furnished mostly in leather. He was watching Dan, who sat under a framed enlargement of a photograph of Freud. An interesting, handsome face, the analyst thought, as he took additional notes. Dan Gunther did not mind the scrutiny, nor did he find the silence worrisome. His whole attitude seemed to reflect that he was already experienced, particularly at listening.

"Moving among us in analytic circles, you have assembled some knowledge of technique," said his analyst. "You know that the couch, which is a convenient and protective device, also provides anonymity. You know that sometimes I shall address myself to the healthy portion of your ego and sometimes I shall address myself to the aberrated portion, which is the residual of the childhood conflict. My job is to uncover in you the deepest infantile springs of conflict.

"Another important thing. I may or I may not answer a question. If I do not, I'll have good reasons—one, I may not know the answer or I may want corroborating data. Two, I may want you to find the answer for yourself. Three, you may not be ready for the answer. Four, I may treat the question as a statement or as a form of free association. And so on.''

The analyst paused, not to collect his thoughts, but to allow Dan a little time. "Please pay strict attention. I am about to instruct you in the basic rule. No secrets. No censorship. I want all your thoughts, your memories, your fantasies, your dreams in complete candor. You are not to miss any pertinent person in your life, including me.

"My obligation to you is also total and I shall hold inviolate all that you entrust to me.''

Dan smiled slightly and waited for the inevitable question. "Do you agree?''

Dan answered: "I'll try.''

"No. That's not good enough. I want your unqualified commitment."

Dan sprang to his feet and took the couch. "All right, I promise."

The first weeks Dan spent pleasant hours. He recited a few nostalgic memories. He did not recall much. Really concentrating, he remembered only one scene way back. "I must have been two. I said to my nurse, 'Feed me.' "

Mostly, in repose, on his back, Dan, serene and talking quietly, told the analyst about Jenny. "My wife is a proud and lovely girl. She is a feminine girl, self-confident and ardent in desire. She has a strong need for tenderness. She makes me feel loved. She does make one demand. 'Love me exclusively and forever.' " Dan never mentioned his two little sons. He related no competitive relationship with his sister.

With the passage of months, Dan began to think each hour an eternity. The monotonous sameness of the room caused him to say once: "I implore you. Tell your wife or your servant to fetch you some greenery and fresh flowers. Let the outdoors enter this stuffy enclosure."

At the start of the sixth month, the analyst said, "Because you are in didactic analysis, I am taking part of this hour to discuss a matter of technique. From now on, we'll concentrate on id interpretations which will deal with your instinctive motivations. The lesson here is: In your dealings with patients, do not give interpretations on the level of deep infantile conflict too early.

"Remember. The analyst gives the push only when the patient is almost ready to see for himself."

The months went by and Dan yearned for the analysis to be done. His resistance evidenced itself in complete amnesia for certain periods of his childhood. He could remember nothing that resembled an Oedipal situation. The analyst knew. Repressed material wants to stay repressed. Once or twice Dan's mind took him into flashes of insight, but Dan did not want to disrupt his life nor did he want to give up the defenses that worked for him, so he continued to fight the unmasking of his unconscious. Mostly, Dan's resistance took the form of defiance.

The analyst constantly interpreted and reminded. The analyst said, "Louder." He asked, "When have you felt this way before? What does this remind you of?"

But Dan needed to be in complete control. He controlled his tears; he controlled his anger. He soft-pedaled issues. Mostly, he was silent.

One hour.
A: "You're being defiant again."
DAN: "I have no symptoms."
A: "All you want is an analytic union card. You don't want to be analyzed."

DAN (in a flash of anger): "You want to rob me of my independence. I'll have to put an end to all this by terminating this relationship of ours."

A: "If you need to be *this* defiant of me, then you are afraid of your own passivity."

DAN: I did not let my old man bugger me. I'll be damned if I submit to you."

A: "Are you still defending yourself against a castration anxiety?"

DAN: "Jesus Christ!"

A: "Are you?"

DAN: "You're trying to deball me just like my old man tried—as far back as I can remember, he tried. But I handled him."

A: "How?"

DAN: "I understood that bastard, so it was just a matter of compromise. I gave him an inch. The rest I made on my own."

A: "You mentioned buggering. Tell me. What comes to your mind?"

Dan turned his head and looked at the man in the chair. "I did not mean that I actually thought in terms of a sexual encounter with my father."

A: "The word 'bugger' came up directly from your unconscious. It probably means a feminine identification."

DAN (with irritation): "Are you suggesting that there is within me a component that wished to cope with my father as my mother coped with him—by submission?"

A: "The idea merits your consideration."

Dan said nothing in reply. His mind went back. At the hour's end the analyst said: "Go on thinking about the strong male—the father—and how he is subdued. Unburden yourself."

Dan nodded in silent answer. As soon as he got off the couch, he was assailed by disturbing thoughts. "Will my sons be exactly like me—always rejecting my best-aimed attempts to be father and friend? Will they greet their mother with happy welcome and me with black fear buried deep?" Partly from a need to be loved and partly from a sincere sense of duty as a parent, Dan made a silent vow. I won't overcomplicate their lives nor will I involve them in unfair competition—my strength against their weakness.

Jenny said, "No I want to wait for Dan."

"What happens if the New York train is late?"

Jenny shrugged her shoulders.

Andrew Gunther hurried over to the telephone in the summerhouse's dining room. He found the number and called. He gave the doctor the news about Jenny. He listened a moment, answered, and hung up. He was just closing the door when he heard a scream. In seconds he was at Jenny's side. White-faced, she was trying to calm her mother, who cried, "Listen to me. If your husband really wanted to be here, he scarcely would have waited until the very last minute. Why didn't he leave with George?"

Jenny looked at her father-in-law.

He nodded and said, "I am sorry, little Jenny."

"Where is George?"

"In the park with Paul. Shall I send for him?"

"No," Jenny said, as she put her hand in Andrew's. He glanced at his watch. "Please let me take you to the hospital."

Jenny shook her head. He saw that there were tears in her eyes. "I'm all right."

But when she tightened her hold and bit at his fingers, he turned to Sara and said, "Tell Clarence to get the car here. Hurry. Then put a call in for the doctor. We're on our way."

Just as they were all set to leave for the hospital, Dan walked in the door. Andrew Gunther said, "For Christ's sake—" Jenny just looked up at him and smiled. "I knew you'd come."

Dan kissed her and then she was in his arms, her hair falling over his shoulder. Together, they left for the hospital.

Their second son was born on September 30 at the New York Lying-In Hospital. Jenny told Dan to write in the name Eric on the birth certificate.

"All right. But will you tell me why?"

"Its the name of your mother's father."

"I know that."

Jenny took his hand. "Your father said, 'Not for me, Jenny. For Miriam. I can see her—her blue eyes looking right at me. I can almost hear her wishing Eric, her father, had a namesake.' "

Dan stared down into her face. He realized how much he loved her.

"Say it." She was looking up at him.

"I love you," he said and gathered her to him. After a while, he said, "I've got to go, Jenny." He eased himself out of the bed, turned slowly, and started toward the door. He laid a hand on the knob and turned. "How strange—Paul looks like my father and Eric looks like Paul." Then he went out.

*   *   *

It was a difficult fact for Jenny to accept. "Truly?" Much as George disliked saying it, he knew that Jenny had better hear it from him. "I know because I grew up here. In Baltimore, 'restricted' means no Jews."

Again Jenny was astonished. "At home," she murmured, "restricted differentiates residential from industrial or from commercial property."

"Listen, Jenny," George said, giving her another jolt, "even in California there are places where Jews are not welcome. Only Californians are quieter about it."

"Maybe. But there is no anti-Jewish or anti-Catholic feeling in San Francisco."

Jenny was mistaken in thinking her own city was completely free of prejudice, George knew. He remembered being told by a newspaper publisher with whom he was having dinner, "Our Jews are social only when seen in the company of social people in social places." George saw no reason to upset Jenny further. They had more important, more urgent tasks ahead of them these first few days in Baltimore. He drove past the hospital, where Dan had just started briefings. People hurried in and out of entrances and exits, and the traffic moved slowly, coming to a halt in front of red and pushing on at green.

"Do you want to go in and have a look around? See where Dan will be spending his days?"

"No, I have no curiosity about hospitals."

George returned to the hotel with her. They killed time in the coffee shop until Dan appeared. He had their mail. "Here," he said to Jenny and held out a letter from her mother. She took it and eagerly read about Paul. Then about Eric. "He is so beautiful with his silken skin and blond hair. And, for an infant, he is powerfully built."

"What does the letter say?"

Jenny smiled at George. "Eric looks like you."

"Now," said Dan, sitting back in his chair. "Can we get organized?"

George said, as he rose, "So long. I'll see you Saturday." He walked to Jenny's side. "If you need Dan and can't get hold of him, call me at the Chevy Chase number. There's always someone there."

Watching her, as she smilingly acknowledged George's considerateness, Dan said, "I heard of a house I think Jenny will like. I persuaded the real estate woman to see us this evening."

"Let me know," George said affably.

The meeting at the real estate office started in a friendly atmosphere. They exchanged pleasantries, and then Mrs. Bishop said, "I have three houses in mind for your consideration. To begin with: The neighborhoods are acceptable—actually, two of the houses are on the same side of the same street. I suggest we look at the smallest of the three first. It is more conveniently located to our best private day school, and the garden is less formal and far more cheerful. And I think the owners will be agreeable to the use of their household furnishings, providing, of course, a suitable guarantee is set aside on deposit in the event of damage."

The Gunthers looked at each other. Jenny let Dan do the talking. "I have been informed by a colleague that a house in Windsor Hills is listed with you. From what I hear, it's exactly what we want."

"You see, Mrs. Bishop," Jenny added with a smile, "our family will be visiting often, we hope, and we need at least three, and preferably four, extra bedrooms."

Mrs. Bishop's surprise was genuine. "Really, doctor, you don't want that house."

"What's wrong with it?"

"Er—nothing. It's a well-maintained house, well set back from the street, with a lovely garden and beautiful shade trees that are a blessing in the heat of summer." Mrs. Bishop saw that her prospective clients, this young couple from California, were mystified. Then, with deliberate candor, she went on. "I take it the person who suggested Windsor Hills is Jewish and rich."

Saddened, Jenny thought, *Oh, my God!*

Angered, though he gave no outward sign of it, Dan said, "As it happens, he is neither."

"Then, I must say, I am bewildered by his recommendation."

A glance passed between Dan and Jenny, and though Dan was well aware that Jenny wanted to leave, he obstinately prolonged the conversation. "I see you consider Windsor Hills out of the question. Why?"

Mrs. Bishop leaned forward in her chair. Her tone a conspiratorial one, she said, "Let me put it this way. Baltimore is only one-third white. Naturally, we have to protect ourselves."

"If I understand correctly, you are saying that you believe Jews are not white."

"Now, Doctor," Mrs. Bishop said, feeling suddenly cornered. "That is an exaggeration, and you are being stubbornly obtuse. You know exactly what I mean."

"Yes," said Dan with a sarcastic grin. "I'm afraid I do." Once outside in the car they sat soberly quiet for a time and then Dan said, "I'm sorry, Jenny, baby. I should have spared you that."

"That's all right, darling. I was prepared for it. George told me that very likely we'd run into it sooner or later."

Dan answered half angrily. "He should have prepared me for it," too."
Then he produced a map of the city and began to study it.

"Dan."

"Uh-huh?"

"That doctor who suggested Windsor Hills—do you suppose he knew?"

"Of course." Dan faced facts. A minute later he said, looking at his
watch, "How hungry are you?"

"I can wait. Why?"

"It's only seven ten. I bet we're barely fifteen or twenty minutes away
from Windsor Hills I heard about. Shall we give it a try?"

"Yes, please. I so want to be settled in, ready for the children by next
week." They drove off along one of the winding roads that radiate out
from central Baltimore. It was a short drive amid trees, with many a stretch
of luxuriously green grass.

After a third ring, a plump little lady with a winning smile opened the
door.

"I am Dr. Gunther." Dan smiled at her. "My wife, Jenny. Can you
spare us just a few minutes?"

"And I am Mrs. Silvers. Come in, please. Come in."

When they were seated in the living room on the green velvet sofa, Dan
wanted to talk at once about renting the house, but Mrs. Silvers said,
"Later. The evening is young. We'll talk. We'll get acquainted. Soon my
Bessie will be back. She'll prepare us a little something to eat." Mrs. Silvers then addressed herself to Jenny. "My Bessie is a preacher—Sister Bessie. She cooks kosher."

And Jenny said to her, "If there is a large orthodox community in Baltimore, then that's something I must learn to do."

"I suppose you come from far away."

Soon Jenny was telling Mrs. Silvers about San Francisco and about her
mother and her grandmother and about Paul and Eric. It was impossible
to resist Mrs. Silver's burgeoning and motherly interest. But when Jenny
mentioned Chevy Chase and Dr. Atlas and Dr. Stein, Dan felt she had
made a mistake, for now Mrs. Silvers began to question her with real zest.

All at once, the infectious rapport between Jenny and Mrs. Silvers was
shattered by the entrance of a small pixie-faced man with thin white whis-
kers. In a voice that sounded as if it erupted from a demon, he asked of
no one in particular, "What's going on?"

"Papa," Mrs. Silvers said, as Dan and Jenny both rose. "Meet Dr.
Gunther from Johns Hopkins and his wife, Jenny."

"A pleasure." His handshake was firm. He kept them standing and talking for a few minutes, and then he told them to sit down.

"In my judgment," Mr. Silvers said, "as long as the garden is not neglected, it's better to leave the place locked up. Besides, how would a young doctor afford a house like this?"

Mrs. Silvers turned on him. "For shame, Papa. How do your five sons-in-law afford Miami Beach and Palm Springs?"

Mr. Silvers laughed uproariously. "So my five daughters have a foolish father, and he makes a slight contribution."

Mrs. Silvers said to her husband again, "My Bessie will still have her home. My precious possessions will stay where they belong. And, God willing, in four or five years the Florida sun will heal my tired bones. I want to die in this house, where I raised my family."

It was settled.

"All right," said Mr. Silvers. "I'll have my lawyer draw up the papers."

Then Dan said aloud the question going through his mind. "The rent?"

This time Jenny answered. "The rent will be fair."

Mr. Silvers shook his head as he looked at Dan from his chair. "Some businesswoman! I don't envy us." Then he said to Dan, "Something else on your mind?"

"Repairs, aside from the normal wear and tear?"

Mr. Silvers smiled. "Don't worry about repairs. I'm in the business. We'll take care of all that."

"The biggest contractor in Maryland," Mrs. Silvers announced proudly. Then she said to Jenny, "I think you ought to see the house." And she invited Dan to join them. A walk through the garden ablaze with lighted torches ended the tour. They both liked the property, not because it was perfect, but there was an undeniable friendly atmosphere. Soon afterward, Sister Bessie called out from the kitchen, "Supper is ready." Mr. Silvers handed Dan a black skullcap. It was the first time that Dan had sat down to eat with his head covered. Before dessert Mr. Silvers excused himself. He returned carrying a gold-framed photograph of his five daughters.

With tea, which was served in tall thin glasses with lemon and lump sugar on the side, Mrs. Silvers said, "I suppose you want the house right away."

Jenny's look was answer enough.

An understanding smile appeared on Mrs. Silvers' face. "You want your babies."

"Yes, I do," Jenny said. "I can hardly wait."

"All right. Move in next Friday. Before sundown."

"Thank you," Jenny said, with a grateful smile.

Dan added his thanks, wondering how to tell Jenny he'd be away from Baltimore that day on a traveling clinic to the Eastern Shore with a psychologist and a social worker. Then the idea of telling George first occurred to him.

As they left, the final practical problem was solved.

"Maybe," Sister Bessie said, "I can find someone to help."

"Please don't worry yourself about it," Jenny replied. "I shall manage. Enjoy your vacation."

Dan grinned at her. "Let's walk before we drive back to the hotel."

They crossed the wide road and entered a park. In about ten minutes they turned onto a narrow path and walked along, under maple and elm trees clean of leaves, until they came to a small artificial lake. They sat down on a wooden bench, both watching the reflection of the gaslights on the water's surface and listening to the muted sounds of traffic some distance away.

"Dan, hold me."

Dan held her.

"Are you worried about something?"

"I don't know, Jenny."

"Do you have reservations about the house? Tell me the truth."

"Only about the rent."

"I don't get it, Dan," Jenny said truthfully. "I thought we settled the money issue in Vienna."

"So we did," Dan agreed, wondering just how much money his father was giving her. Then he put it out of his mind. "Let's go. It's a good house to grow into and the children will be happy in that space."

They drove back to the hotel, where Dan handed over the car to the doorman. In the lobby Dan stopped to buy the evening paper. He caught up with Jenny as she reached the desk to inquire about messages. As she expected, there was nothing, but while they waited for the elevator, the bell captain appeared beside Dan. He had a note and Dan recognized the familiar handwriting as belonging to George. Quizzically, he looked at Jenny and tore open the envelope. The message was brief. "If you succeeded in your house-hunt—as I hope you have—and would like help in moving, just call your unemployed pal, George."

Damn it, thought Dan, *it's almost as if he can mind read.*

When Dan climbed into bed, he was tired. He took Jenny into his arms to kiss her good night. But her hair was falling loose, her long-lashed eyes became deeper mirrors, and her white shoulders were bare. All his tiredness fell from him and Dan was grinning as he brought his mouth hungrily to hers. Clinging to him, she closed her eyes. Much later she whispered his name. Dan smiled to himself and placed a gentle kiss on her forehead, knowing that before he made love to her, he was too wound up to sleep, but that now he would sleep soundly.

Jenny stood aghast. "You mean," she said, "I'm to move in by myself, set up the nursery by myself, meet Sunday's train by myself. I just can't. How can. . . ."

"Stop there, Jenny."

"But, Dan, did you know this. . . . We told the Silvers we'd move in Friday. You can't leave me in the lurch just like that."

"It will be all right, Jenny. I've already made arrangements for George to. . . ."

Jenny cut in icily. "For George to take over at short notice, I suppose. I am ashamed, Dan Gunther. And so should you be!"

Dan shot her a look of incredulity.

"How can you leave me here, in completely new surroundings, leave me alone with two small babies? What do I say to my mother or grandmother when they ask 'Where's your husband?' "

"That shouldn't be difficult. Tell them the truth. Tell them George is delighted to help." Before he could go on, Jenny burst into a flood of tears, her shoulders shaking. More gently, more persuasively, he said, "Be reasonable, Jenny. This Eastern Shore clinic was mentioned even before I actually started work at the hospital. One can't afford to let personal affairs dictate one's professional life. And you know you can rely on George for every kind of help. He's promised to be with you through Monday. I plan to be home that evening around suppertime."

Jenny's reply came as a muffled snort. Dan recognized his foolish dilemma. He was a fool to give Jenny two babies, barely a year apart, before he was ready to take on—he caught himself thinking the word "marriage." That frightened him and he shuddered involuntarily. He knew he wanted Jenny, but he wanted her by herself and for himself until it was convenient to have a family.

Jenny saw that Dan was totally immersed now in his own thoughts. Something came into her mind and she decided it needed to be brought out into the open. "In all fairness, Dan," she said, "I am being unfair. You warned me that the training years would not be easy. And I insisted that I was prepared for them. Under protest you gave me two gorgeous children. *I* wanted them."

Suddenly she was in his arms, smiling warmly up at him. He kissed her hard. They discussed all the details and who was to fetch the babies. Before George appeared, she tidied up the bed so that the room would have a less intimate look.

Dressed in jeans, boots, and a tieless, short-sleeved dark shirt carelessly open at the neck, George found Jenny in clothing almost identical to his; only she wore sandals and her shirt was a flamboyant red.

George's eyes took Jenny in. "All set?"

"I think so."

"Want me to check?"

Jenny looked around the room. "No," she decided.

At this moment the door opened and a bellboy entered wheeling a luggage cart. George helped him load.

"Say," said the bellboy. "Didn't you used to play football?"

George grinned. "Some."

The house in Windsor Hills awaited them in perfect order—flowers tastefully arranged, velvet hangers in the closets, bureau drawers neatly lined. In the bathrooms the numerous towels were sparkling fresh, and in the medicine cabinets were all the little extras that make guests feel valued. And Mrs. Silvers, who took eating seriously, did not forget their stomachs. She made sure the doctor and his wife would dine well on smoked sturgeon and Sister Bessie's superb gefilte fish. As it turned out, she was not here to see her stand-in. However, between the time George said, "Whoever decorated this house knew his business," and the time they sat down to supper, they had spent hours carefully wrapping in tissue and then in newspapers Mrs. Silver's Lenox china, her long-stemmed glassware, her extra-fussy porcelain pieces. George heaved the barrels up to the attic for storage. Then they spent quite a lot of time unpacking Jenny's plainer tableware. By midafternoon, they tackled the nursery. Jenny watched with wide-eyed admiration the ease with which George assembled the cribs and all the things she needed. Even her emergency sleeping cot and her rocker had arrived, crated in sections.

Everything was in order when Jenny said, "Come see the room I readied for you."

"When did you manage?"

Jenny gazed back at him with a smile. "There wasn't much to do."

George looked around. The room was not large. It was carpeted. Comfortably furnished, it held one big chair, one that suited his size, and the footstool was covered with the same subdued fabric. The large window was open and it looked out over the back portion of the garden. George knew that indeed that could be the reason for Jenny's prudent choice. The master bedroom faced the street. And with him, too, that was a point in the room's favor. He wanted to hear no sounds of Dan's passion in the night.

"You like it?"

George nodded.

"Take a peek at your bathroom."

George's mind switched back to the package on the bed. He fixed his glance on it. "For me?"

Her dark eyes smiled at him. "From Dan and me with love."

George promptly opened it. Silk pajamas with a matching robe. The rest of the box bulged with ties, each with a Paris label, and with custom-made shirts. George unwrapped one and held it up—seventeen and a half neck, sleeves thirty-five and a half. Perfect.

"Surprised?"

George stood quite still. Then he moved. For an instant Jenny waited motionless, then suddenly her voice said, "I'll get dinner." George stood a moment more. Then he went into the bathroom, shed his clothes, and turned on the shower. The room was chilly; the shower ice cold.

They ate the soufflé Jenny had prepared and talked.

George was saying, "The big antebellum house was never home. Even after I began to sleep there, Maggie's place was where I belonged."

"Was it for your father?"

"No place was home for my father after my mother was gone."

More time passed in questions gently asked and answers gently spoken. When George was thinking it time for Jenny to get some rest, she surprised him with, "George, do you believe in God?"

"Not with reason, Jenny. With something more than reason—deeper, I don't know—maybe." And then George began to remember out loud. "Friday nights Maggie took me to temple. Saturday mornings, she had me somewhere with an old orthodox rabbi. He told me stories of wise and learned men, of holy men both pious and righteous. But I liked the stories of the fighters, the strong men. I had, even among my favorites, a few rogues and sinners. Every Sunday I was at mass earnestly seeking Jesus. Until I was thirteen years old, I went to Hebrew school three times a week. Maggie pressed me into a Bar Mitzvah—my father really didn't give a damn —and the temple was more than half-filled with Catholics from her parish, including priests in yarmulkes and a scattering of nuns. When the rabbi called upon me to come to the bema and read from the Torah, I became to Maggie the chosen among the chosen. She walked out of that temple on a golden cloud."

Jenny drew a deep sigh.

George took her glass and finished her wine. Presently he was standing with his hand out to her. After the few dishes were washed and dried, he accompanied her to the door of her bedroom. As they had done on the train out to California, they each said good night. George's voice was husky; Jenny turned away from him. He went down to the far end of the hall, then heard the telephone ring. He paused and turned. There was no more sound, yet he heard Dan's deep voice and Jenny, eager and warm, saying over and over: "Dan." George turned again and walked into his room. They did not see each other until nine the next morning, when George greeted her cheerfully the moment she opened the kitchen door and came toward him with a smile. "I smell coffee."

When Jenny was seated, George served an exceptionally good omelette, then he sat down opposite her.

"More coffee," George said, pouring it.

Jenny buttered his toast. "Dan phoned. They're at the State Teachers College in some place called Salisbury."

George nodded. "An industrial and shipping town of about 13,000. It's at the head of the Wicomico River."

"Dan's group is to hold a clinic today in the Department of Public Health."

Again George nodded. "The schools and the juvenile court send their cases there."

"Sunday they meet with teachers and probation officers. Monday morning they hold similar clinics in the surrounding towns. Apparently it's all very progressive; no one's sure of the results."

His glance caught Jenny's and they both smiled. Then he was listening to her plans for their day. "When we get back from Farmers' Market, I'll prepare a divine dinner to which you are invited to present yourself at seven o'clock."

"And after the candlelight dinner?"

"A movie?"

"No."

Jenny turned to him. "A concert?"

"One more guess."

Jenny said, a smile still clinging to her lips, "Dancing?"

George nodded. "Agreeable?"

Her smile widened. "Most."

Then George saw a sudden change, mostly in her eyes. They sat for seconds in silence, then Jenny took a deep, long breath and said, "I want this day to go quickly. Imagine—with the next dawn, I'll have my babies."

At the same time, Dan was sitting with two women at a small table in a restaurant in Salisbury. The psychologist was a brilliant woman. Of medium height and middle-aged, she had a gracious air and a clear voice. Her straight hair was becomingly cut, and her liking for English country clothes of a classic cut was evident. Her name was Lucy Rockford and her husband, Dr. Cleveland Rockford, was professor of anthropology at the

University of Maryland in Baltimore. They were a childless couple, passionately involved with public service and devoted to each other.

Marcia Steele, in her midtwenties, was a startling contrast to her older companion. She grew up in modest surroundings, the daughter of an impassioned supporter of an extreme right-wing group who roamed from one southern town to another, secretly scouting recruits. The mother supported the family by teaching American history in an all-white high school. Marcia was tall with a fairly well-formed body. She had pale eyes in a rather pretty but sexless face. Her expression was normally disapproving, which drew down the corners of her mouth. But now, with Dan, she was making a strong bid to be pleasant, even friendly.

"Do you know," she said, "I have a theory about relief. Our government is too generous nowadays. Most people are out of jobs because they're lazy. Why not be a sponger? Why be a dishwasher or a chambermaid, anything? I repeat—"

Dan cut her short. His eyes moved back to Lucy Rockford. "I'd like you to tell me more about the attitude of the authorities toward young offenders." After she talked for a time, expressing what Marcia considered radical views, Dan asked her about the dependency cases.

"Our foundlings, our orphans, our neglected children, are placed in temporary residences run by the social agencies until formal placements are made in approved foster homes as near as possible to the ethnic and racial backgrounds of the children. Our foster homes are good homes, well selected and well supervised."

"I understand the Jewish agencies take care of their own."

"That, of course, is true, Doctor. So do the Catholics."

Later, when their scrambled eggs and bacon came along with toasted English muffins, Marcia Steele again pursued the subject dear to her heart.

Dan looked at her, his eyes filled with astonishment. "Why are you a social worker?"

"Because my profession is desperately in need of loyal Americans."

Dan made a mental note to use her sparingly. He motioned the waitress. "Check, please."

Later, when Lucy briefed Dan on Marcia, his voice took on a stern tone. "Do we need her?"

"I think you'll find she does her job well."

Dan looked skeptical. "What about her attitudes?"

"She keeps them to herself while working."

"I think I'll have a talk with Miss Knieger."

It was evident to Lucy Rockford that the new doctor had a lot to learn. He seemed to have no idea how the therapeutic team of psychologist, social worker, and psychiatrist worked together, each complementing the other's discipline. Because she liked him, she decided to spare him a confrontation with the chief social worker in charge of all intake, and the liaison person with all other social agencies. Her answer to Dan was "Rebecca Knieger is a cool, detached professional, who gives detailed attention to her staff. She also gives them her support. Unless you have a strong charge to bring against one of her girls, she'll not take kindly to a complaint, thinking yours the typical doctor tendency to deprecate social workers." Lucy Rockford paused. "Another thing. I cannot overrate Rebecca's importance in the hospital hierarchy."

Dan pondered a moment, then said in a friendly voice, "Thank you."

Lucy got up and held out her hand. "Good-bye, Doctor."

Her hand in his, Dan said, "Will you have dinner with me tomorrow? I find that I enjoy your company."

"Why, yes, with pleasure, Doctor."

A smile came to Dan's eyes and a faint grin to his lips. "The name is Dan."

That pleased her.

A driving rain was drumming insistently down upon the roof. George woke, stiff, out of a doze. He looked at Jenny, fully dressed, in a fitful sleep on the sofa. He moved noiselessly to a window and looked out. It was pitch black. He went upstairs into the nursery. Both children were asleep. He carefully picked a blanket off the cot and carried it down. Again, moving very quietly, he covered Jenny. He stood a few moments looking at her, then went out into the kitchen and started a pot of coffee. Then he went into the downstairs medicine chest and swallowed a couple of aspirins. After a while they eased his headache. He tried the telephone. Still out of order, as it had been for the last three and a half hours. When the coffee was ready, he went back into the living room and sat down. It seemed impossible that anything might happen to Dan—not in a car, not in the ocean. He was invulnerable; he knew what life was about. George remembered all the good times they had together, all the things they planned to do. Never, in all of his fantasies about Jenny, did he want her to be his as a result of Dan's death. The thought terrified him and he closed his eyes.

A wild clap of thunder roused Jenny. Her eyes opened and she raised her head. "What time is it?"

George glanced at his wristwatch. "Nearly three."

"George, I'm frightened."

"I know, but you shouldn't be." He was suddenly beside her. "I mean it."

"Aren't you? The truth."

"Not in the least." He spoke very quietly, but his voice was firm. Holding her hand, he said, "Jenny, you haven't eaten anything."

She withdrew her hand. "I'm not hungry."

George rose to his feet. He was quickly back, with coffee on a tray. Sitting up, Jenny drank a little. George began to walk slowly back to his chair when they heard, above the roar of wind and rain, the sound of the front door close. Jenny sprang to her feet and ran. Hatless, Dan stood soaked against the door, his hair glued seallike to his forehead and cheeks.

"Dan!" Tears ran down her cheeks.

He kissed her, comforting her. Then he and George faced each other in silence. George smiled. "You gave us a very bad time."

Her eyes fixed steadily on Dan, Jenny asked, "Are you hungry?"

"I'm starved, but I'm too tired to eat. I left the car a couple of miles down the road—ran out of gas."

Jenny put her hands to Dan's face. "Get in bed, darling. I'll bring you something."

"No, Jenny, dear. I'll come down."

Dan stripped off his wet clothing, showered, and put on a dressing gown and slippers. He passed the nursery, saw the door slightly ajar, and pushed it open. By the light of a single shaded bulb that left the crib area almost dark, he could pick out the curly, darker head of his firstborn and then the tiny form of the baby, round and soft, with golden lashes. His pride in his sons, at home at last, swelled within him. Caressingly, he said in a whisper, "Hello." Then he went down to the kitchen where George and Jenny were setting out a hot breakfast at the counter. Dan was glad that George was there. They sat for a time talking.

It startled Dan to hear that his mother-in-law and Sara were already on their way back to California.

"When did they leave?"

"Sunday evening, last night. Straight from Atlantic Beach, in fact. They said to tell you they wish they could have waited."

"Did they go alone?"

George stole a glance at Jenny who, after an imperceptible instant, said, "Dad had to go to London. He left Sunday, too." Jenny knew that Dan was curious about George's plans, so she went on telling him that George refused to leave her and the children alone, especially after the storm began getting worse.

Dan looked at George. "You were evidently able to cancel your appointments."

"Sure." George did not elaborate. Then he suggested that Dan tell them his story.

"Not much to tell—incidentally, I began calling early this morning." George said, "The phone is still out."

Dan continued. "Sunday and most of today were wet days. The storm was getting ugly when we started for home, but it was on the ferry that we were really battered about. I thought we'd never dock. After we finally got to Baltimore, I had to drive the women home. With Lucy Rockford, I had to tramp through mud that was incredible." Dan stopped. "God—but I'm bushed!" He dragged himself out of his chair.

George turned to Jenny. "Go. I'll clear the table."

Jenny smiled her thanks and consulted the wall clock. Then she stood up and, facing Dan, said, "I'll give Eric his bottle and change his diaper. Paul's, too."

Dan nodded, took her into his arms, and kissed her lips. He went up to the bedroom, where he slept the sleep of exhaustion.

Winter, spring, and summer slipped by, and it was again fall. Temperatures were cooler and rooms were cozier, with the wood fires crackling. In a real sense Dan and Jenny found themselves part of the academic community of the half-northern city with the southern soul, anchored to Chesapeake Bay and within reach of some of the best hunt country in the East. Without ostentation they were welcomed in the drawing rooms of the distinguished and the fashionable. This was not at all strange. Apart from Dan's charm and expertise, and Jenny's style and beautiful manners, it was easily discerned, mainly because they did not push themselves forward, that the young Gunthers had their beginnings in refinement, a quality held in high premium by the residents of Baltimore. Jenny was pleased because she took pleasure in being elegantly entertained and in returning hospitality. But she knew how to do so and was equal to keeping it down to a sensible minimum. That pleased Dan. The social role suited him well and he thoroughly enjoyed it as long as it did not intrude upon or interfere with his interests, for in addition to his professional involvements, he relished his popularity with the medical students. Wednesday evenings were reserved for bull sessions in the Bier Stube in back of the Peabody Book Shop—a favorite gathering place where professor and students alike drank tankards of dark beer and consumed large pewter platters of German sausages. At least once a week, and often twice, Dan met George for long workouts together. After a steam bath and a massage, they went out for an early dinner of soft-shell crabs with white wine and finished off with chocolate mousse or crepe suzettes. Evenings such as these left Dan clearheaded for more hours of study. Jenny often found him alert and still contentedly at work at one in the morning. This rarely annoyed her because he came to her eagerly and with abundant energy.

"Isn't there any way to light a fire under them?" Dan demanded despairingly, eager to get started on his analysis.

Lewis Miller laughed tolerantly into the mouthpiece. "Maybe."

The call from the Washington-Baltimore Institute came soon after that. Dan was given two names and told to make his appointments in downtown Baltimore.

Leonard Calloway nodded across at Dan and invited him to sit opposite him. Remembering how he had been at his first interview, he was watching to see if possibly Dan was as nervous. It was amazing to Leonard Calloway, now a practicing analyst for seventeen years, and he found it hard to believe. He would have given his eyeteeth for a fraction of Dan's poise, the air of calm assurance. Finally he smiled at Dan, and Dan grinned back at him still very self-possessed.

"Tell me about yourself. When did you become interested in psychoanalysis?"

Talking in a low voice, his words distinct and simple, Dan gave a fast biographical sketch of himself. However, he could not help but feel a bit triumphant when he spoke of his friend, Lewis Miller, and a bit proud when he mentioned Jenny and the boys.

"Is there any reason why yours should be a therapeutic analysis?"

"I think not. Frankly, were it not necessary to fulfill the requirements, I'd not submit myself to psychoanalysis."

Leonard Calloway was again reminded of himself. He had not particularly been pleased with the idea of his psyche being dissected, but unlike Dan, he had kept that to himself. He realized now how much more honest and mature Dan's answer was. Still, as a dependable interviewer and a very conscientious member of the powerful "Education Committee," he went on asking pertinent questions. When Dan, in answer to his final inquiry, replied, "I have a fairly good tolerance for frustration," he concluded the interview reasonably convinced that Dan would do fine.

Several days later Dan kissed Jenny, who lay still cuddled up in sleep, shut the bedroom door softly behind him, and drove out amid a blaze of fall colors to Chestnut Lodge to be interviewed by Frieda Fromm-Reichmann. Still youthful and very lovely, she was then about forty-four years old. It was impossible to ignore the admiration in Dan's eyes. Frieda Fromm-Reichmann was touched, but her conduct remained faultlessly professional. After a pause she said, "Good morning, Daniel Gunther. Come sit down by me."

"Thanks," Dan said with a smile.

"I think," said Frieda, "I know quite a lot about you. I have spoken to our mutual friends. Now that I see you, I'm sure you deserve all they say about you. And Leonard Calloway shared his conclusions with me. It is indeed refreshing to find a candidate who is not just another neurotic needing therapy and then capitalizing upon that experience by becoming a psychoanalyst."

As though it were yesterday, Dan heard his mother's gentle voice. Conscious of Frieda Fromm-Reichmann's eyes, he thought she knew. How many times, he wondered, had men like himself responded to Frieda's (he thought of her already by her first name) quiet charm. Immediately Dan felt better in some way.

"I'll not conduct this interview in the usual manner. Why make you repeat what I already know?"

Something of Dan's relief showed in his face, and Frieda went on with a slow smile. "I am, however, required to at least make a pretense of preparing you for analysis. You have much to learn. Everyone does. Heaven knows I did and I still do." She looked at her watch. "Have you had breakfast?"

"I gulped down juice and coffee on the way."

"I invariably forget to eat, especially in the morning, but now, for some reason, I'm hungry."

This sudden prospect of eating with her, of prolonging his visit, pleased him enormously. "I'm glad you thought of food," he said, as though he were starving.

They walked down the corridor to the dining hall not talking. Only one table was still laid for breakfast and when the waitress came, Frieda ordered for both of them. After Dan helped himself to buttered toast and orange marmalade, Frieda said, "I'm sorry I have to talk at you while we eat, but I do have quite a lot to say."

"I know. But it's a privilege and I don't know how to thank you for it."

"I understand," Frieda Fromm-Reichmann said, laying down her spoon and reaching for the coffee pot.

Dan sat waiting.

"You realize, of course, that both Dr. Calloway and I shall say you are right—very right, indeed—and we shall recommend that you be taken on as a candidate-in-training. The full membership will approve our recommendation. They always go along with the Education Committee.''

Dan said nothing, for which Frieda Fromm-Reichmann gave silent thanks. It was always rather embarrassing and rather depressing to watch a candidate-to-be badly act his surprise or be overawed at his good fortune and terribly grateful.

''I think it seemly to tell you now that your total training cost, assuming that you run into no delaying snags, will cost as high as thirty-thousand dollars. That should include, aside from your analysis and supervisory sessions, all other instruction—lectures, seminars, and so on. Here at our Washington-Baltimore Institute you'll be receiving about three hundred and thirty classroom teaching hours per year. I might mention the figures vary. The highest of over one thousand hours—one thousand one hundred and twenty to be exact—goes to Columbia because they interlock clinical out-patient work with teaching.''

Frieda Fromm-Reichmann paused before pointing out to Dan the dangers of the older, smaller, patriarchal training group. ''We—students, teachers, analysts—meet one another constantly. How does one grasp what is real and what is fantasied. This, of course, revolves around the transference. Try, Dan, to keep reality and fantasy apart. Try to admire your teachers for their real learning, not because you are reminded of someone significant whom you once loved—still love.''

''I'll try'' was all he said.

Frieda Fromm-Reichmann gestured to the far side of the room. ''I think we've overstayed our welcome.''

Dan turned and beckoned to the waitress. As he did so, Frieda Fromm-Reichmann rose from her chair and asked, ''Have you any questions?''

Dan stood up. ''May we go back to your office?'' he asked.

''Yes,'' she answered in a low voice.

''You have time?''

''Some. And if I'm a little late for morning rounds, it doesn't matter.'' She smiled over her shoulder. ''You are about to ask me to become your training analyst.''

''That is my intent.''

At the moment her door closed and they were once more seated, Frieda Fromm-Reichmann's eyes went to Dan.

''My answer is no.''

Dan started forward. His mouth tightened. His eyes narrowed. ''Please. You've got to.''

Sensitive to his disappointment, Frieda Fromm-Reichmann recalled her talk with Lewis Miller.

"It'll save everyone a lot of time and trouble if you know that Dan must work through his conflict with a male therapist," he had said, his piercing eyes peering at her over thick glasses. "Were he to start with you, he'd never break away from Mama. As for the breaking-of-the-transference and the termination-of-analysis—" His pause significant, Lewis concluded with: "Matters better not commented upon for the moment."

She felt accused. "Does it occur to you that I may not be his first choice? Or that I have important matters and patients other than Dan Gunther to attend to?"

"Don't look so hurt, Frieda. I, too, am a prisoner of his charm." Lewis Miller chuckled. "And yours."

Turning her thoughts away from Lewis Miller and back to Dan, she said, "The only reason I am turning you down is because I feel you should have your analytic experience with a male therapist. Your conflict is with your father."

Dan knew then that Lewis Miller was responsible for her decision. For an instant he wished he could lay hands upon him. Skillfully he consoled himself: "Maybe it's better. If I satisfy one set of impulses, I'll be doing violence to another." Dan smiled to himself, knowing that in psychoanalysis when one speaks of conflict one is dealing with opposing forces.

Frieda Fromm-Reichmann broke in. "I'd like to see you with Bernard Freitag. We trained together both at Munich and at Berlin. I respect him highly; he is both extremely capable and well trained, especially qualified to deal with characterological problems. Call him in a few days. In the meantime I'll talk to him."

With a grin, Dan replied, "Most likely Mother Hen already has." At her expression, his grin widened.

Frieda Fromm-Reichmann laughed. "My—that is a good name for Lewis. I wish I'd thought of it. Still, he'll get a surprise when we meet next."

"He'll take no notice."

She laughed again, a young girl's laugh. "Very probably."

Slowly Dan got to his feet. Frieda Fromm-Reichmann went to the door with him. "I'd be pleased were you to come back to me for one of your controls."

Dan took a step nearer. "Thank you. Thank you very much for that."

Frieda looked up at him. "Pick a fresh case. By that, I mean a patient who has not been overinterviewed by other therapists."

"A good hysteric?"

"A good hysteric will do nicely," the lady analyst answered with a smile.

Dan lifted her hand to his lips, and without a good-bye, he was gone. Frieda Fromm-Reichmann lingered a moment in the doorway. She was thinking: *You are a charmer.*

Dan was officially welcomed into the Training Institute on Monday evening. Jenny's note was on Frieda Fromm-Reichmann's desk Tuesday morning. She went to the telephone and called Jenny. Their conversation was extremely cordial, and in a few moments lunch was arranged for the following weekend.

"George Atlas, our closest friend, will call for you. You'll enjoy him."

Sunday morning, when George arrived at her home, Frieda was at the door before he rang the bell. She asked laughingly, "Can you detect my anticipation? I am looking forward to meeting Jenny and the boys."

"Good," said George, and continued, "you won't be disappointed." He said nothing to her about the Brotmans. He had no doubt that they had arrived unexpectedly, saying, "Lay three more places at the table," because they knew she was spending the day, and Abe was determined, as was Tascha, to be seen as bosom friends by the great Frieda Fromm-Reichmann.

Less than an hour later, Frieda was in the kitchen talking to Tascha in easy camaraderie and watching with fascination while Jenny prepared lunch of fresh crab and salad. And George helped her. Abe sat in the study with Dan. The three children were running in and out of the garden and through the house, the boys laughing with healthy merriment. Even playing with the two she loved most, there was a grave politeness about Annie. Nothing escaped Frieda's eyes.

After dessert and coffee, Frieda put down her fork, leaned across the table to Jenny, and said, "Let the men entertain Tascha. I find I'd like a few moments with you alone."

Dan looked pleased. Tascha looked surprised. Abe looked annoyed, but only for a moment. He quickly composed his face. Jenny rose at once, and without excusing herself to the others, she led her guest out onto the patio.

"Shall we walk?"

"I'd like to," Frieda answered.

They walked for a time in silence, in the deep alleyway of trees, each glancing now and then at the other, and when their glances met, there was neither embarrassment nor discomfort.

"A funny thing," said Jenny, as they came to the park. "I feel as if I've known you all my life."

"That, my dear, is a charming thought."

They left the sidewalk and walked in the grass until they reached the deep clear-blue lake.

"There"—and Jenny pointed to it—"is my favorite bench."

"Let us make use of it," Frieda suggested quietly.

When they were seated, Jenny looked out upon the water and said, "Thank you very much, Frieda Fromm-Reichmann, for *not* taking Dan on as an analysand."

"A somber remark, young lady, and full of meaning. Explain yourself."

A hint of mischief lurking behind her eyes, Jenny answered. "If I said because then we couldn't socialize, you might not believe me."

"I might. We psychoanalysts are an arrogant lot, certain that socializing with us is enjoyed more than anything. Whose companionship is less hemmed in by bugaboo?"

"You're teasing me," Jenny said good-humoredly.

"Not entirely."

Looking straight ahead, her right hand suddenly clenched into a tight little fist, Jenny said, "I prefer to tell the truth. I'd be jealous."

Frieda Fromm-Reichmann greeted this affably. She had been confronted with this attitude, this passion before, and she understood that the situation was not an easy one for a wife to handle. A husband seeing another woman day after day for years, his admiration and respect for her growing, hurrying to her with each anxiety, taking from her each interpretation, each suggestion appreciatively, taking it as a gift—mother's life-giving gift, her breast.

However, in replying to Jenny, she kept in mind the qualities that made Freud great. Consequently, remaining quite impersonal and detached and with incredible lucidity, she spoke to Jenny of Dan's need to heal and to help, and of the aims he set for himself. Then she went on to say: "In order for Dan to fulfill his professional destiny, he must attempt to uncover his own unconscious childhood memories and trace back their formation in terms of his libidinal investment. He must do this by free association by lying on a couch for periods of fifty minutes five times a week.

"From what I can judge based upon my own impressions and upon what Lewis has confided, your Dan has no neurosis. His analyst will therefore, in the absence of a neurosis, work with the analysis of personality and certain characteristics such as: ambition, stubbornness, competitiveness, revolt. In other words—a character analysis.

"Now, Jenny, I wholeheartedly agree that Dan will probably be better off with a male analyst, one who will, as Freud did at times, use active therapy—biting criticism, if necessary. With Dan it will be necessary to talk about current questions of general interest on the level of a colleague, an equal—to take into consideration his brilliant and fertile mind.''

There was, in fact, little need for her to stress what Lewis had already dinned into Jenny's mind and she knew it, but Frieda, the physician, fully appreciated the unqualified value of fortification by repetition.

Frieda suddenly shivered and got up from the bench, and Jenny realized that, since they had come into the park, the sky had changed. The sun was no longer warm. "We had better hurry home," said Jenny, now aware of the rising wind.

"I haven't touched upon the transference."

"I know. And I know all about the transference. That is: with my head, I know. But the plain fact is I'd still be jealous. I don't want Dan investing the feelings he had for his mother in a woman therapist.'' Jenny moved a step nearer to Frieda, pushing back a wisp of blowing hair. "Funny, I don't mind how dependent he becomes upon a man. There is something I want you to know. Dan's father is a wonderful man who cherishes his family and doesn't want this distance between himself and Dan. Dan's hell-fire resentment is senseless; he really respects his father and loves him deeply.''

"The conflict will be unmasked and resolved in analysis," Frieda assured her.

Jenny looked down on the grass. "I hope so."

Frieda Fromm-Reichmann halted. "Stop worrying, Jenny. You were quick to perceive it."

Jenny looked up. She was smiling.

Frieda took Jenny's hand and gave it a little squeeze. "How do you feel about me in a supervisory role?''

"Fine. Dan's talking to you about a patient is very different from talking about himself, about his parents, about me.''

After minutes of silence Frieda said, "I'm not sure whether I have the right to ask—we hardly know each other." She expected some sort of polite response, but Jenny simply looked at her, raising astonishingly questioning eyebrows. It was brought home to Frieda that Jenny was careful and straight-thinking—far more than one ordinarily expected in a very attractive girl. She reflected and decided: *I may as well.* She regarded Jenny levelly and said, "I am curious about George Atlas. He seems so much a member of the family. Is he? It's plain to see he loves the boys and that they adore him, especially your blond Eric.''

The idea of discussing George with Frieda worried her—not because Jenny felt defensive. The absolute reverse was true. But Frieda was a psychoanalyst and there was perhaps a risk in revealing too little or too much. It would be both interesting and enlightening to examine their relationship with George on a depth level with a trained observer—an oracle —free of prejudgment and personal bias. Jenny spoke her thoughts aloud, looking directly at the older woman.

Frieda replied. "We cannot pursue it now because it's windier and darker and it looks like rain." She started to walk faster, as rain fell in huge drops, then torrents.

"Do you like him?"

Frieda nodded. "Very much." She extended her hand.

A little breathlessly they ran into the house and up the stairs, Tascha following. "We didn't expect you'd wander off so far from the house that you'd come back soaked."

"It wasn't raining when we left the park," Jenny said. "We got caught in a cloudburst."

Aware of her anger, Frieda said, "I'm sorry, Tascha. I'm afraid it's my fault. You see, in our work, we listen so much that when we get the chance to talk, we—"

"I know that excuse," Tascha interrupted. "I hear it all the time."

Taking off her dress, Jenny stood, a slim, pleasing figure in her damp slip. "Stop that, Tascha. You know perfectly well you're being rude."

Tascha turned abruptly to Frieda. "Come on. I'll towel your hair dry." Her glance went to Jenny. "What did you talk about?"

"Nothing much."

The rest of the day stayed gray and wet. The end of their Indian summer. No one minded. Shutters closed against the wind, they sat around the fire—Frieda in Dan's velvet dressing gown—having tea and sandwiches, talking and laughing. It was not long before Abe led the conversation back to psychiatry.

"One thing that puzzles me," said Frieda, directing her remarks to him, "is why you and your fellow militants made so major an effort to establish and maintain a third institute? My information is that, on the whole, the facilities in New York were adequate, and didactic instruction excellent, turning out expert and sophisticated psychoanalysts."

That was too much for Abe. "Come on, Frieda," he shouted, "you know the Old Guard. They've so identified with the Deity that they consider themselves all-powerful, all-wise, all-knowing—the Creators of all thought. Sadly, they're not all-merciful. We younger men didn't stand a chance. They made it impossible for us. They chastised us with castration—the penalty for challenging the Father."

Jenny glanced at Frieda. So did the others. She was smiling. There was

something in the quality of that smile that made Dan awfully sorry for Abe.
"I go along with Abe."

"I should hope so," chimed in Tascha.

Frieda's eyes were on Dan. She was waiting for him to go on. "I don't
know much about it," he said, "except that the American Psychoanalytic
Society went along with it. They set the standards."

Abe resented Frieda. She was too superior, too sure of her worth, too
arrogant. He felt she was dedicated to cutting men down to size. And, he
had—the second she smiled—detected the derision. Abe's eyes seldom
deceived him. His hurt was intense and he began hungering for the pleasure
it would give him to get even. Meanwhile he decided he wanted to know
a great deal more about the famous Frieda. As he became convinced he'd
find something to use against her, his inner excitement grew. Outwardly,
he seemed to have recovered much of his equilibrium.

Sister Bessie came in then and cleared away the plates. "Annie won't
eat her vegetables. And she won't finish her milk. She wants candy." It
was interesting to Frieda that only Jenny got up and went out to the children.
Tascha remained seated and was saying to Abe, "Considering the weather,
I think it's a mistake not to stay over. You can get an early morning train
and still get to your office on time."

Dan said hospitably, "There's no question of anyone leaving tonight."
He was looking at Frieda. "When's your first appointment?"

"Nineish. But, please—"

Dan was grinning at her now. "No problem. No, none at all."

Almost immediately, George followed Jenny. Tascha looked at Frieda
with a smile on her face and told her, "I used to try to help, but Sister
Bessie had terrible things to say about the mess I make in her kitchen."

Everything ready to her satisfaction—the dinner, the dining-room table,
the children in bed—Jenny returned, splendidly arrayed in a peach silk jersey housecoat. George made his entrance moments later. As he walked
across the room, Tascha moved over and made room for him on the sofa.
Frieda saw, at once, that it was no accident that in sitting down he missed
brushing against Jenny by a mere inch, or less. No more than that. There
was a lot more that Frieda Fromm-Reichmann understood. Though she knew
very little about the early life of the Brotmans, she sensed that Abe was
an angry man—a controlled hater. That Tascha had warmth in her and was
capable of deep friendship. That Jenny was an intensely private person;
and that the supermasculine, solid George had suffered some sort of parental
neglect. The one who fascinated her was Lewis Miller's beloved protégé.
She did not question Lewis' faith in his professional future, but Dan disappointed her, too. Perhaps "surprised" was a better word. Why must

he—what drives him to subtly flirt? To feel sure of his own sex appeal? To stave off a feeling of submasculinity, maybe? Surely, he must know how attractive he is.

"Well?" said Jenny. "What did we interrupt?"

In the silence her question seemed to come with dramatic suddenness.

"An argument. Abe was saying—"

"Tascha, let me explain what I was saying."

"I merely intended—"

"Yes," Abe replied, "but that's when you misrepresent my thoughts."

"You flatter yourself, my friend," Dan said with his usual composure. "As I recall, you were quoting Freud's thoughts." He looked then at Jenny and George and said to them, "We were discussing penis envy in girls—that the knowledge that they are creatures without that prized organ leaves them feeling castrated and inferior. Frieda raised some objections, which Abe did not find convincing."

A definite look of derision came into George's face.

With a certain amount of curiosity, Frieda said, "I dare say, Jenny, that Freud's theory of penis envy is not to your liking."

"I don't think it's necessary for me to like it or dislike it. For my own part, I don't feel at a severe disadvantage. Nor do I feel punished because I lack a protuberance of flesh. As far back as I can remember, mine were pure feminine fantasies. To do well at school. To enter into marriage. To enter into motherhood."

"Ah!" Abe interrupted. " 'To enter into.' Perhaps, to penetrate?"

Jenny met Abe's eyes. "That's not my association." Then she turned away and again directed her remarks to Frieda. "I think Professor Freud belittled, ignored, and bypassed the role of women in our society, seeing us as essentially weak, available, and passive. That's a negative view and I object to it. I see femininity as something very positive. I am a woman—I am proud of it. And I believe I can do as much in my way as Dan can in his."

Dan laughed. To Frieda, his laugh said, *You don't need a penis, sweet child. You share mine.*

For the moment, at odds with Dan, Frieda applauded Jenny's views.

"What the devil do you mean agreeing with her?" Abe demanded. "You're a Freudian analyst."

"So I am," Frieda said, comfortably. "I am convinced that one day women will learn to demand that all fields of endeavor, all human experiences, be open to them. And they will succeed."

Dan got up and began walking up and down. He came to a stop in front of Frieda and, searching her face, said, "Come back to the nuclear family.

The Russians are now taking a completely different view of child rearing.''

Dan's reaction impressed Frieda far more than he could possibly have calculated, had he calculated. She would have concurred completely with Lewis Miller's vigorous assertion that never had he met a more innovative mind. When seconds later, Dan again asked her to talk, she said, "Of course, I have never been to the Soviet Union, but all I read leads me to believe that children cared for in nurseries, in kindergartens, in all sorts of child-care centers are not as well off as those children who stay with the mother.''

His face taking on an excited, absorbed look, Dan said, "That's exactly what I think. Multiple mothering, in addition to mother—yes. Instead of—No! Freud knew this. In stressing interpersonal relationships, Harry Stack Sullivan is saying this. And I think the Russians will eventually learn it again and reconstitute the nuclear family.''

Abe felt left out. Feeling left out is an awful thing. That was why Jenny, when she realized, stood up and said, "I hope you're hungry. Dinner is about ready.''

"Just a minute, Jenny. Let me—''

"No, Dan. You go upstairs and redistribute the children. They're all in our bed.''

Dan groaned without conviction. "Not again.''

"I know"—Jenny laughed—"it's a terrible way to keep them quiet.''

So Dan went off.

When George was at her side, Frieda stood up. A sudden merry look in her eyes, she said, "And how do you treat your neurotic patients, Doctor?''

His voice teasing, his reply came quickly. "I operate.''

In constant and immediate contact with some of the central figures—the great men and women—in the psychoanalytic movement, Dan's insights grew. In his own analysis, which he started the year before, he was discovering character structure; he was following the work of colleagues, and no matter what he read or what he heard, he checked painstakingly with his own observations and with his own evolving data. He was learning to coordinate the work of other professionals—social workers, psychologists, social anthropologists. He was no longer too clever, too confident, too quick. He was awed and dizzied by the *all* there was to learn. And most important, Professor Adolph Meyer left him free to choose whatever cases interested him the most, free to visit other institutions.

Dan was grateful to Adolph Meyer, and genuinely fond of him. In the main, he considered him a great humanitarian, for his fine contributions in the area of patient care and changing mental hospitals from pigsty quarters of filth and cruelty, where the insane were left to die, to humane institutions. At the same time Dan could not be a true Meyerian. And though, in time, he learned to pattern Meyer's ramblings and take from them much profound meaning, he was frequently persuaded to imitate the old man. At staff parties, imitating the professor's manners and little affectations, he showed his skill amid peels of laughter, including Dr. Meyer's.

Adolph Meyer's marvelous eccentric humaneness, his wonderful childlike quality, his absentmindedness, his habit of talking to himself, endeared him to everyone. It also made him an attraction. And that is how Dan found himself escorting Queen Marie of Romania into Dr. Meyer's presence. The doctor had been forewarned, and it was assumed that he gave heed to what was said. "The queen looks to meeting only two persons in the United States. Albert Einstein, sir. And you."

Dan tried to draw the professor's attention away from the papers on his desk. He then came to the conclusion that there was only one thing to do. "Professor Meyer! Her Majesty, the Queen of Romania."

Peering over the metal rim of his glasses, Meyer looked at Dan. "Is that so?" Then he fixed his myopic stare upon the queen and, in his falsetto, asked, "How long has this delusion been going on?"

Dan felt himself drawn more and more to another distinguished local psychiatrist, Dr. Harry Stack Sullivan. He was certainly conditioned to the doctor's formidable genius. Lewis had told him, "Harry is an original thinker, a gifted observer, an inspired teacher. Go to him. But don't make a rash statement in front of him. You'll get a very fast, 'As demonstrated by what?' Sullivan becomes positively lethal when confronted with a dishonest presentment or a clinical cliché."

Jenny, whose intuitive estimate of people Dan respected, said of Sullivan, who also seemed to like her, "How gratifying it is to meet a giant who, up close, doesn't shrink into a pygmy."

The knowing Frieda Fromm-Reichmann said, "It's all right for Sullivan to incite intense love and hate reactions in his patients. He knows how to use these sweeping emotions therapeutically."

Looking back, Dan had no doubt that, among his friends, it was Leo Butler who, with his sensitive devotion to Sullivan, pushed him toward the man, telling him, "Sullivan made me the clinician I am today."

About the time the magnetism of Sullivan had Dan mesmerized, Leo Butler came to Washington with his wife Tess to the national convention of the American Psychiatric and the American Psychoanalytic societies. Dan and Jenny were there, too, staying with George. The hotels were crowded.

Jenny and Tess—the children adored Tess—seized the meetings as an excuse.

Since the meetings were long and drawn-out sessions, often extending until well into evening, Jenny suggested to Tess they go up to New York and visit Tascha Brotman. "You will all be busy around the clock. We need a little fun, too! Do you mind if we take the train to New York City for a couple of days?" Jenny sensed some hesitation on Leo Butler's part. "We'll stay with my father-in-law—he knows how to take care of daughters."

Leo laughed. "Then I approve."

"And we'll take the boys—with Bessie. That way everyone is taken care of," Jenny assured Dan.

They left that evening, and Leo moved out to George's home with Dan. It gave them an opportunity to further discuss all the new research in detail. Late one night on their way back after social activities that began with a cocktail party, Leo was comfortably smoking a cigarette. In no great hurry, Dan was driving slowly, enjoying the night. The moon was full and the stars were wonderfully bright. Then Leo turned his head toward Dan and spoke. "It's curious the way the most important events in one's life happen."

"When I concluded my residence, Tess and I took ourselves to Detroit where the prospects for an important private practice were favorable. Tess was large with our third daughter, and I needed money for my analysis, which I started in Chicago with a hard-boiled Hungarian to whom Freud had given the nod.

"All the time, he ate apples and cracked walnuts while I, on the couch, struggled and suffered. He proved disastrous and I became so deeply troubled that I was knocking at Lewis Miller's door. I told him my story. Lewis uttered an astounding oath. 'Give him up. Run for your life. Go to Ferenci.'

" 'Budapest? Why not the moon?'

" 'Money?' he asked, reaching for his checkbook. 'Well, how much?'

"I told him, 'I can't accept,' and he countered with, 'Why the hell not?'

"I was grateful, but—it didn't seem right."

"Lewis quickly abandoned the idea but, as always, had an alternative solution.

"He picked up the telephone. We heard the ring, and then Sullivan's voice, 'Hello.' He heard Lewis out and even I heard his fierce bellow: 'Christ! Not again.' There was a pause; the pause lengthened, then, 'Must I?'

" 'Yes,' said Lewis. 'You must.'

"By then, Harry was at the William Alanson White Foundation in Chicago. I came to Sullivan from Detroit every Friday. I left him Sunday night."

As they neared George's garage, Leo concluded his story. "Even among the greats, Lewis and Harry are a class apart."

Sullivan found in Dan a scholar who could run rings around most of his students, both analysands and trainees. He felt in Dan's mental activity (as he did in the exciting minds of other disciples) a joy as sensuous as most men find in a woman's body. He let Dan study his unpublished notes, encouraged him to look at them with scientific detachment. He allowed Dan a free interchange of views. After some time passed, he got in the habit of dropping in at their home when he was in Baltimore. Jenny always enjoyed seeing him, and he admired her cooking and Dan's fine brandy. After dinner Jenny left them alone, but sometimes, with their permission, she would sit quietly, listening. And sometimes, at his mellowest, he spoke directly at Jenny. The quickness of her mind never failed to impress, though he knew of her keen intelligence from Lewis and from Dan. It was difficult for him to realize that Jenny's kind of girl had her kind of mind. He felt it a waste, and, more than once, he was tempted to tell her to stop playing about in the kitchen and put her brainpower to good use.

During one conversation, Dan said, "I see no great deviation from Freud in you."

"Of course not. The difference between us is one of purpose. His was primarily investigative. Mine is therapeutic."

There was another time, when talking about Lewis, Dan said, "I had a struggle with words before I understood their power. Now I know why Lewis repeatedly insisted, 'Forget the vocabulary. Denude yourself of the mask.' "

Harry caught Jenny's eye and she came right out and said, "Dan is in step."

There was one area in which Dan took issue both with Sullivan and with Lewis, who were working together on the psychoanalytic treatment of psychotics. Sullivan felt, and Lewis agreed with him, that any form of human relationship is better than none. They, therefore, were satisfied to see a schizophrenic patient make an adjustment at a homosexual level. Sullivan went even further in concluding that often a pleasant homosexual attachment was safer for the schizophrenic than a heterosexual relationship.

"Are you offended?" Lewis asked.

"No," Dan replied.

"Then why do you hesitate to accept our formulation?"

"I don't know."

Sullivan, with his uncanny intuition, could see Dan's anxiety. He knew that Dan was not yet completely alert to minor movements of anxiety in himself. With incredible intentness he said to Dan what he had publicly said many times before, "I do know because I am a schizophrenic myself."

Dan answered, "A pity then that there are not more schizophrenics like you." He meant it, but later, on their way home, when Lewis reopened the subject, Dan stared steadily at him and said, "Okay, so Harry is a schizophrenic. What's your excuse?"

Lewis was unaffected by Dan's remark. He said, "I can understand your prejudice. But can you?"

Dan's intuition told him that what Lewis said had something to do with his own relationship with George. He decided to take it up with his analyst.

Lewis smiled a pleased smile, for Dan had not become defensive or angry.

The following hours Dan again discussed his parents, his memory free of distortions.

DAN: "I have a clear recollection of my maternal grandparents. Grandpa, an orthodox rabbi, was a self-satisfied bigot of infinite virtue, who conducted his home like a prison with sufficient food. There only *he* could speak, and the reward for blind obedience was simply to escape punishment. Apparently, grandpa failed to overwhelm Aunt Clara, the youngest of his three daughters. She lives in London, the wife of an Anglican bishop. I'm glad to say he's a special friend of Dad's. The eldest daughter, my Aunt Rebecca, the most brilliant and the least charming of the girls, admired her father. Mother, caught between her sisters, coped with grandpa by imitating her mother. Outwardly, she treated him with all possible respect. She was as self-effacing as possible. Maybe, it was her way of gaining his love. Her behavior pleased her father, but Rebecca remained his favorite."

Dan was silent for a time and then went on: "Mother married a man whom she read as strong and authoritative, but there were enough differences between him and her father to make him acceptable."

A: "Similarity and contrast—to satisfy her compliance and her defiance. This probably was the kernel of her sadomasochistic makeup."

DAN: "I suppose."

A: "What about your father? Are you that well-acquainted with his antecedents?"

DAN: "Only what I've been told. I remember my mother telling me, 'Your grandmother Gunther had a smile like sunshine.' After Jenny came into our lives, Mother made an interesting comment to Dad. 'Remember your mother's beautiful eyes, dear? They danced and sparkled like Jenny's.'

"Dad himself seldom talked of incidents from his boyhood His talk was mostly of West Point and football. He did tell me that his father was a kind, genial, dedicated man—the only man he ever met who was completely without malice. 'I saw him,' he said to me, 'as a saint.' He was a doctor, too. And once he told me he liked watching his mother unbraid her hair and see it cascade down her back." After a pause. "I know—that's why I made Jenny let her hair grow long. It took me long enough to figure that one out."

A: "Dan, in a training analysis, where we're dealing with a fairly healthy ego, we don't always find symptoms and conflicts. We, therefore, look for the elements that entered into the character structure of the analysand. This means the revealing of the introjects—the internalized images of pertinent people—mostly, parents. I suggest, though you became a doctor to please mother, you emulate father. You're alike. Dad's push for power—yours for fame."

DAN: "My drive doesn't compare to Dad's. I have less reason to be that strongly driven because I've got one thing other than my profession going for me. I have Jenny. Had Dad been married to a woman more like her, he'd be a different person."

The analyst shot Dan a quick look and waited.

DAN: "Jenny is a strong and honest woman, and she's marvelously intelligent about people. Even after Dad got rid of Helen, his mistress, I wanted to consider him dead. I wanted only to forget him. Not Jenny. 'I love him,' said she. 'I'm going to find out why he got involved with that woman in the first place.'

"I doubt that anyone ever before dared interrogate father. And then, when Jenny judged I was ready to listen, she told me of Mother's rejection.

"Jenny's story went like this. There had always been women

throwing themselves at Dad, but, to his mind, a marriage is based upon fidelity and he stayed rigidly faithful until one night, when he acted out his anger and frustration, because Miriam, my mother, didn't want to go anywhere with him and because she began bringing me into their bed, saying, 'A tiny child gets frightened by himself.'

"The next morning Dad went to Mother to confess, to explain, to beg forgiveness, to give her his solemn pledge that never again—that no one and nothing could make him betray his vows ever again.

"First he took her in his arms and kissed her. She misunderstood and said, 'I'm tired.'

"Dad said, 'Miriam, my darling. I must ask you to listen. Please be generous. I'll spend the rest of my life making it up to you.'

"He was prepared to beg, to do anything. He expected outrage, jealousy, tears.

"Mother heard him out. Then, mildly, she said, 'Please, dear Andrew, you mustn't be so miserable. You take nothing away from us. I have no reason to complain except perhaps in regard to your ardent nature. A good woman is different from a man.'

"After his own anger subsided, Dad told her never ever to use me for her purposes. He said that if I was frightened, he would stay."

For a long moment, Dan was silent. "That's true. Dad did come to me if ever I cried out."

A: "Your father loved you."

DAN: "I never doubted that. But I always believed Mother condemned Father for his infidelity, that she was lonely and unhappy, and that—though she did not make an open issue of it—his women made life very painful for her."

A: "The pivot of her behavior at the time of his first straying indicates her sadomasochistic nature." Dr. Freitag thought it timely to make a clear comment about Dan. "Now you are seeing your parents as people with childhood residuals of their own."

Dan did not reply.

A: "There are two ways of attaining parity: One, to reduce in size the exalted parental figures. And, two, to build oneself up with self-worth.

"Sit down, Dan."

Surprised, Dan moved cautiously away from the couch and lowered himself into the one empty chair. Then there was silence as Dr. Freitag—for the first time—offered him a cigarette.

Dan shook his head.

"I think," said Dr. Freitag, giving Dan a friendly look, "you are ready to take on a control case."

Dan had a strong impulse to say, "I've been ready for a long time." But prudence was indicated, and so he waited silently for Dr. Freitag to go on. "I've recently been referred a patient whom I've saved for you. I gather the presenting symptom, in addition to her nervousness, is spastic paralysis of some of her leg muscles. I've already spoken to Frieda, who will be your control analyst. You're to call her after you've had your first interview with your patient."

"Thank you," said Dan.

"You're quite a remarkable man, Dan."

"Why?"

"It happens you know your own worth. I like that."

Again, Dan quietly said, "Thank you."

Usually, Dr. Freitag was unable to visit after the hour because of a waiting patient. But today something happened and he had spare time. It was a situation Dan would normally welcome. Today there was something irritating about it—like being kept in after school by a teacher sparing in approval.

A painful thought came to him: "There's something monstrous about the entire infantalizing process of psychoanalytic training. Freud said, 'A glimpse into one's unconscious.' And here I am into my third year of analysis and still my training is unfinished."

Dr. Freitag could guess Dan's mental anguish. He could remember his own heavy resentment but resisted the temptation to mention it. Instead, he said a few words in praise of Frieda Fromm-Reichmann and concluded their visit with: "Your patient's name is Lois Lewis. You'll hear from her. The referring doctor is Richard Blewett. I believe you and he are acquainted."

"Yes, I've played handball with him."

When Dan had gone, his analyst picked up the telephone and called Lewis Miller, who listened as only he could listen, and then he said, "You're not finished yet. You've still got a good year's work before you're done with Dan Gunther."

"It'll be under protest."

Lewis said with a chuckle, "No doubt. That's why I'm profoundly grateful he has a smart teacher."

As he walked out of Freitag's office, the image of an undressed Jenny
again welled up with intensity. Dan remembered he was near her favorite
florist. His walk quickened. He bought a dozen white roses and sent them
with a note. The weight that lay upon him all through the analytic hour
lifted then, and when he got back to his office, he stepped in smiling, ready
for work.

Jenny stood with her face glued to the window. When she saw him
approach, she rushed from the window to the door, but the children got
there first. As he stepped in, she looked at him but did not speak while
Paul said, "We're banished. So is Sister Bessie. We're to sleep at Tiger's
house."

"Oh, you like that, don't you?"

"Sure."

Eric shot him a glance. "Dad, if we have another fight, is it all right
if I give him the black eye this time?"

Dan grinned at the boy. "It's all right with me. But be careful, Pal.
He might not take it lying down."

Eric laid his hand on Paul's. "We're not afraid." But he felt he had
to ask, "Are we?"

Dan stretched out his arms to both of his sons. Then he said softly, "Run
along." As they went out through the door, he stood looking at Jenny and
she came swiftly. Dan drew her to him and they kissed, tenderly, fiercely.

An hour later they got up and took a shower together; they were still
in robes when they came down into the kitchen. Jenny asked if he wanted
cheese in his omelette, and he said yes and perhaps a big green salad with
it. After Jenny fixed their meal, they went into the library where a round
table was freshly set in front of the fireplace. Dan lit the fire and poured
the wine. As they supped, they spoke of the day's happenings.

"I suppose you know, Jenny, baby, that when I came in from the hospital, I had every intention of taking you out to dinner."

"I knew before my exquisite roses arrived that tonight you'd not shut
yourself up in your study."

That brought a lifted eyebrow. Dan's curiosity was genuine and he listened with interest as Jenny told him of her conversation with Lewis Miller.

"Good old Mother Hen. You'd think for once he might allow me the
privilege of telling you about me."

Because it was Lewis Miller, the look they exchanged was light and easy.

Intuitively, they both felt that from him, direct interference was understandable, acceptable, even reasonable.

"Want to hear more?" Jenny asked.

Dan had scarcely time to answer before Jenny was saying, "While Lewis was telling me about the start of your first control case, I heard Dad bellow. 'And about time.' Then Grandma was on the extension. 'Thank heaven, the beginning of the end.' "

That Dan did not anticipate. "Dad? Grandma?"

With a mischievous twinkle, Jenny announced: "And Mama."

"Jenny, I'm absolutely confused."

Delighted, Jenny laughed. "They were changing trains in Chicago, when, on a whim, they decided to surprise Lewis. Now he won't let them go."

Dan shook his head, grinned at her and muttered something.

"It's involved, darling."

"I know. It usually is when you display your typical female habit of starting at the end of a story and telling it backward."

Not in the least dismayed, Jenny responded with: "But when I start at the beginning, you're always impatient for the end despite my well-developed logic."

Dan knew something was going on. He looked at her suspiciously.

"There's nothing wrong with our relatives taking an ocean voyage together, is there?"

"Absolutely nothing. But I don't get it. How did they persuade Mom to go along?"

"Dad tried again. This time he gave her an ultimatum. 'Either we all go or a business deal it's taken me two years to put together goes right down the drain.' You know the one thing Mama simply cannot stand is to lose out on a business venture." Joy mixed with mischievous appreciation flooded Jenny's face.

Dan was both pleased and amused. He went into the kitchen and was soon back with fresh glasses and a bottle of chilled champagne. Then he put a record on the record player. Smiling at her, he said, "I believe this dance is mine." Then suddenly George's name was in the conversation, and he voiced his wish to be alone with Jenny more often.

Dan's tone of voice made his meaning clear, but Jenny wisely chose to ignore it. "Oh, is that so?" she said, smiling up at him. "I suppose I'm the one who cares who beats whom in what round. I suppose I'm the two-handed pinochle enthusiast in this family?"

"I love you, Jenny," said Dan, very surprised at his pang of jealousy. Then he said, "Come, let's finish our champagne."

By eleven they were ready to leave the study. Dan blew out the candles.

Holding hands, they climbed the stairs to their bedroom. Jenny's dark eyes were ardent and loving.

At the head of the table Dan talked youth programs with Laura Mitchell, a psychiatrist who was sitting on his right. Laura's blond hair swung forward over her almond-shaped, hazel eyes and chiseled features as she drank in Dan's new suggestion. At the opposite end of the table, another psychiatrist, Baldwin Brown on Jenny's left, was not only astonishing her but revolting her as he talked about his sex relationship with his eighteen-year-old illegitimate daughter.

Jenny said, "If what you say is true, how do you—a physician and a psychoanalyst—justify your action? It doesn't seem exactly healthy to me."

Baldwin Brown accepted her question without reluctance. "I don't particularly like what I am doing. I am performing a solemn deed. It is the duty of every man who fathers a hideous female, to service her."

George regarded the darkly handsome psychiatrist whom Dan had met at a recent meeting, with scorn. Was he that insecure that he had to shock? Or was he just being a bore? He rose and went in to help Jenny.

In the kitchen he stopped in front of her. "Well, what do you think of Dan's newest associate?"

Jenny drew a deep breath and let it out slowly. "I think she is flirting with Dan."

"I'm sure of it." George picked up the silver tray and left.

In the living room Dan looked at Jenny with an approving smile, but he seated himself near Laura and focused his attention on her. George settled himself down beside Brown and engaged him in conversation, testing him out. Jenny passed the delicate chocolate mint squares, then excused herself to attend to the children. When she came back, Baldwin Brown, who practiced in Washington, was ready to leave. He said "Good night" to all and to Dan, "No, no. Please. Don't get up."

George said, "I'll see you to the door."

Laura barely looked up, but her hooded eyes took in everything. One leg crossed high over the other, a pencil in her hand and a small pad on her knee, she was addressing Dan. "Please, *do* go on." As if she could not wrench her eyes from him, she added, "Your ideas are the most fascinating I've ever heard."

Dan laughed. "They're not my ideas. They're Freud's and Sullivan's and Miller's and—"

Jenny dropped down to the rug gracefully, almost seductively, and laid her head on Dan's knee. "Will I disturb you if I listen?"

Dan stroked her hair.

"I'm sorry. I seem to have hogged Dan all evening." And then as if she really wanted to know, Laura asked Jenny how she amused herself.

Jenny, who had run all day to take care of the children, the dinner, the serving (Dan had forgotten, when he asked them home, that it was Bessie's day off), raised her head. She said, "I talk to the mirror on the wall—you know, like Snow White."

"How quaint!" Laura rose. "Well, I'd better be off." She smiled at Dan. "Please don't disturb yourself. I'll call a cab."

Jenny put her hand in Dan's lap, which prevented him from rising.

Oh, Christ! thought Dan and remained silent, conceding Jenny her victory.

And then George came walking in, Laura's wrap over his arm. "Shall we go?" he asked.

She gave him her sudden smile. "I'm afraid I'll be taking you miles out of your way."

"You won't" was his reply.

Jenny jumped up then. Dan rose and put his arm around her shoulder. As the good-byes were said, Dan seemed to be escorting George to the front door. When the girls were far enough ahead, George fell back. With a grin he said, just loud enough for Dan to hear, "Don't wait up."

Dan's eyes narrowed. He gave George a long look. "I think you're wrong."

"Maybe," George said dryly.

Now Dan's expression was a mixture of sufferance and affection. "We've got a handball date in the morning. Remember?"

George answered bluntly. "Suppose you remember that Jenny's got a lot of cleaning up to do and no help."

Dan nodded. "No problem."

George guided Laura to the car and helped her in. When he was behind the wheel, they sat looking at each other.

"Your place or mine?" George asked finally.

Her heart jumped. "You're very direct."

George did not say anything.

"Talkative?" She was still looking at him.

"No."

"Can I believe you?"

George shrugged.

She leaned closer. "Promise. I shouldn't want anyone to know."

"I promise," George said quietly.

Laura smiled. "I live on Charles Street."

George lifted a brow. Charles Street was a street of elegant town houses, some of the oldest in Baltimore. "You live there alone?"

"In a fabulous guest house." She dropped her head on his shoulder.

Dan was listening to a football game, drinking beer, and eating salted peanuts with George and the boys on the partially enclosed porch of the house; through the screen, they could see the garden, ablaze with summer colors.

On hearing Tiger—so named because he was living proof of Freud's contention that children were by nature aggressive—at the screen door, Dan turned to George with a sigh. "I just decided this is a good place not to be." With that, he got up. "Coming?"

George was not exactly overjoyed at seeing Tiger, but he remained seated, partly because he liked the little redheaded boy, but mainly because he did not want to miss the last play. "Here comes his father," he said suddenly.

"Sunk," said Dan and fetched another chair. Meanwhile, George opened and poured another beer. Tiger's father, Dave Lawrence, accepted both as he pulled his chair alongside Dan's.

As soon as the game was over, he handed Dan the morning paper. "Read," he said, pointing.

"I already have."

"Read it again and read it good. You're my whole defense. Without you, I have no case."

Dan was really looking at him now. "Why?"

"Because I think the man is telling the truth. He needs help. Because I know about murderers and rapists. Because Judge O'Brien asked me to take the case. Because our way guarantees every man his day in court."

This aroused Dan's interest. Furthermore, he liked his chunky, crinkly-haired neighbor who reminded him of Spencer Tracy. And he admired him immensely because a full schedule of private practice and law school teaching did not prevent him from taking on worthwhile causes. So Dan looked down and read; this time it was not just a story of a bartender arrested in connection with the rape and murder of his three-year-old stepdaughter. Tony White had become a real person accused of odious acts, for which, if he were found guilty by a jury of his peers, "The State," in reprisal, would take his life. And Jill White, the little salesgirl, was a real woman, stunned and shocked and sticking fast to her belief in her husband's innocence. "He couldn't have. He loved her."

Dan leaned back, allowing the paper to slip to the floor. He finished drinking his glass of beer and turned his attention to the three children. "There's quite a lot of ice cream left."

"Mom told us before we'll spoil our dinner," said Eric, angelic-looking when it suited him.

"Tell your mother that I think it might be a good idea to serve you now. She'll understand."

"We understand, too," Tiger volunteered.

"Yes, we know all about grown-ups. You're trying to get rid of us."

A sigh fell from Dan's lips. "Tiger, you understand too damn much."

"Dad," said Paul, "it'd be easier if you just told us to go somewhere and play because you've got all those important grown-up things to talk about."

"That, son, is a first-class suggestion very much to the point."

Enormously pleased with the approving wink he got from his Uncle George, Paul grinned suddenly and led the way down into the garden, where he opened the gate into the play area. Eyeing the swing, he said, by right of seniority, "Me first."

After the children disappeared from view, Dan turned. George guessed immediately that Dan was ready to chuck Jenny's plans for the evening. Dan simply said, "I'll not coerce you to take my place. Definitely not."

George got up. "Well, I'll be off. So long."

"Tell Jenny I'm sorry."

George went out to tell Jenny.

She heard him out patiently without comment. At last, she said, "It shall be engraved on his tombstone: 'He had a wife and sons and devoted his time to humanity.' "

Gazing at her, George said nothing. Barefoot, her legs encased in tight western jeans and one of Dan's old shirts over the rest of her, she looked so young George's heart missed a beat. He took her hand in his, watching her face so that he could interpret her true feelings. "Do you think Dave had no business intruding today—that this spot is Dan's home, not is office?"

"Well, I'm not exactly pleased but"—after a pause, Jenny went on—"but I have to admit this *is* important."

"I'm glad you understand that, Jenny."

A grateful look swept over Jenny's face. "You call and invite Babs Lawrence over. I'll get ready."

On the porch Dan, looking very grave, was saying: "I can't go on your instinct. And I can't perform any miracle. Now give it to me from the top. Don't mince words."

"OK, but first, answer this. What sort of man becomes a child molester?"

"You're the public defender. You tell me."

Dave Lawrence rattled off a number of sleek stereotypes.

"Size has nothing to do with it. Dynamically, a child molester is fixed at an early level of psychosexual development. Usually, he has been caught at sex play, for which he has been punished. He grows into a shy, inadequate adult, who cannot relate to a grown woman because he has a compulsion to repeat the traumatic experience. The repetition of the compulsion represents an attempt to find a satisfactory solution to the original trauma."

"Good God, man. How do I explain that to a jury?"

"You don't."

"What in Christ's name then do I do?"

"Go over everything you know. I've got to understand if we're dealing with a miserable pervert. Or are we dealing with a decent guy, who for some damn fool reason left a three-year-old unattended in a tub."

Dave conscientiously went over every fact he had determined in the past three days of investigation.

"Tony worked nights. This enabled him to care for Penny during the day, leaving Jill, his wife, free to bring in a little extra money. She had a job with the May Company.

"Around noon of the day of the tragedy, Tony left Penny in the tub while he stepped out for a few minutes to the corner grocery." Here Dave paused dramatically. He wished he didn't have to tell Dan. But there was nothing to be achieved by holding back a pertinent fact. "Dan," he said, "my client lied to the police."

"Oh?" said Dan, sounding unastonished.

"Perfectly understandable. Fear, panic. Isn't flight a normal first reaction?"

"What was the nature of his lie?"

"He now admits to an absence of about thirty minutes—maybe more."

"OK," said Dan, "so he got home, found Penny, thought her still alive, though limp and unconscious, and called the fire department."

"That's correct. They pronounced her dead and called the police. Everyone assumed it was an accidental drowning owing to his negligence —until the coroner's report revealed that Penny had been sexually molested. The presumption then was that she was held down and drowned."

"Any evidence whatsoever of a mysterious intruder?"

"None whatsoever. Homicide conducted a painstaking search."

"And you still think your client is innocent?"

"Yes."

"OK, let's go to work. The wife first."

Though the traffic was fairly slow, they drove at a leisurely pace through downtown Baltimore. They were in no hurry. Reaching the white stucco house in a workingman's neighborhood, Dan nosed the car to the curb and parked it. The door swung open and they were admitted by a red-eyed, obviously nervous girl of about twenty-five. She was wearing a low-cut sleeveless housedress that revealed a tantalizing view of well-formed breasts.

"You'll have to excuse my appearance," she said, closing the door hastily. She took them to the breakfast table. Casting a glance at the unwashed dishes sitting in the sink, she took down clean cups from a shelf. They drank strong black coffee as they talked.

Dan sensed her fatigue and, smiling, reached over and touched her hand. "No more tonight, Mrs. White."

At the door Jill swung around from thanking Dave to face Dan. "I'm sorry we can't pay you, Doctor," she said, and added angrily, "It's on account of Tony's ex-wife. You'd think, after she took him for all he had, she'd let go. But no. She conned him into adopting that no good kid of hers and now he's stuck for child support."

Dave Lawrence flinched. Dan raised a brow; then, putting his hands on the door, he pushed it shut.

Jill flushed. "Did I say something wrong?"

"Just tell us where we can locate her."

With puzzled eyes, Jill said, "I have a feeling I've done something bad for Tony. Oh, I didn't mean to do that."

Dan reassured her. "Not at all. You may have helped."

Jill named a waterfront bar where Tony's ex-wife usually hung out.

They had a hamburger, then they found the bar, not a very nice one. Considering that it was Saturday night, it was relatively quiet. At once Dan and Dave caught the eye of a sexy-looking blonde, whose appeal, it was easy to see, centered on an extremely well-endowed bosom.

She did not exactly force herself upon them, but when the heavyset, nasal-voiced bartender said, "What'll it be?" it was easy for Dan, who had already surmised her identity, to include the former Mrs. White.

She gulped down her whiskey and restrained her impulse to suggest another. Instead, she fixed heavily made-up eyes on Dan and said, "What brings you and your friend slumming?"

"I am Dan Gunther. I am a physician," said he as he ordered another round. "My friend, Dave Lawrence, is a criminal lawyer. He'll be defending Tony White. Know him?"

"Certainly I know him."

Armed with his knowledge of people, Dan looked into her snapping greenish eyes and said, "Our information, perhaps without foundation, is that Tony has been a disturbed man, literally obsessed with little girls."

In language that would have made a stevedore blush, she gave her opinion of the "jerk" who told them that. "Look, Doc, I've been around a lot and nobody can hold a candle to Tony. He's a real gent and all man, if you know what I mean. Something special. I was a horse's ass to let him dump me for that girly-girl dumb broad. On account of her, look at the mess he's in."

"How is she responsible?"

She had the good sense to answer with a shrug.

"Well," said Dan, as he and Dave strolled out of the bar, "you've got yourself one character witness."

Dave made no effort to be even moderately amused.

With a little wire-pulling, it was arranged for Dan to interview Tony on Sunday. Prepared to wait, Dan sat down in the bare interview room and examined the courtyard below through a window streaked and soiled. At the sound of footsteps, Dan looked away from the window and took measure of the man he saw. Admiringly, he had to admit Tony White was a splendid specimen. Broad, square shoulders, a wrestler's neck, a strong thrust to the chin, a thick head of hair, and the dark eyes were intelligent.

Tony focused hard on Dan until a deputy removed his handcuffs. Then his stare faltered.

"We'll be right outside, Doc," said one officer, and they went out.

Tony's eyes trailed them. Dan ignored the departure. He remained still neither smiling nor offering his hand. He had no wish, at this time, to relieve Tony's tension.

Wearily Tony put his hand to his forehead. "All right if I sit down?"

Dan gave him a brief nod. Then he said, "You know who I am. Do you know why I'm here?"

"To help me."

"Wrong. I'm here to get at the truth."

"Believe me, Doc. I didn't do it. So help me, I didn't. I loved that kid. I'm no goddamned pervert."

Dan just looked at Tony for a while. Then, "If you didn't, who did?"

"How in hell do I know? Some bloody bastard." With a fierce harshness in his voice, Tony said, "Christ, if only—if only I could lay hands on him."

Dan waited until Tony was no longer breathing hard before he said, "You came back and found Penny. What was the first thing you did then?"

"I dunno. My mind was doing weird things. I think I screamed."

Prompted by the knowledge that child molesting occurs only in the face of conflict in the adult heterosexual relations, Dan switched his line of questioning. "How are things between you and Jill?"

"No problems. She's a good kid."

"My interest is more specific."

Slowly, it dawned on Tony. Smiling across at Dan, he said, "T-e-r-r-i-f-i-c!"

"Better than with your first wife?"

Startled, Tony gave a quick look, and then he said slowly, as though the admission were a painful one, "I got to grant. She was good in the sack."

"Then why were you divorced?"

Tony shrugged. Then asked: "Is it important?"

"It is."

"She's a slut."

His mind made up to use the truth serum, sodium amytal, Dan nodded his head. Meanwhile, Tony's eyes were on him—waiting, asking, wanting.

Dan eased himself back in his chair and then said, almost casually, "Knowing in advance that whatever you may say, my lips are sealed, will you agree to take truth serum? Unless, of course, it is in your good interest that I speak, and then I'll do so only with your consent."

"Hell yes! I've got nothing to hide."

Dan smiled. "I'll be back."

On parting, they shook hands.

That evening Dan called Dave Lawrence with regard to this first interview. All he said was "He proclaims his innocence with great conviction."

The following Friday morning, the sheriff himself took charge, and by the time Dan came into the private examining room used by the visiting doctor, Tony, dressed in prison denim and his handcuffs removed, was stretched out on the shiny white table.

With the departure of the sheriff, Dan began his preparations. When ready, he said, "I'm going to shoot this sedative into the vein of your right arm. You'll feel relaxed and a bit drowsy. I want you to tell me everything you are feeling."

"Notice anything yet?"

"I feel woozy."

"You're supposed to."

"I've got a buzz on like I had four V.O.'s."

"Count backward, Tony. Count from one hundred."

"One hundred, ninety-nine . . . ninety . . . eight . . . ninety . . . seven . . . ninety . . . six. . . ."

As Tony jumped from ninety-six to sixty-nine to thirty-three and slurred back to ninety-six, Dan said, "OK." He withdrew the syringe and pressed a wad of cotton over the puncture.

To start, Dan delved a little into Tony's background, to find out the forces that shaped his life. When these disclosures came to nothing, Dan shifted his line of questioning.

"Are you sure things are right between you and Jill?"

"Y-e-s. L-o-v-e Jill."

"Tell me about your first wife."

Dead silence.

"Answer me."

Silences stretched between words, Tony obeyed, speaking in thick tones. "I never should have married that tramp, but I thought that if I put a ring on her finger, she'd—"

Tony seemed tortured.

"Don't be frightened. Tell me what you thought."

"I wanted those big beautiful tits all to myself. I remember—" He switched suddenly and began to talk about the stepdaughter he'd taken on. "At first, I misjudged. What's wrong, after all, for a kid to like her old man?"

"What girl, Tony?"

Tony groaned aloud.

"Trust me," said Dan, "I'm the one person who can help you."

"D'ya think I don't know it was wrong? D'ya imagine I don't feel rotten guilty? C-h-r-i-s-t, I sure as hell do."

After a long pause, Dan said, "Keep talking."

"I don't remember."

Presently, half-scared, half-ashamed, Tony began. "She kept asking for it. D'ya know, it was so I dreaded being alone in the flat with her. I told her mother the kid was making a nuisance of herself. 'She's a horny kid,' I said. Just like her mother, that no-good tramp. Her mother accused me of wanting to get rid of her. She turned away from me and went out to meet some slob." Hesitating a long time, his voice lower, Tony talked about the time the girl got into his bed.

"I struggled out of sleep and there she was on top of me exploring. I must have tried to stop her because she offered me a very good reason for making it with her. 'You slaving all night,' she said. 'And coming home to an empty bed. It's sickening.' Then, she told me she wasn't a virgin. That did it. But—'' Agitated, Tony blurted out, ''I couldn't, Doc. I tried, but I couldn't.''

''Why couldn't you?''

Very agitated now and embarrassed, Tony muttered, ''She didn't have big enough tits. I only get excited by big tits.''

''How old was she, Tony?''

''Fourteen.''

''OK, Tony,'' Dan said gravely, ''you're to remain here for a couple of hours and rest. Try to get some sleep.''

Dan called Dave from the sheriff's office, which the sheriff obligingly vacated for him. ''He didn't do it.''

Dave Lawrence murmured, ''Thank God.'' And then, ''How in hell do we prove it?''

''It's a long shot, but I don't believe the autopsy. I want another postmortem and I want Dr. Elliot Epstein, chairman of the department of pathology, to do it. Get a court order to exhume the body.''

''Holy Christ!''

''Then get in touch with Penny's pediatrician. Five gets you ten she had a chronic genital rash.''

''Due to what?''

''Diurnal enuresis: round-the-clock wetting.''

''That means Penny's death had to be an accident.''

''Just so.'' And Dan added, ''If I'm right.''

The lawyer then asked a number of questions, and when he finished, Dan said, ''We'll talk about it *after* Dr. Epstein turns in his report.''

With a sigh of resignation, Dave Lawrence said, ''For the love of Mike— give me, at least, a clue. I'm in this too. Remember?''

''I suppose you're entitled,'' Dan said as though he were amused. ''What *outstanding* attribute do Tony's wives have in common?''

After an appreciable silence, Dave said, ''I guess I didn't notice.''

With a low chuckle into the mouthpiece, Dan replied, ''You sure as hell did,'' and hung up.

Dan went straight from the county jail to his analytic hour, and, as he opened the door, Dr. Freitag saw at once by the jaunty way he walked into the room that he was unmistakably pleased with himself. Dan strode across the room and took the couch. He could hardly wait to begin. For the next twenty minutes he talked without pause.

A: ''Dan, you presented me with your brilliance in the same

fashion you once presented your mother with a healthy bowel movement. Later, with finishing your spinach. Still later, with excellent report cards. Now you want from me what you got from her.''

DAN: "Nuts!" Dan did not speak for several seconds. "Damn it. Surely we can discuss a man's life on a reality level. Doesn't that make sense?"

A: "Tell me what's bothering you."

DAN: "The dynamics of Tony's preoccupation with breasts. Essentially, it amounts to a fetish. I know it probably has its source in his relationship with his mother—as if he were perpetuating the nursing situation."

A: "That is a naïve interpretation. The continuity is not direct." The analyst used the rest of the hour to talk. "The first layer is the actual mother. This gets repressed and the child breaks away from mother. A substitute gratification ensues. The child clings to his Teddy bear or a rag doll.

"Later, in the phallic stage of development—and we're still talking about a fetish—the substitute object for gratification may be a pet animal. In the unconscious, this substitute-object may be the symbol of restitution for the lost penis—the castration threat.

"The next and last layer is the return of the original repressed wish for the mother's breast. By having a woman with big breasts, Tony has both his mother and his assured masculinity."

Dan got to his feet, eyed his analyst, and nodded his head thoughtfully. "You have made it very clear. Thank you, Doctor."

A: "You did an excellent job. I'm proud of you, and with good reason. The fact is that only a psychiatrist, who is both a physician and a good clinician, is able to see organic pathology as well as functional pathology that has purely emotional origin. Also, because of your medical training, you had the courage and the authority to order the exhumation of the body. And you knew what should be examined. These are some of the reasons we should not permit nonmedical people into psychoanalytic training."

Dan returned to Phipps about twelve thirty that day. A message in his secretary's hand awaited him.

"His Honor, Judge Philip O'Brien wants you in chambers around five. If no message to the contrary reaches him, he'll expect you then."

Dan went to the telephone and called Jenny.

"Oh, it's you, Dan. What happened? Did you get a good interview?"

"Fortunately, yes."

"Is he innocent?" Jenny asked eagerly.

"I think so."

"I'm glad. That man has been in my thoughts all day."

"Listen, Jenny, I called to tell you I won't be home in time to eat with the boys. Judge O'Brien wants to see me. I suspect there have been new developments since I spoke to Dave."

Jenny said, "Don't fret about it, darling. It can't be helped." Then she sent him a kiss over the telephone.

A slim young law clerk greeted Dan with politeness and opened a door for him, then announced him.

The room was fairly large, dominated by a high-beamed ceiling. There were bookshelves filled with law books bound in dark-green leather. On one wall was a large portrait of Abraham Lincoln. There was the judge sitting behind his desk. The three chairs in front were hard, with wooden seats. Dave Lawrence was sitting on one chair. A clean-shaven, well-dressed man in his midforties sat erect on another. Dan guessed he was the district attorney.

Quickly, Dave was beside Dan and was making the introductions. The district attorney rose to his feet and moved toward Dan, his hand outstretched, but his steel-gray eyes cool and remote.

"Gentlemen"—The judge was speaking—"be seated. Smoke, if you wish. First, I should like to hear from Dr. Gunther."

Dan's eyes met Dave's.

Dave nodded. "You may speak freely. I have my client's consent in writing."

Dan then turned to Judge O'Brien, gazed at him meditatively, and said, "If I knew specifically what you had in mind, your honor, I'd know what to focus on."

"Give us all the information you have. I want to find out as quickly as I can if the accused is innocent."

Dan continued to look the judge in the eye. "We won't know that for certain until we hear from Dr. Epstein."

"There is every indication that that should be fairly soon."

"Yes indeed, your honor," said Dave, "everyone quite literally jumped at the chance to help."

The district attorney maintained his silent posture: *I'm here in response to a command. When the facts are in, I'll make my move.*

Dan's eyes never left the judge, although a small smile touched his lips.

He knew what thought lurked in the district attorney's mind. That was perhaps why he spoke as convincingly as he did. Dan always enjoyed rocking complacent skeptics indisposed to set straight a preconceived conviction. He spoke for fully a half hour. Both judge and district attorney kept their eyes on him and listened. Dave listened, too. But he also sneaked a glance now and then at his adversary.

"Tony White was born and reared in a small town in Ohio. His world was not particularly different from that of the average boy born to a low-income family. He went to school. He played ball. He joined the Scouts. He ran errands for pin money and he took an interest in girls. He is not a man of short temper and quick fists, though there is a bit of violence connected with his job. He is not a suspicious man. Never once during our first interview did he glance over his shoulder either casually or nervously to determine how much of our conversation the guards could overhear. The other prisoners shun him and he has endured the insults resulting from their outrage well." Dan's voice trailed off. He mused on his thoughts unhurriedly, then went on. "What I'm about to mention may seem a digression. It is not.

"The two women Tony White married have characteristics in common. Both are conventionally good-looking. Neither is over-bright. Each begot a female child illegitimately. Moreover, each was left to raise the child alone. So far nothing distinguishes these two from hundreds of other foolish girls. What does set these two apart is"—Dan felt the profound silence—"is the size and shape of their breasts, which, I'm convinced, must be near perfect." The atmosphere in the room became tense. Without glancing at the district attorney, Dan saw the malicious grin, the satisfaction flashing from his eyes.

Conspicuously composed, Judge O'Brien said, "You are a born dramatist, Doctor. Do go on."

"The reality of my disclosure, your honor, is: There is always a good reason why a man is compelled to commit a ghastly act of horror, or why he is incapable of doing so. Tony White is incapable of the crime of which he is accused because the only way he can be aroused, the only way he can gain sexual pleasure, is with a full-grown, well-endowed woman. All his sexual energies are concentrated on one particular thing—large round breasts. His capacity for genital gratification is totally organized under the guidance of this 'breast fetish.' "

Judge O'Brien looked at Dan nonplussed. His next question was swift: "How do you explain it?"

Dan shrugged his shoulders. "Tony White may have once during his adolescence seen a woman with large breasts. He became sexually excited

—an accidental circumstance. This, because it is easily remembered, was enough to mask the real causes of the fixation. The unconscious Oedipus complex. The unconscious castration anxiety.''

It was a bad moment for Dave Lawrence when the district attorney leaned back and gave a short skeptical laugh. Meticulously taking a pack of cigarettes from his pocket, the lawyer offered them around and lit one for himself. After the first long pull at the cigarette, he got up from his chair and stood in front of Dan. "To begin with: All this came out in the truth serum interview?"

Dan was staring straight ahead at the judge, and when the district attorney thought Dan was not going to reply, he said, "When I left my office to come here, I was under the impression that you'd take us fully into your confidence. All I've heard are conclusions based upon conjecture. Clearly, there's a lot you've left out, a lot I want explained."

Judge O'Brien nodded his head slightly.

"All right." Dan waited until Dave was back in his chair. He then gave them the full account of his interviews with Tony White. Not once did he refer to his notes. As he finished speaking, he looked around as though expecting some sudden exclamation to come from them. But no one spoke until the district attorney said with feeling, "I'll be goddamned!" Dan found this reaction gratifying.

"It's baffling," said Judge O'Brien. He peered at Dan a moment and said, "I hope you are right—I hope—" He did not finish what he was saying. All at once the door flew open and a stoutish, elated person in a white doctor's coat burst into the room. "I'm here. I came in person. It's incredible. It's fantastic. The little girl was not molested. The inflammation of the vulva was chronic—an infiltration of lymphocytes. Moreover, she did not drown in the bath. She vomited and choked. There was food—vomitus—in the lungs." He broke off abruptly, and turning to the judge, he said, "Your honor. I'm Dr. Epstein."

The judge came out from behind his desk. "Hello," he said with a big smile, extending his hand, "I'm Phil O'Brien and I'm taking you to the University Club for a drink. In fact, I'm buying all of us several drinks." He then put an arm around Dan's shoulder. "If you're not pure genius at deductive thinking, you sure come within whistling distance. Amazing!"

Dan was extremely flattered, but his overwhelming reaction was one of satisfaction. In a head-on challenge from the law, he had fought and won.

As they all began to move out together, Dave Lawrence closed his brief-case and said with a wide grin, "I'll join you *after* I've seen my client." Turning, he said to the district attorney, "Coming?"

"You know I am," the district attorney replied quietly and solemnly.

They parted at the courthouse steps, and as the two men walked briskly toward Dave's car, the district attorney, who had been reflecting gravely, spoke his thoughts aloud. "You know," he said, "psychiatry is truly astounding. There'll be revolutionary changes in the law."

Dave Lawrence assented. "And men like Daniel Gunther will be responsible."

Lewis had just driven up to the house in a taxi when he saw George stripped to the waist, playing ball in the garden with Paul and Eric. A skinny little girl with an intense gaze was watching them, fascinated by their every move.

George seemed surprised to see Lewis at that moment, but he welcomed him and helped the driver with the luggage. The boys greeted Lewis with screams of joy. Eric shoved to get to him first. Paul pushed back and flung himself in front of Lewis. It was not until he was hugged and kissed and questioned—"What did you bring us?"—that Lewis again became conscious of the little girl who somehow looked familiar.

"Whose young bud?"

"Oh," said George, "allow me to present Miss Annie Brotman, one of Jenny's several houseguests."

"Hello, Annie," Lewis said, extending his hand, "I am Paul's and Eric's Uncle Lewis. I am pleased to meet you."

Annie took his hand. "Thank you," she said, permitting herself one of her rare smiles. She was a thin child, plain to look at if one did not notice her beautiful brown eyes. There was sensitivity too in the shape of the mouth beneath the long nose. Lewis decided he liked little Annie Brotman, though he still cordially disliked her parents. Annie must now be the means by which Tascha kept her hold on Jenny.

When the noise at last subsided, George sent the children to the backyard and told them to play there, with no foolishness, until they were sent for. He turned to Lewis, who looked as though he were suffering in a dark, vested suit, white shirt and tie. He said, "I'd better get you upstairs."

"Emphatically no. Not until I've seen Jenny."

"We weren't expecting you until tomorrow. Jenny is marketing."

"Where's Dan? And did you say several houseguests?"

"After you're comfortable, I'll answer all your questions," George said, opening the front door. After Lewis stepped in, he lifted the suitcases.

Lewis proceeded toward the stairway and paused when he found himself staring at Betsy Stein. He had not seen her in years. Barefooted, Betsy's dumpy frame was garbed in a loose smock, the pocket of which was handsomely initialed B.S. She was well into her fifth month of pregnancy.

Though Lewis' attitude toward women was ordinarily negative, even he found it impossible not to like Betsy, and his surprised but friendly look reflected his feeling.

Betsy reached for him and gave him a big kiss. "Oh, thank you for coming. Larry will be thrilled." Then she said, "I'll see you later," and padded out of the hall into the living room.

George laughed aloud at Lewis' frank astonishment. After a bath, as he returned to the bedroom in his robe, he saw George hanging his suits. He eased himself into the armchair and, from a silver cigarette box, extracted a cigarette.

Frowning down at him, George said, "You don't want that."

"I surely do and I intend to have it," Lewis replied, striking a match. He inhaled smoke, peered up at George, and said with impatience, "What's going on around here? Be eloquent."

George dropped casually down on the bed. "Hadn't you better wait and hear it from Jenny?"

"No, I want to be informed now."

George laughed again. "You're here for a wedding. We're hosting about forty guests at the end of the week. They are coming to witness the marriage of Dr. Larry Stein to his wife, Betsy." George did not conceal his amusement at Lewis' expression. "Since it is to be an orthodox ceremony, Jenny has the Silvers coming up from Florida to give the bride away."

"Utterly absurd. I am going home." But there was a smile on his face, and though he did not ask, he listened with amused forbearance to the story of Betsy's six-week stay that spring with Jenny and her conversion to Judaism.

In the seconds that followed, George read his thought. "Don't mock Betsy. She made an important and courageous decision."

"But why orthodox?"

"Larry's father is an orthodox rabbi. I was Bar-Mitzvahed in his synagogue."

Carrying chilled glasses and iced tea on a tray, Jenny entered. With her large dark eyes and a green ribbon holding back her mane of hair, still long, she looked at once capable and childlike. "Lewis," she said, her impatient affection obvious to all, and waited until George took the tray from her. Then she moved to Lewis, took away his third cigarette, stubbed it out, and gave him a resounding kiss on the mouth.

George started to leave. "If you'll excuse me, I'll—"

"Oh, don't go. Let's all have tea."

George glanced at Lewis, who nodded and added quietly, "Stay."

George again took his place on the bed and spoke to Jenny. "Where's Betsy?"

"Resting."

Lewis' brow puckered. "Where's Dan? That's more to the point. Isn't he ever around?"

Jenny finished pouring the tea. "Dan now sees private patients. Saturday afternoons."

"Why?"

Jenny laughed. "He says because I have turned the house into a barracks and myself into a restaurateur."

Lewis chuckled. "What I really want to know is where do we all sleep?"

"Oh," said Jenny, handing him his glass. "Everyone has his place." She moved across the room and sat down beside George.

Sipping his tea, he said, "I'm probably on a cot with the boys."

"That's right. I've claimed your bed for Dan and me."

She turned to Lewis again. "The Silvers get the master bedroom."

An expression of faint amusement on his face, Lewis asked, "And the bride and groom?"

"They have the large guestroom. You remain here. Annie, our olive-complexioned flower girl, is on a couch in Tascha's room. There," she said pleasantly, "it's all arranged."

George rose and stretched. "Thanks, Jenny. I enjoyed the tea immensely." He started for the door.

"George."

He glanced around.

"Dan promised to be home in time to bathe the boys. He'll get them off to bed, too."

George nodded and went out of the room.

Looking at her now, Lewis felt that something was amiss. Jenny was wistful about something, almost unsure as to her next step. Maybe she was holding George there with tea because she did not want to speak freely. He was right. Jenny made a movement to rise.

"Wait," he ordered.

Jenny picked up her glass again.

"Look, Jenny, how often is George in residence?"

"Almost every Saturday afternoon and Sunday. And usually on Thursdays. He comes around six. Why?"

"Perhaps you'll tell my why."

"Gladly," Jenny said, suddenly angry and able to let go with Lewis' supportive presence. "Because Dan has his father, you, and George to look after me."

" 'Go to New York, baby. Have fun. Tell my old man to take good care of you.'

" 'Talk to Lewis, Jenny.'

" 'A movie? Go with George.' He grins that adorable grin of his and adds, 'Don't hold hands. You're my girl.'

"Dan needs you all because he is no longer dedicated to his profession. He is obsessed with it."

Lewis nodded, acknowledging her explanation. He sighed wearily. "All right, Jenny. Now tell me why *you* need George."

"Oh, Lewis, you can be maddening."

"Of course," Lewis said, unruffled. Then he resumed. "Perhaps it is because he is willing to play with the boys by the hour."

"That's part of it." Her answer came unevenly.

"Perhaps—oh, but of course not."

"All right," said Jenny. "Say it."

"Perhaps it is because he struts around here shirtless, his muscles bulging. Is the swelling sweet, Jenny?"

Jenny's cheeks colored. Then she was on her feet. "If you think I could possibly jeopardize my marriage—" She paused. She moved to Lewis and stood by his chair. "You're partly right, dear Lewis," she said softly. "I like the way he looks at me. I like the way he holds me when we dance. I like his constancy and admiration. It feels good."

Lewis nodded. "Yes, I know."

Jenny's smile was warm. "I must go. I want to bathe Annie. Tascha won't be coming till midweek. And Bessie needs a hand with dinner."

"There's plenty of time. I want to talk to you about Dan. Sit here, dear." Lewis tapped his knuckles on the glass-topped table.

"Yes," Jenny said, sitting down lightly.

"You must accommodate yourself to Dan. For you, I recognize, it is very hard. But what he is doing is right for him now. And I think he is working through some crisis in his analysis. Be patient. We are all behind you, you know?"

Looking forlorn, Jenny sighed. "The analysis—when will it ever end? He has been made professor. He has almost completed his seminars. He's already completed one control case. But the analysis goes on and on. I want to go home. I want another child. But when I mention—"

"Jenny!" Lewis interrupted. "Dan's analysis will end when he delivers the solid poop."

Jenny rebuked him. "Honestly, Lewis, sometimes I think you all talk in such graphic vulgarity just to get a reaction. It's sickening."

"All right, Jenny. No offense intended. It's only that you want everything—nice, clean, polite, orderly. However—"

"Lewis! I just remembered something."

The door opened and closed. Jenny looked up and slid off the side of the table. "Why, Dan, you're early."

"Yes, Jenny, dear." He reached for her and kissed her. Then he glanced down at Lewis, appraising him. Then he laughed. "You look OK."

Jenny poured tea in her glass and handed it to him. Lewis saw the change that came over her. Her eyes were shining and she was relaxed, happy.

"What is it?" Dan asked, pulling up a chair. After a moment's pause, "Oh, you're worked up because I canceled out on a patient to get back here early. Believe me, there is no problem."

Lewis looked at him dismally. "Yes, there is a problem. Only it is with you."

Dan grinned. "You're an overbearing mother hen. Come on. Cut it out. Can't you quit harping on George?"

"Go to your sons." Lewis sighed.

Dan grinned affably, said, "See you later," and strode out. After he had gone, Lewis took his medicine.

George came into the bathroom as the boys were getting out of the tub. He reached for a towel, and as Dan took care of Paul, he rubbed Eric dry.

"What did Lewis say?"

"Nothing worth repeating."

Afterward, when the boys had gone to Jenny for their supper, George said to Dan, "Rumor has it you're involved. Anything in it?"

"Involved? With whom?"

"If you don't know, I guess there is nothing to it." George walked back to his own room, whistling gently.

Dan knew. To be seen publicly with Laura Mitchell in Baltimore was a mistake. He left his clothes in the children's bathroom and went to Jenny with a bath towel wrapped around his middle. She was at her dressing table getting ready for dinner. He sat down beside her, put his arms around her. At first, his kisses were tender. He carried her to bed and removed her cotton robe. "You're beautiful."

Jenny half rose. "Not now, Dan. It's almost dinnertime."

Holding her strong, he whispered, "Forget dinner."

"Our guests."

"Let them get their own dinner."

Jenny sank back into the bed and responded to his assurances of love.

"You're all I ever want; you're everything, my sweet Jenny." She let herself be enveloped in his passion and met it with a wildness he cherished. An hour later, as they walked into the living room hand in hand, dinner was announced by Bessie, in her sparkling white uniform.

They were eating the fillet roast when Bessie came up beside Jenny and said, "You're wanted on the telephone. It's Dr. Mitchell."

Dan had difficulty in hiding his displeasure, and it was evident to everyone that it was directed at the caller, not the call. His instructions to Bessie were clear. "Tell Laura her timing is unfortunate. Mrs. Gunther is at dinner."

Jenny ignored him. She rose and walked briskly in the direction of the telephone. Only Betsy kept her eyes on her plate. George's were on Dan. Lewis watched them both. Neither of them met his gaze and both were uncomfortable.

When Jenny got back to her place, four pairs of eyes met hers.

"Well, what did she want?" Lewis took it upon himself to ask.

Jenny swung around, her long lashes lifted, and she answered him in a conversational tone. "She tried to get me to invite her over."

Dan was furious. "Why?"

Disregarding the disturbance in his voice, Jenny went on talking to Lewis. "She said she would appreciate meeting you. I told her that normally you are extremely busy, so that on vacation you value your privacy. She suggested that perhaps we could both meet her for lunch, and then tried to make me commit myself to Monday at noon."

"Of course, you refused."

"Only for myself," Jenny said.

"What makes you think that I should want to lunch with her?"

Jenny's eyes opened wide. "Oh, I don't know." She paused. "You might find it interesting."

"Is she coming to the wedding?"

Jenny shook her head. "She is not invited."

Later in the evening Dan went to his study where it was quiet, but he found it difficult to concentrate. "The hell with it," he said aloud. "I can't work tonight." He went upstairs, thinking of George and his chance remark. Or was it so chance? He went into his room and sat down on the foot of his friend's bed. George sat up and lit the lamp.

"Got a problem?"

"It's unlikely," Dan replied.

"Tell Jenny. She'll believe you."

"There's nothing wrong."

"Especially if there is nothing wrong."

"No."

"OK. Dan, listen to me. I have something to tell you."

"Yes."

George stared deeply into Dan's eyes. "I can take care of everything. Understand?"

Dan drew in a deep breath.

George smiled at him. "Tell Jenny I have to leave the first thing in the morning."

Dan grinned. "We'll miss you more than you'll know." He went out and shut the door.

His groan in the middle of the night jolted Jenny out of a deep sleep. She leaned over him. "Darling, wake up. You're having a nightmare."

Dan looked up at her. His eyes were terrified.

"It's all right, darling. It was only a dream."

"Did I talk?"

"You said, 'Come back. I don't want you dead.' " Jenny smiled at him. "Were you dreaming of me?"

"God, no!"

He sounded so horrified by her question that Jenny did not know what to make of it. He must have dreamed of his mother. She slid down and put her head against his bare chest. His arms went around her and held her, taking comfort from her. After a while, he said, "You know, Jenny, baby, you're lovely. You're nice."

Jenny kissed him. "So are you."

He was able to sleep.

Monday at eleven o'clock he had an analytic hour. He dreaded telling his dream.

DAN: "I am alone in a room. I think it is Jenny's bedroom. The one she had when she was a little girl. It's a happy room." Dan hesitates an instant. "I wonder. Is it silly to call a room happy? Well, it doesn't matter. Anyway—an intruder comes into the happy room. He has a body but no head. I recognize him. I speak his name, 'George.'

"He seems amazed. He answers by pulling out a dagger. I instantly guess his intent. We struggle—the headless body and I, and now it is I who am the beast. The body is helpless against my frenzy. I kill him, of course. Then I look down to see what my enemy has become, and I see a head—no body. Now, the face comes into focus and it is George's face splendidly alive. He speaks to me, 'Oh, God, oh, God. Help me find my body.'

"My mother appears before me. She does not speak. She kneels down there beside the head and says to him, 'My helpless little child. I love you.' Then, in bitter anger, she asks of me, 'How do you bring yourself to use violence against your brother?'

"But the face comforts me. 'I don't need my body. Keep it for yourself.' "

A: "What does the dream suggest to you?"

DAN: "I don't understand it."

A: "You dreamed the dream, therefore the source of the aggression is within you."

Long pause.

A: "The dream says that George is an intruder in your home."

DAN: "Consciously it does not occur to me."

A: "But you are in rivalry with him, aren't you?"

DAN: "Only in games."

A: "A rival is an adversary. Adversaries compete for a prize. What is the prize?"

Dan remains silent.

A: "Repeat the dream."

Dan repeats the dream, this time emphasizing the mutilation.

A: "Were we to translate the mutilation into sexual symbols, we'd call this a castration equivalent."

DAN: "This, then, suggests to me that I want to punish George or whomever he represents—probably my father—for his sexual interest in Jenny, who must then be the representation of my mother."

A: Analyst remains silent.

Dan's next association came to him in the form of a question. "Why was I so terrified?"

A: Analyst remains silent.

Dan goes on: "I really wasn't all that scared at first—or even when we fought. The terror came when I saw that the disembodied head had life. I guess I feared George's retaliatory aggression."

A: "Is this not similar to the fear you had of your father?"

DAN: "Do you mean I feared my hostility boomeranging against me?" Dan muses a bit. "It seems I am reliving the Oedipal triangle."

A: "These associations are helping decode the dream."

DAN: "Then I guess I never really wanted to kill my father. I wanted only to defeat him."

A: "The dream is the expression of your ultimate triumph."

Dan ponders for a time. "It seems to me, Doctor, that a man's ultimate triumph is the attainment of harmony. He is at peace because he need not be at war."

The analyst felt no need to comment upon this conflict-free statement.

Lewis telephoned George from the house. "I am wondering if you'd ask me for dinner tonight."

George replied, "I'll be looking forward to it all the rest of the afternoon."

"Ha, ha! I'll be there around five."

"I'll be busy until about six fifteen."

"I can wait."

When Lewis walked into the suburban office in Chevy Chase later that Monday, the office nurse said, "The doctor is with a patient."

"I am not distressed to hear that. His house key, please."

That made it a bit difficult for the nurse. She said, "Excuse me," and vanished.

In about five minutes George appeared in the waiting room. He had his key in his hand. "I've got a couple of steaks at the house. And I toss a good salad. Will that do?"

Behind his thick glasses, Lewis' eyes rolled. Steak and salad! What could be more mundane? He took the key out of George's hand. "Thank you." He left.

George did not go back to his patient at once. He called Dan.

They sat down to a really good seafood cocktail, baked trout, stewed tomatoes, and, for dessert, a flaky fruit tart. And all through dinner they spoke of ordinary things. They were standing up when Lewis said, "I see you have added to your collection photographs of Jenny and the children."

George said he had the negatives and promised to develop some prints for Lewis.

Sitting down with their coffee in the living room, Lewis, who possessed fine artistic perception, and who rightly judged himself a connoisseur of interior design, took in George's mixture of the old with the functional, which incorporated much of the furniture from his father's house by reupholstering it in country house fabrics of livelier colors.

When they were side by side, sipping brandy, Lewis asked, "Are you personally responsible for the charm retained in this house?"

George smiled. "Jenny suggested the patterned fabrics be repeated in the draperies."

Lewis' sharp eyes gazed at George. "You're good with the camera. Ever try watercolors or oils?"

George smiled across at him. "Oils. Jenny says I'm getting good." His tone was: "I don't suggest that I'm good."

"I hope you let me look at your canvases."

"They are mostly likenesses of Jenny. I paint from her photographs or from memory. She won't pose for me."

"May I see them?"

"I'm sorry, Lewis, but not tonight. They are locked away in the office." George felt a sense of relief that they were in the office and not in the house.

Suddenly—with no prelude—Lewis asked, "What does Jenny fear in Laura Mitchell? She canceled out on our lunch today."

George expected probing, but he was momentarily caught off-guard. "I think," he said, "you are letting yourself be carried away." He saw that Lewis viewed him with skepticism, and added, "Maybe Laura rubs Jenny the wrong way, but fear—no, I don't think so."

Lewis tossed back at him, "Convince me."

That's not so simple, George thought. "Well," he said slowly, "I admit I've heard them exchange a few barbed words, which Dan deadpanned, but that's about it. Jenny, after all, has Dan."

His eyes still watching keenly, Lewis said, "Tell me about Laura Mitchell."

George grinned good-naturedly. "I'd say she's about twenty-nine. She's fairly tall—comes to my shoulder. She has fair hair, large intelligent gray eyes—I think—under aquiline brows." With a pretense of extreme light-heartedness, George added, "She sits with her legs far apart."

"Keep talking."

The smile left George's lips and his eyes swept over Lewis. "She's been married and divorced. She's highly ambitious and she knows how to get the spotlight."

"Do you find her attractive?"

"Nope. Her feet point outwards."

His expression of exasperation made George smile. "I'm serious."

Lewis' hand went up in a gesture of dismissal. Then, after a silent moment, he leaned forward and asked with great intensity, "Does she resemble Sue Palmer? Are they alike?"

"In no way. Sue was pitifully insecure—Laura definitely is not. And Sue, with all her compulsive promiscuity, was not a tramp."

"Is Laura Mitchell?"

George's face had a hard look. "That's the general idea."

"I thought so."

George found himself wanting an explanation from Lewis. "I'm puzzled. How does Sue come into our conversation? It seems a long time since we've thought of her."

"I want to determine in my own mind if Dan has a neurotic need to complicate his life by seeking out this sort of woman."

"Forget it," George replied, dismissing the possibility. "In the first place, Dan did not seek out Sue. She was there and he befriended her. As for Laura—as I get it from Dan, and I accept his word—he's fortunate to get her. She's got a good professional record, and she's a workhorse. That her sex partners come and go is none of Dan's business—unless, of course, her private life intrudes upon her value as a doctor. So far it has not."

Lewis said knowingly, "I sense you've had no difficulty with the lady."

No longer serious, George said with a half grin, "She's not exactly my kind of woman."

Lewis lifted a brow derisively. "Of course not." And now, rising to his feet, he asked George to call a cab.

George shook his head. "I'll drive you. I want to."

On their way out, Lewis took George's arm. "I daresay Jenny and Dan are not entirely wrong about you. You're not so bad."

George made no reply; within himself, he felt immensely pleased.

It was obvious that Tascha had something urgent on her mind as she sat under the trees in their backyard the day before the wedding.

"You must be wondering why Abe couldn't make it, Dan," she said in her direct manner.

"We wanted to see you both," Dan affirmed, moving his chair to face her.

"Well, to begin with, he never turns away a good patient."

Dan could easily imagine that to the Brotmans "good" meant rich.

Tascha took a few puffs then put out the cigarette. "He's involved in politics more than ever. He sees the possibility of becoming the chairman of the Education Committee. That'll give him the power to make important decisions."

Dan couldn't miss the point: "The shit list." He frowned with disappointment. But Tascha was not noticing. She hadn't finished with Abe. She moistened her lips. "We lead almost separate lives these days." She picked up the glass of coke and took a long drink. Abruptly she put it down. "On the one hand, I'm terribly proud of Abe. On the other. . . ." Her gaze dropped and she fell silent.

Dan said, "You've taken a lover, Tascha."

"I simply had no choice."

Dan said nothing more.

Tascha cast him a sharp and defiant glance. "Don't tell Jenny." Dan's silence was his promise.

Without uttering a single word, Tascha's face told him he had let her down. Carefully, to take the sting out of his rejection, he said gently, "If you want to talk about it, Tascha, I promise to listen. I'll not be judge and jury."

"As if you were my therapist. . . . I do want you to understand." Then she set the scene, the only clue to her nervousness being the two bright spots of color high on her dark cheekbones.

"It started last year. At Jenny's annual beach party. Everyone was there —all the regulars, and everyone was happy and having fun except me. Even Abe, under a shade umbrella, was enjoying himself. You were romping with Paul, and I even remember that someone was helping Eric build a sandcastle at the water's edge. Then, something strange happened. Anyway, I thought it was strange, because, as a rule, around Jenny he's so proper. George Atlas scooped her up into his arms, lifted her high into the air, and started running into the surf with her still in his arms. And she laughed up at him, and I knew she was loving it. I was seized by excitement. Then, to my amazement, my hand was in Bill's and he was saying: 'Will you take me instead, Tascha? I'll make you happy.' " Tascha stopped.

Fantastic! Big Bill Reilly, cast in the mold of an Irish hero, with an Irishman's impish charm, now a successful New York doctor at one of the teaching hospitals, and Tascha, the daughter of quite Arabized Sephardic Jews, who from their dismal Yemeni slum, felt uneasy in the comparative splendor of the Lower East Side ghetto.

Tascha moistened her parched lips. Some minutes later she resumed. Dan noticed that as her voice softened, her face went soft, too.

"His hand still closed tightly on mine, we walked the clean white sand, the sun hot on our backs. At the very end of the boardwalk, Bill said, 'We can't ask for more privacy than this.' There was a grin on his face, and I thought I knew his mind. But I was wrong to think that Bill would take me like that, even though he knew I was eager for it. He was even amused, because when he said, 'Tell me, Tascha, when, how, and where shall we conduct our love affair?' I could not conceal my surprise and disappointment from him. But then he kissed me and said, 'You've no idea how long I've wanted to make love to you.' I was astonished at that. We talked of ourselves, of friends, of the need to keep our affair secret. On the practical side, we made plans.

"I told him that I take Annie to my sister's every Tuesday, and that I don't pick her up until after school on Thursday. We arranged to meet the following Wednesday in front of the Commodore. 'Be there at ten sharp,' he told me. 'We'll drive far into the country and search for a place well hidden.'

"It wasn't difficult to find what we were both looking for, up the Hudson near West Point, in a small rural community. It was sheltered by some marvelous old oaks and had a meadow running down from the steps. It seemed it was ours!"

Thinking about the house, about the way Bill leaned across her, about his body warm and hard against hers, about the breakfasts he brought to her in bed, Tascha looked very pretty—more like she used to look in Vienna. Smiling a little, she leaned forward, and watching Dan's face for reactions, she began, "You know Bill. He has to respect himself, respect what he is and what he's doing. He couldn't make my part in his life shabby by taking me each week to some roadside tavern. So he gave me this little jewel of a house deep in the woods. It has a sparkling white kitchen, and three steps up from the living room is the dining room. That's white, too, with a big view window. A small spiral staircase goes to the bedroom."

Tascha's eyes seemed to brighten as she dwelled with endless detail upon virtually everything that went on there—much of which, thinking of Abe—Dan had no stomach for. But to release some of her feelings of guilt, Tascha just had to talk. And Dan, taking refuge in his professional posture—observe and listen—had the discipline to permit her that emotional release.

The wedding of the thoroughly married Larry and Betsy Stein took place on Sunday at four o'clock in the afternoon in a beautifully shaded corner of the Gunthers' garden. The marriage canopy under which the bride and groom stood was made of greens intertwined with flowers. With no deference to her pregnancy, Betsy wore a dazzling white satin gown. A simple square of borrowed lace covered her head. Jenny was matron of honor, for the Steins had insisted upon it. And she looked lovely standing a little to one side with Annie, her eyes filled with tenderness, and a fresh, bright flower in her glossy hair hanging softly around her shoulders. Larry's father, clothed in a yarmulke and a fringed prayer shawl, performed the ceremony, and when he said, "Be fruitful and multiply," a small giggle escaped Betsy's lips. With the breaking of the glass, Rabbi Isadore Stein was curiously overwhelmed. The lusty cries of "Mazel tov, mazel tov" came mostly from the mouths of the goyim Jenny had gathered together.

It was a spirited party that followed. Long tables, set in the shade of beautiful elms, were covered with great platters of smoked sturgeon, salmon, sliced turkey, beef, and tongue. Bowls were heaped high with salads, and there were breads and cheeses, fruits and pastries of all kinds. A good trio was just getting going as the champagne corks popped. The senior Steins and the Silvers joined hands and danced a far from tame kazatsky. Then everyone joined hands. Even Lewis Miller kicked up his heels and danced until he was breathless.

At midnight Jenny stood at the door between Dan and George and waved her arm. "Good-bye," she said, "good-bye." Finally, they went inside, George leading the way, as Dan and Jenny took a last look at the full moon. He turned an eye toward the stairs, wondering if he should look in on Lewis.

Smiling gently, Jenny said, "I'm glad you put him to bed."

"Good night, Jenny." Then, bending, George kissed the top of her head.

"Sleep well," Dan said.

"I'll do that," George said, his hazel eyes smiling.

Jenny and Dan stood gazing after him, then Dan lifted Jenny and carried her upstairs to their room.

Because of his convivial evening, Lewis was late down to breakfast on Monday. With his third cup of strong black coffee, he said, "I think I'll live, though I'm still not sure I want to."

Jenny laughed and got to her feet. She produced fruit, cottage cheese, and dry toast.

"You say you sent the boys away for the day. Why?"

"They wanted to go with Bessie to see the Silvers off, and I wanted you all to myself for a few hours."

When Lewis had finished, they both got up. Jenny suggested the garden, but Lewis turned down sunlight. "Let's go to Dan's study," he said.

There was a great deal they had to say to each other. Lewis listened attentively as Jenny talked about the family.

"Then they'll be leaving California before long?"

"Yes, next week. They want to be in Atlantic Beach, in the cottage they always take, before the hot weather starts." Jenny explained to him Sara's and Dorothy Adamson's plans for the summer.

"I hope to see them before I leave."

"Of course, over the Fourth of July."

"You're going to leave the children there all summer?"

"And Bessie. Now that she has a church to go to at the beach, she likes it there."

Lewis asked, "Will Dan take a couple of weeks?"

"Yes, and a few long weekends."

"I suppose it's silly to ask about your footballer?"

"He'll join us for his vacation while Grandma is away. That way Mama won't be alone."

Lewis already knew that Sara spent the month of August in Martha's Vineyard, where Andrew Gunther still owned a house. What he was thinking he did not say aloud. And Jenny was anxious to avoid talking about Sara and Andrew; she was thoroughly convinced that she alone knew anything of what was taking place between them. Moving quickly to a different subject, she said, "I need to talk to you about Baldwin Brown, the psychiatrist from Washington. What *does* Harry Stack Sullivan see in him?"

Lewis gave her question some consideration. Then he said, "Doesn't Brown conform to your personal standards?"

"That's right," Jenny replied, pushing aside the temptation to elaborate upon her opinion of the man.

"I'd like to ask you specifically what you dislike about him."

"Well, my initial reaction was based upon his behavior the first time Dan brought him home to dinner. Since then I've heard him say the most terrible things. For instance, at one of the Prestons' Sunday brunches, he tore into Sullivan, attacking his reputation. And, at a Truit dinner party, he practically accused his own control analyst of making sexual overtures to that nice schizophrenic boy living in Harry's home. Excluding bad manners, I should like to know what gives him the gall to talk about distinguished colleagues in such a manner."

"Other than yourself, Jenny, who else is agitated by his statements?"

"No one, it seems, least of all Harry. He's the one who gets Baldwin Brown invited everywhere, including here."

"Jenny, even the word 'homosexual' upsets you. Why?" Lewis queried.

"Oh, Lewis, I'm not reacting to a word. I'm trying to find out if there's an element of truth in what he says, and if there is—"

Lewis cut in: "If there is—that horrifies you. Is it because you think it's wrong?"

Jenny shook her head.

Lewis moved his chair around so that he could see Jenny better. Watching her, he began to speak. "Some students of human behavior give credence to the biological factors in the development of homosexuality—these factors being either congenital or a disturbance in the endocrine system. But more important are the psychological factors.

"Normally, the boy is emotionally attached to the mother and ultimately identifies himself with the father. Now we ask ourselves: 'Why does the boy continue to identify with the mother?' " Lewis took a pause to reach out for a cigarette. Jenny struck a match, leaned forward, and lit it for him. Then, again looking over the rim of his glasses, Lewis went on with his lecture. He was hitting his stride now.

"The mother may not necessarily be a good mother. The boy's identification with her may be his way of coping with hostility toward the father. In other words, if you can't fight him—seduce him.

"That is one form of homosexuality.

"Another form is based upon the fear of women."

"The third is a derivative of narcissism. The person falls in love with his own image or the idealized image of himself. Before I go on, do you understand?"

"I think so." Jenny did not add: "That doesn't make it any easier to accept."

"Good," said Lewis, dropping the burned-out cigarette into an ashtray. "I'll tell you now about latent homosexuality—the kind that does not express itself in overt form. This condition, known as the homosexual process, may influence behavior in other ways. In the choice of an occupation. Or it may interfere with a man's heterosexual life. Impotence, promiscuity—the search for a satisfactory sexual relationship with a woman, which is never found."

Jenny was quick to see the point behind the lesson, and Lewis, who was not only innately perceptive but also a trained observer, knew it at once. "All right," he said. "You understand that Baldwin Brown's remarks represent his own fantasies. Naturally, you consider that no excuse. Let's skip that for a moment. We can come back to it another time. You still want the answer to your original question: 'What does Harry see in Brown?' Right?"

Jenny nodded but added, "Of course, if you're tired—"

"You needn't worry about me, Jenny. I enjoy teaching you, telling you about people. You're so easy to be with."

Jenny smiled her pleasure. "Thank you."

Lewis savored her response. "I don't suppose you've seen the inside of Phipps."

"Only Dan's office and Lucy Rockford's. I've never wanted to visit the wards."

"It doesn't matter. I just wondered if you know that ordinarily they do not give long-term residential care." He paused and looked deep into her eyes. "Agnes Brown is the exception—only she wasn't Agnes Brown then. She was Agnes, the breathing corpse, who couldn't talk, who didn't walk. Tube-fed, she incontinently evacuated. She was a stinking mess—a completely regressed schizophrenic kept on for teaching purposes."

Dumbfounded by the implication, Jenny stared.

"Stunned, aren't you?"

Jenny nodded and then listened intently as he went on. "Let's skip back about eight years. Sullivan was then at Phipps where Baldwin Brown was a third-year resident. One morning, on rounds with the medical students, Harry was called to the telephone, so he told Brown to take over for him.

" 'Here,' said Brown, 'is the tragedy of schizophrenia.' He was speaking of Agnes. 'They tell me she was a gifted art student and really quite pretty.' There were murmurings among the students. 'Too strong for my nose. Miserable-looking skeleton. Hopeless.' One girl edged gingerly away, her delicacy offended by the stench.

"Agnes slowly raised her eyes and looked at Baldwin Brown."

"He motioned them to keep quiet. Testing to make sure of her breathing, he bent down and whispered in a voice so quiet even the student closest to him had to strain to hear. 'I'll be back, Agnes.' Then, after a pause, he said, 'If my return holds meaning for you, answer me by blinking your eyes twice.' "

Lewis slapped Jenny's knee. "She answered him, Jenny. Brown caught up with Harry later in the morning. 'You heard about Agnes?'

"Harry frankly expressed his doubts. 'There's nothing we can do,' said he. 'She's been in it too long. Furthermore, she simply can't last much longer. She's in horrible shape.'

"When Brown finished pleading, Sullivan gave in. 'By golly, Brown. You just might get through.'

"Brown stayed with her all that afternoon. He gave her a sponge bath and washed her hair. Before he went off duty that night, he changed her diaper and sat for a while singing to her. When he said good night, her eyes followed him silently. He returned at dawn. By the time he left her at the end of that day, she was drinking milk from a nursing bottle. A week later, at his departing, she sobbed bitterly. With his handkerchief he wiped her tear-streaked face and sat beside her improvised crib for the rest of the night. A few weeks later she was dry and, soon after, bowel-trained. Then Agnes became a troublesome baby. She yelled furiously when he had to leave her. For the slightest reason she spit up her solid food. Month after month Baldwin Brown fought a desperate battle to save Agnes. Then one day Sullivan called him in. He smiled at Brown. 'I think Agnes' therapy must now continue outside the hospital. Will you make the arrangements or shall I?'

" 'I've already picked her residence,' said Brown. Before Harry could say, 'Good,' Brown was talking again. 'I want *you* to take her on as a private patient in a full-scale analysis. I insist upon your getting your full fee. After all, the doctor has to be happy, too.'

"Harry burst out with a compelling, 'Why?' His surprise was violent because Baldwin Brown answered, 'I am marrying her.' "

Jenny's eyes smiled. "Does he love her?"

"Perhaps not in the conventional way. Agnes is still fragile. He keeps his home her sanctuary."

There was a stillness about Jenny that Lewis judged to be expectant; she was waiting for him to say more. He lit a cigarette—this time from his gold lighter. Deep in thought, he smoked in silence. After a while he lifted his eyes to Jenny. "This man-woman thing is a curious business." Then he asked, "What are your feelings now about Baldwin Brown?"

"All mixed up."

"My God, Jenny! You always surprise me."

Jenny answered. "How on earth can the husband of Agnes be the same man who sleeps with his daughter from a previous liaison?"

Lewis rose and patted Jenny's head. Then he burst out laughing.

"Please tell me what's so funny."

Lewis shook his head. "Your prudery is so apparent."

Sighing, Jenny smiled. "Dan doesn't think I'm a prude."

Lewis patted her head again. "With him you are wanton—a minx in silk and scarlet."

Jenny stood up. Lewis' arm went around her shoulder. Peering into her face, he said, "Make yourself pretty. I'm taking you out to lunch. We can talk more when we get there."

Later Jenny raised her wineglass. "It seems queer. Everywhere Dan goes there's one. In Vienna there was Eva Bauer. Then Sue Palmer. And now this Laura Mitchell. All lively, intelligent colleagues—all immoderately devoted to him. What's his devastating charm, Lewis?"

"Troubled?"

"Yes."

Aware of fear, Lewis asked, "What prevents you from telling him so?"

"I tell him, but it's like an accusation to him. It frees him to keep his own counsel. His nature is not to talk."

The wine bottle was empty. The waiter brought the bill.

"Let's go home, Lewis."

"Not until—"

"Very well. Laura Mitchell is a manipulative woman, utterly without conscience or principle. Unfortunately, she is bright. And she is no plain Jane with a shiny nose."

Lewis leaned on the table and tapped his forehead. Then he answered the question in her eyes. "I see no threat in Laura Mitchell. She is a psychopath and she'll arrange her own defeat. Furthermore, Dan reserves his deep relationships for very few people. She is not one of us.''

Jenny did not respond immediately. She was wrestling with a thought.

"Yes?" Lewis asked eagerly.

"I sometimes find Dan difficult to understand. If his authentic happiness is with me and our boys, why does he invariably reveal his appeal to this type of woman? Is he testing himself—indulging himself in an orgy of restraint? Is this, then, his weakness?"

Lewis did not dismiss Jenny's interpretations entirely. They were astute. He shrugged his shoulders and said, "I am afraid it is too soon to know."

Jenny met his eyes. With a note of bitterness in her voice, she said, "I wish there could be an end to his analysis."

Lewis leaned forward and took her hand.

"Tell me truthfully, Jenny. Are you raising the stumbling block yourself—making it difficult by looking at the analysis only from the viewpoint of the wife, the rationalist? Caught, she makes the sacrifices. And gets nothing in return—so she imagines."

"Oh, Lewis," Jenny replied without thinking. "It's not the expense. Dan is the one spasmodically occupied with money."

Lewis let go of Jenny's hand, took another cigarette, and lit it. Presently, he said, "Money popped into your head. Interesting. Possibly because it was so unexpected to both of us. What is the full extent of your resistance? How hard are you fighting the analysis, thereby prolonging it?"

"If the analysis were to terminate, we could go home. I admit to that. Sometimes I feel myself under the strain of playing second fiddle to an all-consuming career. That's hard to accept. In some ways George is more a father to my sons than Dan is. And I suppose I'm jealous—possibly because Dan puts such value on women with special skills. But actually it is I who am doing the real thing, rearing our children, running a home, entertaining at a moment's notice. Laura Mitchell couldn't stand being near Eric and Annie for two minutes, despite all her maudlin talk. Had she wanted to relate to Paul, it would have been useless. He detested her on sight."

As the thought—*I do rave on*—flashed into her mind, Jenny paused. A half smile formed on her lips, and her hand touched Lewis. "If we leave now, we can walk part of the way home. Otherwise, we'll have to taxi. The children will be waiting."

Lewis' gesture kept her from rising. "We'll have our stroll. Very possibly, even Dan will beat us home. But I want more answers."

"Then I'll have a cup of coffee."

Lewis gazed measuredly until Jenny put down the coffee cup. At length he said, "How old is Paul—a little shy of eight?"

Jenny nodded.

Lewis went on staring at her. "You say he despises that female. Why? Has he found his father alone with her—perhaps talking together? It doesn't have to be indiscreet. Children get confused or misunderstand. Father comes home for dinner. He brings a pretty lady. Suddenly Paul is left out. So is Mummy." Lewis' voice became suddenly impassioned. "It's dangerous. Terribly dangerous."

Jenny saw right away what Lewis was getting at. She said quietly, "I don't think Paul saw or heard anything. But I can't be sure. As I told you before, Bessie is getting old. Church nights she's not even there. It's pretty hard to know what's going on in the living room if I'm in the kitchen. As a matter of fact, Dan enters his study and settles himself in one easy chair and his guest in the other; the children are not allowed in. He wants them fed and upstairs so that I can join him. And Paul is sensitive to atmosphere. Paul seems to know"—the pride in the boy showed in her eyes—"with a half glance how I feel."

Lewis said, "About you, Jenny." And his attitude was far from detached. "You doubtless communicate your feelings to Paul. Perhaps, nonverbally, but direct."

"Not necessarily. In the first place Paul is very observant. He is far more poised and more sure of himself than most boys his age and even older. And, like you, he seems to be equipped with feelers getting messages from space."

Lewis had one further question.

"How did Paul disclose his feelings?"

Jenny laughed. "Rudely. Annie was with us and Laura was short with her, but she kept on smiling at Paul. While we talked and Dan left for a moment to get more ice, she asked my opinion of her ensemble, saying she got it at a terrific bargain.

"I said, 'It's lovely.'

"But then she suddenly questioned Paul. He deliberately looked her up and down and said, 'It makes you look the color of vomit.'

"I intervened. But Paul refused to apologize and rushed from the room. After a reasonable interval, he returned polite and delightful, except at bedtime, he kissed his father, George and me, talked to Baldwin Brown, and went away as if she were not there."

"How did Dan take it?"

Jenny smiled. "The way he takes me—with composure."

Lewis grumbled. "Wretched woman!"

Dan picked up the telephone and gave the operator a number.

A little later Frieda called Dan back. "Hello," she said, laughing, "are you the new resident here?"

"Better than that. I'm your new pupil and I've got a red apple for teacher. When may I see you?"

"You've had your first hour with Lois."

"The first two hours."

"Good. That gives us material to start with."

Dan wished desperately that Frieda would say, "Come right now," but he couldn't bring himself to ask it of her. He waited for her to set the time.

"Dan, I've got a meeting of the Education Committee at eight thirty. I can save you a trip out here if I'll not be interfering with your dinner hour."

"Not at all. Jenny is always flexible about time."

"Yes, and very generous with potluck hospitality." Frieda laughed again. "I'll be there fiveish."

"Great. Thank you, Frieda." Dan called Jenny and turned quickly back to his desk and read his notes.

> Lois Lewis, an unmarried, anxiety-ridden, twenty-four-year old white female. Thin pretty face. Odd hairdo. At the onset of her difficulties—age twelve—her condition was diagnosed as poliomyelitis. Her most characteristic feature is her gait, which is spastic, stiff-legged, and pigeon-toed. Not exactly—but approaching—a scissors gait.

At the sound of his secretary's voice, he stopped reading. "Mrs. Gunther wondered whether you'd pick up her order at Geffen's. She phoned in too late for their delivery."

Jenny met Frieda at the door with a happy, warm welcome. The door had hardly closed behind them when Paul and Eric rushed forward, delighted. They were very fond of Aunt Frieda. In the first place, because she really liked them and understood how to deal with children. In the second place, they perceived that, whereas there was a studied politeness in the manner in which Mom received some of Dad's doctor friends, there was no mistaking her affection for Aunt Frieda.

Immediately Eric cried, "It's early. You've come to play with us."

"We've a new game," Paul volunteered. "It's not too easy because it's mostly for grown-ups."

Met by two pairs of wide-open eyes, Frieda felt trapped. Just then she heard Dan's steps on the stairs and, in seconds, he stood in the doorway.

"Dad, Aunt Frieda. . . ."

"Hold on, Paul."

With a big grin that embraced both women, Dan kissed Jenny. He then kissed Frieda's hand. When Jenny asked inquiringly for her order, he said, "Sorry, it's on the back seat. I saw Frieda's car and hurried in. I'll go and—"

"Never mind, dear. I'll send Bessie."

Eric, meanwhile, seized Frieda's hand, a pleading look on his face. Jenny quickly put her arm around the boy. "Dad and Aunt Frieda are home early because they've work to do."

Still staring at Frieda, Paul said, "You'll eat with us, won't you?"

She smiled. "I seem to be making a habit of it."

As Dan flung open the door to his study, Frieda's comment was pointed but not sharp in tone: "For a girl as dainty in appearance, Jenny is a woman of considerable strength. How she manages to accomplish so much with only the help of fat, heavy Bessie is a mystery. Do you, Dan Gunther, know how lucky you are?"

Dan turned and faced her. His eyes told her that he knew Jenny's worth. Seated near the window, they talked for an hour.

"Lois' history, confirmed by her parents, is that she developed this condition suddenly."

"You said: 'Age twelve?' "

"Richard Blewett has determined it was not poliomyelitis because the paralysis was not of a flaccid nature. It is spastic."

"Was she a nervous child?"

"Very. Nervous and frightened—a bed-wetter, a nail-biter. The works. But she got along fairly well—until she was twelve years old. I don't know what happened then. After the 'incident,' she was all at once pampered, overprotected, and indulged by both parents, especially by her mother."

"She spoke of an older brother who, when she was about three, forced her into sex play."

"Did she talk about her paralysis?"

"Not really. Only to say that, in spite of it, or maybe because of it, men are very attracted to her. As a matter of fact, she is very much engrossed with her own appeal. She said, 'Men keep wanting to make love to me. Even married men.' Mainly she harped on—in her words—'nervous spells.' "

"What's her occupation?"

"Legal secretary. From what she tells me—a good one."

"And you mentioned the possibility that her paralysis may have had its origin in trauma. That something terrible happened when she was twelve."

"Yes. She replied, 'I must have forgotten.' But my remark left her shivering. Should I have gone on?"

"No. Never rush a patient."

"Incidentally, Frieda, I told her in some detail, so that she'd not expect a miracle, that because her paralysis has lasted so long, the chances are that some irreversible neurological changes have taken place."

"How did she take it?"

"In stride."

Frieda nodded. "Do you have confidence and optimism with regard to this patient?"

"Yes. She has the personality compatible with the development of a conversion hysteria. I think we can help her."

"Now, Dan," Frieda Fromm-Reichmann said with a smile, "the time has come for me to give you my speech.

"Don't put her on the couch too soon. When she starts to look away because she appears to be embarrassed, then put her on. Let her talk freely, but *don't* pry.

"Be alert to all forms of communication—her speech, her mannerisms, her postures. Even her hiding. That may be the most important.

"Keep careful notes. What the patient says. What you say. Even though the taking of notes may interfere somewhat in your communication, it's unwise to rely on your memory in a control case. It is also important to know, at all times, what your reaction is to your patient. If you find yourself getting angry, you must assume your patient is trying to elicit this in you. Your natural reaction is the guideline by which you judge how other people respond to the patient.

"Watch your own objectivity. It is part of the therapeutic process for the analyst to be given the identity of significant figures in the patient's life. It is quite another thing for the doctor to react to his patient as if the patient were significant in his own life."

Realizing that Dan had heard all this before, Frieda was smiling. "Come see me next week. Once a month I'll come to the pleasant comfort of this room."

Pleased with this arrangement, Dan murmured his appreciation. They then returned to Jenny, and as the clock struck seven, they entered the dining room.

For three months Lois Lewis talked freely but said nothing. Then she told him all she remembered of the first seduction. "He was nine and I was three. It was in the darkness of the barn. We lived on a farm then. Exactly what he did to me is sort of blurred. I think there was a thunderstorm. That's why we were in the barn. The terrible part was what he did to me afterward. 'If you ever tell,' he said, 'I'll put a snake in your bed.' He knew I was terribly afraid of snakes.''

"Did he ever do it again?"

"No," Lois said. She sat up and looked at Dan. "I'm afraid in the dark."

Months later: "I remember. I remember quite well." With each sentence, her voice got louder, her breathing more labored.

"My parents were called away. My brother and I had supper. He gave me wine—lots of it. He led me upstairs to my bedroom. He undid my dress. He was real nice to me. Gentle and nice. He said that because I was tipsy from the wine, he was going to put me to bed. He said I'd feel fine by morning. He took off my petticoat and my pants. I got terrified.''

Each breath far deeper than the previous one, Lois told of the rape with striking clarity. "Afterward . . . I begged him to go away.

"He said, 'We'll do it again in a little while. And you'll see—it won't hurt at all. You'll even get to love it. You'll come begging big brother for more.'

"That's when I made up my mind that, even if I had to die for it, I wouldn't let him. At first, in sheer amazement, he did not defend himself. Then, he hit me hard. I remember my feet felt cramped and tensed. And then all the strength left my body. I guess I fainted.

"When I came to, I loathed the whole human race, especially my mother because she belonged to a man.''

The loud bitterness in Lois' voice increased. Her breathing was rapidly increasing, and Dan saw she was approaching a state of tetany. "Don't talk anymore. You're overbreathing.''

Lois was aware of the stiffening of her feet; nevertheless she finished her story. "I woke up paralyzed. Twelve years later he's still frightened I will tell. That's my revenge.''

As he watched Lois move closer to the wall and fold a handkerchief very neatly over her eyes, Dan felt spent just listening.

In his control hour with Frieda, they speculated.

"It is *now* my clinical impression," said Dan, "that this is not a case of conversion hysteria. If her condition were purely functional, resulting from the rape, she should have shown some improvement after the abreaction of the traumatic experience. Her original spell of tetany was of such intensity it bordered on a convulsion. It affected the circulation of the spinal cord, thereby causing permanent damage.''

"Sounds logical. Most likely there was a thrombosis or a hemorrhage somewhere into the central nervous system, in which case, we may help her neurosis but not her paralysis."

Dan gave her a nod of agreement, then said, "Well, I must be going."

"When will you see Lois?"

"Tomorrow."

At the door Frieda said, "Don't you think it's about time you started your second control?"

Dan stared at her. "You mean it?" Then he felt her hand on his arm. With a shadow of a smile in her eyes, Frieda Fromm-Reichmann said, "Yes, I do."

For weeks, Lois abandoned herself to memories of her brother with passionate intensity. She spoke of him every hour. Then, during one of his control hours, Dan said, "She is fascinated with the subject of her brother."

"You're absolutely right. And it's not because she is afraid. The girl is full of hate and rage."

"Which is quite close to the surface," said Dan.

"It seems to me her paralysis is not a defense since she has no inhibitions in expressing her feelings. I think that from now on, you should bypass the paralysis and find the repressed material about her deformity."

Dan stood up. "Thank you, Frieda. I'll try that."

The next hour with Lois ended with her crying, then screaming, finally throwing a pillow at Dan. He was still very puzzled when he arrived at Frieda's office.

"The scream," said Frieda, "may be a call for help. More likely, it is the expression of rage. The tears are for guilt. The laughter is the distortion. As for understanding, the patient is right. You did not understand—her at least. It comes to her as a surprise that you're not like the others; you are not making a sexual advance to her. Her anger is that of a woman scorned."

"What may we expect next?"

"Analysis proceeds in an atmosphere of frustration. You do not always gratify the patient's instinctual demands. You must, therefore, analyze the transference and demonstrate its true nature to the patient."

The rest of their hour passed in general discussion, and Dan left feeling good, his own anxiety reduced.

A few days later Lois was much more relaxed, aware of her outbursts. Her face red, she went on. "I must be really mixed up. If a man tries to evoke love in me—one way or another, I drive him away. If he's affectionate or friendly in any way, I don't believe him. But if a man is indifferent, then I want him to want me. There's nothing like indifference to bring out the wantonness in me." Lois turned on her side and very cautiously glanced at Dan.

He continued to watch her, waiting for her to go on.

"As I was afraid of my brother, I made brothers of all men, fully expecting each one to violate me. For my own protection, I had to take the initiative—I became the actual aggressor; otherwise sex becomes too frightening. Then I have terrible guilty feelings."

"Perhaps you seek an increase in self-esteem, which means a decrease in feelings of guilt through sacrifice. By becoming the victim of a paralysis, by enduring anxiety, you are paying for your guilt and for your shame. You have arranged your life so that you must suffer."

Lois Lewis was taken aback. She frowned but said nothing. Then she got up to go. "I must think about it," she said, looking slightly dazed.

In the summary of this hour Frieda Fromm-Reichmann gave Dan an approving look and said, "You handled that material well. Your patient has passed the crisis."

Spring soon turned into a hot summer with cloudless skies. Jenny often took the boys on excursions, either to the green coolness of the Worthington Valley with its spacious horse farms or down to the shore near Annapolis. Dan was increasingly involved with his cases. Then the sultry weather hit. One Thursday evening, after a light supper, Dan was at his desk. Jenny was curled up in the big chair, her feet tucked beneath her, reading a Fitzgerald novel.

"Dan."

"Yes," he said, continuing writing.

"Oh, I'm so restless. It'll be so good to get down to Atlantic Beach this weekend."

"Just let me get this down on paper, then I want to talk to you. Why don't you take a cool shower?"

"I'm cool enough. Let's go to a movie. We haven't been in ages."

Dan finished his sentence. Then he twisted around to Jenny. "There's no reason why I can't take the time to drop you off and then pick you up at the end of the show. We'll have a sundae together and"—Dan hesitated before coming to the point—"I'm afraid, Jenny, baby, there's been a slight change in my plans. The choice was not mine, mind you, but I have to leave for the Eastern Shore in the morning. I'll catch up with you at the beach Tuesday night. Wednesday, at the latest."

Jenny knew full well no traveling clinics were scheduled on the Eastern Shore during the summer, especially after July 4. She knew the clinic regulars—Lucy Rockford and Marcia Steele—were both on vacation. She was also aware that Dan had been relieved of that responsibility, with his academic promotion. The Eastern Shore was now Laura Mitchell's territory. So Dan was lying too. Jenny very nearly surrendered to her furious impulse, but her brain cautioned, "Control yourself." She concentrated her gaze on the rug and compelled herself to stay silent. It was a struggle. When at last she looked up, she said, "This may be your very last trip to the Eastern Shore. You have never invited me along—I suppose because it meant leaving the boys. But since they are now at the beach and you picked my weekend to make this trip, I am inviting myself." She promptly pulled herself to her feet. She gave no sign of noticing the flush of surprise on his face, and she began asking his advice about clothes.

"Come here, Jenny." Dan smiled as he took her hands and pulled her down on his lap. Stroking her gently, he said, "I don't know whether I ever told you how dull the Eastern Shore is. Hick-town hotels. Lousy food. Nothing to do. You'll be uncomfortable *and* bored."

"You're utterly wrong. I'm never bored when I'm with you."

"Let's be sensible, Jenny."

She opened her eyes wide.

Dan looked uncomfortable, he always prided himself on handling Jenny right. "I'll be tied up at conferences day and night. And at board meetings for the regional clinics."

"I don't want you to be alone. Just driving up and back with you will be worth it, to say nothing of sharing your bed."

Dan thought: *Christ!*

Jenny glared at him with sudden fierceness. "You *are* going alone, are you not?"

Dan shook his head. He began to talk. "I know this couldn't happen at a worse time, but the call to the Eastern Shore came late this afternoon. Laura has marvelous ideas about day-care centers for working mothers. She prepared a convincing brochure about establishing child guidance clinics on the local level. She's got great ideas in other areas—the training of the handicapped.

"I've made useful friends. I've got to introduce her around. And I have to run interference for her because my chances of convincing the city fathers to part with money are far greater than hers."

"That's all very interesting, but I don't see what it has to do with taking me along."

Dan for once was at a loss for words. He had a remote sense he was letting her down in some way, but he knew he didn't need a chaperone. Taking Jenny away and professional conferences were two quite separate things in his mind.

Jenny's silence encouraged him. "When I come back, instead of going to the beach, we'll go off someplace by ouselves. We'll spend at least half of our time and all of my energies making love."

Jenny felt the crush of his arms. Pulling sharply away, she slapped his face with vigor. Then she jumped up, and in a voice that started full and grew to a scream, she let go the anger and the hurt within her. "With financial comfort provided by others, it is easy to take all the time in the world to attain the professional fame you want for yourself. Your friends push you forward. True, you have all the qualities for success. You're smart. You do the correct things. You even quote the right Freud. And let's not forget your fabulous smile—it makes a whale of an impression, especially on women. But making your professional mark and doing exactly as you please are more important, it appears, to you than I am, than our sons are."

Dan heard her out. "Anything else?"

"Yes, you have thrown away a marriage because I am throwing in the towel. The Lauras win. May there be many."

Dan waited for her to continue. She did. "You may not need a chaperone. Well, I do. Because I am calling George." Tears streaming down her cheeks, Jenny ran out of the study slamming the door in rage.

The realization of the full significance of Jenny's outburst came to him slowly. Like a statue, he sat mulling it over. He recognized the hurt he caused Jenny, and that caused him pain. He saw, too, justification in her anger. He realized a conflict of interests. Then his own self-righteous defiance took over. He tried to reason with himself. "Why the rebuff to Jenny? What am I trying to prove? And to whom?" Some minutes later Dan rang his analyst requesting him not to fill his hours. "I've learned only today we'll not be leaving for the beach until midweek."

Somehow he expected Jenny would be up reading. Instead, he found her undressed for the night in Paul's bed. She had fallen asleep before she could put on her nightgown. Slowly it dawned on him. Jenny had taken a sedative—something she had never done before—in order to sleep. He looked down at her: Color good, breathing even. He waited a full minute, then went across the hall to the bathroom. It was unmistakably evident that phenobarbital tablets were missing.

Dan undressed, showered, and shaved. Presently he was in Paul's room for a second time. Again, before he carried Jenny back into their own bed, he looked at her carefully. Her respiration seemed normal. Carefully, but with a controlled passion, he held her close in his arms. But there was no response from Jenny.

Dan slept only a few hours. Up at six, he shaved again, dressed, wrote a note, picked up his suitcase, went down to the kitchen and got his own juice and coffee. When he pulled up to Laura's house, she was not ready. She came outdoors and said, "You're early and I've still my clothes to pack."

"I'll wait."

"Not in the car. Come inside."

Dan hesitated, then he went in. She persuaded him to eat breakfast. "It'll save time. Besides, we won't find anything decent open at this hour of the morning."

Somehow Dan expected a soggy mess of eggs, underdone bacon, and overdone toast. But even the food she served was a reflection of the perfection with which Laura handled everything, from her career to her sex life. The mushroom-filled omelette was garnished with more mushrooms on top and surrounded with a ring of small sausages. The unleavened lemon biscuits that appeared were hot, and the coffee had a delicious aroma.

Dan made no comment. As he ate, he reflected that perhaps Jenny was right about her all along and that the gourmet breakfast was part of her campaign. That led him to wondering if it was by chance that the call to the Eastern Shore had come just then. Even the fact that she artfully did not intrude upon his withdrawal increased his suspicion.

Dan did not finish eating. He stopped, rose, and pushed his chair away.

"We had better get going." Remembering she had things to assemble, he said, "If you need help with your suitcase, I'll be outside."

With a little smile playing about her mouth, she said, "All right." She turned and went into her bedroom, leaving the door open. Laura had not minded Dan's disinclination to chat. She had five days and four nights. That, she figured, should do it. Or else, why had he come? He knew mental hygiene was a thin excuse—a cover to throw out to Jenny. The thought came to her that for all his sophistication, he was uncomfortable. He saw sex in black and white, and casual fornication as sin. With scorn for guilt and weakness, Laura came strolling out carrying an expensive suitcase and a matching leather catchall.

Dan drove through the streets of Baltimore unable to keep Jenny's words out of his mind.

When they got down to the old inn on the Chesapeake Bay, a restored colonial mansion set among its own magnolias, Dan's fears were confirmed when he found their rooms to be adjoining ones in a separate building near the creek. He marched straight across to the main office.

In the lobby of the big building, the clerk was full of apologies. "I am sorry for the misunderstanding, but on the telephone, Dr. Mitchell asked if I'd be kind enough to hold *her* cottage." The clerk was about to volunteer more, when Dan said crisply, "I want a room away from the parking area and with a double bed. Hopefully, Mrs. Gunther will be here in time for us to have dinner together."

Jenny heard a sound. It came again, sharper. She placed it, but she did not move. And then her eyes saw Dan's note fastened to his pillow with a safety pin.

> JENNY BABY,
> You were already asleep when George returned your call. He'll be here Saturday around three.
> I *love* YOU.
>
> DAN

Jenny stayed motionless until the remote sound of the bell became a piercing ring. She got out of bed, seized her robe and quickly ran down to the front door, which she half opened.

"Mrs. Daniel Gunther?"

Jenny nodded and frowned. The policeman looked at her hard. Eyes big and full of sleep, lips healthy pink, hair pushed back carelessly. The fragrance had to be French. And a long green robe that ended at her painted toes.

"I hope you are selling tickets," Jenny said as casually as she could.

"No, Mrs. Gunther, I am not. May I come in and have a look around?"

"There's nothing wrong here."

"Your husband has been trying to reach you since yesterday morning. He's worried."

"I went to a movie yesterday, a double feature. I came home to a late supper—after eleven—and read for hours. I guess the phone must be out of order." There was only a moment's hesitation in her voice as she recounted her movements.

Without taking his eyes off her, the policeman said, "No, ma'am. It's off the hook."

Jenny appeared startled. For a moment, until she remembered, she really was. "I'll take care of it at once. Thank you so much."

The officer looked down at her and smiled. "Not at all. Thank you, ma'am." He turned from her and went to the street. At the corner curb, curiosity prompted him to look back.

After brushing her teeth and combing her hair, Jenny slipped out of her robe and returned to bed. She spent the next half hour talking to Dorothy,

Sara, and Andrew, and to the boys, telling them nothing except: "Dan did try but—" She promised. "We'll come later in the week. Our telephone has been misbehaving. Don't try to reach me. I'll call you."

After that, to her own astonishment, Jenny obeyed a sudden impulse by picking up the phone again and asking for information. She got the number and called the Crystal Court. She made a reservation for eight o'clock that evening, in George's name. Hungry now, she started down to the kitchen, the green robe on the bed forgotten.

George was not exactly worried at the continuous busy signal, nevertheless, he got himself quickly together, tied a yellow silk scarf inside his shirt, and notified his exchange that, while he could be reached at the Gunther number, Dr. Snyder was taking his calls through Sunday. Less than an hour later, using his own key, he came striding into the Baltimore house, calling out: "Hello." He saw at once that no one was in sight and headed straight for the kitchen where, customarily, messages were left in chalk on a slate. There he found Jenny in her softly seductive coverup still at breakfast. She gave him a brief smile of welcome, and as he walked toward her, eyeing her curiously, observing the sadness in her eyes and wondering about it, the telephone rang.

A step away, George halted abruptly. As he reached, he heard Jenny's voice saying, "It's Dan. Don't answer."

His hand did not pick up the receiver. George was angry at himself. Not because he loved her more than anything on earth, but because he felt the high rise of longing as he looked at her. Consequently, he spoke rather brusquely, "All right, Jenny, what's all this about? Why are you starting your day at five minutes to two in the afternoon? Why was I unable to get in touch with you? Why aren't you at the beach as planned? Mostly, why in heaven's name aren't we talking to Dan?"

Jenny rose to her feet. "Because Dan is with Laura Mitchell somewhere on the Eastern Shore." To counteract his unmistakable disbelief, Jenny said, "He told me so himself."

At his shocked "Why?" Jenny felt the sting of hot tears in her eyes. George's arms went around her, and he was holding her, and it was like the first time he carried her. Her head was on his shoulder, her lips were close to his ear, and she was looking up at him. On their way out of the kitchen, George paused at the telephone. Once more the receiver was off its hook.

There was an excitement in George. This was what he had been waiting for. He was tempted to ascend the stairs. But he dismissed the temptation, though it occurred to him that, in her present frame of mind, she just might be receptive. He turned from the hall into the living room, and when Jenny was snugly propped up against the sofa's cushions, he sat down beside her. He made her tell him everything about the Eastern Shore community meetings, how Dan planned to get public support for adequate budgets for free summer camps and free summer classes, and the programs for training and recreational centers for the handicapped.

"What prevented you from going with them?"

With unsuppressed fury, Jenny replied, "Not the retarded. Nor the underprivileged." As so often happened with Jenny, her mood changed quickly, and she said in a voice hardly above a whisper, "I don't even know exactly where on the Eastern Shore he is. What if I really needed him?"

"Jenny, I am not saying it is so. But if Dan is fool enough to let the likes of a Laura jeopardize and endanger his marriage and his career, then I think I know where he is. If you want to find out, get dressed. We'll make the five o'clock ferry, and I'll have you at the inn by eight—eight-thirty."

"The inn?"

George nodded. "A discreet place, luxury accommodations, elegant dining, and around-the-clock room service from the bar."

With startling directness, Jenny cried, "My God, you've been there with her! Oh, George . . ." Jenny stopped herself; what right did she have to criticize his actions.

George felt a sudden rush of real hope. He thought: She's jealous. She cares. And these thoughts made his head swim. He bent down to her. "Do you want to go?"

She blinked back tears and shook her head so hard a long strand of hair fell across her forehead.

George bent down lower. His hands touched her face. "Darling Jenny, I love you so." He kissed her and Jenny's lips parted a little. George kissed her again and again passionately, and with matching fervor, Jenny returned his kisses. Then she threw her arms around his neck, and moving in close, her face hidden, her body offered itself to him.

With a great sobbing moan, George managed to retain a firm grip upon himself. Gently, he loosened her hold, then he put his arms around her. Jenny lifted her head and, eyes open, surveyed George.

Weak with desire, he hardly recognized his own voice. "Do you know what you're doing?"

Jenny continued to look up at him with big unblinking eyes. "We'll talk about it later." Taking the initiative, she began stroking his face. Another surge of passion mounted within him, and he buried his face in her smooth thick hair. Just as Jenny thought he could no longer restrain himself, George backed away. "Send me away."

"No."

They studied each other.

George sat back on the sofa. He took Jenny's hands in his. They sat there silent for a long time. Then planting a kiss on her forehead, George said, speaking softly, "Darling Jenny, I lie awake at night thinking of you. I wake up sick with longing. 'Please God,' I whisper, 'make her want me.' " He saw her firm chin quiver, her eyes mist over. He forced himself to go on. "I can only take you on my terms."

Jenny began to cry.

"Darling, listen." His voice took on a determined tone. "We're not going to hide. We'll wait and tell Dan and then I'll take you out of this house. You'll get your divorce. I'll get licensed in California. I'll marry you. I'll love you. I'll be faithful to you. We'll share Paul and Eric with Dan because we'll be forced to. But *you* will *never* see him again. For us, he'll be dead."

Sobbing, Jenny freed herself. She rose from the sofa, pulled down the flimsy gown, and with the back of her hand, she wiped away tears. When finally she could talk, she said, "Oh, George. Dear, dear George—if only we were back to where we were one brief hour ago." At the door she turned. "I made a dinner reservation at the Crystal Court. I'll cancel it."

"Jenny, no! You can't do that."

Jenny stared.

"Good God Almighty." George groaned. Within seconds, he was facing her. "We're back to where we were," he said.

Jenny went on staring gravely into his eyes. "I love Dan. I'll *never* stop loving him. I can't."

George took his handkerchief and wiped her face. "I know."

Jenny did not reply immediately. Then she said, "George Atlas, I think you're the nicest person I know." She rose on her toes and kissed him lightly. "Fix yourself a drink while I lay out your dinner clothes. We'll go."

His roguish smile back on his handsome face, George said, "We'll make it a night to remember." He went out softly humming.

They started with champagne. When dinner was over, George ordered more champagne. As they danced every dance, George held her close, and to the pounding of his heart, he felt the swell of her breasts against him. And he believed Jenny sensed nothing.

At one in the morning, just before the band put away their instruments, the bandleader moved up to the microphone. "Ladies and gentlemen, we dedicate the next number to a football hero and his lovely lady."

George led Jenny out on the floor and the guests applauded as they danced the traditional wedding waltz. When they returned to their table to pick up Jenny's purse, there was a magnum of Mumm's and a card: COMPLIMENTS OF THE MANAGEMENT.

"How do you like being a bigamist?"

Jenny laughed. "I love it. Do you suppose I'm just naturally amoral?"

George laughed with her. "It might be interesting to find out."

Outside, Jenny said, "Where to now?"

"How about home?"

"Not yet. Not with a whole magnum of champagne to drink."

"Well, there's not exactly a big choice. I do know an after-hours jazz club, a hangout for musicians. Want to try it?"

"Sounds divine."

A grin lighted George's face. "Why is everything—'divine'—to Californians?"

Jenny raised her eyes to him and shrugged. "I don't know."

"It took me by surprise on the Coast, the first time a fan said, 'You throw a divine pass.' "

Jenny smiled up at him and took his hand. "You sure do."

The next hour went by swiftly in the small bar run by the large woman in a bright orange dress. There was much drinking and minimal attention paid to the jazz band's loud playing, in an exchange of extravagant reminiscences fittingly watered-down for Jenny's ear. But Jenny did not want to miss anything. She finally broke in and said, "Don't spoil the stories. I know all the words." Accordingly, the next story was blunt. It related to what happened after a big game when a party of perhaps ten young prostitutes had invaded the locker room. At the point at which one of the girls decided to give the coach a preview of what was in store for the team, George managed to stop the proprietress, Sadie.

"George," Jenny said, almost embarrassed, "I'm hungry again."

Sadie wheeled toward Jenny. "Good. I'm starved." Then she signaled a waiter and told him what to bring.

The waiter stared at Sadie with no attempt to disguise his disbelief. "Smoked sturgeon! Danish herring in tomato sauce!"

"Tell Louie."

Dawn had come to the city when George and Jenny emerged. And just as Jenny was wondering if her legs would make it to the car, she suddenly felt herself being lifted. She took a deep breath and, looking up, said with a smile, "I think I'm slightly stewed."

"True."

In the car George said, "Put your pretty head on my shoulder and sleep."

Her eyes felt heavy, and closing them, she began thinking, surprised at herself that it was not Dan who came to mind. As they neared the house, she opened her eyes and looked at George with a strange look. Then taking the time to word her idea, she asked George, "Are you imitating Maggie? She wouldn't allow herself a man or a child of her own."

George, who had been preoccupied with his own thoughts, turned quickly to Jenny. "Maybe," he admitted. "But if that's what I am doing, it's what I want."

Jenny said nothing.

George spoke once more. "Though my father never stopped loving my mother, he eventually resumed his former relationship with Maggie. I considered him an intruder and jealously resented him. Years later, when I was trying to find out from Maggie if, given a second chance, she'd live her life some other way, she answered with great feeling in her voice, 'Oh, no.' She reached for my hand and took it to her cheek. Then she said intently, 'When you are truly in love, you'll not reckon the cost.' "

As the car drew up to the house, Jenny was so wrapped up in thoughts that, in the murky gray of dawn, she did not notice the houselights were on. When George put his arm around her and said, "Dan is home," she looked around at him slowly. "I don't care." Her dark eyes were hostile, and her voice sounded extraordinarily remote.

George bent to pick up her shoes and said, "If I were you, Jenny, I'd make Dan sorry."

"I don't need to. He's already sorry."

George bent down and kissed her hair. "Anything I can do to help." He glanced over his shoulder. Dan saw. Outlined in a white silk robe, he was at the open door waiting. George smiled at Jenny. "I think you'd like to be carried."

"Yes, please."

They went inside.

Dan had, in fact, waited long hours anxiously, having arrived at the house minutes after they left. His genuine worry was touched with a complete mixture of guilt and resentment, but prepared to be generous, he managed to look at Jenny as a weary little girl. That explained away George's arms about her.

"Give her to me," he said to George, "I'll put her to bed."

"I'm afraid not," George answered blandly, and he stood motionless. The disapproval in his friend's eyes registered immediately on Dan, and nodding musingly, he waited.

The total silence lasted seconds until Jenny said, "Please put me down."

Since it was obvious that Jenny intended to go upstairs without speaking to him, Dan made a persuasive attempt to stop her. "Have you any inkling of what you put me through?"

"Of course."

"All right," Dan said, "let's consider that settled. I guess, in a sense, I deserved it."

Jenny gave him a look. "I'm moving into Paul's room. Good night." She turned to George and said good night to him, too. But her voice sounded entirely different. After she was out of sight, Dan looked at George with his customary fondness. "Come, I'll make you a nightcap before we turn in."

George caught his breath and let it out slowly. *God!* he thought to himself, overcome with the sudden knowledge that had Dan followed her, he would have stopped him. George turned and, feeling a twinge of conscience, started toward the kitchen.

Dan got out a bottle of brandy and they had a drink; but they did not speak, and it was Dan, more than George, who kept the meaningful silence between them. Then walking past George to the door, Dan said, "I think we had both better get some sleep."

George slept soundly for the next nine hours. For Dan, however, the mild sedative he'd taken resulted in a headache. Dan was angry at himself, at the manifest absurdity of the Eastern Shore fiasco. Dan was troubled—he knew that this time there'd be no magnanimity or angelic yielding on Jenny's part. This was quite clear to him. Then there was his own sense of guilt to deal with.

"Well, if I can't sleep, I can't," Dan said to himself with a sigh and gave up trying.

The straight razor rewarded him with the kind of smoothness Jenny liked. After a couple of hot towels, he splashed perfumed astringent over his face. Feeling slightly more cheerful, he took two Empirin and went downstairs to start the coffee. He fixed juice, hauled out a tray and put two cups and saucers on it. While the pot on the stove was percolating, he got the Sunday paper and started to read. A large headline hit him: NEW DISCOVERY FOR THE TREATMENT OF MENTAL DISEASE THROUGH THE USE OF SURGERY.

Dan read the interview given by Dr. Walter Freeman to the science editor of the Baltimore *Sun*. His heart sank. "Prefrontal lobotomy!" He read the whole thing over again. This time his heart sank even deeper. "Christ!" Dan exclaimed, shaking his head sadly, "another step toward the evisceration of the neurotic patient."

The pot began to jump and the coffee started to spill over the stove. Dan grabbed a towel and transferred the brew from the stove onto the ready tray.

Once she was asleep, almost nothing would wake Jenny, but she was awake now. She heard the knob turn and the door open. She lifted her head and turned unfriendly eyes on Dan.

"I brought the coffee. Am I welcome?"

Jenny did not answer right away. Then she said, "I wish you hadn't asked that."

"In that case," Dan said, seating himself beside her on the bed, "I withdraw the question."

While she drank her orange juice, Dan sat there, his eyes resting on her face. When she lifted the heavy white cup, he said, "I can't understand. Why don't I make a good cup of coffee—like yours?"

The picture of relief, Jenny put down the cup.

Dan laughed suddenly. "Jenny baby—" But Jenny's eyes looked back at him, for once without laughter.

Dan wanted the distance she put between them resolved. He picked up her tray and placed it out of reach. "Do we kiss and talk—or not talk? Or do we talk and kiss later?"

"That depends on the kind of kiss. If it's a peck on the cheek, help yourself."

Dan turned over in his mind the advisability of blaming the entire episode on the analysis—the working out of the early object relationship with mother, the denial of an investment of libido in mother. But, on second thought, he dismissed this idea, because there was indeed the element of truth in the explanation. Dan was fighting impending revelations. Besides, he did not want to further tax Jenny's attitude toward his analysis. For her there were practical difficulties enough.

Jenny was mystified by his prolonged deliberation. Usually he was pretty good at abating her jealousy and then quickly considering the issue settled.

Dan saw that Jenny's eyes were becoming brighter—not a good sign. He wished he knew what to say. And then suddenly he realized that he, too, ought to have an explanation. He decided he couldn't worry over Laura. There were more important things. He looked at Jenny with probing eyes. "Why didn't you want to sleep with me? Because of me or because of George?"

"Because of George." Her tone was such as to discourage further questioning.

"Look, Jenny. It would be better for everyone if you know two things.

Above all else, I love you. And then I want you to know that I never wanted anything from Laura. I have no interest whatsoever in her as a woman."

In a voice rich with scorn, Jenny said, "Liar!"

Her answer came as no help at all. Dan gave a gentle sigh. "For God's sake, Jenny. Stop making yourself thoroughly miserable. It wasn't anything like you imagine."

Jenny sat up to her full height. Eyes blazing, she cried, "I'm fed up with your technical fidelity. I swear I'd respect you more if you honestly admitted to—every now and then—wanting the kind of woman for whom you wait your turn."

"That's crazy. You don't mean it. And I refuse to take it seriously."

Jenny sensed his attitude had changed. He was no longer on the defensive. With concentrated fury, Jenny yielded to an impulse. She picked up her pillow and threw it at him, hitting him full in the face.

Dan had to laugh at her ludicrous behavior. Bending, he grabbed her and kissed her over and over. "I love you."

Jenny struggled, but she couldn't push him away. Finally he released her. "Please, Jenny, baby, listen and believe me."

"I cannot believe you."

Dan's face remained calm, but he did not take his eyes off her. "What are you waiting for? Go on. Tell me."

With an easy pull, Dan took Jenny into his arms. For her part, she stayed quiet. Suddenly Dan's face tightened. "Jenny, my love. Nothing can change what I did, so we'll not talk about it anymore—except to say I had a view of myself I'll long remember."

Jenny's eyes looked somber. "Dan," she whispered, "I had a view of myself, too. George kissed me with passion."

Dan nodded.

"I liked it."

"Don't think about it."

"A priest once told me that in the eyes of God, the will is the deed."

"I understand," Dan said tenderly, "but now everything is as it was before."

"You're not mad at me?"

In a protective gesture Dan pulled her closer.

Jenny stared at him with a bewildered gaze. "No questions? Not a single one?"

Dan's reply was unlike anything Jenny could imagine. To her it was shocking that he said, "Let's slip under the covers. I'll make you forget all about George."

She cried, "No, I can't."

"Why not?"

Jenny sucked in her breath. "It's too soon."

Dan studied her a moment. "What do you mean, it's too soon?"

Still shaken, Jenny said, "Listen to me."

"Go on."

"Were roles reversed," Jenny said fiercely, "and were I to tell George what I just told you, his mouth would tighten into a hard line, his nostrils would flare, and he'd—he'd—"

"And you'd admire that."

"Yes!"

Dan thought it over. Then, with a deceptively moderate air, he said, "I'm not a masterful tyrant. I believe I'm a reasonable man." All at once, to her complete astonishment, she was flung flat on her back and Dan, holding her down, was arched over her. They regarded each other for a long moment, and then Dan asked pointedly the last thing on earth she expected. "When is your grandmother going to make an honest man of my dad?"

"Oh, Dan," she began. But Jenny was too startled. She couldn't go on. But whatever her hesitations, they melted away. Dan saw the soft look spread over her face, the color rushing gladly to her cheeks. It was as if she had gained a new maturity and, in the process, had taught him something.

After several moments he looked at her and asked, "Happy?"

A smile crossed her face as she assured him that she was.

"Good."

"You?"

Looking down at her, he nodded his head.

Jenny laughed. "You're sleepy."

Jenny slipped quietly out of bed. She stayed in her tub a long time, staring at the ceiling and thinking about Sara and Andrew. And about Dan. Apparently, he had known for a long time that they were in love. Why had she been fool enough to think that he failed to guess their secret? It stunned her that she was able to underestimate Dan, and silently she chastised herself. For moments more Jenny lay motionless; then she stirred and showered herself off with cool water. Refreshed, she toweled herself dry, her mind now busy with the prospect of feeding the men a substantial brunch. The next minute, as she opened and closed the door to her bedroom, she saw George. Caught by surprise—she had not expected to find him in her bed—Jenny dashed into the closet, where in quick confusion she grabbed a soft unwaisted sheath and pulled it over her head. Behind the shutter of golden eyelashes, George's eyes watched and marveled.

George paused in the doorway to the kitchen. Dan saw her glance flick to him, her face flush slightly. Then George deliberately took a chair close to Dan. Jenny poured steaming coffee into a cup and gave it to him, her eyes shining with welcome. A flicker of approval crossed Dan's face as he said, "We waited breakfast." George nodded his answer. He lowered his gaze and sipped coffee, his eyes filled with the shrewd suspicion of the inevitable. Dan had once more scored a success; Jenny had yielded some of her anger. Slowly, feeling a grudging admiration for Dan's skillful manipulation, George lifted his head and his eyes followed Jenny through the doorway. Ten minutes later she was back with a platter of old-fashioned sour-cream pancakes topped with blueberries.

George gave his attention to Jenny's pancakes, but Dan hardly paused. "Freeman claims that certain types of cases—the obsessive-compulsive neurotic in particular—are not helped by psychoanalysis. In expounding his thesis, he describes an operation which he has perfected. He reasons that by cutting the connecting pathways in the white matter of the brain, particularly in the frontal lobes, he can interrupt the emotional reactions to thought processes, thereby rendering the patient more adaptable to his environment."

They discussed the operation some more and George said, "A damn shame. I'd as soon let 'em die."

Dan too saw the flaws. "Personally, I challenge that hypothesis. And I can't accept his statement that the obsessive-compulsive cannot be helped by psychoanalysis."

"But—Freud's theory may be as unjustified as Freeman's."

"Perhaps Freud's statement that the obsessive-compulsive state is a regression to the anal-sadistic level is not the whole answer. Perhaps, it is a regression to orality. But as long as contact can be made with the patient, there has got to be a way to relieve symptoms and resolve the well-defended conflict."

Jenny hardly needed to be told.

"The meeting of the Southern Medical Association starts tomorrow. I wasn't planning to attend, but I've got to hear that paper. Right or wrong —what Walter Freeman says is important—because he is important."

George shot Jenny a quick look.

It occurred to Dan then that Jenny hadn't said a word. "I'm sorry, darling. You'll understand how important this could be. I should be able to leave first thing Wednesday morning, but there's no reason why you can't go ahead."

Jenny felt completely cheated. After the fiasco of the weekend, she had experienced a certain relief. Dan had apparently come to terms with his own doggedness and would now come to the beach with her. But at the back of her mind, she recalled that Walter Freeman would, in all likelihood, be Dan's chief examiner in neuroanatomy. The meeting then was crucial for him. Caught between a resurgent fury and her loyalty to Dan, she could only choke on the waves of resentment flooding through her. Without a word, she left the room for the sunshine outside.

Quietly George offered to clear the table.

The scientific meeting in Washington was stormy. Privately, harsh words were exchanged. Generally, the psychoanalysts were not with Walter Freeman, although—to a man—they admired and respected him. But questions were asked. And the dedicated—Dan among them—stubbornly sought the answers.

It was an early morning hour.

DAN: "Our quarrel seems like ancient history. I'd much rather talk about frontal lobotomy. Are you attending the meetings?"

A: "His approach does not interest me."

(Dan shifts on the couch): "Goddamn it, battling with Jenny is hell." He talks for a while about the quarrel. "Jenny was right. I knew it full well, but I sat, grimly nursing my doggedness as if it were the measure of my manhood. I saw her temper as a volcanic eruption. I began to think: She invariably triumphs over me. My hostile feeling toward her made me feel guilty. This led me to look upon her qualities as faults. I let my mind—" For a second Dan hesitates, staring into space. "My God! I imagined Jenny as some creature belonging to a kingdom of higher animals, consistently alerted to all eventualities. Then I began thinking about myself, and with a device not yet invented, I set out to measure intelligence. I found my brain primitive by comparison." Intent upon his thoughts, Dan seems to forget his therapist. "Harry Stack Sullivan saw for himself Jenny's brilliance. Once, he expressed surprise that it was she, not I, who first comprehended his concept of interpersonal relationships." Dan turns and, looking at his analyst, answers the question in his eyes. "Yes, Jenny—perhaps more than even Lewis Miller—persuaded me to find the genuine tenderness in the man, for at the start certain questions, which brought on my anxiety, crowded into my mind. I intermittently spark disaster with subtle jockeyism. I do not want her gaining the upper hand. Then I escape disaster because I am really bound to Jenny. This then is the conflict.

On the one hand, I know the real and I passionately love my own wife. On the other hand, I have unsatisfied narcissistic needs. Still, I avoid any serious experience, and in particular I am repelled by any woman, other than Jenny, who actively seeks genital contact with me.''

A: "Your relationship with your friend George may also be narcissistic in nature—fundamentally competitive and childish.''

Dan admits for the first time: "I don't quite know how to categorize George. But, whether he's friend or rival, the truth is I value him. I do not propose to end our relationship or even alter it.''

A: "One of the elements in your mother's nature was to instantly gratify your primitive narcissistic needs. Is this pampering what you demand of Jenny?''

DAN: "No, my attitude toward Jenny differs completely. On the whole, there is no problematic nature in my behavior toward Jenny. Nor is my attitude toward her rigid and frozen.''

A: "Let us examine the question of derivation. Did you attack Jenny with the kind of fervor usually reserved for attacking mother?''

DAN: "No, I never attacked mother—never had to. Besides, the comparison between mother and Jenny is one of contrast. Mother was passive—she seemed so completely tranquil. Her ways were gentle, always restrained.'' Once again Dan turns. His eyes meet the doctor's. "The flame in Jenny is no ordinary flame—it's mysterious and sudden and urgent. It is complete. It would have terrified mother, who was the cool morning dawn. Jenny is the hot sun.''

A: "Your turmoil is the reflection of your ambivalence to mother—your dependence upon her and your need to be independent of her.''

The screen of repression moves a little. DAN: "Ambivalence starts with bowel training.''

A: "Correct. That's basic. Feces, used to please mother, are also used to attack her.''

DAN: "When Jenny slammed the door, I knew she had made her last appeal. I felt myself grow old. I had to hold myself back from jumping to my feet and going after her. Instead, I forced myself to remain where I was, consoling myself. 'I'll woo her. I'll gather her into my arms. I'll find her warm and eager. I'll win her back.' It's always like this—after a quarrel, I feel an overwhelming urgency—I must make love to her. Then, especially, the satisfaction from taking and giving pleasure is tremendous.''

A: "Just as you did to mother. First, the attack—the stink. Then, the pleasuring—the present. The doing and the undoing.''

DAN: "You put it well.'' A pause. "That night I got no response from Jenny. That did not stop me. Afterward, I had a dream. I was at my mother's grave. It was covered with the black brownness of human waste. I felt sick. I looked around for a shovel. There was none. But I could not allow my mother a blanket of feces. I forced myself to kneel, and using my hand, I began to sweep. Instantly, a curious thing happened. Everywhere, scattered around me, were huge red apples, oranges, ripe tomatoes, yellow bananas, eggplants. Everything good. Everything clean. I felt proud.''

A: "Your mixed feelings toward mother reflect themselves in your struggle with Jenny.''

DAN: "You think my association with Laura was anal.''

The analyst received this statement without comment.

DAN: "I wonder: Is Jenny entitled to this explanation?'' A sudden thought and Dan laughs aloud. "Consider this possibility: Henceforth, if ever I am momentarily drawn to some woman, other than my wife, I am likely to see a mass of uh, h'm-m—''

The analyst chuckles. "Deucedly unromantic.''

With the ringing of the telephone, Dan rises. "I'll see you tomorrow.''

Another early hour.

Dan takes the couch. "There is little left to tell. I went as planned, but I couldn't get my mind off Jenny, nor could I calm myself.'' Pause. "I have led you to regard Jenny as strong and self-sufficient. This is true, but there's another side to her—the little girl side.''

A: "What aspect of the 'little girl' do you refer to? The angry little girl? The sad little girl? The frightened little girl?''

DAN: "I see now the fearful little girl far more dependent than I appreciated.'' A flow of words followed without interruption. "Jenny is always close to a source of emotional support—me, my father, Lewis Miller, George Atlas. No wonder I had a blind spot. Now I understand. Every separation from me is the reactivation of the loss of her father.'' Dan continued for several minutes.

A: "All right. You understand Jenny. What were your needs? What were you satisfying with Laura?"

DAN: "The stolen hours? Maybe I was saying to Jenny, 'Let me breathe.' Maybe it had something to do with my peer relationships."

A: "You don't really believe that."

Dan shrugs.

A: "You were reliving the preadult period of mate selection."

DAN: "I sure as hell deny that."

The analyst then talks to Dan about dependency.

A: "The basic primary configuration upon which all human relationships are established is the early mother-child union. This union repeats itself in many ways and in many guises throughout life. In the child's ego growth, after he has resolved the family constellation, he again duplicates the Oedipal situation with his peer groups. First, he becomes dependent and amalgamates with the group. Later, he differentiates himself from the group. This differentiation is the precursor to mate selection."

DAN: "I know all that. And I concede—perhaps there were sexual undertones to this Laura business, but none of these forces interfere with my faithfulness to Jenny."

A: "Fidelity is the strict observance of a promise. Loyalty is also faithfulness to a commitment, but with a difference. It is a character trait in which the individual makes the contract with his own superego."

DAN: "I accept that. And I confess—I want Jenny clinging and yielding. I also want to feed her flame. That is my well-being. I draw strength from it. But I have eyes. Am I to go through life turning them away because I am foresworn? That is living in a steel box. That is not the price I ask Jenny to pay."

His analyst had no answer for him, but he did have a challenge. "Let's go back to a glaring omission. It is not out of carelessness that in speaking of Jenny's dependency needs, you omitted all mention of her mother and grandmother."

Dan's reply held infinite insight: "Jenny does not need to feed off her mother or her grandmother. There the relationship is true and conflict-free. Her littleness is in relationship to her father—there is the unpaid bill."

A: "That is essentially what I wanted to hear."

DAN (a moment later): "I am taking a clinical position at the University of California Medical School in the fall of next year.

I want to leave Baltimore mid-December. Please, give some thought to our terminating date."

A. (surprisèd): "Clinical? Not academic?"

The reaction was one Dan had already encountered—as if it were downright wrong for the son of a rich man to want to support his own family.

A: "Is it your intention to take on private patients?"

DAN: "On a part-time basis, yes. But I'll still teach, and I'll allow myself time to study."

A: "I have a feeling that what we do may depend upon Hitler. What does your father say?"

DAN: "He does not preclude the possibility of a world war."

Six weeks later.

Dan refuses the couch. He says, with cool self-assurance, "I have proved what Laurence Kubie so correctly states, 'The training in psychoanalytic psychiatry is the longest apprenticeship in medicine—longer even than that of surgery.' I have paid my dues. Good-bye, Doctor." Dan walks out asking himself, "Now, why in hell didn't I tell him that Jenny is pregnant?"

It was then that the analyst picked up his gold pen—the one he used on the completion of a successful analysis. "I'll not forget Daniel Gunther. He is a fine doctor. He understands beyond the obvious. He knows the symbols. What they reveal. What they hide. More than anything else, he is a fine man."

Dinner was already on the table when the telephone rang loud and clear. They both started to get up, Dan saying, "People should learn not to—"

Jenny was quicker getting to her feet. "I'll go."

Dan grinned at the boys. "Your mother's curiosity overrides her good sense."

"Uncle George says it's dumb for Mom to do so much. He worries about her, I think."

"Yes, he did," added Eric. "He told her to go to bed when she's tired."

Dan nodded gravely.

"That's stupid," said Paul. "Mom's never tired."

"Uncle George says that Mom is a very obstinate lady."

Paul looked from his brother to his father. "Is Uncle George worried because Mom's got the new baby inside of her?"

"No, son. He's not worried. He just wants your mother to take good care of herself."

"Dad?" said Eric.

"Yes, Eric."

"I think he's worried."

Dan decided that he had better talk to George. He did not want the boys frightened. Offering them his reassurance, he said, "Your mother is active and happy, and luckily for us all she's endowed with rare good health. Everything is going to be just fine."

Jenny dashed through the door, a big smile on her face. "Dad's on the phone. He wants to talk to you."

Dan frowned and stood up. "You mean he's calling from South America?"

"Yep."

This time Dan was gone for almost twenty minutes. Upon his return, he said, "Hurry boys, get to the phone. You—Paul—take the extension in the kitchen." They bounded to their feet and were off with yells of hurray. As soon as they were out of earshot, Dan said to Jenny, "Dad is arranging to send me a private patient—the son of a dictator. I hope to Christ they're not going to smuggle him in. I don't want a run-in with the authorities—at least not that way."

Jenny ran her hand across her forehead. "You can't see him in your office, can you?"

"No, sweetheart, it will have to be here. And you'll have to receive him as a guest. I want Bessie and the boys out of the house."

"George will be delighted. He loves having the boys all to himself."

Paul and Eric reappeared, at which time Bessie brought in a tureen of soup, full to the brim, and placed it in front of Dan.

Round-shouldered, nearsighted, of nondescript coloring, Alfredo lived—until he was sent to the military academy—a completely sheltered life in a castle which had been in his family for generations. He was the seventh and last child among siblings who were far from close-knit, and the bond between them and him was even looser. Nor did he get along well with his father, who respected only those sons of his who were strong and could fight. His mother was religious, passive, and remote, and left him, from birth, to his ever-changing servants, who complained about his anger, ridiculed the questions he asked, and laughed at his idiosyncrasies—including starvation that lasted for days. On the eve of his eighteenth year was when Jenny opened the door to him, to his physician, who was also his brother-in-law, and to the three towering security guards, and led them into the living room where Dan waited, standing with his back to the fireplace and his face to the door.

In the seconds that pleasantries were exchanged and hospitality offered, Dan sized up the patient, taking note of the cold sweat that broke out on his face. In those same seconds, the guards immediately accepted cognac and cigarettes and lit up, drawing deeply on the cigarettes. The brother-in-law seemed more interested in watching Jenny, as she moved about producing hot coffee, miniature côtelettes pojarsky, a variety of breads, and good stately rounds of cheeses. The patient wanted nothing, but it took the three men a while to get the edge off their appetites, so they were slow to get down to the purpose of the visit.

At the start, Dan spoke privately to one of the guards who described Alfredo as an angry loner. Next, he met with the brother-in-law, whose conversation with Dan was over a snifterful of brandy, which he carried with him into the study.

Dan had spotted at once that the doctor—Phil, as he insisted upon being called—had learned his English in the United States—around Boston, he guessed. Because he himself had gone to Harvard, he suggested to Phil that they were, perhaps, fellow alumni, which indeed they were. This brought on a multitude of reminiscences. As Phil talked, Dan learned something about the man and the family into which he had married. Inevitably, they came to the Generalissimo—El Presidente.

"His popularity is hardly a mystery. He unified our country. He rounded up the bandits and executed them with the same zest with which they robbed and raped." A number of anecdotes followed. In none was El Presidente pictured as warm and compassionate. Rather, a few did reflect the man's savagery just below his surface charm—the charm that sent the populace wild.

Under the glow of the brandy, Phil breezily recounted tales of his father-in-law's cunning. "He knows how to look the other way when the profiteers take over. Just so long as he gets his fair share—" Phil was briefly halted by an interruption in form of a question.

"Well, it's not easy to say why he spends his time in the company of young officers. It seems to me that any man who has Alfredo for a son and my mother-in-law for a wife deserves the pleasure of virile companionship."

"What's wrong with your mother-in-law?"

"Nothing. She's a gracious lady. But, by nature, she is continent. Seven children, and she considers her conjugal duty completed."

"This is all very interesting. Useful, too. At the same time I am acutely aware of Alfredo and his mounting tension. May we put him center stage? Please relate at random or any way you recall his story."

"Alfredo has always been morose, withdrawn, and given to rages. Nor has he ever shown an interest in people, isolating himself for days. He feels inadequate compared with his older sisters, especially my wife, who is brilliant and beautiful and her father's favorite. He is constantly compared unfavorably to his brothers. As his father attained greater and greater power he became more and more frightened of him. At the military academy he embarrassed the family. At a place where his father and his brothers are idolatrized, he was a total nonentity. Then, a few months ago, Alfredo developed a curious affection for a fellow cadet. That, after he was tormented by the very same cadet for declining an invitation to accompany a few sturdy lads to the red-light district.

"To make a dull story short, Alfredo made some sort of advance to the boy. He was rebuffed and reported. The superintendent informed El Presidente of the overture. My father-in-law, who, in this area, has absolutely no tolerance, judged this an odious offense and withdrew Alfredo from the academy. Then he really cracked down on him.

"Since then, Alfredo has become increasingly disturbed, accusing everyone, especially his father, of trying to destroy him. He has threatened to kill the father. 'Before he kills me,' he says."

Dan dismissed the South American doctor politely.

"My guess is that Alfredo has reached a crescendo of agitation. I don't want to delay any longer. Please visit with Jenny. Then we'll sedate Alfredo and talk again."

Under violent protest and flanked by two guards, Alfredo was ushered into Dan's study. He sat down tense with hatred, cursing under his breath in Spanish.

"You may go now," Dan said to the guards.

In unspoken reply they remained standing.

The second time Dan spoke they no longer felt that he needed them for protection. As disquieted as Alfredo was, it was a matter of gratification to know of a man who refused to submit to his father's hired killers. This made him a little easier to deal with. Still, the diagnosis had to be made mostly on history. The actual interview was nonproductive. Suspicious, scowling, and evasive, Alfredo answered in monosyllables or grunts. After a tremendous effort on Dan's part, all he could get out of Alfredo were his systematized delusions.

"I don't know what's wrong. All I know is everyone had made up his mind to talk about me in the worst way. They plot against me."

"How do you know that?"

"Voices tell me. Besides, I can feel it in my bones."

"I hear you had some difficulty at the academy. Do you want to tell me about it?"

Dan found himself the recipient of a look of utter overmastering wrath.

Dan paid it no mind, and asked blandly, "Have you ever had a sexual experience?"

With pathetic eagerness to ward off all talk of sex, Alfredo quickly assured Dan. "No! No!"

It was abundantly clear to Dan that prolonging the interview would serve no useful purpose. "I am sending you back to your Embassy. I want you to take the medicine I give you and get a good night's sleep."

"Wait a minute," Alfredo said, sounding perfectly normal, "don't you know that officially I am not here. The Embassy knows nothing of my presence. Neither does your State Department."

Dan felt strongly troubled. "A hell of a thing," he mused, eyeing the boy. He led him back to the living room. Alfredo went quietly.

The guards rose abruptly. Soon they were across the room, and one of them was holding Alfredo by the arm. They went through the door, leaving it to El Presidente's son-in-law to thank Jenny.

"No trouble at all," Jenny said politely.

"You are kind."

Dan smiled, showing his near-perfect teeth. "About this time in the evening, Jenny is usually ready for another meal and I for a snack."

"But who will put it together? Your servants are obviously not here."

Jenny had no intention of distressing her guest. Holding her fingers crossed, she said, "My servants prepared everything in advance. Just give me a few moments because the food needs heating."

Much easier in his mind, Phil even wondered if perhaps he could help a little around the kitchen.

"Thank you. But there's nothing to do."

In a very short time they sat down to an abundant supper. Outside, the rain began to fall.

They finished eating near midnight. Jenny pushed back her chair. "If I may be excused, please."

Dan rose. Phil rose, too. He came forward, his hand outstretched. Jenny extended hers. Their hands clasped tightly, the doctor said, "You are a lady of great beauty and of great sympathy. We shall not forget."

The color deepened a little in Jenny's cheeks. She gave him her smile and said quietly, "Good night. And good fortune."

Dan's hand touched Jenny's. "If you don't mind," he said to his guest, "I'll see Jenny upstairs. Help yourself to brandy. I'll meet you in my study."

Her hand in his, they reached the second floor. Dan drew Jenny to him and pressed his cheek against her shining hair, marveling at her ability to have everything in readiness. His voice full of emotion for his luck, he said, "Jenny, baby, you make me happy."

Jenny gave him a sparkling glance and raised her head a little, waiting for his lips.

Dan found the study door slightly ajar. He pushed and walked in. A few steps brought him to the chair behind his desk.

Phil took one more puff and crushed out his American cigarette. "Well, what do you think?"

"Alfredo   is   suffering   from   an   extremely   serious   condition—schizophrenia—paranoid form. He has delusions, feelings of guilt and shame, and he is inaccessible. He is too disturbed to be treated outside of a hospital. He requires residential care and intensive therapy. Around here, I recommend without reservation Sheppard Pratt in Towson, Maryland, or Chestnut Lodge, which is close to Washington. Then there's Menninger's. Or Hartford Retreat in Connecticut. Or the famed Austin-Riggs in Stockbridge, Massachusetts. Decide and I'll make the arrangements."

"You obviously don't understand. It has never been intended that a son of El Presidente be hospitalized in a mental institution. That is why we are here."

"I am afraid it is you who does not understand. Your young brother-in-law was humiliated by the exposure. He feels persecuted. He can barely contain his hatred, which is overwhelming." There was a moment of silence. "Alfredo is potentially homicidal," Dan concluded sadly.

The doctor was far less startled than Dan expected. "I think your pessimism is unjustified, my friend. And your modesty, out of character."

"Quite the opposite," Dan replied, giving his guest a pitying smile. "My judgment is that you are being deliberately perverse. Or, possibly, you take the problem of schizophrenia lightly because you do not understand the nature of the malady."

Phil was prepared to admit that in no small degree the role of physician was a sham. Hard-drinking, lusty hell-raiser suited his self-portrayal better. "Dan," he said, "the mysteries of the mind were not revealed to me at Harvard. Since then, I have had more opportunity to study female anatomy first-hand than I have had time to learn the advances that have taken place in medicine. I ask you now to bring me up-to-date."

"To begin with," said Dan, "keep in mind that each patient is different. But, generally speaking, the dynamics of this condition are, on the one hand, a strong tendency toward attachments on a homosexual basis, and, on the other, a denial of these feelings. The denial is based upon rejection—the patient does not want to be a homosexual because he feels the basis for the homosexuality itself is derived from intense murderous wishes.''

After Dan had given him this information, Phil raised a questioning eyebrow. "Maybe I'm obtuse. But let's say I'm merely confused. As I understand homosexuality, one loves someone like himself. Isn't this incompatible with hatred?''

"No, in the paranoid patient, the two are related. He is unlike the true homosexual, who makes his compromises and accepts his libido choice as a way of life.''

Phil accepted Dan's explanation, but it did not alter a thing. He refilled his brandy glass for the third time, toyed with it for a moment, and put it down. "I don't deny we have a problem, but—'' He put his hand into his pocket. A moment later Dan was looking at an incredible emerald. It was magnificent, priceless. Phil's face relaxed into a smile. Offering the jewel to Dan, he said, "For Jenny. For her wondrous face. You will take Alfredo on as a patient, won't you? Oh, I've not mentioned this, but it goes without saying. Our security officers remain with Alfredo.''

There was a dead silence that lasted a long moment. Then Dan said, "I want you to take Alfredo to Chicago to see a friend of mine—a formidable clinician. Perhaps his recommendation will differ from mine, though I doubt it. But there is something to be said for a second opinion.''

"Take the emerald'' was Phil's reply.

Dan shook his head. "I'm afraid you'll have to find someone who wants it badly enough.''

"Listen, Dan, I'll tell you what we'll do—''

Dan rose. "Let's not talk about it anymore. I'll call Lewis Miller in the morning.''

After Dan closed the front door, he sighed: "Phew!'' with feeling.

A few days later Lewis Miller confirmed Dan's diagnosis, rendered a guarded prognosis, and let the party out of his apartment, earnestly urging immediate hospitalization for Alfredo.

El Presidente's son-in-law found, in Detroit, a psychiatrist, a beginning candidate in psychoanalytic training. He did not offer him the emerald, but he did suggest the fee be left open. The psychiatrist had already decided upon that. Still it was pleasant to hear. Their bargain sealed with a mouthwatering advance and a handshake, El Presidente's emissary went home, leaving Alfredo to his doctor and the guards to luxuriate in a stylish part of town.

"Ordinarily," said the FBI agent, identifying himself, "we do not disturb a physician in his home. In this instance, however, we beg your indulgence."

"Please come in," said Dan, leading the man into his study where, after they were seated, he waited for an explanation.

"Some months ago the deranged son of a South American dictator entered the United States illegally. We have reason to believe that he came first to this house."

Veiling his thoughts, Dan did not answer.

"You sent him away. Why, doctor?"

"I was afraid of him and for him. I could imagine him snatching up a letter opener from my desk and wielding it with the strength that came from the hatred he had for his father."

The agent glanced up from under thick brows and shot Dan a look. "You *really* thought that at the time."

"Yes."

"You made your judgment known?"

"I said that he was potentially homicidal."

"To whom did you say that?"

Carefully Dan replied, "To his accompanier."

"Are you prepared to name him?"

"Not at this time."

The agent knitted his brow, paused, and said, "You knew he was coming. You were prepared because you received a telephone call. From whom was that call?"

Dan laughed and said, "Come to the point."

"In a moment. First, tell me what you know about Dr. Samuel Thatcher."

"I never heard of him. Why?"

The FBI agent explained. "Late last Friday night his savagely slashed body was found sprawled on the floor in his consultation room, when the police responded to a call from his wife, who asked them to see if anything was wrong. The wife later told the police that the doctor sent his secretary home early because the identity of his patient was a state secret. That was why we were called in."

"You found the patient's case history?"

"No. Only a scattering of papers torn out of notebooks on which were scribbled bizarre bits from tales of horror."

"In English?"

"In Spanish."

For a long time Dan stared at the rug. He felt frightfully sorry for Dr.

Thatcher and for his family. Dan even had the feeling that Thatcher made his mistake because he was lacking in experience with intramural psychiatry. Finally, conscious of being watched, Dan raised his eyes. "What led you to me?"

"Dr. Thatcher could not resist boasting of his important patient to his colleagues, hinting strongly at his identity. The rest was routine intelligence work."

Dan acknowledged that with a nod. Then, regarding his visitor levelly, he said, "Are you now disposed to level with me?"

The FBI man found himself thinking: *The rest is very movieish.* He fumbled in his pocket for his cigarettes, found them, then asked, "May I?"

"Certainly."

"I am here for one reason: To enlist your cooperation. When I walk out of this room, forget you ever saw me or that you ever heard of an unbalanced lad named Alfredo."

Dan's "yes" was both an answer and a question.

"Please get his record out of your files and give it to me."

To the agent's surprise, Dan said, "I accepted no fee, made no notes, have no record."

Very quietly the agent said, "Strange. Dr. Lewis Miller used those exact same words." He rose. Dan followed him to the door. "May I offer you a drink?"

"No, it's late. Thank you all the same."

As he saw him out, Dan said evenly, "I won't ask how. I am assuming, however, that Alfredo is no longer a visiting alien but a resident of his own country."

The agent answered with an unexpected laugh. "Ask 'how' of your father."

Dan grinned. "Logical."

Dan undressed hurriedly. He went into the bathroom. His eyes softened. Submerged but for her head, Jenny soaked in the tub. Dan knelt beside her and stroked the pinned-up mane of tousled hair.

"I heard the doorbell a long while back. Who was it?"

"A man. He was obviously lost. I let him use the phone."

Jenny knew perfectly well that was not so. She had been on the phone talking to Tascha in New York.

She was turning this over in her mind, when Dan said, "You smell of roses."

Jenny smiled up at Dan, pleased.

George had taken the children for the day, and when they had gone,

Jenny found Dan in his study. He was holding an unopened book and look-ing at the fire when she came in.

"Hello, baby."

Jenny looked at him thoughtfully. "What's the matter?"

"It's nothing more serious than spring fever in the wrong time of the year."

"You don't look happy about it."

"Among other things I've got a couple of lectures to prepare and some papers to grade." He beckoned Jenny to his side. When she reached him, he pulled her down into his lap, where in an unspoken way he com-municated some of his pent-up restlessness to her. "Who's coming over tonight?"

"I told you. The Hills, the Truitts, and Frieda."

"I forgot."

Jenny's eyes opened wide in disbelief.

"Bridge?"

"Yes, for a couple of hours. I'll serve a buffet around ten."

"Know what," Dan said huskily. "We deserve a long nap."

Jenny understood perfectly well. She pretended otherwise. With a quick movement she suddenly sprang up. "You need exercise."

"Exactly what I have in mind," Dan said with a grin.

"I mean outdoors."

"In plain sight of the neighbors!"

With a smile on her lips, Jenny said, "A brisk walk."

"It's raining."

Jenny went to the window, pushed the curtain aside, and peered out. "It's only a drizzle."

With great reluctance, Dan pulled himself to his feet.

Warmly dressed against the chill of approaching winter, they returned to the house toward four o'clock that Saturday afternoon after a long walk under gray skies.

Sister Bessie met them at the door. "Hurry, Doctor," she said, looking pained. "A long distance call."

It was known to them that Sister Bessie had a very sober respect for long distance, so they hurried into the study, where the draperies were now drawn and where the still blazing fire that burned in the grate gave the room a feeling of snugness and comfort.

Sir Abe's call was a surprising one.

"The patient's name is Priscilla Collins. Got it?"

"Yes, go on."

"I've seen her in consultation. She's suffering from a simple condition of fatigue. But because it was essential to the well-being of my patient, a jittery dame, who exaggerates the daughter's condition, I sent her back to Baltimore and had her internist hospitalize her. She checked into Phipps this morning."

"You make it sound like the Ritz."

"OK, OK. Not checked in. Admitted. Satisfied?"

"I take it you want me to see her?"

"Brilliant deduction," said Sir Abe.

"Tell her doctor to call me, and I'll have her put on my service."

"She's probably already there. Go around to see her. You're expected."

"All right. Tell me about Priscilla Collins."

"For heaven's sake, Dan! I can't spend the rest of the day on the telephone. Talk to her doctor, Peter Wood. He lives on Charles Street."

"Where does the patient live?"

"Annapolis. Her husband teaches at the Naval Academy. He's a commander."

"OK, Abe. I'll ring up Dr. Wood."

"Hold on, Dan. Tascha is eager to talk to Jenny."

While the girls chattered of children and winter plans, Dan changed clothes. He went back to Jenny, who was still on the phone.

"I'll not be long."

After their guests departed, Dan sat up late that night with Priscilla Collins' diary. He came to the last entry.

> I don't care what they tell me. I killed Cassandra. I know
> I did. I'll pay for it with my death and beyond my death.

That was written three weeks ago.

The bedroom door was wide open. A light was on. Jenny, in a marvelously silky nightgown, was waiting for him. The sight of her sent the thrill of desire through him. A few minutes later, when she was in his arms, she said, "I've been feeling lonely."

Dan looked into those dark eyes.

Jenny trembled against him.

Dan switched off the light.

Afterward, he did not sleep. He lay awake, thinking: *How did Abe fail to see that Priscilla Collins' misery had reached a frighteningly dangerous pitch?* Dan experienced a queer feeling before he finally drifted off to sleep. A few hours later he was on the phone to New York.

Abe Brotman heard him out. "I cannot be overly concerned," he replied. "However, take all steps necessary. The parents are loaded."

Knitting his brows in astonishment, Dan said, "That I shall." Then: "So long, Abe. I'll keep you informed."

Monday morning, outside in the corridor, Dr. Wood and Commander Collins were waiting for Dan. They decided to go to the coffee shop for their talk.

"I believe your wife to be very ill," Dan said to Commander Collins.

Dr. Peter Wood concurred. "I am of the same opinion."

The commander did not flinch. "That's not exactly what Dr. Brotman thinks and he's a Park Avenue specialist. The best."

Dr. Peter Wood smiled.

Dan gazed at Commander Collins for several moments, and then said, "Is there anything you can add that'll help us understand your wife's illness?"

"She got drunk after Cassandra died and she stayed drunk." The commander sighed audibly. "That's why I had to ship her off to New York, or else she might easily have become the topic for gossip at the academy. I have to be especially careful, you realize."

"How did you feel about Cassandra?"

A mocking grin on his face, the commander said, "I thought you'd ask that."

"We're trying to piece together the events and the emotions that led to your wife's collapse."

"Christ!" said the commander, his temper blazing. "Who wouldn't cave in? She stayed with Cassandra day and night—nursed her around the clock."

"It appears," said Dan, "that you willingly allowed your wife to wreck her health in a useless fight against terminal cancer."

"I behaved like a decent man." He could see in Dan's face that Dan did not think so. He turned to Dr. Wood. "What do you think?"

Dr. Wood shrugged. "It's hard to say."

With no anger left in him, the commander surprised both Dan and Dr. Wood. "You see," said he, "Cassandra was a delightful, luscious girl, intelligent and verbal. She was a wonderful friend, who brought a richness to our lives. We all loved her. Everyone did."

Dan then said, "Thank you, Commander."

The commander rose. "May I see my wife?"

"Of course."

In the next half hour Dan heard Dr. Wood's report.

"I've known both girls since they were in nurses' training together. They were inseparable. I recall that Cassandra insisted on protecting Priscilla. I noticed that the first time I saw them on a case together. I questioned Cassandra. At first she adamantly refused to admit that she carried a far greater share of the work load. Then, finally, she confided, with the understanding that I'd not betray her confidence, that Priscilla had been tubercular, which accounted largely for her parents' overprotection.

" 'Yet you must remember,' Cassandra said to me, 'that, in spite of all the money, all the pampering and spoiling, Priscilla decided to become a nurse and live a useful life serving others. That, over the disapproval of her family and her doctors.' " Then Dr. Wood went on to tell Dan that Cassandra was all that the commander described her to be and more. "She played the piano. She sang delightfully. I must say I was a great admirer of hers, and, whenever possible, I put in a request for her."

"What about Priscilla?"

"She's not as pretty as Cassandra was, not as talented, and not as openhearted. I may add, I didn't know her as well. But immediately after Cassandra was admitted into the hospital, I had reason to reevaluate Priscilla on a number of points. She did the work of three nurses. Her devotion was so great, her supportive care so intense, that Cassandra was able to approach death with an amazing calm."

"How much was Cassandra suffering toward the end?"

"She was getting a grain of morphine every half hour."

Dan reflected: A lethal dose! "How can you be sure she was getting that much?"

"Read her chart. It's all there."

"And who administered the morphine?"

"Priscilla did."

Now Dan understood why Priscilla wrote into her diary, "I killed Cassandra. I know I did."

He did not see Priscilla again that day, but on Tuesday he spent two full hours with her.

"I had a dream, Doctor."

"Tell me about it."

Priscilla's lips tightened. She said, bitterly, "I was wonderful to her. Kind, tender, and caring. The staff knew it."

Dan nodded. "That's right. You were." Then he listened as Priscilla stumbled through her dream.

"Cassandra and I were on white stallions. We were carrying swords. We began playing a dreadful game. A battle to the end on horseback. We each slashed the other's mount, and then, after the stallions were badly wounded, we made them jump. I can't remember why we stopped. Next,

Cassandra came over and touched me in a loving way. Sexually aroused, I responded to her as if she were a man. She came closer and stroked my neck. Then I saw the knife. Maybe it was a can opener. I trusted her. I knew she was only teasing me. But—then—that knife-thing—opener—was at my skin. Cassandra slit my throat.

"I woke up."

"Priscilla, I want you to tell me the first time you got drunk."

Priscilla's lips closed.

"Tell me."

Priscilla closed tight her teeth.

"Tell me, Priscilla."

Priscilla glared at him and kept her lips together.

"You have got to tell me."

Suddenly Priscilla cried out, "The day she died." Panting, she screamed, "I hated her." Then Priscilla burst out crying. "I could never hold a candle to her no matter how hard I tried." A terrible coughing spell ended their visit. When she was quiet, Dan left her. A minute later a nurse brought in the sedation.

Before leaving the ward, Dan called Frieda.

"Are you free for lunch?"

"Only if you can drive out here. I'm due at staff meeting at two thirty."

"Is twelve too early?"

"No, Dan. Twelve is fine."

"I'll see you."

"In the dream she has both affection and hostility toward Cassandra. Her own throat is slashed as punishment for her sexual and murderous impulses."

"The same is indicated to me, Frieda. But, I'm not concerned with the strong homosexual tendency shown in the dream. I cannot escape the feeling that she'll destroy herself by reactivating her tuberculosis."

"Yes," said Frieda quietly, "that is entirely possible. As Sir William Osler said, 'It is as important to know what goes on in a man's head as what goes on in his chest, in order to predict the outcome of pulmonary tuberculosis.' "

"I came here to ask you to help."

"I'm at your service."

"I want to transfer Priscilla here to Chestnut Lodge and I want you to take charge."

"All right, Dan. But I'm telling you now, I'm not optimistic."

Dan thought for a moment and said, "Well, do what you can. Maybe we'll get lucky."

Nothing Frieda tried worked. Finally, she had to tell Priscilla, "You must go to a sanatorium."

Priscilla started to cry.

Weeks later they buried her alongside Cassandra.

It was a long, hard day—gray and dismal. Dan was going home. He particularly needed to go home to Jenny. Just as he got up, the telephone rang, and the only reason he lifted the receiver in answer to the ring was habit—a habit formed out of training and tradition.

The caller was Dr. Lewis Hill, an independent, hard-working, exceedingly well-thought-of teaching analyst. Mrs. Hill also felt a special tie to Dan, as she was in therapy with Dr. Freitag.

"Hello, Dan. Are you getting anywhere in your search for a second control case?"

"No, not really. I thought I had one, but when I told her that I'd be using her disclosures in my own training, she judged me sadly limited and decided to find a doctor who—in her words—'already knows his stuff.' "

After a hearty chuckle, Lewis Hill asked, "What about a second control analyst?"

"I am still waiting to hear, the official attitude of the Institute being: 'All in good time, dear boy.' "

On his end, Lewis Hill reached for the glass on the coffee table in front of the large sofa. Dan stared into the mouthpiece of the telephone, puzzled. After a while, he inquired, "Are you there?"

"I'm thinking."

Dan waited.

Finally, Lewis Hill said, "I have an idea. Do you know Al Coventry? He just recently transferred to our Institute from the newly organized New York Institute of Psychoanalytic Medicine."

"I've met him. Is he a friend of yours?"

"I barely know him."

"Are you recommending him?"

"He's got free time. Check him out with your friend Abe Brotman."

"Thanks, I shall."

"Tell me something, Dan. Are you willing to take a chance on a really tough case? Or do you favor one quick and safe?"

"I like challenges."

"Fine. I've got a humdinger. He's been totally impotent for five years, and unless you make him function, I can't get anywhere with the wife, who is my patient.''

"Is he a latent homosexual?"

"I have no idea."

"What's his profession?"

"He's a diehard, methodical physician married to an outspoken woman who, at the university, had a few well-publicized clashes with the authorities. 'Because of my concern for the working classes,' she claims."

"Sounds interesting. What more?"

Again, Dan heard Lewis Hill's chuckle. "Plenty. I'll send you a confidential report on the wife."

Dan grinned because obviously Lewis Hill was enjoying himself. He then asked, his tone serious, "How old is the doctor?"

"Roughly, thirty-six. They've been married eight years."

"Any other symptoms?"

"Undoubtedly." Lewis Hill went on, "I'll tell you what. Why don't I have Henry Bottinger call you. Get the facts from him directly."

"OK," Dan answered and added, "thank you—thank you very much."

"Don't mention it." There was a pause. "We'll see you Saturday."

"Yes, we're looking forward to it."

"So long, Dan."

Dan put the receiver slowly back on its cradle. He walked to the door, down the flight of stairs, and out into the street. He drove deftly through the early evening traffic. As the car drew up in the driveway, Jenny walked around the house to meet him.

"You're late, darling."

"Sorry."

Jenny held her face up to be kissed.

Dan put his arms around her and drew her to him, grateful for her smallness and warmth.

"You look tired."

Dan released her abruptly. "I must go call Abe."

Jenny's eyes widened. "Anything wrong?"

"No."

"Darling, let's eat first. The children are waiting."

"Later," Dan said quietly.

Jenny gave a deep sigh. "I'll feed Paul and Eric and get them ready for bed." As they ascended the stairs, Dan said, "Lewis Hill referred a good case to me, and I think I've found a control analyst."

"Oh, Dan!" said Jenny. "I'm so glad." There was pleasure mixed with relief, a real relief that the end was in sight. Jenny sped back to the children.

Tascha answered.

Dan found her habit of shouting into the phone deafening.

"Tascha, lower your volume. Please."

"So I haven't got your soothing voice. Sue me."

Dan replied with an easy laugh.

"Do you want to talk to Abe?"

"Yes."

"He's in the shower. Talk to me."

"Listen, Tascha. I'm calling to get some information about a teaching analyst. Tell Abe to call me back and reverse the charges."

"Who's the teaching analyst?"

"Al Coventry."

"He's a jerk." Then Tascha said, "Hold on. I'll get Abe."

A few minutes later, Abe was saying, "Al Coventry. He's my friend."

"I'm considering calling him."

"Not a bad idea."

On the extension, Tascha came in with, "It's a lousy idea. It's also stupid. He's a jerk. He unloaded an abundantly satisfactory human being to latch onto a rich bitch."

"Hold on, Tascha. The poor bastard had bad luck with his first two wives."

"He's not a poor bastard. He's a. . . ."

Abe's voice rose higher. "The good thing about marrying a patient is you, at least, get to know her before you've given up your freedom."

"Baloney!"

"T-a-s-c-h-a, please—"

Dan intervened. "Tascha, I don't want his personal biography. I just want to know everything pertinent to his professional qualifications."

"How do you keep them apart? If you buy yourself a louse of a man, you've got yourself a louse for a teacher."

Abe was dying to say, "Shut your trap. Dan wants to hear from me." He couldn't quite do it. But Tascha herself said, "Good-bye, Dan. Give my love to Jenny."

Without waiting for Dan to say good-bye to Tascha, Abe started on a rundown of Al Coventry's background and activities, including the fact that he had taken a leading role in organizing the New York Institute of Psychoanalytic Medicine.

"Does he really know his stuff?" was Dan's next question.

"He's a top classical Freudian, certified in Berlin."

"What made him move to Baltimore?"

"Two former wives and kids. A new wife. You understand. Besides, Ceci comes from Virginia. Baltimore's more convenient."

The silence that followed bothered Abe. After a short while he said, "I want to know. Have you decided?"

"I have certain reservations."

"For Christ's sake, Dan. Let me give you a piece of advice. Go to him and get it over with. It's about time you stopped being the eternal student."

"I suppose you're right, Abe."

A few minutes later, the immensely informed Lewis Miller was offering his opinion. "I haven't one good word for him. His career has never taken on an ounce of grandeur."

"So he's not likely to win the Nobel Prize in medicine. But Abe tells me he's bright and well trained."

"He's not bright. He's got an incredible memory. And I challenge the statement that he's well trained. You'll find few teachers of skill and wisdom—fewer who'll carry psychiatry forward as a dynamic science in this country. The rest content themselves with slight therapeutic results."

"As for Abe." His annoyance beginning to rise, Lewis counted off the number of times that he—Abe—clamoring for importance and recognition, reduced his own professional usefulness with exaggerations, half-truths, and fanciful fabrications. And when Dan said "I can remember when you saw promise in his brilliance!" Lewis answered, "He finished himself off years ago. Don't you ever learn? Have you forgotten that Abe thought Priscilla Collins was only suffering from fatigue?" Dan said nothing, remembering only too well. They talked more about Al Coventry.

Dan was troubled, trying to sort out what would be most beneficial to his career, and yet mindful of Jenny's years of waiting. Lewis Miller listened to the silence, feeling a gratitude for the fact that Dan was weighing the situation.

Gradually, Dan became conscious of the passing of time. More to give himself confidence than to dispute Lewis Miller, he said, "Surely, Lewis, were he unqualified, the elite Baltimore-Washington group would not have accepted him as a training member of the institute."

"There's where you're wrong." Lewis Miller then explained the inherent weakness, as he saw it, in the training institute. "On the one hand, each institute—within the requirements of the American—wants to set its own standards and be autonomous. On the other hand, it wants to integrate its training program with those of other institutes so that its members may move with full status into a sister group." Lewis Miller remained silent for a

moment. "With Al Coventry, the slipup was in New York, where they
have the distorted notion that a European training automatically equals good
training."

After some deliberation, Dan said, "It's difficult for me to believe that
Abe—"

Lewis interrupted. "Mark my words well, Dan. Your friend, Abe Brotman, is no friend. Jenny made something of Tascha—how, remains a mystery to me. But for you to be swayed by that ambitious—" Lewis' voice
rose with his temper. When he started to wheeze, he had to stop and rest.
Dan leaned back into his deep chair and waited for the wheezy sound to
subside.

Lewis Miller continued, directing more disparaging remarks against Abe,
until Dan had to laugh. "Mother Hen, you're at your best when you're
tearing someone to shreds."

Unabashed, Lewis Miller ignored Dan's remark and continued. "It seems
to me you put the cart before the horse. Line up a good case first, then
concern yourself with a control analyst."

"I have a case."

Lewis Miller sounded moritified. "You haven't talked over a new case
with me!"

It seldom happened, but there were times, and this was one of them,
when Dan felt exasperated by Lewis' possessiveness. His next words betrayed an indulgent rather than a resentful tone. "As soon as I have something to report, I undoubtedly will make you my confidant. OK?"

Lewis was by no means offended. Immediately he began to foist advice
upon Dan. "Listen to me, Dan. Steer clear, at this point, of a patient requir-
ing character analysis."

"Why?"

"Too many subtleties to analyze."

Dan shook his head and grinned. "You mean—there are neurotics
aplenty. Grab an easy one."

After a slight pause, Lewis asked gently, "Will you follow my advice?"

"I'll think it over." Dan thanked Lewis Miller and hung up the telephone.

The boys were waiting in their rooms. In the course of the next half
hour, Dan romped and played with each child in turn, encouraging their
enthusiasm. Then as each boy grew quiet, Dan tucked him in, pleased and
proud of their growing individuality. After that, he showered and went down
to Jenny in a silk dressing gown over pajamas. It was nine o'clock when
they sat down to a meal which Dan thought Jenny had kept with utmost

care. He was mistaken. She had taken the trouble to put a small club roast in the oven, to steam fresh vegetables, to stew dried fruits into a delicious compote. She sat listening intently, and until he had informed her of everything, she remained silent.

"What do you think?" Dan asked.

"It seems to me that the one being who knows what's best for you is Lewis. Be guided by him without misgiving."

"Nonsense!"

Jenny had the nasty suspicion that Dan might choose Al Coventry just to prove something to himself. "Darling, talk it over with Dr. Freitag."

Dan, sunk in his own thoughts, said, "Mother Hen has you thoroughly mesmerized."

Jenny's dark eyes smiled.

For a while they both ate and kept still.

"Jenny."

"Yes," she answered.

"You know, even if Al Coventry is as mediocre as Lewis insists, it's of small consequence. I'm not at his mercy."

A faint frown crept over Jenny's brow.

"I've come a long way from Vienna. From now on I'll learn from my patients, from the literature. Even from my mistakes. There's not much more anyone can teach me. There's no reason why I should not be a full-fledged member by now. It's taken me longer than most, even though I've worked harder and know more."

Jenny waited before answering, stirring a little, choosing her words with care. "Maybe that *is* the reason."

"How so?" Dan asked slowly.

"Dan, darling. You've got the whole world. Perhaps there are those who ask themselves, 'Why should he have everything? He should wait.' "

"I don't believe that. The people we know aren't like that."

"But maybe Al Coventry is. Maybe Lewis was telling you that your brilliance will be an overwhelming threat to him. Maybe he has the kind of self-image to maintain that you cannot possibly anticipate."

Dan sat gazing into Jenny's eyes. Finally he said, "More wine?"

Jenny rose from her chair. "I'll get the coffee."

Dan listened to the sound of her steps die away. When she came back, he said, "I'll talk to Al Coventry and see."

He did and it was not quite as he had expected. Al Coventry had more than his share of charm and preening self-confidence, but instead of contributing in any significant way to his chosen field, Dan found him disdainful, almost uninterested in his evaluations, and then bored with his insights into a highly intelligent patient's impotency. Dan had been working away, seeing Henry Bottinger regularly. Still the clinical clue would not come and Al insisted Dan was missing something. It was as Jenny had predicted—a test of strengths. Finally Al curled his lip at Dan's new diagnosis and suggested he go back to the couch to resolve some of his own difficulties. Dan kept his temper and resolved then and there to write up a paper on the significance of deep-seated inhibitions established in the preverbal period of the patient's development, and to present his findings to the society.

It was Frieda finally who warned Dan that Al Coventry was going to make it very difficult for him to be fully approved by the Education Committee and that he planned to recommend that Dan be suspended from the training program. By now Dan's guard was up, but he managed to grin.

"What do you think the Education Committee will say?"

"Don't worry on that score. You are endorsed all the way. You did a good job with me. What I do want to know is: Will you keep your promise to Jenny after that?"

Dan's face relaxed as he became aware of a genuine friend's concern. "Of course. If I have to, I'll transfer to the Topeka group and finish training in San Francisco. Berliner, Bernfeld, and Erickson are all there now, so there is nothing to worry about."

Dan then brought out a journal for her to see in which every hour with his patient, Henry Bottinger, was documented and summarized. Much of the journal was devoted to innovative ideas that might provide useful tools for understanding the rudiments of human behavior.

In reading the journal, Frieda had her first clear recognition of the significance of Dan's thinking. It was as if the lid to a treasure chest, that had been hidden, had been opened and one looked down upon precepts and concepts as if they were shining but dear jewels.

"Marvelous, Dan. Undeniably brilliant. But I would like to know exactly how you put it to Bottinger. After all, you didn't say: 'Look here. I am very displeased with you because you are a therapeutic mess.' "

"After several hours and a monster dream, I stated, 'You have defiance. You have compliance. What you don't have is alliance. So, you don't have a working relationship with me. You're not helping me help you defeat your problem.'

"He had an intense reaction to this. At all other times there was an apparent lack of external response. I immediately told him that in this lack of alliance between us—the therapeutic distance he put between us—he was repeating the distance reflected in his relationship with his parents and with his wife.

" 'You're right,' he said. 'I'm the same with my own patients. Distant. I don't see them as people—only as disembodied illnesses.' "

All sorts of questions were running through Frieda's mind, but she waited calmly.

"Henry is now able to face some of his early infantile fears. I think he'll be able to release his hold on his total symptom complex."

"Are you suggesting prognostically that Henry Bottinger will eventually see his wife as his mature object choice?"

"That's his goal."

"And you told all this to Al Coventry?"

"Yes, but he remained adamant. Each new idea I presented seemed to repel him. When he spoke to me, his tone was annoyed or derisive or plain perfunctory."

Frieda Fromm-Reichmann was a gentle, completely feminine woman. But she knew when to square her shoulders. And she was acutely aware of superiority, of courage, and of the value of thinkers willing to take a chance. "Dan," she said, "Al Coventry's behavior is shocking. It's incredible. I'm appalled. Nevertheless, when he presents his case against you in front of the whole society, he'll be supported by some who have no love for you—or for Jenny."

Dan's eyes narrowed and hardened.

Frieda went on as if she hadn't noticed. "Look, Dan, let's be utterly honest. Compared to you, some of our colleagues are dolefully lacking in any distinction. Among these, some are married to the righteous daughters of the middle class. Compared to Jenny, their women are plain. Compared to her, they're unaccomplished. Moreover, with you and George she is dead center of an imposing trio. Add to that Lewis Miller's devotion. Let's not forget Coventry's group either. Until he appeared on the scene, not one of them had so much as a peep into the inside of the society or a chance at the kind of parties the new Mrs. Coventry has both the money and talent for."

"Agreed," Dan said thoughtfully, "but we can't precipitate this move. It'd be more useful to—" Dan interrupted himself. The frowning look was gone. He said, "I don't want to be torpedoed out of membership in the Baltimore-Washington group. I'll be guided by you."

"I have an idea. Write a paper on infantile fears to read before the entire society. I'll prod the chairman of the Education Committee into calling a general meeting. It may very well counteract the negative attitudes against you.''

''I'd like to present the paper on the Perceptual Preverbal Superego.''

Frieda shook her head. ''Too startling. Too innovative for a candidate-in-training.''

''It annoys me very much that I have to soft-pedal my ideas.''

''You don't resent it any more than I do. But we must be practical; otherwise you'll be in a worse position than you are now. School yourself in restraint until you're voted in. Then no one can ever again override you.''

Dan nodded.

''Write your paper on the 'Precursors to the Superego.' I'll go over it with you.''

''Thank you, Frieda. That'll be very helpful.'' Weary of sitting, Dan rose. He held out his hand to Frieda. As she got up, Dan leaned forward and lightly touched her lips. ''I've always wanted to do that—from the time I first came here.''

''Good night, Dan.''

When he got home that night, it was very late, but George and Jenny were still up, playing backgammon. Dan burst out with, ''Of all my friends, I've never had a better friend than Frieda.''

''Sit down, Dan. Tell us about it.''

''Tomorrow.'' But then Dan looked at Jenny. And he looked at George. ''We'll sleep tomorrow. We'll sleep the whole day through. Jenny needs rest, I know.''

George grinned. ''What about your sons? A short while after you called, Jenny promised them you'd all go out.''

Jenny laughed. ''But not until afternoon.''

When Dan had finished his story and sat silent, George said, ''Even when I played pro-ball, I never roughed a man up unless I had to. I'd sure like to get my hands on this Al Coventry.''

With a grin, Dan replied, ''I'm out of practice. I haven't slugged anyone since high school, but can I help?''

Many thoughts ran through Jenny's head. After a while she inquired, ''If, by Friday, you've not heard from him, what do you plan to do?''

''Pay him a call.''

Rumors of a major infight got wide circulation and spread rapidly. Psychiatrists began talking about making sure they got to the meeting early.

Seated among those members he had courted and entertained, Al Coventry smiled with satisfaction. This combined gathering of the teaching faculty with the total psychoanalytic community was, in fact, his debut into the prestigious Baltimore-Washington group. If the men chose to back him in preference to the in-power boys—prima donna Frieda Fromm-Reichmann included—that gave him an edge over them. He was, after all, the new-comer. Al Coventry had a dual purpose. His ultimate goal—and he estimated it would require a few years before he attained national recog-nition—was to become president of the American Psychoanalytic Associa-tion. That it had come into existence in Baltimore as early as 1911 added to its status.

The more immediate purpose in his plan to destroy Dan had to do with his own countertransference about which he himself was unaware. In his unconscious, he saw Dan as a hated sibling—younger, brighter, and favored. No one yet had sent him back to the couch.

Dr. John Warren, the zealous president of the Baltimore-Washington Psychoanalytic Society, somewhat nervously eyed the people jammed into every available space in the large room as he opened the meeting.

"Gentlemen and ladies, good evening. Once more we are here assembled to vote into or deny to membership a fellow physician psychoanalytically trained. Allow me to remind you that our candidates, carefully selected, have spent much effort, much time, much money for training—usually with excellent results.

"I say with pride that we, as an organization, have been and are the proud standard-bearers of therapeutic techniques of demonstrated worth. I also say with pride that—though we are indeed ardent disciples of Freud—we offer a forum for the consideration of new ideas in the psychoanalytic movement. We are *not* stagnant, frozen purists, as demon-strated by the original thinkers among us. In particular, I have in mind our celebrated Harry Stack Sullivan. I now want to introduce the name of Dr. Daniel Gunther. In the opinion of many of us, he is professionally extremely well trained. His own analyst, Dr. Bernard Freitag, reports that Daniel Gunther worked well with him. Dr. Freitag considers him success-fully analyzed and eminently qualified. He advocates that today we vote him into full membership.

"Dr. Frieda Fromm-Reichmann concurs. In fact, she strongly supports Dr. Freitag's recommendation. In her report to me and to the Education Committee, she states that Daniel Gunther is a man of rare intelligence, a man who has great and quick empathy for his patients. She further states that he is dedicated in his persistence to unearth psychological causes.

"However, Dr. Alfred Coventry, who was Dr. Gunther's second control analyst, strongly differs with both Dr. Freitag and with Dr. Fromm-

Reichmann. He claims that Daniel Gunther's shortcomings as analysand and candidate demand serious attention. Dr. Coventry's feelings are so intense, he has asked to be heard. I call upon him now.''

Looking as if he had stepped from an *Esquire* advertisement, Al Coventry rose to his feet. He knew the powers of his charm, and it had never failed him before. He strode briskly to the rostrum. In a show business way—like a performer about to affect a patter—he looked around, waited until he was sure of his audience, and then began. "Am I mistaken perhaps?" Again he paused. "I don't see Lewis Miller here. Perhaps we ought to postpone this meeting.''

Aghast, Dr. Warren spoke from his chair. "Unless you have something particular in mind, please be done with innuendo.''

In a voice meant to allay doubts, Al Coventry said, "Sorry. I fully expected to confront Lewis Miller. I'm not minimizing his clinical achievements, but I was under the impression that he devotes much of his energies to smoothing the way for his protégé.''

"That is a surmise which we shall not discuss.''

Everyone perceived the hostility beneath Coventry's ill-judged remarks. Al Coventry himself quickly reflected upon the coldness of his audience and immediately tried another, less blatant, tack.

"Frankly, I find no quarrel with Lewis Miller. Never did. But I submit that he doesn't see Dan Gunther for what he really is. It isn't something you learn about a charmer—a charmer with brains, if you like—until you've worked with him. On the couch, I might add.''

Dr. Freitag glared at Al Coventry across the huge room. "I worked with him.''

Someone yelled, "So did Frieda.''

"I admitted he's a charmer.''

Several faces froze. Eyes hardened. Someone yelled, "What are you saying?''

"Look," said Frieda quietly to the man who yelled, "I don't need protecting. I'll do my talking later.''

Dr. Warren gravely used his gavel. He turned to Al Coventry. "Please state your case. Then return to your seat. There are others here who petitioned for time.''

Realizing he had gotten himself into a stupid situation by coming on so strong—perhaps these Baltimore types were not as sophisticated as the doctors he had known in New York—Al Coventry fumed. He quickly pulled himself together. "I meant no offense to Dr. Fromm-Reichmann. Actually, I was paying Gunther a compliment. He compensates for his inadequacies with a beautiful façade. Cut that away and you'll find a man who by instinct and habit is arrogant, overly ambitious, and basically dishonest. I'm even suspicious of his motives in dealing with patients."

He went on and on, his flow of abuse constantly interrupted by hot-tempered hissing and name-calling from the floor.

Al Coventry lost control. Repeatedly, he thumped the table in front of him with his fists. "The cheeky bastard has you all duped. The plain honest-to-Jesus long and short of it is: Dan Gunther is not analyzed. He does not know how to adhere to Freudian teaching. He takes the poor patient around the barnyard with his screwball ideas and leads him deeper into confusion."

Bernard Freitag rose from his seat. "Look into your own aggressive behavior. Observe your own belligerence. Investigate your own destructive thoughts." He paused for breath and continued. "You had a hundred hours with lay analysts and you consider yourself analyzed. Really?"

"I had no neurosis. I went to Budapest and then to Berlin to learn." Al Coventry lacked information about Bernard Freitag's training. He assumed, looking at Freitag's graying hair, that he had become a teaching analyst before there were organized standards and established institutes. That he came into the psychoanalytic community as a founding member. He paused long enough to enjoy in advance Freitag's exposure. He said, a derisive light in his eyes, "I suppose you had more than a hundred hours of didactic psychoanalytic training. Or was yours a therapeutic analysis?"

Bernard Freitag, who ordinarily avoided any discussion of his own analysis, suddenly felt exultant. It was beautiful. "Like Dan," said he, "I had a character analysis. Like Dan, I saw my analyst five times a week for the first three years of my analysis. In my fourth year, I tapered off to four times a week, then three. I taught Dan everything I learned in my years with Professor Sigmund Freud. I also saw patients under the supervision of Karl Abraham and Ferenczi."

All Al Coventry could storm was, "My friends in New York correctly forecast this would happen." His shoulders were not set so square.

Without comment Dr. Warren turned to Al Coventry and said, in his well-bred voice, "Thank you, Doctor, for your comments, but not all teachers have the same way of looking at an analysand. Obviously, we must hear from Dr. Fromm-Reichmann. But first I call upon Dr. Sullivan, who also has been involved with Daniel Gunther."

Even as he left the rostrum, Al Coventry was not exactly pessimistic about the outcome of the meeting. He was quick-witted enough to relish a fight. At the memory of other victories, he felt his hopes surging on. Then, too, it was natural for the men to think that where there is smoke, there is fire. It was natural for these men to distrust anyone controversial.

In spite of Frieda, in spite of Freitag, Dan Gunther would not go unscathed. As for Harry Stack Sullivan, he'd amble through his Sullivan thinking, much of which made no sense anyway. He couldn't imagine Sullivan getting seriously excited about Dan Gunther's professional future—or anyone else's.

As Harry Stack Sullivan approached the rostrum and took his drink of water, a total quiet filled the room. There was no doubt that this round-headed, unassuming-looking man—not Dan, not Al Coventry—alone dominated the scene.

Harry Stack Sullivan made no introductory remark. He stared straight ahead and talked.

"On the strength of his paper alone—without knowing him, without knowing anything about his training—I'd say this man has capabilities far beyond the average candidate. He has the spark of individuality, which will advance the science of psychoanalysis. I admire his courage. He stood before us last week and presented a departure from the old ruts.

"Dan Gunther has a real feeling for interpersonal relationship. I believe he is correct to emphasize the early superego on a perceptual level—just as I believe Lewis Miller is correct in insisting we spend too much time talking about content and not enough time understanding the total con-figuration—just as I believe Melanie Klein's work is correct.

"Dan Gunther has been criticized for quoting her. But his exposition gives me added respect for her contributions. Freud took as a major premise: 'All mothers are good.' Melanie Klein differed from Freud. She is right in verbalizing the concept: 'There are good mothers and there are bad mothers.' She is even more right to divide every mother into two segments —the good and the bad. The child builds the forerunner of his conscience by internalizing the 'no-no' mother—the inhibiting disciplinarian.

"As Dan Gunther emphasized in his brilliant paper, this force acts as an internal restraint at an extremely early age. Many of us here are losing sight of the fact that Dan Gunther arrived at his conclusions through his own intensive work with children. Through his play method, which is largely original, he learned how to communicate with children. Sadly, many of us are lacking in this skill."

Here Sullivan pulled and tugged at some papers in his pocket. He arranged the crumbled sheets and his quick eyes ran over them. When he reached Dan's summary he reread that portion that stressed the important point in the formation of the primordial superego.

"In conclusion, let me say that Daniel Gunther's thinking is comparable to Einstein's search for a unified field theory in physics. He is thinking as Selye, who brought us the idea that there is a common factor in all forms of illness, both physical and emotional."

The room burst into thunderous applause. It had nothing to do with Dan. The society was honoring Harry Stack Sullivan. He paid no attention to it. He stuffed his carbon of Dan's paper back into his pocket and returned to the seat.

Lewis Hill stood up. He waited with patience until the room was again quiet. Then he asked to be heard. He spoke from the floor and the membership listened as their attention was increasingly gripped.

"I sent Dan Gunther the patient in question. The wife is in therapy with me, and I know what's going on. Admittedly, the presenting symptom has not been alleviated, but he is better in many ways. His wife is sustained by the progress he is making. He is less shy and more assertive. He has more feeling for people. He is even writing a scientific paper to present to the American College of Surgeons. Something he could never have done before therapy.

"Now—before I sit down," Lewis Hill said calmly, "I'd like to say that it was I who sent Dan Gunther to Al Coventry. For this I have great regret and for this I extend to Dan—*in absentia*—my sincerest apology."

Al Coventry's lips spread slightly in suggestion of a contemptuous grin.

Then the chair recognized Dr. Leonard Calloway. He had a worried look on his face. "If we fail to elect Dan Gunther into our society, I suggest we consider our worth in continuing our educational program." He sat down. He looked at Frieda, mutely indicating it was now her turn. She rose and started down the aisle.

Frieda Fromm-Reichmann spoke clearly with quiet dignity, and it was evident that she was confident.

"Mr. Chairman, members of Baltimore-Washington Psychoanalytic Society. When one considers the averagely trained doctors admitted every year into institutes and societies and into the American, it is shocking to even consider a case against Dan Gunther. He has one of the finest, keenest intellects I have ever encountered. And he has a shrewd grasp of the human situation. Aside from Harry Stack Sullivan, I have only once met a contemporary of ours more brilliant. There is nothing obscure as to the identity of the man to whom I refer. Nevertheless, I shall name him. Lewis Miller. But in the recorded history of our profession, Dan Gunther, not Lewis Miller, will be remembered. For Dan writes. His use of language is superb. The written word is forever."

Frieda paused. "I find, though there is a great deal more to be said, that it is not necessary to go on in praise of Dan Gunther. I think you will not fail him. You will not fail us."

Frieda's serious and serene composure gave way to a smile and unexpectedly she said, "That's all."

Al Coventry groaned inwardly. He knew he was licked, but he had to wait until the ballots were counted. *At least*, he told himself, *it won't be a unanimous vote*. That didn't help much, as he left quickly.

A half hour after the count, an elated Frieda Fromm-Reichmann was standing at the Gunthers' door, with Lewis Hill grinning like a schoolboy at her side. "Look what Frieda had hidden in the trunk of her car." Lewis chuckled and handed the magnum of champagne to Dan as he opened the door.

"It's warm," said Dan.

From behind, George reached for it. Hugely pleased, he said, "Give it to me. I'll exchange it for one that's cold."

As Jenny threw her arms around Frieda, she said, "I think I'm going to cry. Thank you, thank you." And for once Jenny broke down in uncontrollable sobs.

Part IV

CAIN AND ABEL

FOR Dan it began on a rainy afternoon well into the fall, when his secretary, who knew when and when not to interrupt, put through Tascha Brotman's call. Dan listened intently to Tascha's "Abe has disappeared."

"Look," Dan said quietly into the phone. "Abe is not the sort of man who walks off without leaving some indication of his whereabouts. And he is not one to run out and leave you and Annie."

"I know that."

After a silence that seemed to last a long time, Dan said, "You say he left the apartment Monday? It's now Thursday."

"That's right."

Perplexed at the lack of appropriate anxiety or agitation, Dan tapped gently on the desk. "I take it the police have checked out the hospitals and the morgue."

"The police! What's the matter with you, Dan?"

It sounded to Dan as if Tascha did not grasp the seriousness of the situation. That, too, worried him. All he said was "Sit tight, Tascha. I'm on my way." Dan heard her cradle the receiver before he buzzed his secretary, Mrs. Philips, to give her instructions.

It was now more than three months since the big feud with Jenny. Since that time, there had been no reason for—indeed he had given no thought to—any excursions without Jenny. He knew he wanted her and needed her

317

beside him. She'd be disappointed now, but she'd understand. "Sweetheart," he said as she answered the phone. Then he told her what little he knew, and Tascha's inexplicable reactions.

"You sound scared."

"I think I am."

"Well," Jenny said, "Tascha needs help. I'm glad she called you."

"You'll be all right?"

"Of course. Make your arrangements. I'll bring your suitcase down to the office and drive you to the station."

Dan said with a smile, "That's my girl."

George's voice sounded polite but preoccupied; he was with a patient. Dan offered to call back, but George told him to hold on. For minutes Dan sat swinging his feet; then George's voice came over the wire. "What's up?"

Dan described his conversation with Tascha.

"Sounds sinister."

Dan's mind was on the same track. Still, in a lilting voice, he said, "Another of your hunches?"

"How did Tascha allow almost eighty-four hours to pass before calling you?"

"I have no answer for that either."

Knowing what was coming, Dan said, "I'm going to New York, George. On the four twenty."

In his office George leaned back in his chair and swiveled it toward the window. The thought of Jenny alone for the weekend, her disappointment that Dan had reneged on a promise, gave his big voice the crack of a whip. "Galahad to the rescue. Have you forgotten your—"

"Nope." At his own desk Dan surprised himself by reaching for a cigarette. He rarely smoked. "Why don't you take her?"

Concealing his gladness—a surge of emotion he did not want to think about now—George said, his voice turning sarcastic, "I thought you'd never ask." Dan's chuckle was that of a man amused and friendly. His concern for Jenny particularly acute, George went on. "What happens after you get to New York? Will you stay there until the situation is resolved?"

Dan's reply came back quickly. "I think so."

George's irritation with Dan began to ignite again. "I think Jenny should go home. She's overdoing it—and two rambunctious boys—"

"Jenny is perfectly fine—blooming, in fact. And, based on her previous pregnancies, I say, 'Let her enjoy her marvelous energy.' "

"That," George cried, "is sheer rationalization—something you want to believe. I advise you, Doctor, to remember that Jenny is thirty—not twenty-two."

"Nonsense." Then Dan got an idea suddenly. "Say, why don't you stay with her? That is, if you don't mind the daily commute to Chevy Chase!"

Thinking himself a featherbrained ass for looking a gift horse in the mouth, George answered, "I guess you're not completely out of your mind at that."

Dan said easily, "Thanks, George. That takes a load off my mind."

Before he hung up, George remembered to caution Dan. "Stay at your old man's. I don't consider Tascha a suitable roommate for a married man."

Dan resented George's remark about Tascha a little. Yet all he said was "So long." He walked up and down waiting for Jenny. His thoughts turned to Abe, and he started to theorize. On a white sheet of paper, which lay on the desk before him, he wrote down the two words he could not help thinking and yet could not entirely accept either. Both had to do with death. He heard the quick light footsteps for which he was listening and scratched out his scribble. He wanted to confront Tascha with a completely open mind.

Headlights on and horn honking, the taxi crawled through heavy traffic along the rain-soaked streets of New York. Finally the driver eased past a delivery truck and pulled up in front of the Park Avenue apartment house in which the Brotmans resided on the ground floor; the foyer and parlor served as waiting and consultation rooms for Abe Brotman's patients. Now, having eaten off trays, Dan and Tascha faced each other across Abe's desk. With quiet earnestness, Dan was talking. "You say that the doorman was sick and Abe called the cab company. Because of the rain, they were in heavy demand and were taking no orders; so Abe decided to stand outside and take his chances at getting a passing taxi."

"Yes." Tascha's face betrayed no emotion and Dan was trying to decide whether it was from nonchalance or extreme fear. There was a curious passivity in the sharp profile that Dan had long admired, even though the dark hair was flecked with gray. Still a good-looking woman though.

"How is it possible, Tascha, that you did not know until today, Thursday, that Abe never went to his meeting, that his Education Committee waited a reasonable length of time, concluded a bit of business without him, and adjourned early."

"I wasn't here."

Dan looked at Tascha in profound surprise. "Do you care to explain that?"

"It's a long and involved story."

"Well," said Dan, "I've come a long way to hear it."

To his astonishment, Tascha said, pushing back the hair that fell over her face, "I have to go back to the beginning of my marriage, giving you details I thought I'd never again reveal."

His professional nod was Dan's only reply.

Tascha began her account with the years before her marriage, and naturally she remembered her miserable childhood only too well, and made a good deal of it. Though Dan gave a sympathetic ear, he asked no question about the struggle, the suffering, the sacrifices, the degrading poverty. It was a story he had heard a number of times before. But finally fearing that Tascha would wear herself out, Dan suggested she leave the details of those bad years.

Tascha turned her head away. "Absolutely right."

Automatically Dan glanced at his watch. It was getting late. "I wonder," said Dan, "if—"

Tascha looked back at him, her expression taut. Something complex was on her mind. "I haven't finished."

"I'm listening."

"When I married Abe, I never knew a man, not even him—really. I thought his fumbling was sex and I was disgusted. Gradually, we both managed the act a bit better, but still I was far from thrilled. But he was working hard—I was working hard. We were always hot and tired or cold and tired. Grateful for a few hours of sleep, we didn't think too much about lovemaking. Time passed. He completed his internship. I saved enough money and we sailed for Europe third class. Steerage would have suited our budget better. And don't think we didn't try to find a ship that still took travelers steerage.

"In Vienna I began having doubts about Abe. Until then, I thought all men were the same. Now—no longer constantly fatigued, listening to psychiatric concepts day and night, moving among people experienced in the art of living, I came to feel real desires. I assumed they were directed toward Abe because he was my husband and I loved him. Thinking, I'll find out and then I'll teach him, I confided our ignorance to one of Joe Garafalo's girls—Daisy. Do you remember her? She used to preface everything with 'Ich bin ein Modell.' "

Dan's grin softened his expression for a moment. "Indeed I do."

"Her first offer was to arrange a rendezvous for me with a man she considered a very able performer and whom she trusted as completely dependable.

"I declined.

"She urged me. 'No risk at all.'

"I said: 'No. You must teach me with words, with diagrams, with pictures.' She said, 'I doubt if that will be as good as the real thing, but I'll try.'

"Shortly after the start of my tutelage, you came. Do you recall that the very night of your arrival you dined with Dr. Wagner-Jauregg, and Jenny partied with all of us? Well, sometime during that evening, Daisy dragged me off to the powder room. She said: 'If you want to learn how to make a man hot, watch that Jenny. She's a natural.' I answered her warningly. 'We only met today, but we're friends. Don't you dare talk like that about her.'

"Daisy laughed. 'I pay her tribute.' She pulled me to the mirror. 'Look up at a man the way she does,' she said. 'Moisten your lips the way she does; then make yourself laugh—the way she does—so easy, so natural. And when you dance, let your feet know more than you do, like they have a life of their own.'

"I watched, I practiced, I tried everything I learned on Abe. I might just as well have tried to unload my need, my yearning, on a four-legged donkey. He had a new tactic for avoiding sex. 'You've got to remember,' he said, 'we were raised almost as brother and sister. It's natural that I should think of our relationship as an incestuous one in this stage of my analysis.'

"I almost toppled over. Me—taboo! I felt I could kill his analyst. In that moment of rage I gave Abe an ultimatum. Somehow he drew some strength from somewhere, and that night Annie was conceived. But that same night, I came to a full understanding: Abe was not only unskilled; he was also underendowed. I found his smallness revolting and I never again communicated my need to him in any way."

Tascha reached for a cigarette, and Dan deliberately took time striking a match. After an uneasy silence, Tascha said, "Don't think that Abe and I have been unhappy together. He has his practice; he is a wheel among the local analysts. He excels at chess. We both have Annie. And Abe is really generous. There isn't anything on earth too good or too expensive or too much for me and Annie."

"And," said Dan, "you still have your lover."

"Yes," Tascha answered without hesitation; and for the first time that evening, animation appeared on her face.

"Bill and I saw each other on Wednesday this week as usual; in fact, it was a wonderfully dear day in the country. I didn't return to the apartment till today."

Dan had listened up till now with a sense of remoteness, as if he had been watching a movie. Now he cut in sharply. "All this no doubt can explain why it was close to four days before you missed Abe."

"Yes, Wednesday is the night Abe is especially removed from all awareness of me. It's his chess night."

There was something unnatural about Tascha's narrative, and about her lack of agitation. It puzzled Dan because he could not fit the pieces together. What was really going on—something sinister, perhaps?

How was Tascha capable of slipping from detail to detail without once mentioning Bill's wife? Dan reflected before saying, "I'm curious. How's Helen?"

Tascha met his direct look and, in a strangely impersonal tone, said, "She is terminal. She has lost all use of her muscles and is totally incontinent. Her speech now is so thick it is unintelligible and her optic nerves are entirely degenerated. She is blind, Dan."

Dan could not help but see them again on their wedding day barely seven years ago. Bill and Helen laughing—running from the steps of St. Patrick's Cathedral into a bombardment of rice and confetti. Dan dismissed the vision. It was time to ferret out the truth, and this was what he was in New York for. "Fill me in," he said, "to the minutest detail—from the time Abe left the apartment until your call to me."

"Monday I did not stir out of the building, with the weather so awful. And because of the downpour, Annie was home and underfoot. Patients kept calling to cancel appointments and that didn't help my mood. On top of everything else, the janitor slipped on the wet pavement. The hospital finally sent an ambulance. When the message came that he had a broken hip, his wife went absolutely hysterical." Tascha pushed the hair from her brow. "I was goddamned glad when the day was over and Abe finally left for his institute meeting. I listened to the radio in bed and then read until I fell asleep.

"Tuesday was another dim, equally miserable day. I got Annie off to school; then I removed myself from the telephone."

Dan glanced at her curiously.

"I'm always restless on Tuesday—waiting for Wednesday, you know." Tascha took a second. Satisfied that Dan understood, she went on. "I went window shopping in the rain. I took in a movie. I killed time until I picked up Annie and took her to my sister's, where I decided to stay the night. Wednesday morning, ten sharp, I—"

"Tascha, please—"

Her brows lifted. Her chin lifted. And Dan could tell that she wished he'd postpone the questions until after she finished. Dan pushed that aside and put the question to her. "Didn't you miss Abe Monday night? What about breakfast Tuesday morning?"

"Want some coffee?"

"No—just answers."

"Do I have to spell out the obvious?"

Dan nodded at her. "You do."

"My God, I thought you understood. I don't go into his bedroom. He doesn't come into mine."

"Breakfast, Tascha. That's important."

Tascha summarized their routine. "Abe takes a bite at six forty-five. I breakfast with Annie around eight. Our cleaning woman fixes his lunch. Mondays and Wednesdays he eats out. Tuesday night he visits his mother up in Riverdale. She feeds him. For years now we seldom met until Thursday evening."

"I get the picture," Dan said in a factual tone. "Go on."

Tascha detailed Wednesday. "As I started to say—ten sharp I was in front of the hotel, and it couldn't have been more than a minute later that I was seated beside Bill and we were on our way. I said, 'I was so afraid you wouldn't come.' He answered. 'It doesn't help my conscience to leave Helen now, but I couldn't stay away. I need you, Tascha.' We didn't talk after that until Bill remarked offhandedly, 'Incidentally, what happened to Abe Monday night?'

" 'Nothing. Why?' "

" 'He never showed at our New York Institute meeting.'

"I explained that he had trouble getting a cab.

"Bill dismissed the whole thing, saying: 'There were so few of us, there was no sense in staying. I guess he got there after I left.'

"I didn't give Abe another thought until last night—it must have been about ten thirty—when I walked into a dark apartment. Before leaving for his chess club, Abe always turns on the hall light for me. I went through the dark into the kitchen, and then I saw the note on the table. I walked over and read it. It was from the cleaning woman. She complained that we forgot to tell her that the doctor was away, and she had rushed to make coffee and refrigerate a salad for lunch—all for nothing. I went to Abe's bedroom and turned on his lamp. The bedspread was still on the bed. I searched his closet and his drawers. Nothing was missing. Next I came in here. Again I turned on a lamp. Everything was in order—everything in its proper place. I decided against alarming anyone. My reasoning was I'd better wait—someone would call, either Abe or the police.

"I picked up the phone and got my sister. I asked her to keep Annie because I was coming down with a chill. Then I went to bed. Anticipating nightmares, I slept the most peaceful sleep. This morning I sent the cleaning woman away, telling her we wouldn't need her for a few days. The next thing I decided had to be done was call Abe's patients. What I heard is most perplexing. In each instance I was told that very early Tuesday morning, a man, speaking in a tutored voice—slightly foreign—canceled the patient's appointment, saying, 'Dr. Brotman is called away unexpectedly. Upon his return, your hours will be resumed.'

"Next I looked through Abe's checkbook. It told me nothing. I went to our bank by subway and had a talk with the manager. I said, 'I believe we've made a large withdrawal and now I'm wondering if our balance will cover the checks I must write.' The manager examined our account and assured me that no withdrawal was made. I insisted. 'Then the money was taken from the savings account.' He said: 'I'll inquire.' He was soon back, a look of amazement on his face. 'Mrs. Brotman,' he said, 'you are very much mistaken. The savings account is intact.' I came home. I waited. I watched the clock. Then I called you. I was worried by then."

"What about insurance policies?"

"One policy is large—for one hundred thousand dollars. It contains a double indemnity clause. It is gifted to me, and, of course, I am the sole beneficiary. I have it in my personal safety deposit box and there is no way in the world for Abe to put his hands on it. The second policy, for ten thousand dollars, also double indemnity, lists Abe's mother as first beneficiary. Should he outlive her, I am to hold the money in trust for Annie. And that, too, is in my custody."

At first, it gave Dan a shock to hear the size of Abe's insurance policy, but thinking about it, he concluded: *I might have guessed. He earned that much.* They talked a little more and drank their coffee, while Dan's thoughts centered on the why and how of Abe's disappearance. The answer might lie with the tutored voice. There was a definite possibility, and Dan was almost sure that the voice belonged to a brother psychiatrist. Who else would give himself the trouble of remembering an appointment between patient and doctor? Dan stored the idea; he was not ready for it yet. Instead, he made his mind go back over each point. He thought about Abe's mother. Knowing what he knew about her, it did not seem likely she'd remain silent. The question to Tascha was hardly out of his mouth when Tascha exclaimed, "Oh—that's so stupid of me! But I plain forgot. She's in Providence this week with Abe's sister."

Christ! *That's pat—too pat,* was Dan's thought.

Tascha had gotten a cigarette and glanced at Dan for a light. She found his eyes watching her—speculative. Does he think me hard, or uncaring perhaps? But she needed his unsentimental wisdom right now.

"Well? More third-degree? You're looking holes through me."

Dan blew out the match and put it down. "Tell me," he said, his hard gaze still on her, "is Bill Reilly in good financial shape?"

With no hesitation at all, not even for a fraction of a moment, Tascha answered, hiding nothing. "He is not only flat broke, but he is deeply in debt. It's probably five years now that Helen is bedridden and in need of around-the-clock nursing seven days a week. For the first two years of her sickness, Bill had slashed his practice to be near her, and he did this before he finished his own analysis—while it was urgent for him to earn money. Then there's my house. That cost Bill a pretty penny."

Dan was tempted to call Bill every kind of cursed fool. He got up and opened a window. He breathed in deeply the cool air smelling of rain. After a while he closed the windows and went back to Tascha, placed his chair very close to and directly in front of her, and said, "Tascha, you and Bill are in one hell of a mess. And unless we solve this puzzler fast, you'll both be dragged through the mud. And, at best, Bill's career—at least in New York—will be over."

Tascha turned pale. "Don't say that. Not a soul knows about Bill and me."

"I hate to disillusion you, Tascha, but how long do you suppose it'll take the police to round up someone who sees you every Wednesday morning at ten in front of the Commodore? Finding that little jewel of yours is mere routine—pathetically easy. What about your cleaning woman? Do you think you've completely pulled the wool over her eyes? What's more— more than anything—why aren't you concerned about your husband? Don't you want him found?"

Tascha couldn't answer that or perhaps just did not want to. Impulsive as whe was, her thoughts were focused on Bill and her own immediate problems. She had spent one night thinking of Abe and that was it. He had not shown up. There was too much else to think about.

Dan let her think, while he picked up the phone and asked the operator to connect him with the Bureau of Missing Persons.

A Sergeant Brown took the call and let Dan state his inquiry with the relevant details.

"Hold on, Doc."

Dan glanced over at Tascha. "I've just interrupted a gin game, I believe." On the other end, there was a click and a murmur of "Count your points." Then the sergeant was on the line, briskly this time.

"You say your friend dropped out of sight sometime Monday evening?" Dan confirmed this and answered some questions and dodged a few. He made it sound as if Tascha was beset with anxiety. The policeman was appropriately sympathetic. "OK if we drop by for a photograph—say, in about an hour?"

"I think it better be tomorrow. Mrs. Brotman is heavily sedated. I want her to sleep."

"Just as you say, Doc. Meanwhile, we'll put out a missing persons bulletin."

"Thank you."

Tascha looked at him defiantly. "That's not the kind of smart thinking I expected from you."

"Don't worry about me, Tascha. Worry about the police—maybe the district attorney. If they start asking, 'Who gets the money? Where were you?' you'd better have some smart answers."

Tascha waited and then said worriedly, "Dan, you've got to prevent that."

His voice sober, Dan said, "I'll try. And you're going to trust me and do as I say. Agreed?"

"I promise."

"All right. Tomorrow morning we start the hunt. I have one hunch to go on. You call each of Abe's patients and give everyone an hour, his own."

"I don't think you'll find anything there. Abe's rich, rich females are devoted to him."

Dan looked at her sharply. "Are you asking me to believe that the chairman of the Education Committee of the New York Institute doesn't have a few bright candidates in training—that he doesn't have some real tough cases—really sick people in therapy?"

"Not Abe. He concentrates on the money crowd—a steady stream of dolls with a pain here and a few extra pounds there. He's got the wife of a millionaire industrialist who pays him one hundred dollars an hour. He once told me they just sit and look at each other for fifty minutes, and she claims that no one has ever done as much for her as he has. She wants her husband to endow a chair for Abe so that he'll never again have to worry about money."

"I can't believe it." Motives of professional jealousy and money hunger were beginning to crowd in on Dan's mind.

"It's true."

Bone-certain a murder had taken place, Dan's suspicion that a brother psychiatrist was somehow involved strengthened. Sorting ideas, speculating, he brought Bill Reilly back into the conversation. "I guess Bill avoids Abe."

Tascha pursed her lips. Her eyes narrowed. "Leave Bill out of this—he had absolutely nothing to do with Abe's disappearance."

"You're not a fool, Tascha. Don't talk like one. And get rid of the stupid notion that your adulterous affair with Bill is your private business."

"But—"

Dan's face hardened.

"Oh, all right."

"That's better."

"You were asking about Abe and Bill." As Dan nodded, Tascha reached for another cigarette. She inhaled deeply. "Socially there is no need for Bill to avoid Abe. We never did meet much, after Vienna, except when Jenny invited us together or when we ran into each other at regional or national meetings. Then Bill always made his way to me and asked me for a dance.

"Professionally, Bill despises Abe and is very critical of him. However, as you would expect of a gentleman, he hasn't publicly allied himself with Abe's enemies. He spoke to Abe directly, and, believe me, Abe has no illusion of what Bill thinks of him." A cynical smile came to Tascha's face. "If I could blush, I'd blush. I am not a bit perturbed to disclose Abe's lack of virility, but to repeat what Bill says of Abe makes me feel disloyal. Do you think that's funny?"

"It's awkward for you, I know."

"Bill doesn't approve of Abe's kind of practice."

"How do you feel about it?"

"Well, if I had been born rich, maybe I—" Tascha studied Dan's expression and stopped.

"What else has Bill told you?"

"Bill says it's dishonest that Abe, with inadequate training himself, has maneuvered himself into this position of supervising training, and cowardly that he covers his lack of total analytic qualification by avoiding patients who need real depth therapy."

Dan's brows went up. "I find that hard to believe. And as Jenny is fond of saying, 'There is no use pretending otherwise.' I remember Abe in Vienna—the brilliance with which he expressed himself. Next to Lewis Miller, he was openly acknowledged to be the most gifted of us all. I also remember my pride in him when he wrote that his analysis in Vienna seemed incomplete and he was therefore undergoing a second analysis here in New York."

"Not true," Tascha insisted. "Once when I suggested more analysis, he said, 'What in the hell for? In another year or two I'll be head of the Institute's important Education Committee and I'll have them all by the balls.' "

"He takes no analysands in training under him directly?"

"That's right. But that makes him plenty popular. He is in the position to fill everyone's hours."

"What about control cases? He can't possibly avoid them and still head the Education Committee."

"He takes one a year—bluffs his way. It's not hard. He's quite a talker and he knows the literature."

Dan said, "I'll be damned." Suddenly weary, he rose to his feet. "Tascha, how about a beer and something to eat—anything—a piece of cheese?"

Tascha answered. "I suppose I can find a can of soup and tuna, but I'm sure there's no beer. Another coke?"

Dan walked to the window and looked out. The night was black but the rain had stopped. He decided to take Tascha out for a midnight snack.

Friday morning Dan went to work at seven, and he finished at seven that evening. With no more of Abe's patients left to see, Dan reported to Tascha. "You were right—nothing incriminating there."

"Were they counting on you to fill in for him?"

"No. All loyal. All willing to wait. And since no one admitted to a disorder more serious than 'a little nervous,' I was quick to tell each of the ladies, 'You'll hear from Mrs. Brotman. It won't be long.' "

"What next, Dan?"

"I concentrate on Bill."

Tascha accepted that with a nod. "I want to be there when you do."

"No," Dan said.

Tascha knew that Dan Gunther was not the man to give in. Still, she made one more try. "Will you see him here?"

"Definitely not."

She was just going into the kitchen when the phone rang. It was the police. Dan took the phone, listened awhile, and then nodded. "I see. Thank you, Sergeant." He turned to Tascha, whose eyes opened wider. "The police have come up with nothing. They say if they do not trace Abe within the next forty-eight hours, an alert for 'missing person, presumed dead' will go out to all five boroughs and the adjacent counties."

There was no audible response from Tascha.

Andrew Gunther's manservant admitted Bill Reilly and led him into a comfortable room, where Dan was standing, his back to the blaze of a wood fire. The men's greetings were friendly, and Bill said, "Sorry to keep dinner waiting, but I couldn't leave."

"How is she?"

"She can't possibly last the week."

Dan let his expression speak for him.

After a pause Bill said, "I suppose there's no use in asking about Jenny. She's always in such marvelous health." He expected no comment and went on. "Do I have time for one quick Scotch?"

"Plenty of time."

Just then the servant reentered, wheeling a cart. He made Bill's drink strong and Dan's weak. When he left them, Bill asked, "Where's your dad?"

"He decided to go to his club for the evening. He knows that I have some things to talk over with you."

"Care to start?"

Dan put his hand on Bill's shoulder. "Let's eat. Everything is ready."

When they had made their way back to the study after good steaks, Dan closed the door firmly. "Edward is discreet—nevertheless . . ." Dan took one of the big armchairs and pointed to the other. After Bill had poured himself a brandy and was seated, Dan stated, without preface, "I know about you and Tascha, and Abe is still missing."

Bill showed no feeling but shrugged slightly. He shifted his big frame in the armchair and sipped his brandy. Then Dan told him in detail all he knew and all he feared.

His voice somber, Bill asked, "Do you suspect me?"

"Don't be an ass, Bill."

Bill eyed Dan with affection.

Dan went on talking. "It's possible the police will think you removed Abe."

"I'm beginning to realize that."

"It's almost a corny situation!" Dan said. "A dying wife, a missing husband."

Bill's mind reflected what the tabloids could do with a scandal involving psychoanalysts. Certain that the same thoughts occupied Dan's mind, he said, "It's almost as juicy as finding mother superior in bed with the parish priest." He emptied his brandy glass. "Mind if I have another?"

"Pour two."

Bill reached for the bottle and another snifter. "How do we get around this mess?"

"Find Cain fast."

"Oh, sure."

"He has got to be someone both you and Abe know."

"If true, where do we start?"

"Suppose we start with Tascha. I think I'd like an explanation of your attitude toward her."

"How does that fit in with this mystery?"

The question sounded like How is that your business? Dan said softly, "Don't be unnecessarily sensitive, Bill. I'm only asking for the gist of what I consider a family matter. In a way I've become your go-between. I'd like to know what I am representing."

Bill looked at Dan gravely for moments. "Everything between Tascha and me is right."

"Meaning?"

Their eyes locked: Bill's troubled, Dan's solemn.

"It's just that I don't like talking about Tascha, even with you, even with a possible murder hanging over us, while I have a wife who still breathes."

"Sorry, Bill. But we don't have time to be delicate. We have to find Abe and whoever has done away with him before the police get there."

The stubborn part of Bill thought: *All the same—*. His practical part reasoned: *Why make a fuss for nothing?* "OK," Bill said decisively as he again reached for the brandy bottle and poured a few ounces. As he drank, he talked. "To begin with, we were a convenience for each other. It's not like that now; it hasn't been so for a long time. We've come to love each other."

"Is it your intention to marry Tascha?"

"As promptly as possible."

"What?" Dan asked dryly, "if Abe is alive?"

"I had some trouble convincing Tascha. Divorce is repugnant to her. Still—we've known all along that as soon as Helen—" Bill left the rest of the sentence unsaid. He took a quick sip of his brandy. "It is also my intention—and has been for a couple of years now—to get away from New York. It shouldn't be difficult to establish a practice in southern California."

Dan's face lit up. He raised his glass: "That's what I wanted to hear. To a good future, Bill."

Bill drank, unsmiling. A couple of moments later, Dan was again completely serious.

"Let's consider the facts. A few right guesses will save us a whole lot of headaches. Who had reason to be Abe's enemy? My theory is that the enemy is a brother analyst. And I think we must proceed on the presumption of insanity."

A low whistle escaped Bill's lips. "Jesus, Dan, I think you are onto something." Bill hesitated a second, then said, "I'm not sure. I'm just conjecturing. But—"

Dan said, "I'll trust your hunch. Who?"

"Peter Rice."

Dan's eyes narrowed. "Is he still in the East? I thought we'd lost track of him."

"Where did you get that idea?"

"I don't remember now. No matter—fill me in."

"Look, Dan, when I talk of Abe, I'm not talking about our Sir Abe—not our buddy with whom we studied in Vienna and to whom we listened. That Abe vanished a long time ago. The Park Avenue Abe is a money-grabbin' so-and-so who steals ideas, makes dirty deals, holds grudges, castrates the candidates, and gets his kicks from destroying people and the power he wields. If I didn't know what I know about Abe, I'd think your Cain and Abel theory a piece of fiction—pure fantastic fantasy."

"Hmm— I'm beginning to think there is no Abel. Cain destroyed Cain who then killed Cain."

"I follow you. Abe did commit psychological murder over and over, and one of his victims was Peter Rice. It all started a few years ago. But I can't say for sure—let alone prove—that Peter killed Abe. Could he have done that—and why?"

"Let's not concern ourselves with proof just yet."

Bill sat back in the large armchair and loosened his tie, ready to embark on the whole story. *What a straightforward and sane guy he is,* thought Dan, measuring his friend. He let Bill begin.

"About four or four and a half years ago Peter Rice, at Abe's insistence, made application to the New York Institute to become a candidate in training. As a then newly appointed member of the Education Committee, I was one of his two interviewers. I did not consider him a suitable candidate. He had a dearth of object relationships. I suspected, from the Vienna days, that he had deep-seated hostilities. I thought him basically detached from external objects. I regarded his full-time job in geriatrics as a reaction formation to his own aggressive impulses. I therefore recommended a therapeutic analysis as a prerequisite for candidacy. Abe shouted me down. Nor did he hesitate to communicate his enthusiasm for Peter to Peter. Later, when they were no longer friendly, Peter swore to me that Abe had said, 'Bill Reilly was against you. Fred Mason was on the fence. I got you in. Stay on the right side of me and in you stay. Get out of line, and I'll throw you out on your ass. You'll be through—finished.'

"The break between Abe and Peter occurred over a paper. I was there, sitting in the audience. I remember thinking Abe's paper superficial, unimaginative, repetitive, and a put-on. I was surprised that the paper wasn't turned down. When I saw that Peter Rice was the discussant, I thought: What's the use of staying? Abe picked a man who knows his stuff in geriatrics to back him up. Very clever.

"Well, within the ten minutes allotted to Peter, he not only tore into Abe's paper and pulverized it, he used part of his time to present his own ideas on the psychodynamics of the aging process—he'd been involved in prolonged research himself and had carried out clinical studies of people advanced in years. He was damn good and the audience gave him a hand.

"Knowing Abe, I knew he was outraged, and I supposed he would lash out at Peter. But I'd forgotten how clever he is. He cradled his anger and filled the two minutes of his summation time with an amusing anecdote. Relieved that Abe had handled Peter lightly and that there was, at least, no public unpleasantness, I nevertheless prepared myself for the crackdown. It did not come. The bastard waited for Peter to finish his analysis and complete his controls. That way he had more to take away. Imagine kicking a guy out at the very end of training."

"Didn't you go to bat for him? Didn't his analyst?"

"We tried. It didn't help much. Abe used his power to question the competence of Dr. Steinhardt, Peter's analyst. He influenced the other members of the Education Committee by pointing up defects in Peter's psychological makeup. He was quite brutal. With careful stirring-up, he persuaded the men, over whom he already had a lot of domination, to vote Peter down and to label him unstable and unsuitable. Abe said to Peter, 'There might still be hope for you. Why don't you have yourself committed for a few years? If you don't want your family in Canada to know about you, I've a friend who is a judge and who is always anxious to do me a favor.' "

Bill's summarization of the disintegrating relationship between two of his brother psychiatrists, together with real worry over a possible scandal and his intense pity for Helen, left him feeling drained. Yet there was more to tell. He had to explain his own position so Dan would understand why he had not resigned from the Institute in protest of Abe's cruelty. And he had to convey to Dan that Peter, broken by that cruelty and by the seeming abandonment of his therapist and his control analysts, was living up to all of Abe's labels.

Bill wanted another drink, but this time he made no move for the bottle. He sighed a deep sigh and began his unpleasant task. "After what was done to Peter, I felt that I ought to remove myself from Abe's committee. But first I wanted to talk it over with Tascha. She made her usual excuses for Abe and suggested that I put a little distance between my disgust and

Abe's offense.'' Bill paused, then said, ''A man goes a long way to please a woman.''

With a look of great compassion, Dan nodded. He offered no comment.

Bill raised his empty glass, in a gesture of salute. He put down the glass, and his eyes fixed on Dan's, he continued: ''I finally caught up with Peter in a dismal room of a dismal rooming house within walking distance of the Hospital for Chronic Diseases, where he works. What struck me then was his clinging to the parent figure—and his sense of abandonment. He spoke of Abe as 'Big Brother.' He said, 'I put my trust in him. With him, I did not need God. That's why I wanted to be a member of the institute. I'd be by his side and never be alone. But Abe, just like my real brother, was bad. With the expectation of becoming the Almighty Father, he demanded all the rights, all the power. My father thought me a nonentity, too.

'' 'Now I've satisfied them both—four years on Steinhardt's analytical couch did not succeed in changing what I am into what I should have been.'

''I wanted to make some comforting remark. I said, 'No mind is ever fully free from its original dependence.' I reminded him of our past friendship. He turned on me. 'Go worship Abe. He deserves it. He is the God-sent son worthy of his destiny.' I left Peter sobbing like a lost child.

''Two months passed. I looked for Peter. A neighbor informed me of his move. At the hospital I was told he had resigned his position and left no forwarding address. I remembered he had an old house that stands on wooden piles near the ocean, its back to a street, its front to Freeport Bay. I drove out to that part of Long Island. There was a thick fog rolling in. The house was shuttered and locked. I pressed the bell a couple of times; no one answered. I had the notion that he was on his boat and that the fog would bring him in. I waited. As I expected—''

''Just a minute. How long has Peter had a boat?''

''I don't know. Seems that he has always had a boat. He picked this one up for a song from an ex-rum-runner. As I remember it, Peter bought the house from him, too. It's great. The boat docks right under the house. One push opens a trapdoor above, and presto—you're in the living area.''

''Have you ever been on her?''

''Sure. Deep-sea fishing. She's a beauty—steady and fast—built to carry fifty cases of booze and still outdistance the Coast Guard.''

Dan felt a sensation, not exactly a pleasant one. ''Well, we know where Abe is.''

Slowly Bill let out a sound. ''Jesus!''

''Tell me,'' Dan resumed. ''What was Peter's mood when you last met?''

''Elated.''

"How long ago?"

Bill made a quick calculation. "Fourteen days ago—exactly."

"That worries me. It's too neat, altogether."

"Dan, we're just guessing. We're not sure."

"He did it. And the deed does not surpass explanation."

There was the authority of certainty in Dan's voice that Bill didn't attempt to question. After a moment of profound quiet, he exclaimed, "Good God, Dan, how long can we keep secret what we already know—and how long do we leave Peter on his own? Maybe he has already skipped or committed suicide."

Dan shook his head. "Peter has triumphed over a detestable brother, and having done what he had to, he is now empty. Until someone turns on him, there'll be no excitement." Dan got up then. He went to the telephone and reached his father. He spoke very briefly. "Hello, Dad. Can you call me back on a pay-phone? Thanks."

Bill stretched and lit a cigarette. "I'm mystified. Why would Abe go out in the boat with a man who no longer had any use for him? Abe Brotman liked only adoring associates."

"Peter will tell us why." Dan took the phone as soon as the first ring came. He faced toward Bill as he gave his father a condensed but accurate account of events thus far. When he was silent, it was clear to Bill that Andrew Gunther was asking penetrating questions. Dan's answers were cautious; then he nodded his head. "That's what I'd like, Dad. But tell them that Peter Rice must not know he is being watched. Warn them, too, that in his probable state of paranoia, he'll be way above par in detecting sounds or any sort of movement out of the ordinary."

Again Dan listened. "Just a minute. I'll ask." After he repeated Bill's direction for getting to the house on South Bay Street in Freeport, Dan thanked his father. "It's really kind of you, Dad. We'll see you Thursday in Baltimore. The boys are so looking forward to it."

"Private detectives?" Bill asked.

"Yes," Dan said. "My father will manage to have them out there tonight. They'll keep vigil."

They drank and talked some more, Bill more relaxed as if some load had been shifted from an already heavy burden. Dan keenly outlined the next steps.

"We'll be considered accessories after-the-fact."

"I will. Not you. Don't let it concern you. My dad knows people in important places."

"I'll be damned, Dan, if I let you go this alone."

"You've no choice. If you want to marry Tascha, you've got to stay out of it. Incidentally," Dan added, "I don't want to leave Tascha alone in that apartment. She can move in here in the morning, before I talk with Dr. Steinhardt. I've a spare key for you to come and go as you please. It's safe. Edward starts his vacation. The doorman will be off over the long weekend—and, fortunately, the elevators run themselves."

Bill said, "If I knew how to thank you, I would. Maybe someday I'll find a way."

Dan's grin came slowly. He did not answer.

"When will you come back to confront Peter?" Bill asked.

"Unless there is a foul-up here, I won't spoil Thanksgiving for Jenny and our houseguests. Also, I'll have the chance of taking Lewis and Leo into our confidence. We'll need their help. Lewis is, unquestionably, the most important behind-the-scenes dictator of policy. And we need to handle the institute as tactfully as possible. So we'll clear with the American Psychoanalytic through Leo Butler. His influence is big, even now, and he is moving up fast."

"Aren't you supposed to be flying to San Francisco with Jenny after Thanksgiving? How will you do that with this problem to solve here?"

"Jenny won't be alone. Dad's going. And Paul and Eric are most resourceful for their ages. They'll all take good care of her."

"Are they excited about the baby?"

"Sure are. And the questions they ask!"

Bill smiled. "What sort of things?"

Dan started to laugh. "Paul says that he knows I planted the seed. What he doesn't understand is how. I drew pictures, which he later shared with Eric, who then astonished me and embarrassed Jenny by asking, 'Daddy, are you really long enough to reach all the way into Mom's belly?' "

Bill chuckled. "I'd like to hear your answer."

Dan laughed again. "I believe in answering questions with the truth. I modestly admitted, 'With inches to spare.' "

Bill's eyes smiled and he said, "It must be nice to have sons. Now I wish you a daughter. Small and delicious like Jenny, and with her marvelous vitality."

Dan said, "Thank you," and got to his feet.

Bill glanced at his wristwatch as he rose. "Are you sleeping here?"

"No, I promised Tascha I'd come back. She'll be waiting up, I know, for my report."

"I'll give you a lift."

The call came as Dan was opening the front door. Bill, closer to the telephone, took it. He said, "I am Dr. Reilly." He listened, then turned pale. He put his hand over the mouthpiece. He said to Dan, "My answering service. Helen is dead."

Dan took the receiver from Bill's hand and replaced it on its hook. He led Bill back across the room. "Sit down. I'll fix you a drink."

Bill remained standing. "No, thanks." His face was like stone. His eyes were dry. His hands trembled. His mind saw Helen, the woman he had married, when her eyes were shining and her breath was sweet. His heart cried and the tears brought him no relief. "Come," he heard Dan say, "I'll drive you home." He went, glad that it was Dan and not Tascha who was witness to his private sorrow.

Dan's appointment with Dr. Steinhardt had to be postponed for a day, not because it was morning when he left Bill, but because Tascha, disgruntled, became difficult. Dan was taken aback by her heartlessness. "Why is Bill playing the role of bereaved husband when, in actuality, we've lived with the thought of her death for years?"

"Tascha, you cannot put a lock and chain on Bill's feelings. Don't try."

"Well, what bothers me is that, suddenly, Bill is caught up in death rites and all that sort of rubbish. It never occurred to me that his freedom wouldn't blow him right into my arms. It is I who have been his real wife these last few years."

"Tascha, take a moment and think."

"About what?"

Dan shook his head at Tascha's stubborn self-solicitude; he had already told her of the growing certainty of Abe's murder. He let the words escape with a sigh, "Your husband—"

Tascha replied, "Well, I agree with you there. We'd better get busy and sell his practice. I know an Austrian refugee analyst whose Aryan wife turned him in to the authorities for recommending a therapeutic abortion. Then. . . ."

"Tascha—for God's sake—do only money and nerve-end sensations make clear sounds to you? Don't you know any other values?"

"You're an analyst. You can't be judgmental—nor should you attitudinize."

"The hell I can't! Listen, Tascha, I came here as a friend of long standing."

Dan took hold of Tascha, somewhat roughly, pulling her to her feet. His eyes were blazing with indignation and as his voice cracked out, she dropped the bland, unemotional façade she had been maintaining, as some of the headlong spirit, evident so long ago in Vienna, reappeared. "Get into that kitchen and fix us something decent to eat before I call Bill and tell him what he may very well already know—that is, to leave you and your restless dissatisfaction and start his life in Los Angeles free to meet someone new—someone like Jenny—born and bred to make a husband happy."

Dan was weary. He wanted a few hours of sleep. And he was hungry—hungry enough to eat out of Tascha's cans. He said, "Tascha, while we eat, I'll talk. You'd better listen to me."

Tascha's reply was defiant. "I'll throw something on and you can take me out. There's nothing in the house. Had I known you'd always be wanting food, I would not have sent the cleaning woman away. She markets and fixes things."

Dan thought: *Tascha Brotman, what sort of woman are you?* And he wondered: *Bill, are you making a mistake—the greatest mistake of your life?* But there was nothing he could do about it.

Another thought plagued Dan. He spoke to Tascha of it. Standing at her bedroom door, she gave him her answer. "I don't think of him as dead— just out of my way. Don't forget—he caused me to become an adulteress. Had I drifted into an affair with someone other than Bill, perhaps my lover would say of me, 'She is nothing but a whore.' For that, I'll never forgive Abe.

"But more important, I'll help Peter Rice—with money—in any way at all. Now I won't have to go through the disgrace of a divorce. And Abe can't shame Bill. And he can't take Annie away from me or make me out cheap in her eyes."

Dan said, "I see." He thought of all the years and all the dreams and all the things that Abe and Tascha had shared. Right from birth, they had shared and struggled together. But because nature made Abe small and soft, he took his revenge by developing a genius for retaliatory evil. And Tascha, in healthy rebellion, despised him for making her eat at another's table. Now all facts pointed to Abe's death. Peter Rice, if he escaped the electric chair, would spend his life in an institution for the criminally insane. And disciplinary action would be taken against those who walked with Abe and thereby shared in his guilt.

Dan asked of himself, *What lesson can we learn from this? But Tascha is going through some kind of elaborate confusion. Actually, were she on the couch and I in the chair, it would be easier on both of us because I wouldn't be trying to jam my values onto her.*

Dr. Steinhardt's night had been a sleepless one. Bill Reilly had said over the telephone, "We need your help." Well, probably the bright young man who was coming to see him about Peter was also coming to size him up as the foreigner who was not a medical doctor but only a lay analyst, whose degree was in pedagogy. Later, Daniel Gunther would report his impressions to the high-ups—the older men in the national organization—who set standards and policy in American psychoanalysis. Dr. Steinhardt was frightened. He had lost his practice in Germany, not because he was a Jew—he was not—but because he was a Freudian, who held tight to his scientific beliefs and who could not bear to give allegiance to any new divergences. Now when everything was going right for him, he was again threatened.

Dr. Steinhardt dressed, sucked an orange, drank a glass of hot milk, and when the bell rang, he himself brought Dan into the consultation room, where the picture of Freud, in an ancient gold frame, hung on a stark-white wall.

Dan accepted the offer of coffee and a sweet roll and waited until they were served before opening the conversation. "It is good of you, Doctor, to give me part of your holiday."

"To tell the truth, I don't like giving it any more than you like taking it. But I was unlucky enough to be handpicked by Abe Brotman to be Peter's analyst; so ask your questions. I'll try to answer them. If what you told me on the phone proves true, I may have to explain how I did not recognize the symptoms of actual psychosis."

"I come to you as a fact-finder. The Peter Rice I know, or knew rather, was not a violent man. Yet it appears almost totally certain that he committed the ultimate violence. I have pieced together the story of outside events. From you, I want his real story—his history, his inner world. I want to know how a neurotic stability broke down into a sudden loss of ego control. What reactivated infantile conflict might drive Peter to commit an outrageous deed?"

Dr. Steinhardt shivered involuntarily as he settled himself in the chair, carefully making sure his stockings were pulled up. A glance at Dan's not unfriendly features reassured him, and he launched into Peter Rice's background, consulting old notes every so often.

Peter was the middle child of three brothers, close together in age. The mother was restless and irritable, but the father, a successful retail merchant, was well liked, and handled affairs at home as well as his business. Intensely attached to his father, Peter felt rejected by him because of repeated favoritism to the bright, good-looking elder brother. He began to search for a father substitute by developing attachments to brother images. The elder brother was quite indifferent to the shy, sensitive Peter, who soon felt left out, too, by his aggressive younger brother.

It turned out that Abe Brotman had personally brought Peter to Dr.

Steinhardt, who was a little surprised to find that the candidate had never seen a private patient but had worked primarily as a neurologist since leaving Vienna. In the analysis Peter's extreme hostility to his brothers was brought to the surface, as well as his attachment to his father. Probably there had always existed fratricidal impulses in Peter's background, but the sibling rivalry was pretty well worked through in the analysis and Peter gained strength. Eventually, he was able to attack Abe Brotman's paper to the institute, not because of his hostile feelings toward a brother figure, but in the clear knowledge that its content was weak. When Abe did not immediately counterattack, it gave Peter considerable happiness, for, to him, it meant that the secure brother image was unruffled by criticism.

At this juncture Steinhardt paused and shifted his position before mentioning his own frightening quarrel with Abe Brotman. Realization came to him of Abe's libidinized aggression, that he got real pleasure from hurting someone.

"I was immediately aware that I'd better put my new insight to use. I called Peter and asked him to come see me. He refused, giving as his reason a quite incoherent statement. This alarmed me. But I never dreamed that his ego boundaries were shattered and that he had regressed to his infantile position."

"Do you recall what Peter said?"

"Not exactly. But it had paranoid coloring."

"And you did nothing else?"

There was the imperceptible shrug of the man who no longer gets involved in other people's messes.

"What could I do?"

Later that week they slipped away from their friends, gathered for the holiday, to the quiet of their bedroom. Dan glanced around. Even in winter Jenny kept the room bright with flowers. "Come here." For a long moment he just held her, looking down at her full belly thinking: *This time, I hope it's a girl.*

Jenny smiled up at him. "Do I pass inspection?"

Softly Dan said, "I love you, Jenny."

"No one else? Just me?"

Dan nodded.

She reached up and kissed him and then gently pulled herself free. She walked over to the chaise and sat down. Dan followed her. He didn't really want to talk about Abe and Peter and, least of all, about Tascha. But Jenny was anxious and knew there were unexplained dangers on the New York scene. She did not say so directly, but he knew she was frightened. George had been told, and he had plenty to say on the subject. Not in front of Jenny and the others.

"Dan," Jenny asked in a small voice, "what if Peter sees his younger brother in you—he may make another try."

"I'll be careful."

"Promise."

"Do you know the district attorney?"

"No."

"Get the lowdown on him from Dad's lawyer. Don't take him into your confidence until you're sure of him."

"Dad's report is a good one."

"Dad merely said that the district attorney enjoys a warm family life. He could be charming to his wife but a complete bastard to you. You can't afford to make assumptions."

George, Leo, Lewis, even Leo's wife, quiet, gentle Tess, all were giving the same advice: "Don't give anything away to the district attorney until you are certain that he is trustworthy. Act with Peter as you would with a patient in a locked ward for the violently insane. Keep those private detectives within the sound of your voice." To each Dan gave his word. "I'll be careful."

"Baby, it's almost time for me to go."

Jenny turned away. "I hate partings."

Dan took her into his arms. He started with gentle kisses on her hair, her eyes. When his lips reached hers, the kisses became less soft. And when, at last, he let her go, Dan said, "Do you think I'd take the chance of losing all this?"

"I doubt it." Jenny was talking with more cheer. "All the same, don't feel you have to act the hero single-handed. I need you, too—remember that!"

One hour after Dan left for New York, Jenny and the boys, accompanied by Lewis Miller and the Butlers, boarded the plane for Chicago. There she was to meet Andrew, and Jenny was to go on by train to the West Coast to await the baby's arrival. Normally, the boys were geared up into high spirits at the prospect of a trip. This time Paul's fists were clenched and Eric's eyes were filled with tears. "What about Uncle George?" they wanted to know. "Why isn't he coming with us?"

Luck was with Dan. He was able to talk to his father's friend, a distinguished and urbane lawyer, who arranged a private meeting with the district attorney, Philip Walker. But the lawyer voiced his puzzlement as to why Dan was getting involved. To him, it was a messy situation.

Dan had no interest in spending the evening explaining himself. Still, his father's friend and adviser was asking questions and he was no mean judge of men. Dan said, "To my mind, my actions are reasonable. One friend is dead. I feel I want to help his widow for whom I have a strong liking. Another friend—a casual one, to be sure—is—and I must say 'probably,' although I'm not positive—in a complete paranoiac state. He needs a physician to lead him from his house. As far as our worry what this tragedy could do to disturb the growing harmony between psychiatry and the rest of medicine, between psychiatry and the public—well, I'm here. I have the time. I think, and my friends agree, that I'm qualified to represent our profession."

Impressed with Dan's confidence, Charles Norton Pritchett III said, in an admiring tone, "You're a lot like your dad. I'm glad you and he have come to a warm understanding of each other." Dan grinned.

In trying to discover what kind of man the DA was, Dan discovered he would be dealing with someone who had no political aspirations, whose attitude toward punishment was not primitive and yet who understood the relationship between psychiatry and the law. It was a relief, and Dan was more than grateful to know where the law stood. He hated uncertain factors in a situation like this.

Dan drove the rented car along the narrow streets and pulled up to the back entrance of the house on the bay. He turned to his companion, a man of enormous bulk, most of it hard muscle, and said, "You stay out of sight. After I'm in, I'll somehow throw open a shutter, raise a shade, do something that will let you see in. Remember, if I need you, I'll need you badly, so move fast."

"I don't like your going in there alone, Doc."

Neither do I, Dan thought, as they waited for the detectives to appear and make their report. They had only a minute to wait before a man dressed in workman's overalls, a heavy pea jacket, and rubber boots trudged up to the car. "Dr. Gunther?"

"Where's your partner?"

"Guarding the boat."

"Same story?"

"Yes, sir, it's been the same for six days. Up at dawn. Sits around inside all day, sometimes in an old overcoat, sometimes in a robe. He doesn't come out until dark. Then he makes his daily excursion to the village, look-ing over his shoulder all the way. He buys milk, rolls, a couple of apples—things like that. And he picks up all the newspapers. On his return trip he moves so fast he practically runs all the way.'' The detective wrinkled his brow. ''He sure searches those papers. I wish I knew what he was look-ing for.''

Dan said, ''Thanks. Stick around. I think Dr. Rice will be coming out with me.''

The detective shook his head. ''My advice to you, Doc, is to call the cops. That fellow in there is a genuine nut—keep clear of him.''

Dan flashed the detective an inquiring glance. ''What I don't understand is how you keep track of him. You must have X-ray eyes.''

''We have ways in our trade, same as you have in yours.''

Dan grinned. ''That explanation will do for the present.'' He turned once more to his companion, who reminded one of a prison guard but wasn't. ''Our friend here has a way of looking through closed doors and shuttered windows. He'll send you in if it appears necessary.''

''Let me go in with you, Doc. I'll have him in restraint before you can say seventy-seven.''

Lighting a cigarette, Dan took the time to answer. ''Thank you, John. However—no. Restraint is precisely what I do not want. You see,'' Dan went on to explain, ''the signs are good. He's been eating. That means he still has the wish to live. He's been scanning the newspapers. That means he is still in possession of some departments of his thinking apparatus.'' Dan put out the cigarette and tossed it into the street. ''We're all right,'' he said. ''Dr. Rice is hanging on to what he has left of his reality sense long enough to unburden himself.''

''OK. But you should have someone in there listening to his story. The police may not believe you—at any rate, not without a witness.''

''That makes sense, Doc.'' The detective, who was smoking, inhaled deeply. After he blew out smoke, he said, ''Those homicide boys, they don't fool around. Kindness to a friend. Balls! And they are not going to be too kind about your outwitting them either. They haven't even drawn the scent because of your putting Mrs. Brotman off limits.''

Dan knew the police—tough professionals to a man. ''All right. Move in after I've had the chance to engage Dr. Rice in conversation. It's possible that he won't care who hears his grim tale.''

Dan stepped out of the car into the damp cold of a Long Island morning. Gulls were wheeling and crying mournfully in the mist. The wind seemed to be blowing him directly to the door. As he expected, his ring went unanswered. *Peter has waited because he feels compelled to speak,* he reasoned. Therefore, he tried the door—to discover his reasoning rewarded. The door opened.

Dan said, "Hello, Peter." He stamped his feet to make certain Peter was aware of his presence. He couldn't make out a thing in the gloom. He said, speaking loudly, "Peter, it is I—Dan Gunther. Do you remember me? May I come in?"

"Yes, yes." The voice sounded weary. "But hurry and shut that door. You're letting in the ethylene gas. Abe's stooges are outside. They bottle it and force it through all the openings."

The muscles in Dan's abdomen tightened. Leaving the door open, he crossed the threshold cautiously. He inched his way to a window, unlocked a shutter and threw it open.

"Stop, stop!"

"Where are you, Peter?" Dan asked in a low voice.

"Here."

Dan looked back into the room, fear creeping up the back of his neck at what he would see. Peter was sitting on a heavy wooden chair, which stood at the far end of the long narrow room; in the center of the uncarpeted wooden floor was a trapdoor. Dressed in an unprepossessing flannel robe, a woolen blanket flung over his knees, Peter was shaved and his hair was combed. He looked pale and haggard, but not undernourished. He said, "What took you so long?" His voice was expressionless, reflecting in an uncanny manner his hollow appearance.

"Were you expecting me?"

"It's about time you came. Jenny is on his shitlist. She said something uncomplimentary about him in Vienna. He owes her for that." His eyes on the floor, Peter spoke as if he were neither alive nor dead. With the same odd indifference, he continued. "It's all in his little black book."

Wondering exactly what it was about Jenny, Dan said, "You have Abe's black book. That's good, Peter. Where is it? Can I see it?"

Suddenly attentive and eyeing Dan unpleasantly, Peter said, "There's someone else in this room. Did you bring your father? I made him a carved chest, but he hasn't seen it because he never sets foot in the woodshop. He goes to football games. Football has status."

"Please, Peter, give me the black book and whatever else you have of Abe's. You have no idea how important it is that I have his things in my possession."

Calm once more, Peter's voice was quite flat. "They're in my bureau drawer—the shitlist book, eighteen dollars and forty-five cents, and his appointment book. I couldn't let the patients come and wait for nothing. That seemed very wrong."

As if addressing a small child in need of praise, Dan said to Peter, "You did well to cancel his appointments. Now tell me what you did."

"I killed him. Rolled him in canvas. I weighted him with iron bars. Then, in the middle of the night, I took him far out to sea and fed him to the fishes."

"I need to know more than that, Peter."

"What's that man, standing inside the doorway, ready to jump at any moment? He makes me feel frightened, standing like a football player—like my brother. There is no need for a brother now. Father is dead. I made him dead for sure. The night was cold."

"Yes, Peter. But Abe was a fairly husky man. How is it he did not escape your attack? Did you fire a shot into him—or stab him with a knife?"

"No." Peter's voice was bored. "Have you no imagination at all? Listen. And warn that guy over there that if he makes one false move, I'll release all those poisonous gases I've been breathing and that'll be curtains for him. Get it?"

Dan thought he detected a slight rise in Peter's voice. He knew he was treading a very thin line of calm. He did not want Peter to reach a stage of extreme tension, which only violence could break. In his effort to keep Peter calm, he reassured him, "John is a friend. He came with me. But if you want him to leave, he'll leave."

Peter debated. His face looked agonized. Then he said, "Let him stay. Later, if I want to kill him, I will."

Dan moved closer to Peter and, facing him, blocked John a bit out of view. "You were about to tell me, Peter. Remember?"

For an instant it seemed that Peter had lost all interest in them. His chin fell to his chest and his eyes, downcast, stared at the bare floor. Then, with a dull conformity in his tone, the nightmarish story came, as he sketched the planning and the committing of his deed.

After Abe's revenge had come, Peter Rice came close to committing suicide. But, in a sane moment, he reasoned that in so doing, he would provide Abe Brotman with yet another excuse to curl his lip in disdain, to say he could have predicted such a turning of aggression inward. Peter swore that Abe—the Judas—would never get the chance to justify his perfidiousness. But if it is true that "corruption is a tree, whose branches are of an unmeasurable length"—then, so is hate. Peter reasoned further: Better he than I.

There were two things that hastened Abe Brotman's demise. The first was dreams. In these dreams Peter destroyed his father, and his father had Abe's face. Later, the voices came. They came wherever Peter happened to be—in the shower, in the middle of a movie, at a restaurant—and they not only told him to kill; they left him red-eyed and exhausted. Nearing five o'clock one chilly morning Peter heard a new voice. This voice, Peter remembered, sent a shiver through him; it filled the room like an explosion. Peter knew he need no longer muzzle his murderous impulses. The order to kill Abe came directly from God. A great weight was lifted, and his brain began to plot the details.

Peter began following Abe. He got very good at it. He was never too tired. It was never too early, never too late. He discovered that, as a regular pattern, Abe left his apartment building alone three times a week—on Monday, Tuesday, and Wednesday nights. And though he had no quarrel with Tascha, he easily found out about her Wednesdays. He devoted no particular consideration to this; if anything, there was a mild satisfaction in it. What he concentrated on was this: He had, each week, three separate occasions when he could happen by in his old car and offer Abe a lift. He decided to surprise Abe one stormy night when taxis were scarce.

That settled, he really went to work. He started at the New York Public Library by searching the newspapers for unsolved murders. The number surprised him. But none caught his attention—they weren't clever enough—until he came across a murder which took place in a bar and grill speakeasy on Lenox Avenue near 116th Street, back in 1932.

It was necessary for Peter to secure a trick boutonniere with a rubber bulb, which could be concealed under one's garment, and which, when pressed, squirted water out of the flower. This proved singularly hard to find, but Peter persisted. Uptown, downtown—he went everywhere, in taxis, on foot, by subway. He searched toy stores and novelty shops. Ironically, in a little stationery store, on Lenox not far from 116th Street, he found the rose boutonniere. He filled the rose with strong potassium cyanide solution, which he had already obtained from the laboratory. He was ready. All he had to do was wait for a bad storm. It came on a Monday.

Abe Brotman walked out of his apartment in a rage. But Abe wore his charm outward and his anger inward, releasing his anger only occasionally and, even then, as an actor would if the play's lines called for such a display. The immediate cause of Abe's black mood was the storm. He loathed rain. And he had quite a lot of belligerence directed to the cab company for its to-hell-with-you Mister attitude. Even when he went on rapidly explaining, "I am a physician," the dispatcher replied, with complete lack of respect, "Sorry, buddy—no orders."

Peter Rice made certain there were no taxis in sight before he pulled over. He lowered his window and peered out. Abe remained unaware of his scrutiny until he called out, "Abe, can I drive you somewhere?"

Abe remained standing under the canvas awning and kept looking. "That you, Rice?"

Peter, trying to suppress his sense of elation, opened the car door and stepped out so Abe could see him. Abe, never to be caught off guard, was wary: "What do you want? You surely didn't happen to pass my door in this miserable rain just at seven thirty when I have to leave? What errand brought you here?"

For a moment, all Peter felt was alarm and a foreboding that he would not be able to go through with his plan. Then the fact of Abe's unquenchable ego came to him. Stepping into the circle of light in front of the Brotmans' doorway, Peter allowed himself a smile before firmly grasping Abe's hand. "Good question. Look, Abe, I owe you an apology. I know that tonight's your committee meeting, and I figured that somewhere between here and there you would accept my apology."

Abe stared at the rain pelting down. He rolled up the collar of his English mackintosh, pulled down the brim of his hat, and ran to the car, slamming the door behind him. Trench coat flying, Peter followed and pulled himself in behind the wheel. He had just enough time to start the engine before Abe said, "So you've come to beg forgiveness. Isn't that charming?"

Peter stared at his knuckles, white on the steering wheel. "I want to put my whole future back in your hands."

"You've had enough, have you?" Abe said with a smirk. "Well, second chances are hard to come by. What fine inducement do you intend to offer in payment for my forgiveness?"

Peter's head dropped a little lower. The long breath he drew gave Abe the impression he was searching for the right words.

Abe prodded him and Peter responded. "You handed me my

big chance when you invited me to discuss your paper. I was wrong to offer that much criticism.''

Abe was suddenly a happy man again. "You were a horse's ass.''

Peter nodded, and after a brief silence, he said, "Give me another chance, Abe, and I'll never step out of line again.''

"I haven't forgiven you yet. And I've promised you nothing. But I'll let you come in with me and tell the Education Committee what you think of yourself. But don't think reinstatement will come that easily—if at all. You have to remember—I am the best friend you ever had.''

"At least, we're speaking.'' Peter made an abrupt stop at the curb. "I'm cold. Let's have a schnapps.''

"Good idea,'' said Abe, biting off the tip of a long cigar. He reclined comfortably back in his seat, expecting the bottle to be brought out; then he noticed that Peter merely sat—if anything—a bit closer to him, not making a move. Still somewhat taken aback, Abe said, "Who's got all night—where is your schnapps?''

"Right here,'' Peter said, pointing to his rose.

"Ha, ha! Some joke.''

Abe knew about Peter's occasional inventions and gags. Some were really clever, and at parties he could be counted on. "If you open your mouth, I'll give you a swallow of the best orange brandy you ever tasted.''

"To put it delicately''—Abe laughed—"you're nuts.''

"Try it!'' Peter said gently. "See how my latest gadget works. I guarantee you it's good brandy.''

Through the thick of his cigar smoke, Abe humored him. "What have I got to lose?''

Only your miserable life, Peter was thinking. Abe opened his mouth. Peter pressed. The rose sprayed straight into Abe's mouth. An intense wheeze and one quick gasp and Abraham Brotman slumped down. His body twitched in a couple of uncontrollable spasms; then he looked like a man fast asleep, the sleep of death. Peter stretched out a hand and got rid of the cigar. He switched on the ignition, pushed his foot down hard on the gas pedal, and the little car accelerated with astonishing speed.

The ride to Freeport was without incident. Once in his own neighborhood, Peter made a careful survey of the area. It was empty. He unbolted his back door, opened it, and in the darkness dragged Abe's body noiselessly through the mud. After he garaged the car, he wiped clean with a wet rag all traces of Abe. After that, his activity increased, and, as if he were automated by some superior being, his hands performed his will without command. His scheme had been perfectly rehearsed.

In rain and heavy ground fog, Abe Brotman's remains went to sea. Ten hours and fifteen minutes later, at exactly 8:02 A.M., Peter Rice was home. He built up a fire, brewed some coffee, and went straight to the telephone. After Abe's appointments were politely disposed of, he took a hot bath. Too weary to worry about retribution, he slept. It was his last normal rest.

Dan did not imagine for a moment that Peter, drained by his recital, would remain quiet, staring into space indefinitely. He was stunned by the elaborate details of the plan, by the fantastic ingenuity that the deranged mind had access to. Dan consequently moved fast. He sent John, whose job it was to help handle Peter, for blankets and the detective to the bureau drawer for Abe's effects.

"Don't press your luck, Doc," the detective advised. "Leave them where they are for the police."

Dan thought on this a moment. "OK." He then turned his full attention on his patient. "Peter, I brought a drug to help you, to relax you. Then I am going to wrap you comfortably in blankets and take you to a hospital, where everyone will take good care of you. The authorities will want to speak to you, but they'll wait until the doctors say that you are ready to speak to them."

There was no response from Peter.

Dan rolled up his friend's sleeve. He wiped the skin with alcohol and jabbed the needle in gently.

Peter's vacant eyes stared straight ahead. He remained silent. John lifted him and carried him out. He had no difficulty. It was like carrying an awkward, top-heavy bundle. Dan walked alongside as they went out to the car. His impulse was to weep for Satan's child.

Dan Gunther liked what he saw. A compact man with an honest face, whose shy smile often succeeded in making one forget to take respectful heed. And Philip Walker, district attorney in the State of New York, a seasoned observer of men, was attracted to the professional integrity in Dan's manner. Quite soon that wintry Wednesday afternoon in early December, the two partly affirmed antagonists, only about six or seven years apart in age, were on a first-name footing.

"Sit down, Dan. I'll have coffee sent in." They had left the club's dining room—where Dan had told him the bare facts of Peter Rice's deed—and were in the library. The coffee poured, Philip Walker measured Dan steadily.

"If I were to tell myself what you just told me, I would not believe myself."

"In your business and in mine, we run across some pretty incredible doings."

The district attorney moved closer to the coffee table. "Dan, I know something about you from Charles Pritchett—a friend of your father's, I believe. I know you're a first-class doctor. I know you're smart. What I don't know—though your points of emphasis compel my admiration—is why you felt you had to solve this disappearance all by yourself."

Dan gave no sign that he was aware of censure. He said in reply, "We knew Abe Brotman was missing, but there was no proof whatsoever. How could I name his murderer before I had the whole truth told me?"

"Well, I still think you might have taken me into your confidence. Legally, you are not on exactly safe ground."

"Maybe, but I have another reason for requesting this meeting."

His interest again aroused, Philip Walker looked sharply at Dan. "I'm listening." And during the next half hour, it came to him that Dan, in weaving the several threads into an understandable whole, was communicating a staggering point. A new one for the law.

"So you see," Dan concluded, "you can't possibly try Peter Rice for the murder of Abe Brotman."

Philip Walker became the formidable opponent. "The hell I can't," he said in a voice packed with authority. "By your own admission, Peter Rice committed several highly coordinated, well-thought-out acts. As a matter of fact, viewed in totality, I'd say Peter Rice is an extremely intelligent man who very nearly enacted the perfect crime. I'd also say that his reasoning power is very much intact, and that I can easily establish him as personally responsible. In legal talk, your Dr. Rice knew the difference between right and the wrong of his particular act, and therefore—based on the McNaughton rule, proclaimed back in 1843—he fits well into the legal definition of sanity.

"I will go before the grand jury. They'll bring in an indictment. And I'll get a conviction, too."

Dan shook his head. "I don't think so. I don't think you'll even try. I refuse to think you that unwise."

"That's interesting." Eyebrows raised, the district attorney said, "Go ahead, Doctor. Tell me why I won't do my job."

Dan recognized the challenge in Walker's retort and ignored it. He felt convinced by the rightness of reasons above and beyond the law, but it was necessary for him to convince the public servant.

"How shall I put it? You believe this is just another murder case. I have to prove to you that this is more than a murder case; that neither Abe Brotman nor Peter Rice are terribly important as protagonists; and that we must —at all cost—avoid a newspaper blast. Because, if this tragedy is reported, we can expect a violent explosion, and the real victims will be the emotionally ill—thousands upon thousands of them—who look to psychiatrists for healing."

"You're a terrific convincer. But I have a sworn duty to the people of the State of New York to investigate crime and to prosecute the wrongdoer. When I walk into a courtroom, I ask the jury to mete out justice."

"Justice? Whose justice?"

Philip Walker did not answer.

"I really haven't reached you, have I?"

Philip Walker shrugged.

Dan said, quietly, "Listen. It's hard to explain, but there are other factors operating in this instance."

"Go ahead. I'm here to listen. I'll spend the night, if necessary."

"Thank you." Dan glanced momentarily at his wristwatch, then his eyes came back to the district attorney. He began to speak and his voice took on a professional quality. "In plays and in legend, murder grows from madness. Take Macbeth—or Medea. So Peter Rice's act of fratricide—the curse of Cain—grew from fear, humiliation, and hatred, triggered by childhood memories, and this fear in turn let loose primordial drives and desires. Once obsessed with the idea of destroying Abe—or his brother image—Peter was driven to enact his fantasy. That fantasy was a psychotic wish of a delusional nature because Peter Rice interpreted Abe's rejection of him as the repetition of the early events in his life which brought about his original struggle with himself. In the killing of Abe, he was committing not only fratricide but patricide, too."

"That's fascinating. But I don't see how it changes the legal situation. Did Peter or did he not know right from wrong when he squirted potassium cyanide into Abe Brotman's mouth?"

"Right from wrong! That damn half-baked formula. It discloses nothing."

"It's the law. And I'm only asking for information. Did he or did he not?"

"Peter Rice was still in the stage of superficial normalcy at the time of his confession. However—"

"Well . . ."

"Wait. Let me finish." Dan drove his ensuing remarks with intense forcefulness. "Peter Rice is now nicely tucked away in a sanatorium for the mentally ill. Would you dare drag a very sick man before a grand jury? A man, mind you, who bears all the marks of physical exhaustion. And—for the sake of argument—were you to succeed in getting your indictment, I am willing to appear in any court, as is Dr. William Reilly, as are others —all highly reputable physicians—and swear, under oath, that Peter Rice did *not* know right from wrong when he committed the act of murder. He was *not* in adequate contact with reality. I will say, 'Link fantasy, patterned on an infantile death wish, with action and you have murder.' I'll make it sound good. Other expert witnesses will testify: 'There is clinical indication—or, in legal language, presumptive evidence—that the psychotic process had been going on for some period of time. All of Peter Rice's actions which resulted in the killing of Abe Brotman, the evildoer, were part of his delusional system.' A third psychiatrist, whose good reputation is firmly established, will swear, 'Peter Rice's act of violence was in conflict with his identity as a physician. He was delusional when he committed the killing.'

"Well," Dan asked, after a pause, "what do you think of your chances for a conviction?"

Philip Walker thought: *You clever son of a bitch.* He smiled, withdrew his smile quickly, and, in a voice hardened by derision, said: "Are you telling me, Daniel Gunther, that you and several of your highly respected colleagues will, under oath, prevaricate?"

"Indeed not. There is a penalty for prevarication under oath. Furthermore, I am enthralled with the inner truth—in the case of Peter Rice, it serves justice marvelously."

The district attorney, a pragmatist, began to think. Remembering all that he'd been told about Daniel Gunther, he took cognizance of the warmth of Dan's personality, of his grin, of his ability to sense people's reactions. He saw himself in a courtroom, and he had a very shrewd foreknowledge of how Dan's idealism and integrity would impress both judge and jury. Too, he realized, he'd meet head-on the legal eloquence of a Liebowitz. Philip Walker, district attorney, concluded he had encountered a worthy adversary. He began to talk to Dan again, making his shift gracefully. "You are absolutely right. If Peter Rice cannot understand the nature and the consequences of his statements, he cannot be brought to trial. And if, as you believe, he already is in a paranoid panic or a catatonic stupor—well. Why pursue a lost cause?" With this, the district attorney shrugged and expected the matter to end. He was wrong.

Dan was thanking him for his interest, and even more for making the decision he made, when the door opened and one of the uniformed menservants stepped across the room to face Dan. "You have a call, Dr. Gunther."

Just as Dan got up, Philip Walker said, "Switch it here."

Dan walked over to the telephone and picked it up. Meanwhile, sitting relaxed in his chair, Philip Walker picked up a magazine. Skipping from page to page without stopping to read, he did not notice Dan's face turn white. He heard Dan draw in a deep breath, heard him say, "Good God!" Then: "Brief me."

He looked up quickly. He had the sudden feeling that Dan, though he had straightened up and his face was expressionless, almost taut, was reeling under a blow. It seemed forever before Dan finally hung up and, slowly turning, said quietly, "That was Charles Pritchett."

Philip Walker knew enough not to ask immediate questions. He moved forward, clasping the magazine in his hand, and as he observed Dan, his certainty of disaster increased.

Dan was silent a moment longer until he realized they were alone. "Tascha Brotman took the call from the hospital. She had the sense to call Charles Pritchett. Peter Rice committed suicide. He saved some of that potassium cyanide—had it tied into his handkerchief. There's a long letter he left behind. They found it in his robe pocket. The envelope is addressed to 'No-one-in-particular.' "

Genuinely sorry, Philip Walker walked over and put an arm around Dan's shoulder, saying, "Let's go."

They made the long drive out to the Westchester Hospital in an official car but, at Dan's request, without the district attorney's regular driver. As they moved through the streets away from Manhattan, Dan never for an instant took his eyes off the road ahead. "I should have foreseen this. Perhaps I did. Perhaps I even wanted this end for Peter Rice. There was no way out for him." They stopped at a red light. Dan turned to Walker. "I don't think I've ever thought of this before. Suppose there never was an Abel—suppose each of us is, in his own way, Cain? Generation after generation of countless Cains." The light changed. They drove on.

"That's an astonishing thought, Dan."

Dan nodded. "It would explain the meanness, everyday common meanness of man toward man—the corruption, war, destruction."

The district attorney said, "That needs thinking about."

"It's a lousy thought, my friend."

For some minutes they were silent. Philip Walker brought out his pipe from his breast pocket. He sucked, then looked at Dan from the corner of his eye. "Accidents happen. There's no way of avoiding them. Don't blame yourself."

Dan lowered his window and drew the chill air into his lungs. "Do you know why I'm at fault? Because I treated Peter Rice in a way different from the way I normally treat a patient. Ordinarily, I don't drop off a seriously disturbed person at a small private hospital, whose appeal is distance and a reputation for discretion. I pick a teaching hospital with top personnel. I stay and make damn sure that my patient is properly searched. I protect him from himself. *I* start the medication, and sometimes it's hours before I take off. That, my friend, is my usual pattern."

Philip Walker surmised Dan's immediate need to judge himself harshly—it was therapeutic. One thing he was convinced of. Peter Rice was better off dead. "Think of it this way, Dan. Peter Rice had nothing left to live for; either he had to remain insane and stay locked up or he had to go—if not to the chair—to prison for life, with no parole. I'd have seen to that."

"I know. Reason says: 'Be glad Peter is done with hurt and fright.' But—somehow it's hard to meet death with reason."

Philip Walker struck a match, cupped it with his hand, and lit his pipe as they drove on to the hospital.

> Sell everything I own. Add the ensuing proceeds to my bank savings and to the contents of my safety deposit box—Morgan City Trust—blast the thing open. Turn the total estate over to Tascha Brotman. My brother gets my ashes.

> There was a P.S.

> I never gave a thought to the wife and child. For that alone, I, Peter Rice, deserve to burn.

Both bone-tired, Dan and Philip Walker were stretched out in the apartment, besieged by questions from Tascha, Bill, and Andrew Gunther, who had been there for hours waiting.

Bill said, "We're infinitely grateful to you."

Dan said, "Go home and hit the hay—you're beat."

Andrew Gunther said, "I let your wife know. I knew she'd be worried about you."

The last forty-eight hours had proved a strain for everyone. Dan wondered why he always got into things so deeply but was convinced of the rightness of his action; Bill felt spent and unable to contemplate the future; Philip Walker, the imperturbable lawyer, realized that he had come across another fine shading to the human success story. Everyone had talked. The piecing together of Peter's deed, his capture, and his demise fell into orderly sequence as the disjointed events were revealed. The sad chapter had ended.

Tascha on the whole behaved well, taking in Peter's suicide with quiet restraint and adjusting to the newly acquired windfall. It seemed that she was sensibly weighing the prospect of her future without Abe, until she startled Philip Walker with: "Just a minute! How about my life insurance? I want . . ."

She got no further. "I understand, Mrs. Brotman. I'll do all I can to cut the red tape."

Dan thought: *For Christ's sake! There's no stopping her.* He moved past Tascha and opened the door into the corridor. He walked out alongside the district attorney, following him into the elevator. He fully intended to express his deep appreciation. All he said was "I've run out of words." When he went back to the apartment, he went and sat down directly to write to Jenny.

Midway down the page:

> I felt numb but I went on talking to him as if he were alive. His lips stayed locked. No answer came.
>
> Was he psychotic? I saw with my own eyes that he was. And I watched for malingering. I really did, Jenny, my own. But now —I'll never know for sure—will I?

There was more.

> Tascha wants to sell Abe's practice to that refugee analyst from Austria. I suppose I'd better tell you that, at this moment, I'd like to throw her in for good measure.

Dan dropped the pen. He grabbed the telephone. A businesslike voice said, "Number, please?" Dan gave a San Francisco number. The girl on duty said, "I'll give you long distance." Dan repeated the number. Soon he heard Jenny, her voice a sweet mixture of sleep and heedfulness.

"I needed to hear your voice."

"M-m-m"

"What are you doing?"

"Now?"

"Yes, Jenny, now."

"I'm smiling."

In San Francisco, it was exactly nine twenty-seven in the evening.

Dan fell into bed. He dreamed about Jenny, but then he had no time for her, because he had to find a cure for Tascha's greediness. At the end of the dream, Dan was in a place empty of all people and all things except for a single tower—tall and imposing, rising up to the heavens. Even in his dream, Dan understood the tower quite clearly—he knew it to be his ambition.

It snowed in New York the next Monday, and a cold wind blew the snow in all directions. Dan said, "Their plane is almost certain to be late." It was.

In quick impatience Bill stamped his foot. "Christ, it's cold."

Dan turned up the collar of his coat. "Let's go inside. We'll watch for them through the window."

But Bill was determined to wait it out. Ten more interminable minutes and the plane landed. Leo Butler was the first to emerge and clamber down the wooden steps. He was alone. Lewis Miller had not come.

"What went wrong?"

"What we all need, Dan, is a hot cup of coffee."

Bill picked up Leo's overnight travel bag. They went over to the coffee stand and were served right away.

"Thank heaven I got to Chicago in time to prevent him. He shouldn't move for the present." Leo was speaking. "I promised we'd stick with his plan and that we'd keep in touch by phone."

"His asthma?"

"Yes," Leo admitted. "A wretched attack. It's worse—allows him no rest."

Bill asked, "His heart involved?"

Leo nodded.

Dan glanced at his watch. "We'd better get down to business." He turned back to Leo. "He understands what has to be said to the institute here. Do you really think his ideas best?"

"Yes, I do."

Bill agreed.

Dan seemed pleased. "Just before we go, I have something to say." Leo and Bill waited and Dan went on. "I think it might be best to let Bill carry the ball."

Smart, Leo told himself, and while Bill thought about it, he said, "Of course, it's perfect—a solution coming from one of their own members will arouse less shame. And if they don't heed Bill, I'll take the floor."

Dan did not envy Bill his job as he and Leo followed him in through the columned doorway of the former town house that served as home to the New York Institute of Psychoanalytic Medicine; all three of them unwrapped the layers of clothing made necessary by the winter's first cold snap before entering the conference room. If Bill was nervous, he was able to disguise the fact.

It was a large room, dominated by an ornate stone fireplace, and with several portraits as well as sepia photographs hanging on the walls. About eighteen men, most of them in their thirties and forties, were sitting around the table talking in low tones. At one end loomed the tall, Lincolnesque figure of Yasha Atwood, distinguished to look at but disconcertingly at odds with the flat, nasal voice that emerged. As presiding officer, he rather lamely introduced the two visitors and then reminded the members gathered that this was their third emergency meeting. His eyes avoided Bill Reilly's completely.

Yasha Atwood directed his next remarks to Dan, seated between Bill and Leo at the long oblong table. "It seems incredible to us that you were able to solve with such astounding accuracy the senseless murder of one of our members. Please may we have the account of what happened from you? What made you decide that Abe Brotman was dead? Precisely why did you perceive in Peter Rice the murderer? Tell us about his capture and of his suicide. How did it all come about?"

Is he trying to create a diversion? Dan thought: *Throw it to the floor.* Determined that he should not succeed, Dan said coolly: "Bill Reilly and I did our thinking and planning together. I can bring you nothing fresh. And since you have been reliably informed, I see no need for rehash."

Yasha Atwood cursed silently—the big shots meant business. "Quite right," he said, sounding proper and portentous. "We're here to discuss the issues of scientific integrity, professional training, and so on." With a slightly obsequious smile, he turned to Leo. "Will you honor us, Dr. Butler? We want to hear what messages you bring us from the American Society of Psychoanalysis."

Leo Butler stood up and looked around him at the noticeably European set of the faces, some angry, some resentful, others bitter. This was a society dedicated as they all were to furthering analytic training, which had allowed the inherent weaknesses in psychoanalysis to take over and evolve into gross injustices. For that he had no sympathy nor any particular liking. But ever a just man, he knew certain facts had to be faced, and he started talking about the Baltimore-Washington group, of which he was still a member, and his teaching in Chicago.

"We esteem our candidates and therefore they develop self-esteem. We can do this because our process of selection is geared to finding emotionally stable, intelligent, highly motivated young men and women. We turn down the applications of bright, even brilliant neurotics. We might never have taken Peter Rice. If we had, and had he completed his didactic analysis to the satisfaction of his training analyst, and had he satisfactorily completed his controls, his acceptance into our society would have been axiomatic. Never, in my group, would a man be carried for the full training period and then summarily rejected. Why was this humiliation inflicted upon Peter Rice? And I want to know why you allowed Abe Brotman—an opinionated man, afraid of new ideas, originality, and openness—his high position. This leads me to ask, not officially, what kind of men are you? I ask for myself, for my own curiosity.''

Leo Butler ignored the whispers that went around the table and continued. "Perhaps I'll say more later. I am hopeful, however, that, after taking a long, hard look at your situation as it now stands, you will arrive at a conclusion that can be equated with solution. Otherwise, gentlemen, there will be another emergency meeting held, this time by the American Society, which has a duty to society in general, and to all the members of the profession. From their decision, there will be no appeal.''

The president thanked Leo Butler and turned quickly to Dan. "Do you, Dr. Gunther, wish to make a statement?''

"Yes,'' Dan answered mildly, "with your permission, I should like to add something. I am skeptical about training psychoanalysts in society and institute settings. They share in all the shortcomings but lack the virtues of university training centers. I object to psychoanalysis isolated from the other behavioral sciences. And not unmindful of the genius of men like Siegfried Bernfeld, I am completely against nonmedical psychoanalysts. Abe, although we knew each other well in training, is someone I cannot be proud of. I'm stabbed by the lies he told me. And I don't understand how he managed to keep your confidence or why you cooperated with him.''

The fierce uproar that greeted him, though not entirely unexpected, was more than Dan had bargained for.

Yasha Atwood stood up to quell the scene of disorder and bellowed above it: "Quiet! Each of you will have his say in due course.'' As quiet was restored and the flood of voices became a mere trickle, he addressed Dan with a surprising degree of dignity. "We owe you a debt of thanks for undertaking a dangerous and extremely delicate mission and for handling it with skill. We expected you to walk in here as our friend, receive our gratitude, and act as our counselor—no more. But you have chosen to challenge us on grounds that do not rightly belong here. Are we to conclude that you share Dr. Butler's low opinion of us as a group?''

"Ideas that have to do with standards and with training belong at all times and affect us all," said Dan simply. "We cannot, as doctors, allow injustice and personality struggles to become malpractice."

Bill Reilly rose, glaring almost past Dr. Atwood as he spoke. "If—as you point out—Dr. Butler has a low opinion of us, I submit that we may well deserve it. We kept Abe Brotman in power and, by our silence, permitted him to proceed with his malicious intent, even condoned it. What did we do for Rice? Hardly played the Good Samaritans, eh? This guilt is our guilt."

Yasha Atwood surprised everyone by shaking his head and saying, "I know. I know." He sounded weary; he looked defeated.

Leo Butler broke in. "Dr. Reilly has something further to tell you."

Yasha Atwood smiled bitterly. "Go ahead, Bill. Out with it."

Slowly Bill's eyes went from face to face. They reached Leo and rested. "Forgive me for pulling this surprise on you. Until a few moments ago I wanted to talk to you all, but for reasons I'm not going into, I have decided I'm not the man for the job. I'm sorry."

"All right, Bill. If you consider me better suited to speak, I will gladly do so." Leo Butler turned. "Mr. President, I am not averse to orderly intervention. Anyone who wishes may raise a point or ask a question. I'll be pleased to listen—willing to answer."

Their gazes met and held. "May I remain seated?"

"Surely."

Leo Butler took a full pack of cigarettes and a small box of matches out of his pocket and put them on the table. "Let's get started. I have no speech to make. This will be most informal—a kind of in-the-family talk. A possible solution. How many of you know Lewis Miller? H'mmm. So few! Well, how many of you know *of* him?" Leo Butler nodded his head vigorously. "Everyone. That's more like it. Well—"

The first interruption came. "I've heard he is a meddler."

"I take it that you say that as censure."

The speaker shrugged. "How else?"

"We're all meddlers. How we meddle is the important thing." Leo Butler made sure no further comment was forthcoming before he continued. "Lewis Miller is a priceless man—a man of excellence. Some of our most brilliant, most productive colleagues—from coast to coast—brag: 'I trained with Lewis Miller.' Although no one has ever been able to press Lewis Miller into holding office in official organizations, his influence is beyond appraisement." Leo Butler heard a sound. He leaned forward and looked down the table, made extra long, and said: "How's that?"

"I said: Eyewash! I'm entitled to my opinion, I guess." The speaker was a German-trained analyst, formerly a surgeon.

"If it pleases you to be rude." Leo picked a cigarette from its pack. "I mention Lewis Miller because what I have to suggest comes from him. And because it comes from him, it will receive support—if not here, then higher up, where it counts. I want you to think about that when you're making up your minds."

A hand went up.

"Yes?"

"Lack of air and hours of talk. We're all breathing too heavily. There's a kitchen down the hall. The urn there holds about forty cups of coffee. Platters are filled with Danish pastries. Let's take a rest. While we refresh ourselves, we can open a few windows. Here—and—" the speaker tapped his forehead—"here."

A few voices dissented.

Yasha Atwood's gavel sounded. "We'll take a break."

In twenty minutes they reassembled. Leo Butler lit still another cigarette. Eyes turned on him, and Leo Butler began. "You are a comparatively young institute whose history, until now, has been unimpressive, so your activities went unnoticed. The nightmare you are now faced with, because it is real, made a quiet investigation of your membership necessary. We found that the majority of you are European-trained; understandably, you take the European position of following the one in command.

"Abe Brotman, a bright, aggressive, and rather shrewd man, after a short analysis in Vienna, moved into the institute early. Because he possessed a quick wit and charm, because he was an American and a doctor of medicine, because he named Dan Gunther and Lewis Miller among his pals, and proved it, by bringing Bill Reilly into this group, his progress to privilege was fast. But Abe Brotman had unsolved problems. He had unresolved animosities, especially toward his colleagues, his siblings. And he was insecure. This made him a dangerous man.

"To recount events is unnecessary and useless. What concerns us is not this particular society, but the reputation and progressive professional standards of American psychoanalysis in general. Consequently, we don't give a rap for the who, the whom, or the why of this mess. This is no cover-up. It is a deliberate attitude, carefully inspected. I hope you don't think that because the good interest of patients and the future of psychoanalysis are of paramount importance, we lost sight of you as individuals. You are, all of you, of notable significance.

"Lewis Miller masterminded a sagacious plan. His suggestion is to dissolve this institute—and I cannot recommend strongly enough that you follow this. State briefly, in an official letter to the American Society of Psychoanalysis, that your candidates-in-training are few—that several of you intend to leave this area and apply for membership in other societies. For instance, Bill Rielly is moving to Los Angeles. He is asking for admittance from Topeka. By the end of this evening, one of you may decide to come to Detroit. I will gladly make time for one or two of you as analysands. Lewis Miller will immediately fill the hours of anyone who might be interested in the Chicago area. San Francisco is bound to become one of the great training centers. Who among you would like to make his way there? We'll help you—that is, if your credentials and qualifications are in order.

"Most of you will, of course, choose to remain here. That is entirely natural. Fortunately, there exists in New York—not one, but two magnificent groups. For those of you who are already members of the American, transfer into either of the other societies will be arranged without difficulty. Who among you will retain the status of teaching analyst is a matter that rests with the respective Education Committees."

Leo Butler paused and was silent a moment. Then: "If, among you, there are a few—and I think there may be—who need more analysis, then I say, get it. It's a blow, but better a blow now than a big mistake later. It's up to you."

Leo Butler, a grave look on his face, looked around at the dismal faces. He said, "I've talked quite a lot. Yet if I may have a few minutes more—"

There was no reply; for in many heads, thoughts were racing wildly, each man considering his own situation, assessing his own feelings of guilt. Stay? Go? Take a chance? Play it safe? It had been a fair, certainly a justifiable, suggestion.

The sound of Leo's voice intruded upon their thinking. "Earlier this evening Daniel Gunther went on record on a very touchy matter. He refuses to share the practice and the teaching of psychoanalysis with anyone lacking the prerequisite licensing in medicine. It happens that some of our foremost analysts disagree with him. It has crossed my mind that when Jones has stepped down from the international scene, more and more analysts will go over to Dan's point of view. I myself don't know exactly where I stand. But these last couple of weeks I've been thinking about it, and I know I've moved a long way toward Dan."

"Why?" The question came from all around the table.

"Because doctors are trained to make decisions, decisions that affect physical beings as well as our minds, to act upon those decisions, and to take full responsibility for them. Who but a full-fledged physician would have dared to do what Daniel Gunther dared to do with Rice? Those of you who feel attacked by Dan, answer to yourselves the question I just raised.

"Gentlemen, in conclusion, I want to thank you for your courteous attention—and for inviting us here. Something good may come of this double tragedy, if we think of it not as an end but as a beginning. God bless every one of you."

There was intense quiet.

Yasha Atwood was first to speak, and it was in dejected resignation. "I will entertain a motion to the effect that inasmuch as the New York Institute of Psychoanalytic Medicine sees no useful purpose in its existence, it votes itself into oblivion."

"I so move."

"Second?"

"I second the motion."

"Opposed?"

There was silence.

"Approve?"

There was a groan, a nod, a nervous cough, a furious upward jerk of a hand. The overall effect was of unhappy, subdued assent.

"Motion carried."

In the hours that followed, Lewis Miller committed by telephone large sums of money to those who needed assistance in order to reenter the official family of psychoanalysts. Dan made generous, noninterest-paying loans. And Leo Butler, who had no large private income, who had neither rich father nor rich wife, pledged help wherever it was needed. Bill believed that Tascha, after he talked to her, would make a generous gesture—perhaps in memory of Abe and Peter Rice.

This time Bill's faith in Tascha was rewarded. She came through with a lump sum.

In the window seat looking out at the great stretch of clouds below him, lulled by their anonymity, George was content with his thoughts. They were not new thoughts. He was thinking of Jenny, thinking of the simple fact that he loved her.

Dan, on the aisle, read and dozed and read. The hours on that flight seemed long and the air miles to San Francisco stretched endlessly on. The print blurred before his eyes. Turning his head to George, he dropped his book. "When will you make the decision?"

"Sorry, Dan, I wasn't listening."

Dan repeated his question.

"What's to decide? There's nothing to hold me in Washington. I need only to sell the house and find someone competent to take over my practice. That shouldn't be difficult. A large number of well-qualified physicians have managed to get away from Hitler's Germany. One is coming to see me as soon as we get back." George flashed Dan a smile. "I'll be ready to leave with you."

After a moment's pause Dan pulled a letter from his pocket. "Say, why don't I move in with you? This is from the Silvers. In a nice way they ask if it is possible for me to vacate our house right after the New Year."

"I thought about suggesting that—then decided it was your move."

Dan gave him a quizzical glance.

George's answer came with a grin. "If you suddenly get fed up with commuting, you can't blame me."

"You trying to suggest anything else?"

"Well, buddy, what?"

"A bachelor's life is such that he doesn't need a boarder around."

"I see the difficulty, but I'll be as discreet as can be."

At this point Dan made a comment, meant to be taken lightly, that met with real annoyance. He mentioned that there were those among his colleagues who considered George's attachment to Jenny not such a good thing.

George gave Dan a hard look. "Of all the crap I've ever heard, that's the crassest."

Surprised at the passion in his voice, Dan dropped the Silvers' letter back into his pocket and said mildly, "People like to speculate."

George's annoyance persisted. "That bearded genius gave you people a vocabulary and a panacea for everything. Dredge up dreams. Blame everything on someone other than yourself—preferably mother."

Dan had known George long enough, and well enough, to know that he blasted psychoanalysis because he did not want to come to grips with his own conflicts. So Dan did not defend Freud. He said, "In your case, I'd say father and the circumstances of your birth. By loving a wedded woman, in the medieval sense of courtly love, you protect yourself from matrimony. You don't want to inflict upon a girl the misfortune that befell your young mother."

"Very interesting." George's voice sounded pooh-poohing.

Dan's grin appeared. "A little oversimplified."

"Dan," George asked with reasonableness, "how is it that you keep the door to your own psyche closed?"

"Meaning?"

Watching Dan's face, George asked, "Why do *you* let me share your life? We are like brothers. Or perhaps not?"

Dan's eyes looked at George with sudden interest. Then his expression relaxed and he smiled. "Let's say that in all conflict-free areas, I'm prepared to be generous."

As George was puzzling over a hot retort and realizing that Dan's insights had the validity of good judgment, not just smugness, the hostess came to inquire whether the gentlemen were ready to begin supper.

Paul pulled himself to his full height, which brought him close to Jenny's shoulder. "There they are, Mom. Coming through the gate." Jenny was aware that the three of them made a handsome picture standing in the main lounge of San Francisco's airport. Her elder son, with his dark hair, ruddy cheeks, and eloquently flashing eyes, had all the physical attributes of a superb athlete yet was sensitive beyond his years to what went on in the world of grown-ups. She could always rely on his ready understanding, and, on this trip to California, Paul had effortlessly moved into the role of man of the family. Eric, on the other hand, was like a ball of quicksilver, with his mercurial temper and infectious grin. At seven he considered life one grand adventure, especially if Uncle George was around to share it. His hazel eyes lit up in sudden joy as he started to run. As if to avoid a contest, Jenny held back a minute, giving silent thanks for the safe landing.

Finally, Dan lovingly dismissed the boys and they rushed to George, while Dan made his way to Jenny. He was marveling that, almost at term, she could still look so slim and graceful from a distance, in her long mink coat. Jenny walked the remaining steps, and they met with an embrace that left George and the boys plenty of time to catch up. As Dan released her, Jenny turned to George with a warm smile. "I'm so glad to see you." Then she kissed him.

George silently gazed at her, not even bothering to conceal his feeling for her. He knew in a curious way it was reciprocated.

That was the only pause there was. After that, Dan took her hand. "Let's get a cup of coffee. Boys, how'd you like a sundae or something?"

Jenny gazed up at him, an undercurrent of puzzlement in her voice. "That's an odd suggestion. The family has waited months to see you, you know!"

Dan continued to look at her, saying nothing until George lifted both boys, one in each arm, and said, "I'll get us a table."

"Dan! What's the matter?"

"Nothing, Jenny." He laid his hand gently on her shoulder. "I have an appointment in Vancouver with Peter Rice's brother, who is flying in from Prince Rupert. After I've handed over the urn of ashes, I'll turn right around and come home. I'll be with you tomorrow evening.''

Troubled and tremendously disappointed, Jenny felt the baby's strong stir. Unsmiling now, she pulled away. But something told her to hear Dan out, whatever his reasons might be.

Conscious of her hurt feelings, Dan said, "George offered to go in my place, but I don't think that's right. I feel I have to deliver the urn."

"Why?"

"Because, Jenny, I let him die."

"That's not true," Jenny cried. Her anxiety all for Dan now, she said, "That's a terrible thing to say; you can't assume that kind of guilt—nobody can. Give me your promise that you'll not—"

Dan interrupted her. "All right. My word of honor."

Jenny thought suddenly of Paul's and Eric's inevitable disappointment. As her mind raced to an idea, she said, gripping his arm, "Listen, Dan. Take the children with you—if only you knew how they've been counting each day."

"You're a little genius, my love. Now why didn't I think of that?" Dan kissed her full on the mouth. Then he said, with a rising inflection, "I don't suppose you'd permit us a few extra days so that I can really show the boys something of what that area is like?"

Jenny laughed. "Leave time between planes in Seattle to buy pajamas and jeans and heavy shoes. They'll need socks and underwear, too. And be back on the twenty-fourth for sure. You'll ruin Dad's surprise if you're not."

"What has he bought now?"

"Be patient."

Dan and Jenny separated. He went to make the arrangements for the Vancouver flight. She took the boys over to watch two Cessnas going into the nearby hangar. An hour later the Seattle plane took off, and Jenny found herself alone with George. "Did you ever see such happy little boys?" she asked.

"They'll have a ball together." A smile spread over his face. "What a wise woman you are, Jenny."

It was nearly dinnertime when they reached the Adamson house on its hillside.

"You mean to tell me—" Andrew Gunther stormed.

"Dad."

His eyes wandered to Sara. "I'll be damned if I understand my son."

"Poor Andrew." Smiling directly into his eyes, Sara said, "You even look handsome when you growl."

Everyone laughed. And Andrew's temper passed.

Jenny drifted into sleep thinking of the house Andrew had built just for Sara on her wild seacoast up in some wonderfully lonely acres. The ultimate retreat, it was an extraordinary, quite special house—contemporary and vital—with high, open-raftered ceilings, cool stone floors, and great windows, offering a breathtaking view of the Pacific Ocean. Convenient and practical, without sacrificing elegance, it was filled with beautiful things well placed, and with dramatic, vivid colors against redwood and native stone. To the back of the house, away from the ocean and looking out on the surrounding forest, was a heated swimming pool, a secluded garden of potted plants in seasonal blooms, and a rustic patio fully equipped to accommodate visitors. Jenny loved the house with a passion even she had trouble putting into words; and inseparable in her mind were the sheer rocky cliffs, the drift logs, the seabirds, the swell of great rollers in the stormy winter months, the seals out on the rocks. And the mist, the fog, the ocean breeze—it was like magic to her.

The morning of December 26, a bright and windy day, Jenny did not keep them waiting breakfast. And no one lingered over the meal because Paul and Eric were popping with excitement. Their grandfather was taking them up to Lake Tahoe for skiing and sledding. They loved snow. A laughing, happy Jenny was too excited to finish eating. For her the prospect of five days up in Sara's house on the Sonoma Coast made her wide eyes shine with anticipation. Dan and George, who looked at her with doctors' eyes, shared her plans but not her enthusiasm. Neither did Dorothy, who, after plates had been pushed back and cleared away and they were alone, made her feelings known to her mother-in-law. Sara advised silence. "After all, my dear, she is married to a doctor."

"More like *two* doctors, I would say," remarked Dorothy.

Sara nodded her head slowly a few times and retorted, "Well, then, let them both take care of her."

"Mother."

"Yes, dear?"

"I don't mind being alone. It's only for a few days. Please tell Andrew you'll drive to the mountains with him."

"I'm not invited," Sara answered cheerfully. She linked her arm in Dorothy's as they left the dining room. "Come along."

In Jenny's room a heated discussion was going on.

"Listen, Jenny. You're nearer than you think. I don't see how we can—"

"You're being tiresome, Dan."

Dan was convinced that Jenny had miscalculated again, and he felt that it might have saved further argument if Jenny's obstetrician had not run off to Hawaii for the holidays. "Why in hell did Kelly have to go on vacation now?"

Jenny, in front of the looking glass brushing her hair, turned to him. "Because I won't need him until mid-January. Now hurry. I want to drive up before the fog sets in."

Dan relented. "OK," he said. "I don't know about now, but I used to be pretty good at home deliveries."

Jenny laughed and sprayed Joy perfume on her ears, then accentuated her lips lightly with a pink lipstick.

Meanwhile, in his room, George inspected his medical bag with a professional and critical eye. Not enough—not even the right things. He went to find Sara.

"Come in." Sara, at her dressing table, smiled at him in her glass and murmured a welcome. But her smile died away as her eyes rested on his face. Offering him a chair, she turned to him with a question. "What makes you so serious?"

"I'm troubled. Jenny ought not leave the city right now."

"Her mother shares your opinion."

"If you were to talk to her, she'd listen."

"Perhaps," Sara said quietly, "but I'm not prepared to spoil anything for Jenny, particularly because I believe she wants this child to open his eyes on the blue Pacific. Besides, with you and Dan to attend her, I'm not concerned. Let nature take its course."

George approached Sara. On her dressing table he laid a white sheet of paper, upon which was written a long list of things. "Please call your druggist in Jenner as soon as we leave." George paused. "He will deliver, won't he?"

"Yes, of course." Sara looked down. Then she turned her marvelous dark eyes on George. "Catgut? Green soap? Lysol? Heavens!"

Smiling now, George teased. "I suppose there's no use in again asking you to marry me."

Filled with tenderness for the man, who reminded her so vividly of her dead son, Sara responded with, "None at all, but you needn't stop asking. It keeps Andrew on his toes."

Tactfully, George failed to make the obvious comparison.

They took the inland route as far as Petaluma. Years ago, when the country was young, it contained many such tranquil towns. Now there were few such places left. Petaluma always delighted Jenny. She loved the farmhouses painted white, and the barns brilliant red, and the special whitewashed wood shelters, perfect housing for the fat hens producing their double-yoked eggs. Eager to share her enthusiasm with George, Jenny made them stop near a small creek that splashed and played over mossy rocks. They walked a stretch along a dirt path until they came upon a farmer leaning on his fence. They greeted the farmer.

His eyes went directly to Jenny. "Hi!"

She said, "We want to have a delicious feast. Have you a chicken or two to spare—and some eggs?"

The farmer remarked, "Chickens and eggs all over the goddamned place. Help yourself."

They took the Petaluma turnoff to the Coastal Highway. Driving slowly, they wound along the rocky shore through unspoiled hills. With the windows rolled down, it was cool but not too cool. They heard the roar of breakers. They saw the pelicans soaring above. They passed sheep on the hillsides. And all the while, Jenny was talking, telling George about *her* coast—what it meant to her.

"It's not as overwhelming as Big Sur. And our hills don't drop off as abruptly or to such great depth. But it is sublime nevertheless. You should see it on an Indian summer day at sunset when the red of the sun inflames the blue of the sky. You should see it on a misty winter morning just before a storm when the ocean is thundering in. Or in the spring when the rhododendrons are in bloom."

Behind the wheel, Dan smiled.

George pressed her hand warmly. "You left out summer."

Jenny suspected she was being teased. It did not matter. "Summer is divine. The sea otters are gone, but great herds of seals sun on the rocks. There are sheltered coves and tide pools to explore, and trails from beaches to pine meadows."

They came to Bodega Bay.

Dan pulled up to the wharf and parked. After that they walked, passing seafood restaurants serving all sorts of enticing dishes. They arrived at the edge of the pier in time to see a lumber schooner rocking on huge waves. Slowly they strolled along, eyeing fishnets stretched to dry and old weather-beaten fishermen resting on the bollards. The nets lent a colorful air to the somber tone of the rocks.

"Jenny," Dan said finally. "If you want to make Jenner in time for lunch, we had better move on."

"All right," Jenny said.

When they came to the mouth of the Russian River, where it empties into the Pacific Ocean, they were in Jenner, a fishing town unsheltered from the wind and, through most of the year, bathed in coastal fog. They stopped for lunch at a restaurant with a view of the fishing boats. On entering the dining room, they were led to a table set with a checkered cloth, with glasses, and with two bottles of local wine—one a delicious red, the other a cool dry white. Sitting down right by the window, they felt as though they were enjoying the terrace breezes on a summer's day.

The men ate breaded fried clams, and before the crab came from the outdoor brick broiler, they devoured sourdough bread hot with melted cheese.

Jenny ordered only an endive salad.

"What about an entrée?" asked the young waitress.

"Nothing, thank you," replied Jenny.

This was quite out of character. Somewhat concerned, the men exchanged glances. Then, his eyes going from George to Jenny, Dan asked, "What's the matter?"

Jenny smiled gently as she answered. "Nothing." She turned to George. "I want Dan to drive slowly from here. I don't want you to miss a thing, especially the church at Fort Ross. It's spare and simple." She sighed and continued conversationally. "Really worth seeing."

George laughed; resting his hand companionably on her head for a moment, he said, "You'd make a first-rate tourist guide."

When coffee came, Jenny excused herself. She was gone an uncomfortably long time. Dan waited quietly, his grim expression the only clue to his apprehension. George forced himself to remain calm. Finally, Dan pushed aside his cup and beckoned the waitress to their table.

"If you're ready for dessert, sir, the apple pie is home-baked and very good."

"Will you please see whether my wife is all right? She may be indisposed."

"Yes, sir." The waitress departed with quick steps and headed for the rear of the restaurant where the rest rooms were. She returned moments later to say, "She's gone."

George's eyes shifted anxiously to Dan.

Dan was angry. He took his wallet from the inside pocket of his jacket and placed a twenty-dollar bill on the table. The men rose and walked silently to the door. As they started to descend the stairs to the street, Jenny came into sight carrying a paper sack. Coming to them hastily, Jenny said apologetically, "I had an errand."

"I want you to tell me what's going on," Dan said, his sharp gaze resting on her.

"The baby is coming sooner than I thought."

Quite obviously, Dan was annoyed. "Did you have to go for Kotex your-self?" Before she could answer, he said, "Do you need help?"

"No, the druggist let me use his washroom."

Suddenly realizing, George went white. *Good God,* he thought, *a dry delivery.* After a silent second he said, "I'll get the car."

Jenny looked at him intensely with a serene look that unnerved him even more. She put her hand on his. "Don't be scared."

Dan glanced at Jenny's hand. His eyes softened. His annoyance vanished. "I'll go."

Jenny, as usual, sat between them. Dan, intent on the road, noted that she was very quiet. "My immediate instinct," said he, "is to get you to the nearest hospital, which would serve you right. But then we'd have to take a chance getting up over the mountains to Sacramento."

Jenny turned and looked at him, her dark brows arched. "Why are you mad at me?"

"Because you did *not* miscalculate, you *knew* the baby would come before mid-January," Dan turned the corner and headed for the mountain pass, using his horn around turns to frighten away deer. Twice he had to slow down almost to a stop to ease his way through flocks of sheep, scrambling off the roadside in confusion.

Suddenly, Jenny giggled. Dan stared ahead. George stared at Jenny.

"Better tell us what's so funny."

Jenny again turned her gaze to Dan. "I'm happy. I have you to hang onto. I have George to deliver me. And for an anesthetic, I have the rustle of trees against the roar of the sea. What could be better?"

George looked startled, but no words formed. He gazed hastily down at his hands. He licked his lips. "Me to—"

Dan cut in. "The baby is my job."

Because she was disappointed—in her mind the job she assigned to Dan was far more sanctified than the one he was choosing for himself—she asked somewhat curtly, "Why you?"

Dan gave George a sideways glance. His strained expression, his total silence, told Dan that George was numbed by the thought that his life cost his mother hers.

Jenny nudged Dan. Frowning at him, she repeated, "Why you?"

Dan answered lightly, "Because I am one hell of a delivery boy."

George felt an immense relief. Jenny looked at him then. Her eyes were sharp and she saw the change in him. George caught her eye. He gave her a brief smile, and then, with no modification, he disclosed the secret he thought he could never admit.

"I very nearly did not graduate from medical school. I flunked obstetrics."

Dan shifted his gaze from the twisting road. "You're kidding."

"No, I'm not—unfortunately. My first exposure was a home delivery. I set out on time—I thought—but I had trouble finding the place. I got there too late. I took one look at the God-awful mess the woman made of herself. She was moaning, 'I wish I were dead, I wish I were dead.' By nightfall she was dead. The next day they buried the child with her. That finished obstetrics for me. I didn't even bother to show up for the final. The next year, my senior year, the professor offered me a second chance.

"I said, 'No thanks.'

"He said, 'Can you give me one good reason why, after working for four years, you are throwing your whole career away?'

"He soon realized that whatever the real reason, I was not about to divulge it. He dismissed me. I couldn't get my mother out of my head. I kept thinking of Maggie. I thought: Well, that's the end of everything now. A few days went by and the professor called me in. He said, 'Let's go over to the Golden Rail. I'll treat you to a pastrami on rye.'

"After we were seated, he said, 'Speaking of football, you've just picked up a fumble on your own thirty-yard line. You've got the ball. What are you going to do?'

"Startled, I answered, 'Run like hell!'

"Grinning from ear to ear, he said, 'Congratulations, you've just passed your course in obstetrics.' "

Dan couldn't remember exactly when he had laughed so hard.

Jenny was incredulous. "George Atlas, is that true?"

"Now you know," George replied, putting his arm around her and feeling the enormous relief of sharing his burden.

Jenny sat close to Dan and leaned her head against him. In the long silences the hours passed. A strong wind was tugging at the trees outside. The room grew dark. The pains grew stronger.

George checked. Everything was in readiness. Moving softly, he built up the fire and put hot water bottles between the sheets in the bureau drawer where the baby would lie.

Suddenly Jenny cried out involuntarily, "Oh, Dan." She rose heavily. "Help me."

It was George who removed her robe, helped her onto the bed, and covered her with a sheet. Then he knelt beside her, and passing his hand lightly over her hair, he prayed, "Dear God, please let it be all right."

Dan was on his way to scrub with green soap. He came back into the room, turned on all the lamps, and without a word he bent over Jenny and pressed his lips to hers. Then he went to the foot of the bed.

The men worked well as a team, and Jenny held back screams and did as she was told. When her pain seemed past bearing, she dug deeper and deeper into the hand she held in her grasp, and from time to time she pulled it to her mouth.

George was concentrating hard and a certain professional pride was guiding his actions. When he judged it time, he turned to Dan, who nodded, and then he gently disengaged himself from Jenny and injected her with a sixtieth of a grain of morphine. After easing her suffering a little, George gave her back his hand. She welcomed it with both of hers and clung to it, gasping now and then for breath. A shaking seized George then, and color flooded his face.

Dan looked up slowly. "Ether."

Once more in control, George freed his hand, and placing a gauze mask over her nose and mouth, he poured a little ether onto it. Then smoothly, softly, he whispered, "Take a deep breath. Bear down. Bear down with the pain." It was a firm voice and Jenny confidently obeyed. An eternity later—one minute—he whispered again, "Breathe, Jenny. Breathe deeply. Push."

Dan hooked his finger under the baby's chin. "Put her to sleep." Minutes later Dan held the infant by the feet. A gentle slap to the buttocks brought the first bellow and turned the skin a rosy pink. Another miracle of life had happened. Dan looked at his son with a profound sense of awe. He handed the pink bundle to George and moved back to deliver the afterbirth. Fortunately, there was no indication of a tear. That relieved Dan of the one task he was not looking forward to. With a sigh of satisfaction, he pulled off his rubber gloves and went over to the improvised crib. The baby was clawing blindly in the air, moving, reaching out.

George rose to his feet. "Congratulations, Dan. You're quite a delivery boy."

Studying the child, noting the perfection of his tiny limbs and features, Dan replied, "For a guy who flunked obstetrics, you're not so bad yourself." He went back to Jenny. They both watched her; then Dan called to her. "Jenny, darling." She stirred. "We have another son." She opened her eyes. "Fetch him." She kept her eyes on Dan until he came back to her.

Jenny looked at her baby. "He's dark. He's beautiful." Her eyes and the little smile that played about her lips showed them all she felt. But she did not need to be reminded that she was exhausted. "His name is Andrew," she whispered. "I promised Dad."

Dan kissed her then and once again took his son and turned away.

"George"—she gazed up at him—"did I hurt you?"

George laid his lips on her forehead. "Yes, darling Jenny, you did."

For a long moment she was silent, then she asked him to show her his hand.

Staring down at it, she said gravely, "You have teeth marks." Then she closed her eyes. She looked so little in the big bed.

It was a night of a full moon and myriad flickering stars in a pale sky, and up from the sea the wind blew the scent of salt. Dan and George sat contentedly sharing dreams and drinking Jenny's drink—champagne over ice. Thousands of miles to the east and thousands of miles to the west, evil men were already calculating their next moves in the conquest of the world. The United States was three hundred and forty-six days away from Pearl Harbor. Meanwhile, up above the rocky coastline pounded by the unceasing surf, a mother and her newborn charge slept on.